WHEN
SHE
REIGNS

BOOK THREE
OF THE FALLEN ISLES TRILOGY

By JODI MEADOWS

The Fallen Isles Trilogy
Before She Ignites
As She Ascends
When She Reigns

The Orphan Queen Duology
The Orphan Queen
The Mirror King

The Incarnate Trilogy
Incarnate
Asunder
Infinite

The Lady Janies Series
Coauthored with Cynthia Hand and Brodi Ashton
My Lady Jane
My Plain Jane

WHEN
SHE
REIGNS

BOOK THREE
OF THE FALLEN ISLES TRILOGY

JODI MEADOWS

KATHERINE TEGEN BOOKS
An Imprint of HarperCollins Publishers

Katherine Tegen Books is an imprint of HarperCollins Publishers.

ISBN 978-0-06-246946-5

Typography by Carla Weise
19 20 21 22 23   PC/LSCH   10 9 8 7 6 5 4 3 2 1
❖
First Edition

For those seeking hope

THE GREAT ABANDONMENT
selections from
the holy books of the Fallen Isles
during the first through fifth years of the Fallen Gods

When the rains are too much and too little, when the fields turn fallow, when the harvest of hope is small: the Great Abandonment has come.
    —*The Book of the Daughter*

The greatest calamity comes in the night, when the people are not listening.
    —*The Book of Silence*

Love survives death.
    —*The Book of Love*

A true warrior faces the end with strength and honor. However, there is no dishonor in fear.
    —*The Book of Warriors*

Remember: fire cannot exist without something to burn.

    —The Book of Destruction

The brightest lights yield the blackest shadows, but even during the darkest day, the shadow soul of the dragon reigns.

    —The Book of Shadow

They called me Hopebearer.

Because hope was too heavy a burden for them.

The *Drakontos celestus*

THE END OF THE FIRST DRAGON WAS THE BEGINNING of the Great Abandonment.

Millennia ago, six constellations vanished from the sky. Then, fireballs streaked through the night and crashed into the sea with a thunder that rattled the world.

The wounded ocean opened wide, its depths evaporating and scattering into the sky.

Blazing debris rained from shattered heavens, and all across Noore, the air ignited and whipped into firestorms that burned until there was nothing but ash. Desperate people took shelter in caves and stone houses, but for many, it was too late. The fires had won.

And in the middle of the ocean—

As sister moons eclipsed the sun—

From the molten rock of nascent lands—

The first dragon erupted, star-scaled and crackling with divinity. A child of Fallen Gods: fire and death and sky incarnate.

1

• • •

SOON AFTER, THE Great Abandonment began.

When humans set sail across the sea, with unadulterated worship shining in their eyes and promises falling from their tongues.

When they looked down and prayed, overcome with a sense of belonging.

When they looked up and gasped, because there were dragons in the sky.

And when they looked back at where they'd been and found more people coming—these with weapons drawn.

A war began for the Fallen Isles, between those who'd come first, and those who'd come second. Generations were born and lived and died at war, but after hundreds of years of defending the islands from the kingdoms and clans of the mainland, a solution was decided upon.

The first dragon led a wing of her brothers and sisters across the sea, where they laid waste to everything they found. Fire spun from their open jaws, burning all that had been built since the Great Fall. Houses crumbled to the ground; forests went as black as night; even the rock ran liquid, hissing where it hit the sea. They left nothing as they blazed up and down the coasts, burning and burning and burning, unstoppable.

Until.

A poison-tipped arrow slipped between the scales of the first dragon. She screamed at the stars as her flight faltered, though her wings pumped to gain height. Then more arrows found their marks in her brothers and sisters. Another polyphonic screech ripped from the first dragon. Fury. Shock. Grief.

The dragons dove, death beating in their inferno hearts. Flame ravaged the earth beneath them, searing the archers' names from history, and it was there—among the still-burning bones of their enemies—that the dragons collapsed to the ground and slept for a century. And then they, too, died, the first dragon last of all.

THE GREAT ABANDONMENT could have been prevented. But it was not.

PART ONE

THE HARVEST OF HOPE

CHAPTER ONE

THE GOD SHADOW STRETCHED ACROSS THE SEA, CAST-ing the city into an early, unwelcome twilight.

I shivered, unable to look away from the length of umbra that darkened everything, or the immense god hunched over on the horizon. Sunlight strained long and golden around his curled shoulders, his bent head, and his lean body—a nightly eclipse that caused a deep, anxious hush to settle across the city of Flamecrest.

Gerel elbowed me. "Stop looking at the sun. It's not good for your eyes."

"It doesn't hurt my eyes anymore. Not since . . . you know." I didn't want to talk about the dragon rescue. Not here. We were perched on a roof with ten strangers, all of us hoping to see new ships arrive in the harbor below.

This was hardly the best time. "Besides, the sun is hidden. That's the problem."

"Try not to stand out. Once the ships arrive, we can go back to the hotel and you can be as odd as you want."

I sighed and looked back toward Flamecrest Port. No one could say what—or who—was on the ships rumored to arrive tonight, only that they brought hope. And with the god looming on the horizon, bent in contemplative silence, hope was the one thing everyone wanted.

One god had risen. Abandoned his people. Killed most of them, too.

Any island could be next.

This one, maybe.

"Do you think the others had any luck finding Nine?" I spoke softly, but Gerel still glanced around with a worried frown.

Fair. Nine was a spy from the Algotti Empire, and it was dangerous to talk about them in public, but no one was paying attention to us. Rooftops and balconies were packed with people trying to get a good view of the port, while the streets were even more crowded. Anticipation knotted through the crush below, with pale blue noorestones dotting the sea of dark faces and bright headscarves. Even with the god-shadowed hush, there was still enough ambient noise to obscure our conversation.

"We'll find out when we get back." Gerel glanced north, toward the Fire Rose Hotel, where we were all staying. "I don't like so many of us being out at once. Altan could easily overpower Chenda and Zara. And Aaru is in no state to help."

She said it without judgment, but just thinking about Aaru and his state was painful. He'd been physically present but emotionally absent ever since the earthquake.

"Altan could have left after"—I lowered my voice—"the battle at the ruins. But he didn't. He stayed with us." Maybe he'd been compelled by honor, but more likely he still needed something from us. He'd wanted to help us free the dragons, but I didn't imagine he'd genuinely changed since his attack on Crescent Prominence.

"And he's been useless ever since."

I couldn't argue with that. While we'd been going out in pairs to search for Nine, we kept Altan locked in a closet. Partly because we weren't sure what to do with him, and mostly because we needed information, which he refused to give. Like where he'd sent Tirta and Elbena, who'd betrayed me, or Kelsine, the *Drakontos ignitus* we'd befriended.

"What do you think is going to happen when we find that spy—"

"Nine," I said.

"Nine. Fine. Whatever. What do you think will happen when we find them, anyway?" Gerel asked.

"We'll ask a thousand questions." To start with. I needed to know more about the Algotti Empire, but that need was impossible to explain to the others. At least right now. Ever since we'd destroyed the ruins above Flamecrest and set the dragons free, something had been different. My dreams—previously just dreams of flying—felt stranger. Older. More powerful.

Gerel just shook her head. "I hope you're making a list."

"Of course."

"It just doesn't seem like enough. Listening to gossip. Looking for Nine. Keeping Altan locked in a closet. What are we doing here, besides waiting for the world to finish falling apart?"

"Trying to find a way to put it back together."

"Unless you know something I don't, I'm afraid that's impossible." She dropped her gaze to the noorestone in her hands. "Nothing better to do, though. I'd rather die doing something meaningful, but I'll settle for staying busy."

I'd never heard Gerel so morbid. For a moment, I considered telling her about my dreams. The dragon. The moons passing before the sun. But as the god shadow settled deeper over the city, casting the twisted streets into a premature darkness, a child began to cry. Followed by another, and another.

"I wish people would take their children inside before sundown." Gerel fidgeted with the noorestone, making light bounce across her strong features. "How do you explain to them what happened? How do you tell them the world is ending, and there's no way to fix it? Better to let them have some peace before the Great Abandonment takes them, too."

"Ignorance isn't the answer." I looked at Gerel askance; she was the last person I'd have expected to advocate for sheltering children, but maybe that was because she'd never been sheltered. "But I am glad it isn't our job to explain what's happening. It was hard enough telling Ilina's mother."

Gerel gave a soft snort. "Seven gods, that was—"

At her oath, we both went quiet, a beat of discomfort drifting between us.

I pushed past it. "Even Zara took it better." Perhaps that was unfair to my sister; she'd been uncharacteristically subdued these last five days. "I'm sure it won't be long before her shock wears off and she starts demanding silk gowns to wear to the Great Abandonment."

"I wish we'd sent her on the *Chance Encounter* with Ilina's mother." Gerel sighed. "But I understand why you said no."

Mother had promised Zara that I'd protect her, and that was the last we'd seen of either of our parents. For all we knew, they were dead, killed when Altan's warriors attacked Crescent Prominence and destroyed the council house. I might be the only person my sister had left.

I dropped my gaze to the noorestone-lit harbor, where dockworkers bustled around piers to prepare for the arrival of these new ships. Aside from the workers and their supervisors, the port was empty. All the crowds had been pushed outside the gates, held back by fences and squads of soldiers in flame-blue uniforms. Even the berths were mostly vacant; every ship that wasn't in need of repairs had left as soon as possible, weighed down with medical supplies, food, blankets, and cots—whatever could be spared. It seemed impossible that anyone could have survived the god of silence rising up from the sea, but people had to search. Just in case.

"How long will we have to wait?" someone on the other side of the roof asked.

No one answered; no one knew.

Then.

I felt it.

Power called to me, and I answered.

I climbed to my feet, careful on the smooth tiles, and strained my eyes to peer farther into the god-shadowed sea. The sunset sky burned like hot iron over the water, and to the south I could just see the barest scrapes of land: Damyan, perhaps—the god of love. It was from that direction I could feel . . . something.

Noorestones.

Not just any noorestones. There was something different about these, something I couldn't quite identify. Then, what I'd thought was land in the distance grew; it wasn't land at all, but ships coming closer. They carried noorestones. *Loud* noorestones.

Most felt alike: they set a hum against my thoughts—making me aware of their presence without becoming intrusive.

But these would not be ignored. They were powerful. Old. Slightly . . . wrong, like a note just out of tune, not quite reaching true dissonance. They drew my thoughts into a current of uncontrollable curiosity, dampening the sounds of the city and surf.

I listed forward, the toe of one shoe thumping on the guardrail.

"Mira." Gerel's whisper was sharp, like it wasn't the first time she'd said my name. "What are you doing?"

My heart thundered as I shook back into myself. I'd forgotten she was here; I'd forgotten anyone was here.

"It's the noorestones." My fingers curled around the cool iron rail. "They're on the ships, coming toward us."

As soon as the whisper left my lips, a shock of excitement traveled through the crowd. *"There!"* people cried, pointing toward the water, where ten enormous ships slipped into the god shadow. *"Hope is on the way!"*

The ships were huge, bigger than any I'd ever seen, save the *Star-Touched* and the *Great Mace*. They were ocean-crossing vessels, powered by immense, unstable noorestones that had—in one case—interacted badly with a dragon, causing an explosion that had taken the *Infinity* four and a half years ago.

But that wasn't the truth. The imperial spy called Seven had told me the explosion of the *Infinity* was a test, a way to gauge the destructive potential of these giant noorestones.

He'd also said the Anaheran government was behind it.

"Do you think the noorestones are weapons?" Gerel's question drew me back to *now*.

I glanced around, praying no one had overheard her, but voices rippled all around us, teeming with cautious optimism. On rooftops and balconies, people had lifted themselves up to get a better look at the huge ships. They weren't just unusual; they were *shocking*.

Gerel tried again. "Do you think they plan to use the noorestones to hold cities hostage?"

I shook my head. "I think, for now, the noorestones are being used to power the ships."

She frowned. "Doesn't this class usually require three noorestones?"

"Usually." I bit my lip, listening to the excitement build around us; the promised hope was almost here. "I think these will be slower than the *Star-Touched* or the *Great Mace*, but they'll be able to outpace any other ship in any Fallen Isles fleet."

Her frown deepened. "I wonder how they'll match up against the black ships."

"If we ever find Nine, we can ask them to race." Right after we found out what they knew about Anahera's role in the Mira Treaty. Seven had given us what information he possessed, but Nine had been working in Anahera for months.

A short, barked laugh escaped her. "I'm sure that's what spies do in their free time."

"Without a doubt." My smile faded as I watched the ships come closer. "Remember when we first saw Seven's ship?"

"I remember." She crossed her arms over her chest as a sea breeze lifted from the water. "Chenda said she thought Anahera was building a new fleet. This is it."

"That seems like a fair guess." These were almost identical to the design of our other ocean-crossing vessels, made from wood, rather than metal like the imperial ship. "I suppose," I murmured, "my question is *why*? Why build a fleet of ships this big? What use could anyone have of ships capable of crossing the ocean? There's nowhere else to go."

"There is the Algotti Empire." Gerel's tone was low, frightened, almost. "What if, on top of everything else, Anahera wants to take us to war against the Algotti Empire?"

Dread deepened inside of me. "Why?"

"There's a lot about Anahera that doesn't make sense." She kept her voice soft so that the Anaherans around us wouldn't overhear. None of this was the people's fault, I kept reminding myself. We all had corrupt governments. We'd all been betrayed by the people sworn to protect us. This was just . . . so big.

I let my eyes travel across the city, to the Red Hall. Like most of Flamecrest, the capitol building was made from red sandstone, its upper walls adorned with polished rubies that shone like fire during the day.

That was where High Magistrate Paorah lived. Where he ruled. I'd been to the Red Hall during both of my previous visits to Anahera, and while my movements had been carefully monitored, I knew that much of the building was private, sectioned off not only for the high magistrate and his family, but for other purposes as well. Darker purposes, some claimed.

As the sun set fully behind the god of silence and dipped beneath the horizon, the ships moved into the harbor. They were brilliantly lit—almost cheery—with noorestones covering the decks and masts. *Hopeful*, at least as far as most people were concerned, but the dark chord of the giant noorestones slipped through the back of my head.

Something was deeply wrong. High Magistrate Paorah wouldn't introduce this fleet here, now, without some reason. And I doubted *hope* was his true intention.

Excitement jumped like static through the crowd, intensifying as blue-clad guards bade people back off Revis Avenue, one of the seven major thoroughfares that radiated from the capitol building. Soon, a straight line from the port to the Red Hall appeared, along with fresh whispers about who or what was arriving. Regardless, the high magistrate would receive his delivery tonight, under the eager eyes of his people.

Then, a magnificent horsecarre—painted flame blue and detailed with gold—came down the newly cleared Revis Avenue. A team of white horses pulled it along the cobbled road, and though I couldn't hear the clatter over the distance and noise of the hundreds of assembled onlookers, I could halfway feel it, rattling in the back of my head, along with the noorestones.

"That's the high magistrate's crest," said someone on Gerel's other side.

Another horsecarre followed the first, and then another, until fifteen waited along the road, just a short distance away from the port. Liveried guards stood at regular intervals along the road, their spines straight with attention. Swords gleamed in the steady light as they all faced the port entrance.

The gates opened wide, waiting.

Slowly, carefully, the ships drew up to their berths, glittering with the cool light of ten thousand bright crystals. The crews worked. Gangplanks were lowered. And handfuls of people—it was hard to tell how many from this far away—stepped onto the main decks of the immense, unfamiliar ships.

Whispers grew from our rooftop as people passed around a scope, like the kind Captain Pentoba used on the *Chance Encounter*:

"That one looks Bophan."

And: *"Is that one Hartan or Daminan? I can't tell."*

And: *"Those are Khulani clothes."*

At my side, Gerel tensed, but didn't speak.

I wanted to ask the others if we could use their scope, but I didn't even know their names, and Gerel had permitted me to come on the condition that I didn't draw attention to myself. She didn't want anyone recognizing my face, and while the long scar Elbena had given me provided a measure of anonymity—few people would see me as the Hopebearer—it also made me stand out in a new way. So I didn't ask. I just leaned against the rail, heart pounding, and squinted through the gloom of dusk.

By the time the figures began moving down the gangplanks, full dark had arrived, and the bright glares of noorestones made it difficult to see details.

Without us asking, our hosts passed the scope to Gerel. She held the metal tube to her eye, and her breath hitched with alarm. "Seven gods." She handed the scope to me.

For a moment, I saw only a dizzying blur of people and lights and water, but finally I figured out where to aim. And I saw.

There were three Khulani in warrior uniforms—

The familiar profile of First Matriarch Eka Delro—

And the stiff posture of Lady President Dara Soun.

The hope that High Magistrate Paorah had promised was the remaining governing bodies of the Fallen Isles.

The scope slipped from my hands. It would have fallen to the ground, crashing two floors down in an explosion of shattered glass and twisted metal, but Gerel snatched it from the air and returned it to the owner.

He—the owner—shot me a nasty look, but didn't say anything as he went back to his friends.

Gerel turned to face me, using her body to block me from the others' view, keeping her voice low. "What do you think this means?"

I wished I had a good answer, because it should have been such a comfort to see them down there. Given the cheers breaking out all through the streets, most people *were* comforted. They probably believed our governments had decided to do something about the Great Abandonment and—at last—take real action to preserve what was left of our world.

But they'd had that chance with the Mira Treaty, and they'd squandered it.

"He's using their hope against them." My voice fell flat, muffled under the din of speculation. "He'll tell everyone this gathering is to find a way to stop the Great Abandonment, but—"

"It will be a lie," Gerel finished.

Below, the officials strode past the guard-blocked crowds, their procession bracketed by delirious applause. Perhaps some were believers in the high magistrate. Most, even, since he'd been elected again and again. But all of these people?

A cynical part of me wondered if he had agents planted within the crowds, meant to guide group reactions.

I stared hard, watching as the officials began to reach the opulent horsecarres the high magistrate had sent for them. They didn't get in yet, just stood and waved as the cheers escalated. Unease twisted through me as that place in the back of my head—the one that always counted whether or not I wanted to know—ticked off the number of people brought in by these giant ships.

It was difficult to make out individuals without the scope, but there seemed to be a lot more than I'd anticipated. Had the *entire* Twilight Senate come? The *entire* Matriarchy?

What a thought—all of the other islands without their leaders. The Luminary Council was gone, as far as I knew. And then there was the Idrisi government—the Silent Brothers—who had died along with the rest of the people of Idris when the god of silence lifted himself from the ocean.

Excitement built in the assembled crowd, hope in their voices. Even the other ten people on the roof with us spoke in eager tones.

"Finally, we'll get some answers."

"It won't happen to us. We're not like Idris."

"I knew High Magistrate Paorah would have a plan. He is so wise."

A shiver ran through me. They didn't know, I reminded myself. They didn't know that the high magistrate had effectively made all the other Fallen Isles his, thanks to the Mira Treaty.

Below, at some sort of signal I was too distant to see or hear, the officials began to climb into the horsecarres, ready to go to the Red Hall and join the high magistrate. Strange that he'd chosen to remain there, rather than come greet them.

Maybe it was just his way of putting himself above them. He was too busy, too important, to come down to the harbor. Besides, he'd gotten all of us to come here on his behalf. *We* were the greeting party.

"I think it's time for us to go," Gerel said. "Hopefully we can make it back to the hotel before anyone else has the same idea. We've seen all we needed, right?"

"Yes." But even as the word came out, a familiar figure caught my eye. Tall and slim, dressed in a blue dress that swirled around her legs.

I must have gasped, or cried out, because Gerel straightened and followed my line of sight. "What is it?"

Confusion spun through my head, and my heart lurched between hope and grief. I'd know her shape anywhere: Mother.

Mother was *here*.

She was *alive*.

But where was Father?

I staggered, kept upright only by Gerel's strong grip.

If Mother was here but Father was not, that could only mean that he was dead. That he'd been killed.

"All right, Fancy," Gerel murmured, "we're going now. Give me just a moment."

My fingers ached from clutching the railing, but I nodded and she went to say good-bye to our hosts, thanking them for allowing us onto their roof to watch the ships' arrival.

My mother's arrival.

I had to tell Zara. And then I had to get to Mother.

All of the officials had climbed into their horsecarres

21

by the time Gerel returned. Her tone was gentle as she guided me to the ladder. "Whatever it is, you'll be all right. For now, let's focus on getting back to the others in one piece."

She went down the ladder first, onto the narrow balcony, then held it steady for me.

Three rungs. Four. Five.

Then—

Boom. Shocks rippled through the ground, and I dropped down the last rungs and spun to look toward Revis Avenue.

A spiral of smoke bloomed into the sky, so thick it blacked out the stars.

A house had exploded.

CHAPTER TWO

SHOUTS OF EXCITEMENT SHIFTED INTO HORROR AS, like a plague, panic caught and carried through the people-choked streets. A roar of terror spilled over the night, pierced with screams and the siren wail of children crying.

"Dear Fallen Gods," I breathed, stuck in a moment of pure shock—until I remembered my *mother* was down there, in one of the horsecarres careening wildly down the avenue. I had to help her.

"Let's *go*, Fancy!" Gerel grabbed my sleeve and yanked me through the balcony doors. But even before we were inside the house, another great *boom* shook the city, like an attack of thunder.

This one was nearby. On this street.

Chaos escalated as people pushed and pulled, everyone trying to get somewhere safe. Wherever *safe* was anymore.

Thousands of terrified screams were sharp on our heels as we raced through our host's upper dining room, silk curtains fluttering in our wake. Questions flickered through the back of my mind, but right now *who* and *why* didn't matter. The only thing that mattered was making it through this alive.

My heartbeat rushed in my ears as we hurtled ourselves down the curved staircase (fourteen steps), through three silk-covered archways, across one braided rug, and past two heartwood end tables. The numbers narrowed my thoughts, focusing me as I followed Gerel through the front door.

The streets were pure chaos. Fear and smoke saturated the air as people ran in every direction, shoving one another to get away from the black plumes twisting into the dark sky. A dirty, bitter scent coated the back of my throat. I gagged, staggering back toward the doorway, but a body slammed into mine, spinning me against the wall. Gerel grabbed my hand and pulled me north, toward the hotel.

She didn't let go as we pushed through the crush of people. Our progress was terribly slow, and I had to fight my instinct to make way for others. There were too many people, and not nearly enough of us running in the same direction, but Gerel was a force: she didn't hesitate to shove others aside and drag me along with her.

A third *boom* rattled the street, and a bright flare of fire lit the skyline ahead of us.

My heart kicked, and I tried to keep close to Gerel, but half the people who'd been running *with* us now turned and fled in the opposite direction.

"Mira, hurry!" Gerel was ahead of me, her fingers tight over mine. I pushed harder, trying to squeeze between a pair of burly men, and then—

My fingers slipped from Gerel's.

One of the men shoved me aside, into another person. We tumbled, staggered, and by the time I looked up, Gerel was nowhere in sight—swallowed up by the chaos.

"Gerel!" My voice was lost under the cacophony of mass panic. "Gerel!"

As thousands of people grabbed and pushed around me, I scanned the tallest people nearby, but I couldn't see her. She was gone.

The air soured with sweat, while dust and ash fell like mist. I coughed and gagged, catching myself as people plowed into me. I couldn't stay here. I had to *move*. But Gerel . . .

I shouted her name again, but it was no use. The calamity was getting worse, and Gerel wouldn't want me to waste time looking for her. She'd tell me to go straight to the hotel. She was probably halfway there already.

North. I searched for familiar landmarks and pushed through the throng, toward the Fire Rose Hotel. Gerel would be there when I arrived. She would be safe. Ilina and Hristo—who'd been wandering the markets looking for rumors about Nine—would be there already, too.

They had to be.

IT SEEMED LIKE ages that I fought my way north, block by block, pushing myself between terrified people. But eventually, the crowds thinned as others took side streets or ventured indoors. And, when no more explosions sounded, the mass panic began to ease.

Still, a bitter stench smothered the streets, and every crack or shout made me jump. Every flare of light felt sinister. Even the people skittering about the streets seemed filled up with potential danger. If only I had a knife. There were thousands of noorestones nearby, and I could use them to defend myself if necessary, but a knife would be obvious protection.

My heart pounded in my ears as I searched the flat-topped buildings for the Fire Rose Hotel. There. Two buildings down, gold flowers painted on the walls shone in the glow of streetlamps. I slowed to a walk, struggling to catch my breath in spite of the dust and smoke that hung in the air.

The double doors were solid bloodwood, bright with gilt vines growing up the polished surface. Extravagant, Gerel had called the hotel, but Captain Pentoba had warned us that less expensive places would be more of a risk, should anyone working there discover our identities.

In Flamecrest, the wealthier innkeepers could afford to be loyal to their guests; they had far less incentive to talk to anyone about the people staying with them.

Of course, if the high magistrate wanted to know, anyone would tell him anything.

One glance over my shoulder—nothing but dust and darkness—and I pulled at the front door, ready to race up the stairs and make sure all my friends were accounted for.

The knob wouldn't turn. Locked.

New fear spiked in my chest as I balled my fist and pounded on the door, trying not to think about what would happen if I couldn't get in. Upstairs, LaLa whined; I didn't hear it with my ears, but I *felt* it through our bond, which had only grown stronger since we'd rescued those dragons from the ruins.

"Go away!" a man shouted from the other side of the door. The owner. I recognized his voice; it sounded too deep for someone so wiry.

"I'm staying here. Please!" A wild note of terror edged my words, but I couldn't stop it. "Tanhe, please!"

The lock clicked, and Tanhe peered out. At first, it looked like he didn't remember me, but then his eyes caught on my scar; he hadn't commented on it when we'd arrived five days ago, but he'd definitely been curious. Everyone was.

"Forgive me." The door opened all the way, revealing the dark lobby. Everything held its breath, still and waiting for safety: the gold silk draped over the reception desk, the velvet covers over noorestones, even the sounds. A hush hung over the building, like everyone here was too afraid to even speak. "When we heard the explosions, I feared people would rush in and invade all the rooms, and our guests—you—would have nowhere safe to return to."

I stepped inside, noting the sword clutched in Tanhe's right hand, and the dagger still in its sheath. He had that backward, given the closer quarters. It didn't inspire much confidence in his ability to protect his guests. Anyway, we were far enough away from the explosions that it was unlikely anyone would have come here seeking shelter, but no one knew if the explosions would continue, or if they'd spread farther throughout the city.

My boots tapped on the flame-blue tiles, crossing the lines of gold that swept into elaborate lala flowers. Days ago, coming to the Fire Rose had felt like a good omen—as much of a good omen as anything could be, with the god shadow swinging across the city every evening and our entire world falling apart. Now everything felt prickly. Dangerous. Nowhere was safe.

Tanhe quickly shut the door behind me, locking it. "You left with a friend, didn't you?"

"I did." I glanced at the vine-like staircase that grew in the center of the lobby, like a garden of iron bones. The steps were empty, at least on this level. "She didn't get here before me?"

"I'm afraid not. There's been no one."

My heart sank. She should have arrived already. Gerel

was stronger, faster. If she wasn't here yet, she must be hurt.

I'd have to go back out and search for her.

Tanhe shifted his weight. He was a tall man, with deep brown skin and a narrow frame, and clearly uncomfortable with his height. His shoulders curled inward, ruining the lines of his fine linen jacket. "The two of you went to the harbor, didn't you?"

I nodded, nerves jangling inside my head. And now that we were closer, LaLa's worry tugged at my heart.

"What was on the ships?" Tanhe asked. "Did you see?"

Traitors.

But I couldn't say that.

"Governments." My voice sounded thin—wispy with smoke. "I saw the Twilight Senate, the Warrior Tribunal—all the others, except for the Silent Brothers and the Luminary Council."

Mother had been there, though, wearing the same dress as when I'd last seen her. I wished I knew what that meant—if she'd been taken against her will, or if she was being treated well. . . .

Worry darkened Tanhe's eyes. "I wonder if the explosions were meant to harm them in some way."

"Perhaps," I said slowly. "But no one knew who was coming."

He nodded.

"It seems more likely that the explosions were meant to cause chaos among the people. There were thousands of us out there." I didn't know who would do that, though, or why. Then again, it wasn't my job to find out. I had more important things to worry about, and surely High Magistrate Paorah and the Fire Ministry would make a thorough investigation. "My friend is still out there. I'm going to get someone to help me look for her, but if she arrives before we come down, please make sure she's allowed in."

He nodded. "Of course. It will be my honor."

What a strange thing to say. I narrowed my eyes at him as I moved toward the grand stairs in the center of the lobby.

"All of my guests are like family," he said. "Those on the third floor especially."

Suspicion clawed at me, but I didn't waste any more time. I took the stairs two at a time, climbing to the top floor.

Chenda stood in the doorway when I arrived, holding out LaLa's tether for me. I took the worn leather—and LaLa—and stroked my little dragon's head. Together again.

"Where is Gerel?" Worry twisted Chenda's words into a sharp knot. "Is she hurt?"

"I'm not sure. We were separated during the stampede. What about—"

I didn't have to finish the question. Hristo pushed past her, into the hall, and took in my torn dress, the bitter stench of explosives clinging to my hair and clothes, and the shortness of my breath.

"I should have gone to look for you." With his good hand, he took my arm to steady me. Beyond him, Ilina watched us from the parlor, relief clear on her face. "I'm sorry."

"It's fine," I said, pulling LaLa closer to me. "It's good you came back here. We'd never have found each other out there."

He didn't look convinced, but he didn't press.

"We have to go find Gerel," I said. "I just came up here to get one of you."

Hope lit Chenda's eyes, but Hristo was already guiding me into the suite. "Not like this. Rest for a minute and give her time to get here. If she isn't back in half an hour, I'll look for her."

"But—"

"No." He spoke firmly. "Give her half an hour. This is Gerel. If anyone can handle themselves out there, it's her."

Exactly. And if she wasn't back yet, then something had clearly happened.

But there was no use arguing with Hristo when he was acting as my protector, and for ten years I'd been told to obey Hristo in emergencies. It was hard to ignore that kind of training. "Ten minutes." My knees buckled as I walked. Not much, but Hristo's grip on my arm tightened, and LaLa squawked with renewed concern. "Ten minutes," I said, "and then I'm looking for her, with or without you."

He sighed but nodded. "Fine. Sit, though. Before you fall."

Chenda flashed me a tight smile as she shut the door after us, but she didn't move far from it.

I sank into one of the cushioned chairs and focused on breathing. Knots loosened. My heartbeat eased. When Ilina knelt beside me with my bottle of calming pills, I shook my head. "I'm all right now. It's passed."

She squeezed my arm, then went back to her own chair, where she'd fastened Crystal's tether. The dragons must have been terrified by the noise if Ilina had put their hunting gear on them, but it was probably the best choice.

Zara stood by the window, holding the gauzy curtains closed. She'd been looking outside again, most likely, even though she knew how dangerous it was. But I couldn't be mad at her, not knowing how relieved she'd be to learn that Mother had arrived on one of those ships and that she wasn't completely alone after all.

"What?" Zara wrinkled her nose at me. "Why are you staring like that?"

I breathed deeply, letting the fuzz of adrenaline slip away. Quickly, I told the others about the noorestones, the ships, and the government officials marching down the street. "And then I saw her." I looked at Zara. "I saw Mother."

My sister's jaw dropped, and a second later, she sat on the floor. Hard. "You saw Mother."

I nodded.

"Liar," she whispered.

"I'm not lying."

"Mira, are you sure?" Chenda's tone was gentle. "You said everyone was far away. Maybe you only thought you saw her."

"Did you see Father?" Zara's eyes were wide, eager. "Was he with her?"

"What about *my* father?" Hope deepened Hristo's voice.

I shook my head. "I know it was her. I'd know her anywhere." I looked at my sister, then Hristo. "But she was alone. I'm sorry."

His eyes went glassy with tears, but he just swallowed and gave a single nod. Both of us knew that our fathers' absence meant they were likely dead.

"Mother is here." Zara pulled her knees up to her chest. Tears trickled down her cheeks, but she didn't bother to wipe them away. "How do you think she ended up on that ship? Do you think the warriors let her go because of her charm? Do you think the high magistrate went to save her? Do you think the explosions were meant to hurt her?"

"I don't know."

"When are we going to get her?"

"I don't know," I said again. "She's with High Magistrate Paorah."

"Did you even try to get to her?" Zara scrambled to her feet. "Did you even *want* to get her? All the gods! You care about everyone else more than you care about Mother and me."

"That's not true." But my protest was too slow. Too late.

Before I could say anything else, she'd stormed through the door to the room she and I shared.

Slam. She let out a muffled scream, and something crashed, but then the washroom door slammed, too.

I started after my sister, but Ilina took my elbow and pulled me back. "She'll come around when she's ready."

My sister hated me. She would never come around.

"What's happening out there?" Altan's bellow came from his closet in the boys' room. "What were those explosions?"

"He's been yelling for an hour." Chenda glanced at the door. "Just ignore him."

That was what we usually did.

I dropped my face to LaLa's and breathed in her smoky scent.

"Let's find Gerel," Chenda said. "I'll get the medical kit. She might be hurt."

I stood, looking for a place to fasten LaLa's tether; she would not be coming with us. "I'll see if Aaru can listen for her." It seemed unlikely, since he'd barely moved for five days, but maybe he could hear her and give us a direction, or—

Thuds sounded on the stairs, coming all the way up to the third floor. My heart wrenched up into my throat as Chenda rushed for the door and threw it open just as Gerel reached the top of the stairs, her face dark with unease. Dust coated her clothes and skin, but she was whole.

"Gerel!" Relief soared through me. Thank all the gods

she'd made it back. "We were just coming to look for you."

"No need." She glanced through the room, making sure everyone was accounted for—although Aaru was still in his room, Zara was in hers, and Altan was locked inside a closet. "Everyone's safe?" she asked.

"Yes, we're fine." More or less. I turned my chair—now with soot smears marring the cream fabric—so that she could rest, but she waved it away.

"What about you?" Chenda took Gerel's hand. "You're all right? Not hurt?"

Gerel scoffed and lifted her chin, as though to say she was above getting hurt. But she squeezed Chenda's hand nonetheless. "I'm fine. Sorry to worry you." Those last words were for Chenda, mostly. To the rest of us, she said, "I took a detour to find out what happened."

"You left Mira alone," Hristo said. "You shouldn't have done that."

She rolled her eyes. "Trust her a little more, will you? I knew she'd come straight back here. No one was looking for her out there. They were all too busy trying to get themselves to safety."

"I was all right." I touched Hristo's arm. "I was more worried for Gerel than myself."

"You're always more worried for other people." Hristo looked down at me. "That's why I worry."

I couldn't make myself smile, because Gerel's expression turned grim.

"People were killed in the explosions," she said. "And

others were injured during the panic after. I don't know how many, but I know it's bad out there. People are terrified."

Of course they were. They should be. Back in Crescent Prominence, Altan's warriors had caused a massive explosion that had taken out the council house, and my noorestone power had almost destroyed the Lexara Theater in Val fa Merce. How could people have known whether this one was connected to the others or not?

"Everyone thinks High Magistrate Paorah will put the entire city under martial law." A muscle ticced in Gerel's jaw. "Curfew, checkpoints, and limited movements. The last time they were under martial law, people were discouraged from leaving their homes except in emergencies, and even then a guard might detain them for looking suspicious."

A chill ran through my entire body.

"What do we do?" Ilina blew out a breath. "What *can* we do?"

"Did you have any luck finding Nine?" Gerel asked.

"No." Hristo frowned and readjusted his sling. "Nothing. Nine is so well hidden they may as well not exist. And it's going to be even more difficult to find them with martial law."

The high magistrate was in control now, not just of Anahera, but of all the remaining governments of the Fallen Isles. "He brought them here for a reason," I muttered. "For *hope*, he claims. Everyone thinks he's going to

36

do something to prevent the Great Abandonment."

"How?" Chenda shook her head. "The gods are already rising. Is it possible to make them stop? Is it possible to make them lie down again?"

"I don't know." A memory tugged at me. Or a dream. Fire and bones brimming with power. I shook it away, even as LaLa nudged at me with keen excitement. "If he brought all the other governments here, he has a plan to share with them. We need to be there, both to hear firsthand what he tells them, and to find Nine." Not to mention, my mother would be there. She was *alive*.

"Because an imperial spy wouldn't miss that kind of meeting for anything." Ilina nodded. "All right. Then we need to figure out when they're talking, and how we'll get in."

"That's the easy part, isn't it?"

Everyone looked at me, question in their eyes.

"I'm the Hopebearer. I'll announce myself and walk in through the front door."

The *Drakontos celestus*

SOMEWHERE—

Sometime—

In a deep and distant memory—

Great bones slept beneath the earth.

The anatomy was unusual, at least to anyone who'd studied dragons before. The shape of the scapula, the length of the ulna, and the curve of the keel: all were different from any other dragon on record. Indeed, in a certain light, these bones even seemed to have iridescent scales.

Such a strange dragon, locked away in the crust of the earth, buried under layers of mineral-rich strata. She didn't belong there. Her place was somewhere else, in a land made of fallen stars and undeniable gods.

But across time and distance and death, the first dragon reached.

"BRING ME HOME."

CHAPTER THREE

"Definitely not."

"That's a terrible idea."

"Why would you even suggest that?"

I waited until their comments were finished before I said, "It's the most straightforward plan."

"It's the *worst* plan," Gerel muttered. "You've been hiding your identity for decans. Why expose yourself now?"

"We want to find Nine, don't we?"

"Not at the expense of your safety," Hristo said.

I smiled a little. "We were running from Altan. Now he's locked in the closet. Anyway, I don't think my identity is as secret as we thought. Tanhe knows who I am."

"What?" Ilina's mouth dropped open. "Are you sure? How do you know?"

"We've been using the papers we bought in Val fa Merce." Chenda crossed her arms, and she had the look of someone already composing a letter of complaint.

I perched on the arm of the sofa and sighed, pulling LaLa toward my shoulder. She started licking my face, as though to wash off the stink of explosions. "He didn't outright say anything, but it seemed like he was hinting that he knew."

"Then we can't be sure," Chenda said.

"I can get answers." Gerel's tone was dark.

I held up a hand. "No, it's all right. He clearly understands that we're trying to keep our identities secret. We used false papers, and he said it's important to protect his guests. It shouldn't be a surprise, though. Zara looks similar enough to me. And my scar doesn't make me look like a different person."

"And we paid with dragon figurines." Ilina dragged her hands down her face. "That was stupid."

In addition to Captain Pentoba's influence (she knew everyone in every port, and they all seemed to owe her favors), we'd given him a few of the dragon figurines I'd brought from my home in Crescent Prominence. They were worth a small fortune, as some had real gemstones embedded in them, while others were made of precious metals. They were exquisitely detailed, crafted with care, and on Anahera, they were worth thousands of lumes.

"I agree with Feisty," Gerel said. "It was a poor move on our part, but we were in shock after the earthquake."

We were *still* in shock.

"Which is why we need to think about this," she went on. "Mira, regardless of Altan's whereabouts, you were still a prisoner in the Pit. We were *all* prisoners there. Exposing yourself puts everyone at risk."

I closed my eyes and exhaled slowly. "You're right. But if we want to make a difference in the world, we have to take risks. We can't put our own safety above the survival of the Fallen Isles, and Nine might know how to help us."

"How so?" Gerel leveled her scowl at me.

I couldn't answer that without sounding crazy, but I *knew* that finding Nine was the first step. I dreamed of dragon bones and eclipses every night, and even if my human self couldn't put together all the clues—not yet—this dragon side knew something important.

LaLa clicked urgently and thumped her nose against my jaw. She knew, too: we had to find Nine to find the bones.

"If we knew there was a way to prevent the Great Abandonment from progressing, I'd agree with you." Chenda's tone was gentle. "But we must consider our own safety."

"No one else has to go," I said. "We can take measures to protect everyone, but sooner or later, someone—not just Tanhe—is going to recognize me and ask questions. I'd rather do this on my terms."

The others were quiet a moment, and finally Ilina nodded. "All right. We'll find out when the meetings will be."

Hristo just sighed, but he didn't fight me again.

"One problem." Chenda studied my face. "There's a false Hopebearer somewhere out there."

Tirta. When I'd refused to follow their orders, the Luminary Council dressed her up as me. And people had believed the charade.

"Then we find her," I said. "We'll put her in a closet, too."

"Our closets are getting awfully crowded." But Gerel smiled a little, clearly pleased to have a task. Without waiting for anyone, she marched into the boys' room and threw open the closet door where we'd been keeping Altan.

The rank odor of unwashed warrior filled the room.

Ilina made a faint retching noise. "Don't you let him bathe?"

Hristo shrugged. "We let him out to relieve himself, but this is a desert. The sign in the washroom says not to waste water."

"Consider this a necessity," she said. "Tanhe is going to kill us when he finds out we've been keeping dragons here, *and* a stinking warrior."

I followed behind the others, while Ilina and Hristo talked, and Gerel pulled the gag off Altan.

Aaru was sitting on his bed, motionless, same as he'd been since we'd arrived. As far as I knew, he got up to use the washroom and bathe, and sometimes the food we left for him disappeared, but he was losing weight. His skin, once a warm brown, deeper after all the sunshine, had a gray cast to it now. I sat next to him every

42

day, just being present, but I could never tell if it made a difference.

"Fancy." Gerel glanced over her shoulder. "Your turn."

I passed LaLa to Chenda, then squeezed around Ilina and Hristo to stand next to Gerel. She had a hand resting on her knife, but she didn't draw it. Not yet. Altan's wrists were cuffed behind his back, and the burn scabs on his face were freshly bandaged; they'd come open during the fight in the ruins and begun oozing something foul. Still, somehow, he stood inside the closet as though he was the one in charge.

"Hello, Hopebearer." He grinned. The reek of his breath was almost unbearable.

I didn't waste time with niceties. "Where are Tirta and Elbena?"

He raised an eyebrow. "Didn't I tell you? You can have them when I get what I want."

"You're not one of us," I hissed. "You don't get to know the things we know. You are a prisoner."

His shoulders lifted slightly in a faint shrug. "Very well. Then I suppose you'll just never know where I've put them."

Fury blackened the edges of my vision. "You will tell me," I breathed. "You will tell me *now*."

"Will you torture me, Hopebearer?"

No, I wouldn't. He knew I wouldn't. I wasn't like him. I wouldn't hurt people to get what I wanted. But maybe I could give him an incentive. "What about a bath?"

"I'm not interested in you like that," he said. "But it's thoughtful of you to offer."

Gerel drew her knife halfway from its sheath. "Watch your tone."

"Tell me where they are," I said, "and you'll have a nice half hour to bathe. The hotel has a lovely jasmine-and-honey soap you might consider using. We'll even make sure your closet is aired and cleaned."

He lifted his shoulders and sniffed. "I don't mind a little bit of filth. All I want is to know everything you know."

I sighed, regretting it instantly. We all knew he was getting a bath no matter what.

"High Magistrate Paorah has gathered up all the remaining island governments. Since your warriors killed the rest of the Luminary Council, the high magistrate will be searching for Elbena. It wouldn't hurt him to have Tirta, either, since she's pretending to be me."

If there was anything redeeming about Altan, beyond his devotion to dragons, it was that he was smart. He put things together. He knew what I wasn't saying, even if he didn't understand that Anahera was behind the Mira Treaty, not the Algotti Empire like he believed.

"You don't trust the high magistrate."

"I don't have a reason to trust most governments right now," I said. "So no, I don't want him to have any version of a Hopebearer to parade around. Who knows what he might use her for?"

He glared beyond me, thinking. Then, finally, he said,

44

"All right. They're in a house on Weber Street. But you have to go yourself. My people will speak only to you or me, and I don't expect you'll invite me to go with you."

"Not a chance."

He shrugged. "Your loss."

I turned to Gerel and Chenda. "Tonight. The longer we wait, the more likely it is the high magistrate gets to them first."

"We'll get ready," Chenda said.

For the first time since the earthquake, I felt . . . *good* wasn't the right word. How could I, with a risen god on the horizon and the boy I loved so devastated he could barely move? But I felt resolved. Determined. Focused. We had a goal and a plan. And—if my dragon dreams were real—maybe we had a reason to hope.

HRISTO PULLED ME aside before I left.

"I wish you'd take fewer risks," he said.

"You heard Altan," I said. "His warriors won't give up Tirta and Elbena for anyone else. I have to go."

He sighed. "Not just this time, but earlier. Anyone else could have gone to see the ships. Gerel could have gone by herself. And all the times you went to the markets . . ."

"You don't have to worry about me," I whispered. "Besides, it's only fair I do my share of the work. I can't ask anyone to go anywhere I'm not willing to go."

He just looked at me sadly. "I know you have incredible power over noorestones and dragons now, but that doesn't mean I won't worry. I'm not just your protector, Mira. I'm your friend. Never forget that."

I hugged him as tight as I could, and then Gerel cleared her throat from the doorway. "Are we actually doing this tonight, or are you just going to share feelings until Paorah finds us here?"

I rolled my eyes, but I pulled away from Hristo. "I'll be careful."

Together, Chenda, Gerel, and I crept down the stairs and through the lobby. It seemed so mundane. Part of me had wondered if we might rappel out the window, or climb up to the roof and jump from building to building, but of the three of us, Gerel was the only one with any of the necessary skills.

"Excuse me." Tanhe appeared from behind the desk. "Where are you going?"

"Nowhere you need to know about," said Gerel.

"Martial law is—"

"Are you going to tell anyone?" I lifted an eyebrow.

"If the high magistrate asks—"

"Does the high magistrate come here often?" I asked. "Do his guards usually have reasons to ask questions about your guests?"

He sputtered a little. "No, I— No, of course not."

I angled my scar away from him, so that he'd only see the Hopebearer, and I offered the kind of warm smile that put even the most nervous of people at ease. "We're only going to find a couple of friends. After the explosions earlier, we want to make sure they're safe. This *is* a safe hotel, isn't it?"

"Absolutely," he assured me. "I'll stay up, of course. And wait for you. In case you need anything. Something to eat or extra toiletries for your friends. Whatever you need."

Again, I flashed the Hopebearer smile. "Thank you so much for your help," I said. "And your discretion."

Then, Gerel, Chenda, and I went through the front door.

"And to think," Gerel said, keeping her voice low, "you claim you don't possess Daminan charm. But if I didn't just witness it there . . ."

I shook my head and smiled. "That's not charm. Just the Hopebearer effect. No, if you want to see charm, you should see my mother. Even Zara, when she tries." My throat tightened up at the thought of Mother in the high magistrate's hands. From here, we could just see the tops of the Red Hall, its noorestones lighting up the gemstones.

"All right," Chenda said. "Hush, both of you."

Though only a couple of hours had passed since the explosions, the streets were dark. Empty. Even so, we kept to the side streets and pockets of deepest shadows.

The air smelled wretched, like dust and smoke and a thousand other things I couldn't fully identify. A deep, fearful part of me wondered if I was smelling the bodies of people who'd died, but I didn't let that thought finish forming before I squashed it back down. It was too horrible to contemplate.

Gerel and I kept close to Chenda, letting her shadows darken around us. Having Aaru's silence would have been useful, too, but this wasn't the time to ask him to use the gift of his god.

I didn't even know if he *could* anymore.

Worries haunted me as we made our way through the dark, dust-choked city. I had never seen it so deserted. During the day, even with the horror of the Great Abandonment sitting on the horizon, the narrow, twisty streets were always filled with a steady roar of voices, punctuated by occasional shrieks of laughter or outrage. On corners, people usually begged for spare coins, but everything was empty now. Even the heavy carts that were pressed up to the sides of buildings had no merchants standing there, no one calling out for buyers seeking silks or honey or spiced cloudfish. There was no clatter of horsecarres, no tolling bells, no shouts of police struggling to create orderly traffic.

The quiet was eerie. Uncomfortable. Unbearable, so soon after disaster. That was why people had gathered together after Idris rose up from his seabed, rattling the bones of the earth and causing the western horizon to darken with a silent promise: worse would come; the Great Abandonment was upon us.

People had needed community. Companionship.

But now, just two hours after explosions rang through

the streets of Flamecrest, there was nothing.

"We'll have to run," Gerel said as we reached Revis Avenue. We had to cross, but there were no shadows to hide in, no crowds to get lost in. "One at a time. Keep your steps light, and aim yourself there." She pointed to a pocket of darkness between an abandoned food cart and a bank. "Mira, you first."

My back was pressed against a building. I hated the thought of crossing the street, so exposed to anyone who might be looking down from a building, but I'd made the decision to come out tonight. I had to do this. And I had to do it first.

I sucked in a deep breath and set my eyes on the food cart, and then, nerves steeled, I pushed myself off the wall and sprinted. One, two, three: I ran on the balls of my toes, keeping my breaths long and even. I felt too slow, too clumsy.

And when I reached the middle of the street, I could look to my left and see the Red Hall all the way down the illuminated stretch of road, glowing so bright it washed out the stars.

The building was immense, imposing. It seemed like an eye that stared straight down at me.

My mother was in that building.

Then I was across the street, tucked away in the shadows Gerel had indicated.

Chenda came next, graceful in her long strides. She crouched next to me while we watched Gerel.

Then I heard them: footfalls. The steady cadence of guards patrolling the area came from behind Chenda and me, moving straight for Gerel.

Chenda noticed at the same time as I did, and I knew she didn't think—she just acted—because at once, shadows fell across the street where Gerel was running. A moment later, Chenda hissed, realizing her mistake. The sudden darkness would make Gerel *more* obvious than she had been before.

A small shout sounded. The footfalls sped up. The guards had noticed.

I squeezed myself between the building and the cart, trying to make myself as tiny as possible next to Chenda.

We needed a distraction. Something to hide *this* shadow and let Gerel through.

As the guards went rushing by, I reached out with my mind, touching all the noorestones nearby—and pushed their inner fire away, toward noorestones farther down the road.

Darkness rippled, spreading both ways down Revis Avenue. Lights dimmed and went out.

The guards stopped on the other side of the cart, and in the moonslight, I could just see the tops of their heads. They looked from side to side, shifting their weight.

"What happened?" asked one.

"Can noorestones do that?"

Both stood there, letting their eyes adjust to the darkness, while Gerel slipped behind the cart with Chenda and me. It was cramped, but we kept as quiet as possible.

I wished we had Aaru's silence.

Now that she was safe, I allowed the noorestones to shine again, one at a time.

"Strange." The first guard took a few steps forward.

"Lots of strange things today." The second followed a moment later. Both, I saw now, had their weapons drawn. "Those explosions, the raids, martial law. Now this? Do you ever wonder—"

"Don't finish that question." The first guard looked sharply at his friend. "You know better."

The second guard sucked in a deep breath. "Right. Sorry." They were quiet a moment, still creeping forward as the last of the noorestones illuminated once more. "Maybe they will fix this at the summit," he said. "The Great Abandonment, I mean, not the noorestones."

"Wouldn't hurt if someone fixed the noorestones, too, though." The first guard shot a nervous smile over his shoulder, and then they were taking long, steady strides across the street.

Huddled in the shadows behind the cart, my shoulder pressed up against Chenda's, I let out a long sigh.

"Sorry," Chenda whispered. "I panicked."

"It's all right." Gerel took Chenda's hand and squeezed. "They didn't see us."

We watched the guards until they disappeared down the road, and then we drew ourselves up to walk the last few streets. How would we get Tirta and Elbena to the hotel like this?

Finally, we reached the house Altan had told us about.

51

Weber Street was quiet—residential, with all the curtains closed as far as I could see. Not a hint of noorestone light shone anywhere except on the streetlamps.

I steeled myself and crept up to the door.

And listened.

Wind breathed down the street.

Noorestones hummed in the back of my head.

And my heartbeat thudded in my ears.

No sounds came from inside the house, but maybe everyone was sleeping. If Aaru had been here, he'd have been able to say for sure.

Cautiously, I gave a soft knock, waited, and when no one answered, I knocked again.

Nothing.

Gerel and Chenda exchanged worried glances. "Try to open it," whispered Chenda.

I tried to turn the knob, but it caught. Locked.

Gerel shifted us all around so that she stood closest to the door. She tested the knob, as though confirming I wasn't just terrible at opening doors, and then gave a sharp twist. The door swung open, and the smell hit.

It was a terrible, sick odor, like someone hadn't made it to the washroom in time. The stink rolled from the front door and knocked all three of us back a couple of steps. "Seven gods." I coughed. "That's vile."

Chenda's face was drawn with disgust as she pulled her shirt up to cover her nose and mouth. "It smells worse than the sewage holes in the Pit."

Even Gerel looked ready to vomit, but she just shook her head, silently ordering us to stop talking, and pushed the door open wider.

It was dark inside, but there was a covered noorestone on the wall right beside the door. After checking that the door was shut behind us and the window curtains drawn tight, I lifted the velvet away and let cool blue light shine across the parlor. Empty. Except . . .

Red-brown streaks marred the golden hardwood floor, making a choppy trail into the hall. Gerel knelt and held out a hand for the noorestone, which I gave to her.

"It's blood," she said. "Dry now."

The three of us went from room to room, finding only bloody trails—evidence that something terrible had happened here. The stench of bodily waste grew stronger as we reached the back of the house, and that was where we found them:

Four warriors had been laid out on the floor of the back bedroom. Dead.

There was no sign of Tirta or Elbena, and suddenly I realized what the guards had meant by "raids."

High Magistrate Paorah had known they were in the city. He'd sent his soldiers looking for the last Luminary Councilor and the false Hopebearer. Now he had them.

We were too late.

CHAPTER FOUR

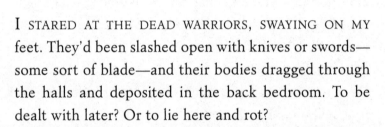

I STARED AT THE DEAD WARRIORS, SWAYING ON MY
feet. They'd been slashed open with knives or swords—
some sort of blade—and their bodies dragged through
the halls and deposited in the back bedroom. To be
dealt with later? Or to lie here and rot?

The overwhelming stink of blood and feces scraped
the back of my throat, then slid down until my stomach
turned over. I wanted to heave, but not here. Not next to
their bodies.

I half stumbled, half ran from the room, threw myself
out the back door, and vomited into a scraggly bush.

They were killers, I knew. Monsters, like Altan. They'd
worked under him, and they may have been part of the
group that destroyed the council house in Crescent Prominence less than a decan ago, but still.

Still.

I vomited until my stomach was empty, felt through my pocket for my calming pills, and held the cool glass bottle in my hand. I didn't need a pill right now—I didn't have anything to swallow it with, anyway—but knowing they were there helped.

"Fancy?" Gerel touched my shoulder. "We should head back."

She was right. We couldn't stay here. Not with bodies. Not with martial law.

After I spit the taste of bile from my mouth, I pulled myself straight. "Sorry," I said. "I've never seen anything like that."

"That's a normal way to react." She squeezed my shoulder. "There's no reason to be embarrassed about it."

I took a gulp of fresh air before moving into the house again. It was strange what the mind and body could get used to in such a short period of time, because the stench didn't seem quite so bad as I marched through the hall, making sure to avoid stepping in the congealed blood.

On the walk back to the hotel, I couldn't get the sight of those warriors out of my mind. High Magistrate Paorah must have sent scores of soldiers in there. Warriors—even those away from Khulan—were not easy to kill. And now, Tirta and Elbena were in the high magistrate's hands. He had his own Hopebearer, and it was impossible to say what he would do with her.

"We should have gotten to them sooner," I said. "I

should have forced Altan to give them up days ago."

"He wouldn't have revealed anything." Gerel led us around a corner. Our hotel glowed cheerily just a block away. "You'd have had to tell him the truth about the empire and Anahera, and I assume that's not something you're willing to do yet."

"I want to tie a rock to him and throw him in the deepest part of the ocean."

"I can arrange that." Gerel looked hopeful.

"He still has Kelsine." Even as I said the words, I wondered if the *Drakontos ignitus* had been in the house, too. But I hadn't sensed her presence, nor had I noticed molted scales or talon scrapes.

Then, we reached the hotel. I knocked a quick pattern, and Tanhe ushered us inside. "Your friends?" he asked.

I shook my head. "I need a favor."

"How can I help?" The end of his question held an unspoken *Hopebearer*.

"High Magistrate Paorah is holding a summit to discuss the Great Abandonment with the other island leaders."

Tanhe nodded. "That's good. Perhaps there's a way to preserve our islands after all."

"Perhaps." I offered my warmest, most patient Hopebearer smile. "I'd like to attend the summit."

"Of course. You belong there, what with the Luminary Council being . . ." His shoulders curled inward. "Excuse me. I only meant that someone needs to stand for Damina."

Gerel shifted her weight, and Chenda frowned. I let the beat of silence persist just a moment into uncomfortable, and then I said, "I'm afraid I didn't intend for anyone to learn my identity."

His smile didn't falter, but the light in his eyes dimmed. "The attack. That's why you're in hiding."

I bowed my head, not outright lying—Mother said I was a terrible liar—but allowing him to believe I was confirming his suspicions.

"I was so sorry to hear about that," Tanhe went on. His gaze slipped toward Gerel as she walked partway up the stairs, watching the landings above for signs of anyone eavesdropping. This wasn't the best conversation to have in the lobby, but moving it to his office would invite more questions. "Such a tragedy. And now you've come to Flamecrest, only for everything tonight . . ." He waved a hand toward the front door.

"It's been a difficult decan for everyone," I said. "And since you've cleverly found me out, I must ask your help in keeping my secret."

"Of course. Guest privacy is a priority at the Fire Rose. As is ensuring our guests' needs are anticipated and met."

I smiled. "Then you already know what I'm going to ask."

"You'll have everything I can find by tomorrow afternoon."

"The Fire Rose came very highly recommended. Clearly its reputation is well deserved."

Tanhe bowed as Chenda and I followed Gerel up the stairs.

"Was that wise?" Gerel kept her voice low. "Can we trust him?"

"I don't know," I said. "But we need help."

"We should make a plan in case he betrays us," Chenda said.

"We should." Gerel glanced over her shoulder. "But first I'd like to hear what Mira thinks she's going to do. You really think it's possible to get into the summit as anyone other than yourself?"

"Now that he has Tirta, I can't go as me. Imagine the chaos of two Hopebearers." I hauled myself up the last few stairs. "No, I'll go incognito and look for Nine. It will give me a different sort of freedom, not being myself."

Gerel nodded slowly. "I hate this idea, just so you know. It's stupid, going straight into the Red Hall when fake Mira was just kidnapped—again—and all her guards killed. But I can't think of anything better right now, so I'll help you."

"That's nice of you," I said.

"I just mean that I've gotten used to having you around, so it would be a shame if something terrible happened because you're bad at plans." Gerel opened the suite door to where Ilina and Hristo were waiting for us to give them the news.

"YOUR BREATH STINKS."

Zara, tactful as always, was standing in the washroom doorway, watching me as I peeled off my dusty, sweat-streaked clothes and dropped them into a laundry basket.

"I threw up." I was tempted to start gnawing on a bar of soap; it smelled of honey and lala flowers.

Zara's eyebrows arched. "You haven't thrown up in years."

I looked at her askance. "One: it's weird that you know that. And two: Mother said it would ruin my teeth, and you know what it's like living with her."

My sister shrugged. "She never cared about my teeth, or anything else about me."

I rolled my eyes and turned on the tap in the tub. Water gushed out, luxurious beyond measure in this desert climate. "Of course she does."

"Not like she cares about you." She said it like a fact she'd learned long ago. Like she'd accepted it. "When are we going to rescue her?"

"I'm not sure."

"You said High Magistrate Paorah is bad. You said he's behind all the things you accused the Algotti Empire of doing."

"That's true."

"Then we need to rescue Mother. We can't leave her with that monster." Her eyes were bright with tears. "I just want to find her. I want to go home."

"I know. We have a plan, all right?" Telling Ilina and Hristo—and Zara, who'd been lured out by her insatiable need to know things—had gone as well as expected. No one liked the plan of trusting Tanhe and sneaking into the summit under false names, but like Gerel said, we didn't have much of a choice.

Unless we wanted to hide out here until the world finished ending.

"Your plan is stupid," Zara said. "And you didn't once mention rescuing Mother."

"Tomorrow. We'll have a better idea of our options tomorrow."

She gave a dramatic sigh, then spun around and went into the bedroom she and I shared. (Ilina had been sharing with her mother, but now that she had left, I was seriously considering moving in. I just couldn't tell if that would make Zara more or less angry with me.)

I sank into the tub, water so hot it should have scalded my skin. But, like looking at the sun, it didn't hurt. Not anymore.

When I closed my eyes and listened, I could hear Zara move around our room before she flopped onto the bed. Springs groaned. My sister let out a short, hitched breath, and at once I realized she was crying. Because of something I'd said?

I listened harder, hearing voices rumble in the parlor. The conversation earlier had been quick, because everyone was exhausted, but I knew Ilina and Hristo weren't happy about my decision to go to the summit. Not as myself, and not in disguise. But I'd meant what I'd told Hristo earlier: If I didn't go, who would? Who else *could*? Seven had been willing to talk only to me; we had to assume Nine would feel the same.

And then I stretched my senses even farther, until I heard—or imagined I heard—tapping. ::**Strength through silence.**:: Desperate prayers from someone whose god had already abandoned him.

I listened to his prayers, over and over, and wished more than anything that I could help. But there was nothing I could do to ease the pain of his loss.

When Zara's cries quieted, and the voices stopped, and even the tapping faded, I realized I would fall asleep in the tub if I didn't move. But somehow, the water was still hot, and the jasmine-scented air was relaxing.

Grudgingly, I finished cleaning myself and climbed out of the tub. Then I noticed it: water steamed off my skin, and before I had finished wrapping myself in one of the plush towels, I was dry.

A shiver of unease worked through me, but I put on my nightgown and wrapped my hair in a square of cool silk.

In the bedroom, Zara was already sleeping, the covers twisted around her and half spilling onto the floor. One leg was stretched onto my side, but if I moved her, she'd wake. Zara only looked like a deep sleeper; if my experience these last few days was anything to go by, she startled awake at the slightest touch.

Or maybe that wasn't normal, and she was only like this now because she was terrified.

I watched her a moment longer, my heart softening—and then she grabbed up all the blankets and hugged them to her chest. Greedy. This was why I always tried to go to sleep before her.

I hesitated, then went into the parlor. I could stretch out on the sofa and sleep.

The noorestones had been covered already, so the space was all shadows when I entered. But one shadow seemed off—not a sofa or chair, but a person, I realized, as my eyes finished adjusting to the darkness.

Aaru.

I kept my footfalls as soft as I could make them, but of course he heard me. He looked up, eyes round with questions. He didn't speak. He didn't even tap in the quiet code. He just . . . looked.

"May I sit with you?" I kept my voice to a whisper, but even that seemed too loud in the strange hush that smothered the city.

He moved a pillow to make room.

Carefully, as though he might run, I perched on the edge of the sofa. "My sister was taking up the whole bed, and I didn't want to wake her. I thought I'd be less of a bother out here. I didn't realize you had already claimed it."

He glanced at the door to the room he and Hristo shared.

I wished I could interpret that look. Did he mean he might go in there now, leaving the parlor for me? Or was he saying he had come out here to be alone? My heart wrenched with not knowing. "Aaru," I whispered, and brushed my fingertips across his chin. "I wish I could help. I wish I knew what you needed."

Grief crashed over his expression, so raw it hurt to look.

There were so many things I wanted to know. What did it feel like to have one's god abandon the world? Empty? Hollow? Or like some incorporeal and previously unknown limb had been ripped off?

At home, I'd sometimes felt a pull toward the earth, deeper into Noore, where my gods rested in the seabed. I'd sometimes felt rooted there, filled with a powerful sense of belonging—not to the people around me, but to the very gods whose bodies gave us life. I couldn't bear the thought of never again feeling that—of knowing there were places lost to me forever. The sanctuary. The temple. Because, yes, terrible things had happened there—the sanctuary had been plundered and the temple was where I'd been arrested—but those places still existed. I could make new memories in them.

But for Aaru . . . Idris, as he knew the island, was *gone*. His god had raised himself up, casting countless people into the sea.

I couldn't imagine what that felt like.

Even if there had been an evacuation, it seemed impossible that everyone would have been saved. Thousands of lives had surely been lost. Tens of thousands. And

Aaru, for all his importance to me, did not come from an important family. He came from a disgraced family, one the community leaders wouldn't prioritize.

Then, slowly, as though he'd forgotten how to move in front of other people, Aaru put his arm around me and drew me closer. We sat there stiffly, but soon our breathing synced and our muscles relaxed.

"Can I tell you something?" I whispered.

He didn't respond.

Maybe I shouldn't. Maybe it wasn't right to burden him any more.

But then he tightened his arm around me. Slowly. Gently. I let in a shaking gasp. He hadn't spoken a word— not in quiet code, and certainly not aloud—since we'd first seen Idris on the horizon. Well, maybe those prayers I thought I'd heard earlier, but maybe not. When we'd come to the hotel, he'd gone straight into a room and closed the curtains, the door, and sat alone for three hours until Hristo had gone in there with his bags. And later, Altan.

So this—a soft squeeze—was more than anything I'd gotten from him in five days.

I closed my eyes and switched to quiet code, my fingers tapping softly against his wrist. ::I've been having dreams since we escaped the Pit. At first, it was only after I used noorestones. I dreamed I was flying.::

Silence. Stillness.

::I dreamed I had great wings and fire.::

Again, nothing.

::But it's changed since then. Since the ruins. I still

dream I'm flying, but I see things. I know things.::

Another faint squeeze, this one in question.

My heart pounded.

::Do you remember when Gerel told us about the Celestial Warriors?:: I left a space for his reply, but he didn't offer one. ::On Khulan, after the god's eye, we stopped at an obelisk, and Gerel told us how the Celestial Warriors flew to the mainland on *Drakontos titanuses* to fight off the clans and kingdoms. I dreamed I was there. And I dreamed I saw the Algotti Empire.::

Aaru was as still as ever.

::I dream about an eclipse a lot—both moons passing in front of the sun, one after the other. And it seems like I'm supposed to know something. Be somewhere. Do something.::

It was impossible to explain the feeling of urgency present in the dreams. Everything seemed so immediate. So imperative. But trying to articulate it always fell short.

::And I've dreamed about islands. Ships. People moving toward coasts and building ships. And the other night, I dreamed about dozens of tiny boats dotting the ocean, a little girl inside each one. The girls didn't speak out loud, but I thought I saw . . .:: My fingers stilled as I reconsidered telling him that I thought they'd been using the quiet code. It might upset him more. ::They're just dreams, though.::

His breath hitched, like he'd felt all the words I'd kept trapped inside my fingers, and slowly he pulled back to look at me.

Three stuttering heartbeats. Four. Five. His eyebrows

were drawn in, his lips parted with a question he couldn't speak.

"Sorry," I whispered. "They're just dreams. I shouldn't have said anything."

He took my hands in his and tucked our tangled fingers beneath his chin. His pulse thumped against my knuckles. One, two, three . . . He studied me, like he could see all the ways those dreams of stars and flight and ancient past were tugging me forward.

But that was all. After a moment of looking at me—*looking* for the first time in days—he just leaned back on the sofa and pulled me with him.

I rested my cheek against his chest and didn't mind that our position was a little uncomfortable. He wanted me nearby. That was enough.

And then the dreams came again.

The *Drakontos celestus*

AFTER THE GREAT GOD OF SILENCE ROSE, THE OCEAN dipped and swelled, rushing outward to flee such wrath. But a knot of stillness hung in the tormented waters nearby, shadowed by great wings and an angry god. In a space where everything was chaos and movement, this quiet was out of place.

Closer inspection revealed a dozen small humans in tiny boats, hands clasped fast around one another's. None of them spoke aloud, but their fingers tapped and tapped around their circle, relaying information and passing on encouragement.

They were so little. So determined. They were a testament to humans' desire to survive against all odds.

Higher up again, they became mere specks of life on a vast ocean of chaos, notable only for their stillness and silence.

So strange.

CHAPTER FIVE

Dragons, as it turned out, were not very good at doing nothing.

In the morning, while we waited for Tanhe to get back to us, Altan got the bath he'd been promised, and then the others went out to listen for gossip about the summit, the explosions, or anything else that might affect our plan.

That left me with the dragons.

They hadn't been able to do much flying over the last few days, since we didn't need anyone wondering why two small dragons kept going in and out our window. So LaLa and Crystal were restless, and over the course of the morning, I had to stop them from chewing on the curtains, lighting fire to the chairs, and stealing noorestones to add to their nest.

Zara was just as bad. She roamed the suite, restlessly moving objects *just* out of place, like she was a particularly bored cat. She tilted a painting, nudged a vase off center, and left cabinet doors ajar.

Aaru, at least, was easier to manage. When we awakened this morning, I was still pressed against his chest and our fingers were laced, but it almost seemed his heart beat a new rhythm. He stood at the window now, curtains parted just enough to allow him to look outside. For a little while, I stood with him, watching people bustle about, shouting and waving, darting through the busy market nearby.

Shortly after lunch, the others returned, faces shining with the heat of the day. Chenda dropped an envelope on the table. "Tanhe came through."

I clicked for LaLa and gathered her up in my arms. My sweet dragon weasel pressed her nose against my breastbone and puffed smoke, then snuggled onto my lap when I sat on the sofa.

"I don't like this," Gerel growled. "I don't know what he had to do or say to get this information. If he told anyone that the Hopebearer is staying in his hotel—if he even *hinted*—we'll be in trouble."

"I'm not worried." Chenda sat beside me, her expression thoughtful. "If word were to get out that he doesn't care about his guests' privacy, no one will stay here. Not with the prices he charges. It would be too big of a blow to his business to betray us."

"I can't believe we're relying on other people's greed for safety," Ilina muttered.

Chenda gave a quick shrug. "Money is a powerful motivator." She turned to me. "Interested in taking a look?"

Careful not to squish LaLa, I leaned forward and pulled Tanhe's envelope off the table. There wasn't much inside, just two sheets of paper: a schedule and a note.

> On the ninth day of Suna, in the 2205th year of the Fallen Gods
> Sunset, Upper Gardens—Memorial for Idris and the Idrisi people.
> Immediately following, Great Hall—Ball: fancy dress, light refreshments provided by the high magistrate.
> On the tenth day of Suna, in the 2205th year of the Fallen Gods
> At the ninth hour, Council Chambers—Summit to discuss the events on Idris, and how to prevent the Great Abandonment from affecting the other Fallen Isles.
> Lunch will be provided by the high magistrate.

The note accompanying the schedule was brief, in a long, slanted handwriting:

> Most esteemed guests,
>
> Enclosed is the schedule I've acquired on your behalf. Unfortunately, the summit will be quite impossible

*to attend, as attendees are limited to government
officials only. However, I was able to acquire two
invitations to the memorial and ball, and I can offer
transportation in the hotel horsecarre.*

*Below you will find a list of dress shops and tailors, if
you need suitable attire. You know where to find me if
you require anything else.*

*Yours sincerely,
Tanhe*

"Who throws a ball at a time like this? It's so insensitive." Zara threw a glance at Aaru, who was still standing by the window. He wasn't moving. He didn't seem to notice that attention had shifted to him.

"High Magistrate Paorah does," Chenda said. "It's a way for him to show off his wealth and power."

"If he is truly the one behind the lie of the Mira Treaty"—just the words hurt my throat—"then he needs to be seen as doing something *kind* and *generous*. He needs his people to believe he is good, and any measures he takes that limit their freedoms, like enacting martial law, are because he cares about them."

Ilina nodded. "It's a long, carefully planned act." She frowned at the schedule. "It's a shame we can't get to the summit, but the memorial and ball sound promising."

I leaned back and crossed my legs. LaLa huffed and readjusted herself, this time with her belly up for scratches.

I obliged. "If Nine is at the memorial, perhaps they'll be able to help. There's not a chance in all of Noore that they'd miss the summit, so they must have a way in."

"Agreed." Chenda tapped her chin. "With the invitations Tanhe procured, getting into the memorial and ball is a matter of altering residency papers and having our false names added to the guest list."

"Oh, is that all?" Gerel shook her head.

"I didn't say a *simple* matter." Chenda smirked.

Gerel turned to me. "It's dangerous. What if Paorah recognizes you?"

"He won't. It's been three years since I last saw him. I look different now."

Chenda snorted. "That scar isn't as good of a disguise as you imagine."

Ilina nodded. "You still look like you. And you'll still look like the Hopebearer if you go in dressed appropriately. Not a hunting dress and leggings, but something nice."

"Something like one of the gowns *you* told me not to bring because they required too much effort."

"Exactly." A smile touched the corner of Ilina's mouth.

My fingers drifted over the ridge of scar tissue on my left cheek. It *felt* like it should alter my entire appearance, but they were right. Wearing hunting dresses or cheap clothes, I could usually hide who I was. People expected the Hopebearer to dress a certain way, so they rarely noticed me otherwise.

"We could ignore the invitations and I could go as a

servant," I said after a moment. "Like you did, Ilina, in the Shadowed City. No one would expect me like that."

She shook her head. "Even more impossible. The high magistrate is paranoid, so all his servants have been with him for years. My father said he employed entire families, not out of generosity, but to ensure he always had the right kind of pressure over the people who worked for him."

I rubbed my temples. I believed her, of course, but it was difficult to comprehend someone so thoroughly awful. "Then what do we do?"

LaLa looked at me, then scrambled up to butt her head against my knuckles. As I petted her, the knot of frustration eased.

"While we were out," Hristo said, "I found it interesting how unconcerned people were about martial law. I got the sense that it's a regular occurrence, sometimes after protests or labor strikes. People are confident this one will end soon—a couple of days at worst."

"Aren't they worried about the explosions?" Zara asked. "If they haven't caught whoever planted the explosives, it could happen again. It could happen *here*." She gestured around the room.

"I wouldn't worry about it happening here." Ilina's expression grew hard. "Plenty of people are blaming it on anarchists who've apparently done things like this before, but others are suspicious of the guards. They think the guards occasionally set explosives to give themselves more power and control in the city."

"That's . . ." I shuddered. "That's horrible."

"That's Anahera," she said. "At least the leadership." Uncomfortable quiet dropped through the room, and then she said, "I told you my father escaped Anahera. And that I was told never to come here."

"Yes." I was dying to know what had happened, but I didn't want to press.

"People usually have two thoughts when it comes to Anahera: it's either an island of manipulative schemers, or an island of crafters. The truth is that it's both." Ilina took a steadying breath. "My father grew up here, in Flamecrest, working with dragons. He showed a rare talent, and eventually, Minister Paorah—now High Magistrate Paorah—took notice."

Zara scowled. "But doesn't your father have a Daminan name?"

Hristo glanced at her, one eyebrow raised. "I have a Daminan name."

My sister's face darkened. "I know that."

Ilina kept her tone even. "My father changed his name when he left Anahera, but you're making me skip ahead."

Zara hunched her shoulders. "Sorry."

"Paorah was obsessed with dragons. He wanted the best sanctuary in the Fallen Isles, and he was incredibly selective in who he decided to elevate. It was a huge honor that he chose my father." She looked down, scratching at Crystal's chin. "Father went to three of the best universities on Anahera in order to study, and when he came back to Flamecrest, he was put in charge of a breeding program that focused on *Drakontos sols.*"

I'd never seen a *Drakontos sol* in real life, not even during my visits to various Anaheran sanctuaries. They were desert dragons, able to absorb sunlight and convert it to fire energy. But because they didn't need to eat as often in order to maintain their fire, occasionally they starved to death.

Like all dragons, they were at risk for extinction, and they were only found in the Anaheran deserts, so a breeding program made sense.

"Unfortunately, Paorah was more focused on the numbers than he was on the dragons' health. He encouraged inbreeding, which might have temporarily increased the number of *sols* in the sanctuary, but my father was concerned about the long-term effects." She curled her lip. "Plus, dragons don't usually mate just because a human tells them to. They have standards."

"So your father said no?" I asked.

"He said no." Ilina straightened her spine. "They threatened him, and his family, but he was firm. He thought the work they wanted was unethical, so he fled to Damina. He walked all the way down to Crescent Prominence, and when he got there, he offered his services to the Luminary Department of Drakontos Examination in exchange for asylum."

"That was brave," I said.

She nodded. "They helped him change his name so it would be more difficult for regular people to find him. Of course, Paorah became the high magistrate a few years after Father fled, and it wouldn't have taken much effort to find Father, but the Luminary Council was protecting him. I suppose when the dragons in the ruins started getting sick, the council didn't mind letting Anahera take him—and my mother—again, in order to treat them. And if I'd been there . . ."

She would have been taken, too, because if the high magistrate wanted dragon people, he wouldn't have just left Ilina. He'd have put her to work in those ruins. Or worse: kept her as leverage against her parents.

"He wanted the dragons to make sure Anahera will be the last to rise," I whispered. "He thinks if he collects them here, it might save him the pain of what just happened to Idris."

No one spoke for a moment, and I wished I knew what they were thinking. Maybe it was the same thing that kept running through my head: *how selfish*. Instead of working to ensure we were all safe, instead of looking for wiser methods of raising the dragon population, instead of truly embracing the Mira Treaty . . . he'd tried to take everything. The islands' sovereignty, the dragons, and our futures.

At least we had denied him the dragons.

I dropped my eyes back to LaLa, letting my thoughts work while I petted her.

"We still have to get into the Red Hall," I said after a few minutes. "And if posing as a servant isn't an option, that leaves the invitations. I'll find a way to disguise myself."

Gerel sighed, but I couldn't tell whether it was in agreement or resignation. "The second invitation should go to someone who can protect you."

"I can protect myself, in case you've forgotten." At once, all fifteen noorestones in the parlor brightened, and then stretched tendrils of fire toward me. Beads of hot energy spilled toward my waiting fingers, and a white-blue nimbus flickered around my hands. "I can control it now." I released the light, sending it back to the crystals with a flick of my wrist. "Where there's a noorestone, I'm safe. And there are noorestones everywhere."

"Mira, please." Hristo gazed at me imploringly. "None of us go anywhere alone. You know that."

"I'm just saying I don't need to be *protected*."

"Then I should get to go." Zara sat up straight. "Because Mother will be there and I should get to help save her." She stared at me, as though daring me to suggest that rescuing Mother wasn't a possibility.

"If I can free Mother," I said, "then I will. But you should stay here. She expects me to protect you, not let you go prancing straight into the halls of our enemies."

"That's stupid. I wouldn't be prancing, and you don't *let* me do anything—"

"I'll go."

My heart lurched.

Everyone went silent.

One by one, we turned toward the window where Aaru stood, still looking outside. He hadn't moved, but the words had been his.

He'd been so quiet, practically invisible while he listened to the rest of us plot and bicker. The others had probably forgotten he was there; it was so easy for people to overlook him, as quiet as he was. Even I hadn't realized he'd been paying attention, because for the last six days he'd been a shell of the boy I'd known before, locked away in his room, caught up in his unending sadness. But here he was, not just listening, but participating in the conversation. He wanted to be the one to go.

That was when I realized.

He hadn't said it in the quiet code.

He'd spoken *aloud*.

"Aaru," I whispered. I stood, pulling LaLa up to my shoulder. "Aaru."

He turned his head, and light shone bright around the contours of his profile. I followed the line down his forehead, his sharp nose, and full lips. It was so hard to believe that after decans of no sound passing those lips . . .

Even when he'd wanted to speak out loud.

Even when he'd *tried*.

Nothing. Until now.

Aaru reached up and pulled the curtains all the way closed. Then he turned fully and met my eyes. Again, his voice came, soft and careful. "For the memorial."

Of course. Of *course* he should go to the memorial for

his people. I should have thought about that first. I should have invited him—

"*You can talk?*" Zara's words were piercing in the quiet parlor.

"Shut up, Zara," I muttered, unable to rip my gaze from Aaru, his lips, the place on his throat that must have vibrated with his voice.

His voice.

I stepped forward, like I might be able to catch his words in my hands. I'd *missed* his voice, the careful, deliberate way he spoke, the thoughtful softness of it, but mostly I'd thought about it because *he* clearly thought about it. Whether or not he ever spoke aloud again—that didn't affect the way I loved him, because it didn't affect who he was. He was Aaru. That was all that mattered.

But now he could speak aloud again, after so much effort.

Now he could speak aloud again. Because . . .

I stopped moving, letting my hands drop to my sides as I thought about that evening on the *Chance Encounter*, right before we'd kissed, and he'd tried to say my name aloud.

There'd been a part of me—a deep, secret part of me I'd never wanted to acknowledge—that had thought if he ever used his voice again, it would be because of our love. I'd believed, somewhere in my selfish depths, that the first time he used his voice again, it would be to declare that he loved me, or to speak my name, or something else silly and romantic.

Disappointment washed through me, hot with the shame of my greed. My throat and cheeks burned as I looked up at him. "You and I will go."

He gave a single, small nod, and then walked into the bedroom. The door shut. And a moment later, we all heard a long, grief-stricken scream.

CHAPTER SIX

THREE MORNINGS LATER, ALTAN WAS GONE.

It started with a shout.

At first, I thought it was just noise from the streets below. Every morning, the city sprang awake like this might be the last dawn, and the cacophony never ceased to amaze me. Carts rattled, people yelled, bells pealed, and horsecarres clattered. And today, being the day of the memorial and ball, pushed even more urgency into the clamor below. I caught a few hacking coughs, someone hollering for another person to hurry it up, and also the chime of laughter.

Then the shout again: "Everyone get in here!"

I startled up from my sliver of Zara's bed. That had come from inside the suite.

"Where is he?" Ilina's words came as a snarl now.

Adrenaline jumped through my chest as I kicked a blanket free from my ankle and stumbled through the parlor. LaLa careened through the room to land on my shoulder with a soft *thump*.

Chenda and Gerel were already running toward the boys' room. I followed, rubbing sleep from my eyes.

From behind my friends, I couldn't see much besides Hristo standing near the washroom door, a towel crumpled at his feet. (He was dressed, thank all the gods.) Aaru stood beside him, expression half watchful, half cringing from all the yelling.

"How did this happen?" Anger steamed off Ilina in hot waves.

"What?" The closet door was open, but it still blocked my view of the interior. "What's happening?"

"Look." Her voice went low. Dangerous.

Dread filled my stomach as I slipped around the foot of the bed and looked over Ilina's shoulder. Inside the closet, there was:

1. *A pile of blankets.*
2. *One noorestone.*
3. *An empty water bladder.*
4. *Nothing else. No one else.*

Hristo and Gerel didn't waste time. They left the hotel without a word, knives and daggers tucked into their waistbands.

I rested my fingers on LaLa's back. "I should go with them. I should help." But the words were just that: words. I didn't know how to find him. I couldn't guess where he'd gone.

"No." Chenda shut the closet door. "You have other duties today. If you go running after this enemy, then you won't be ready to visit the Red Hall this evening."

"I know him best." A weak argument.

"No." Chenda's tone was steel. "Gerel knows him best. She will hunt him. She will capture him."

I sighed. She was right. But still, I felt like I should be doing more than getting dressed up for a ball.

"Let the others do their parts. Make sure you do yours. Don't allow yourself to be distracted by things that you cannot control. Focus on the things you can affect."

This was why Chenda was a better political leader than I would ever be. She weighed her problems. She allowed herself to delegate. She didn't feel the need to *do* everything because she trusted the people around her to do their jobs.

"All right." I hated to concede, but she had a point.

Ilina hadn't taken her glare off the closet. "Maybe I—"

"No." Chenda touched Ilina's shoulder. "You will be more useful here."

The tension in Ilina's shoulders didn't exactly ease, but after a moment, she nodded and looked at me. "Fine. We'll get Mira ready. Just know that I'm mad about it."

"Noted." A faint smile turned up the corner of Chenda's mouth.

"Who will help Aaru get ready?" I shifted my gaze to my silent friend, but he was just looking out the window, as somber as ever. If he felt anything about Altan's escape, he didn't show it.

"It won't take Aaru all day to get ready, and Hristo will return in time." Chenda strode toward the bedroom door. "Let's go."

Ilina set her jaw. "When they do get back with him, we're wrapping a chain around the closet doorknobs. He won't escape again."

"Flawless plan." I was still furious at Altan for escaping, but Chenda was right. What could I do besides get in Hristo and Gerel's way? They were good at what they did, and I needed to trust them.

Zara, who was leaning on the doorframe, just scowled around the room. "What I want to know is: How did he get out? I didn't hear anything. Did you?"

I shook my head. "Nothing but your snoring."

She stuck her tongue out at me.

"Not me," said Ilina, and Chenda shook her head, too.

"Aaru?" I looked up.

He looked at me.

And I saw it.

There, buried under the trauma of grief, was the truth: he *had* heard Altan's escape, and he hadn't stopped it.

But . . . but Aaru was on *our* side. He wouldn't.

He had.

Why? Why would Aaru, of all people, let Altan escape

84

into a city full of innocent people? Aaru knew what Altan was: a monster. Perhaps, sometimes, a useful monster, but a monster nonetheless.

He was the man who'd locked me in my cell all by myself, starving me for four days.

He was the man who'd transferred noorestone fire into Aaru in order to make me talk.

He was the man who'd pursued us across the Fallen Isles—hurting LaLa, stealing Kelsine, destroying the council house, and threatening to kill Aaru on the *Chance Encounter*.

Altan's effort to free dragons from the ruins above Flamecrest didn't make him any less of a monster; it just made him into a monster whose goals occasionally aligned with mine.

Oh.

Aaru's chest expanded with a long breath, and my question died in my throat, because I suddenly knew *why*.

The two of them—Aaru and Altan—shared a goal. Or at least they had goals that lined up.

Aaru had a goal that he hadn't shared with me. But he had shared it with Altan.

Something inside my chest cracked. I turned back to Chenda. "You're right. We have a lot to do today."

She looked surprised at my sudden reversal, but she just pressed her hand to my free shoulder. "Don't worry. Gerel and Hristo will find him. He couldn't have gotten very far yet, and you *know* Gerel is the best."

"At everything." I forced a smile, but Chenda was underestimating Altan. And we had all underestimated Aaru.

Before she could drag me out of the room, I shot Aaru one last glance over my shoulder, praying I hadn't made a mistake: I'd just protected his secret instead of telling anyone—including my best friend—that *someone* might know where Altan had gone.

DISCOMFORT SURROUNDED ME like a fog while I bathed and washed my hair.

Carefully, I combed soft oils through the dark strands, letting moisture soak in. In spite of the nightmare of the last decan, it felt good to take care of myself, to focus on making myself clean and pretty. It also felt like an undeserved luxury during a time when gods were rising and governments were falling, and when our enemies were allies and our friends were . . .

It hurt, thinking about Aaru.

He'd been present for every meeting in the parlor over the last few days, but if he'd spoken aloud again, it wasn't within my hearing. Still, he'd been there, tapping in the quiet code like before; I'd interpreted, but a couple of times, Ilina had responded before I finished; she was starting to catch on to his language.

All three nights, I'd drifted into the parlor, hoping to find him alone once everyone else had gone to sleep. But the first night, after he spoke, after he screamed, I'd perched on the sofa and waited for hours, only to awaken to Ilina poking my nose, LaLa snuggled in the curve of my shoulder, and dawn glowing beyond the curtains.

The second night, after shopping, planning, and having our papers adjusted, I'd slumped onto the sofa and hoped, but the only thing that happened was a fight with a blanket that wouldn't lie properly. And I lost.

The third night was the last night before the memorial, and I'd thought he might want to talk. But he hadn't come out of his room.

I'd gone back into mine.

And then Altan was missing.

Aaru didn't owe me any kind of explanation—aside from what happened with Altan—or a doorway into his feelings. But we were in love, weren't we? Even if he didn't want to discuss his voice—its absence or its return—shouldn't he want to be with me? We didn't have to talk at all, but wasn't this supposed to be the part of our relationship where we tried to be together all the time?

He was grieving, yes, but this was something different.

He wasn't pulling away from anyone else. It was only after he spoke those five words—only after his anguished scream into his pillow—that he'd pulled away from me specifically, and I couldn't help but wonder if I had done something wrong.

With a shiver, I rose from the water and wrapped myself in a soft, cream-colored robe. I closed my eyes and exhaled, long and slow.

One.

Two.

Three.

Four.

When my whirling thoughts began to settle, I took myself into the parlor. Ilina and Chenda were already there, waiting with their supplies, while LaLa and Crystal perched on the back of a chair, clucking and squawking at each other.

The door to the boys' room was closed, and I couldn't hear anything beyond it. If Aaru was up and moving around, he wasn't making any noise. Of course, he never was.

Until the other day.

The pain in my chest shifted again. Had Aaru talked to Altan? Had he shared his voice with Altan? Altan, who'd *taken* it two months ago?

My head swam. My heart hurt.

Chenda beckoned me toward the chair they'd placed near the window, giving them plenty of light to work by. "Come on. We're not growing hours over here."

I lurched into motion. "Where's Zara?"

"I sent her out to buy the last part of your disguise." Chenda glanced at Ilina and grinned. "We have grand plans. Now sit."

"Better hope Zara doesn't take this as her opportunity to run," I muttered, but obediently took the chair. When they began their work, my gaze slid back toward Aaru's door, and unwanted thoughts cluttered my mind:

Was he still in there?
Why had he freed Altan?
Did he know I knew?
Could we trust him?
Could *I* trust him?
Did he still love me?

CHAPTER SEVEN

As Hopebearer, going to balls and other formal events, I'd often worn my hair long and loose, because Mother said it made me look younger—more innocent. Of course, Krasimir had braided my hair plenty of times over the years, but that had been for the everyday, meant to be put up or down, depending on weather or mood. The braids had often felt tight the first day, but they'd been simple to care for. Easy, even when they'd been time-consuming.

This—what Ilina and Chenda were doing—was something else entirely. More elaborate. More beautiful. More *everything*.

The sun pulled high above the city while Chenda and Ilina worked, discussing laws surrounding dragon sanctuaries, regulations Ilina thought prevented proper care for larger dragons, and what could be done about the dwindling population of every species.

When I was finally allowed to see their work, I gasped. My friends had given me a thousand tiny braids, weaving them into intricate patterns through and around one another, like the perfect decorative knot. I resisted the urge to touch it, to feel the texture of braids over and under, to count the true number.

"Do you like it?" Ilina squeezed her hands together.

I loved it. It felt like armor.

"Yes," I breathed. "Yes, it's amazing."

Ilina practically glowed with the praise.

Chenda smiled. "This is an older Bophan style. Not two years ago old," she clarified, "but old enough that it now signals class and elegance. Before I was sent to the Pit, some of the younger girls were starting to wear their hair like this again. They think they invented it."

I twisted to inspect their masterpiece from another angle. "It reminds me of the tattoos."

"Good. It's supposed to."

It wasn't long before Zara returned, a small paper packet clasped between her fingers. "You don't look awful."

I opened my mouth to sting her back, but then I caught it: a small, hesitant smile hiding at the corner of her lips. I let my bitterness melt away. "Thank you. Ilina and Chenda deserve all the credit, though."

Zara's smile widened as she turned to the others.

"You're doing a good job, considering what you have to work with."

Ilina threw a comb at her, which Zara dodged.

As the afternoon wore on, my fingernails were trimmed and filed and buffed, and then my face was brushed and powdered and shaded. As the cosmetics went on, a new Mira emerged.

Mother had always told Krasimir to make me look soft and sweet, like a delicate lala flower. But after two months living in the Pit and running from isle to isle, my face was no longer *soft*. And my friends didn't try to pretend.

They sharpened the lines of my cheekbones into beautiful knives, and shadowed my eyes into deepest night. I began to look like someone else—like a stranger—and then Chenda reached for Zara's package.

It was just a powder, bronze in color and sharp on the eyes, but when Chenda dipped a damp brush into it and began to paint across the dips and swells of my right cheek, I understood.

"Tattoos are individual," she murmured, still working. "Not all Bophans have them, of course. It costs money. Most people think that the different pigments signal different class levels, and in some ways, that is true. But it has more to do with what people can afford. The white pigment a lot of people use, for example, is fairly inexpensive.

"You are going as a lady of wealth and importance," she went on. "You'd have a higher-quality pigment, something chosen to complement your skin tone. Unfortunately, we don't have time for an actual tattoo today—"

"Not to mention she'd be stuck with it for the rest of her life," Zara muttered from the doorway.

"I like my face the way it is, thank you."

"Even if there were someone who could do a real Bophan tattoo here, it would need time to heal. But I think I can create a reasonable facsimile for tonight. It should stay put as long as you don't go rubbing your face on anything."

When she dipped the brush into the pigment again, I said, "I'll try not to turn into a house cat while I'm there."

Ilina smirked.

"What do the patterns mean?" I asked, before Chenda touched the brush to my face again. I couldn't see all the details because her body was blocking the mirror, but every now and then I caught a flash of bronze against brown, bright swirls against dark cosmetics. It was a striking contrast.

Chenda tilted my face sideways; the touch of her brush was soft but deliberate. "Different lines suggest different meanings, but there can be more than one interpretation of every tattoo. It's individual to the person, and sometimes private, with only a suggestion of pain or joy or some other feeling associated with what the tattoo actually means to the wearer."

"What are you putting on Mira's?" Ilina asked, though she must have been curious about Chenda's tattoos now. Like me, she'd grown up reading *The Book of Love* and wouldn't ask for personal information that wasn't offered.

"Dragons," she said. "Hope and power and voice." She pulled back and smiled at her work. "I would have liked to draw something completely misleading, to add to the disguise, but that would be tempting the Deepest Shadow. To wear a lie is to poison oneself with other falsehoods."

"It's not a permanent tattoo," Ilina said, "just a drawing."

"Perhaps, but why risk it?" Chenda shrugged. "Besides, no one will be able to read all the true meanings. Bophans will respect that, and outsiders won't ask."

As we were finishing, the suite door opened and two pairs of footfalls came in: the even cadence of Hristo's long stride, and the angry thunder of Gerel's.

I started toward the parlor, but Ilina caught my hand. "Not yet."

"But—"

Ilina shook her head. "Get dressed."

It had been almost physically painful to buy a gown from a shop—partly because I had a better idea about what things cost now, and also because I had never worn a premade dress and I was certain everyone would be able to tell. But shopping in Flamecrest meant there was so much competition that shopkeepers were willing to bargain, and if anyone knew how to get a deal, it was Ilina. In a display of Daminan charm rarely seen, she talked the seamstress into selling us the gown for half the price.

We were fastening the last of the buttons into their

eyelets as Gerel walked into the bedroom, a dark look on her face. "Nothing. No idea where he went."

I sighed. "I'm sure he'll turn up the moment we think we're free of him for good."

"When he does, I'm going to gut him." Gerel crossed her arms.

"That's reasonable." Chenda stepped back from me. "But will you at least acknowledge what *I* have accomplished?"

Ilina cleared her throat.

"With Ilina's help," Chenda added.

Gerel's eyebrows lifted. "Aaru is going to combust when he sees you."

I couldn't imagine what Aaru would think. He had never commented on my appearance before, though the way he looked at me made me *feel* beautiful. Thinking of him now, knowing Altan had evaded Gerel and Hristo . . .

"Maybe he'll reconsider how slowly he's been moving." Ilina's smile drifted into a frown. "I mean, it makes sense right now, after Idris, but it's so clear that you and he want to be together. Don't think I didn't see how you two held hands every night on the *Chance Encounter*."

My face went hot with embarrassment.

Chenda sat on the bottom corner of the bed and beamed. "We can all rearrange rooms if you need. Just say the word."

Gerel waved that away. "You know what? Don't say the word. We'll rearrange anyway. I mean, they will. Chenda and I are staying together, obviously."

"That puts me with Zara." Ilina sulked. "Or Hristo, I suppose, but honestly, this seems so unfair to me. Nevertheless"—she looked at me—"I'm cheering you on."

My skin burned so much I thought I might explode. "You know he can probably hear us, right?"

The three of them looked at one another and erupted in laughter. "Good!" Gerel grinned. "Maybe he needs some encouragement, too."

"His fault for eavesdropping." Ilina shook her head.

They teased me a few minutes more, until a knock sounded on the door. Everyone sobered. "It's time to go," Hristo said.

"All right. You look beautiful. Go combust him." Ilina swung the door open, and they all shooed me into the parlor, where Aaru waited.

I couldn't breathe.

From the first moment I'd seen him in his cell, skinny and dirty and dark-eyed, I'd known there was something compelling about him. About the way he carried himself, about the depth of his gaze, about the shape of his mouth: even then, he'd been magnetic, and I hadn't wanted to look away.

And now.

He'd shaved, so his jaw was smooth and sharp. The cut of his suit was all clean lines that accented his slender build, and the fabric was deep blues and black, with hints of bronze embroidery that popped around his cuffs and collar. So unlike an Idrisi. Even his fingernails were clean, trimmed neatly into pale ovals over his warm brown skin. I *couldn't* look away.

Then I realized he was staring at me, too, and his careful unreadability was gone. His lips had parted. His eyes were wide. His breath moved short and fast.

I must have looked like a stranger to him.

With my hair braided like this, my entire face was clear, as if I wasn't trying to hide my identity at all. It revealed the bronze lines of Chenda's artwork, which twined across my right cheek and down my neck. On my left cheek, my scar stood as clear as ever. And then there was the gown.

When I was the Hopebearer, my gowns had been elaborate creations, lovingly designed by my family's personal seamstress. Mother had always intended me to look beautiful, young, and distant. Like a painting. The gowns had reflected that by style and color and level of complication. I'd been meant to be seen—heard when appropriate—but not touched.

This was something else entirely. It was simple. Elegant. Cut in the flowing Bophan style, the black gown hugged my chest before flaring down into loose ripples that showed hints of my shape when I moved. I'd chosen it because Mother wouldn't have, and because I liked the way the silk felt as it slid over my body.

The entire ensemble made me into another person. Older. Sharper. Stronger.

Aaru's mouth moved, but he didn't speak. Slowly, he

packed away his surprise: his lips closed, his eyebrows fell to their normal height, his breathing evened out. Then he approached me and offered a hand, as though to ask if I would dance.

My heart thundered so loudly he *had* to hear it, but as I accepted his hand, warmth spread through me at his touch, and I knew—no matter what he'd done earlier—that I still loved him. I would still do anything for him, if only he asked.

"Are you ready?" My voice came from deep in my chest, thick with longing.

Aaru squeezed my hand. "Yes."

PART TWO

THE GREATEST CALAMITY

CHAPTER EIGHT

IN SILENCE, WE TOOK THE HORSECARRE TO THE RED Hall, where the memorial was to be held on the largest rooftop garden. My hands rested on my lap. Aaru's stayed on his knees. Knots of anxiety tightened between us, and I wanted to ask him about Altan—surely he had a reasonable explanation—but that worry kept coming back. I'd been betrayed too many times.

I distracted myself by watching the red sandstone buildings pass by, listening to snatches of dialogue from people on the streets, and praying that no one at the memorial or ball recognized me. I looked different, I knew that, but anyone who cared to *see* me would know the truth.

The Red Hall rose ahead of us, its jewels glittering as the sun eased toward the west. We pulled into a long drive, lined with springy grass and bright dragon flowers, until we reached a grand stair that led up to the south face of the building. Daminan-style columns stood sentinel around a huge patio, and windows—dozens of them—glittered in the hot glare of the sun.

Our driver stopped behind private carriages and other horsecarres, and Aaru reached for the door. I held up a hand. He hesitated, but a moment later, the driver came around and opened my door for me.

I slid out. Aaru slid out. A blue-jacketed porter strode toward us, his palm up as he asked for our invitations and papers. Aaru produced both from within his jacket pocket, then hid his shaking hands behind his back while the porter studied everything as though the high magistrate were watching.

When he looked at my paper, then my face, my heart pounded painfully. The drawing had my scar, but not the false tattoos. There was just a box checked—facial markings—and nothing more.

"You look familiar." He glanced at the drawing again—I looked more like me there—and frowned.

"You would be surprised by how many people think they know me." Not a lie, but then I had to say the next part to solidify the story. "They always say I look like—"

"Mira Minkoba," he finished. Hearing my name sent spikes of fear down my spine, but the porter was nodding, grinning. "Yes, I can see the similarities now. Maybe you're distantly related to her."

I forced a smile. "Perhaps."

Finally, the porter handed the papers back to Aaru. "Follow the signs to the memorial. There will be attendants along the way in case you get lost."

What he really meant was: *Don't wander because we will be watching you.*

As Aaru and I followed a line of Anaheran elite up the stairway, my heart began to slow to a normal speed. The others had coached me on how to deflect that sort of attention, but I hadn't thought I'd need it right away. With the *porter*, of all people. This promised to be a very long evening.

Cool air enveloped us as we stepped inside the entry hall. It was just as I remembered, lavishly decorated with art from all over Anahera: paintings of dragons in flight, intricately woven rugs made from talopus down, and wooden baskets filled with obsidian knapped to look like dragon eggs. I'd always liked those eggs, especially the ones that had been cut from the inside, too: the black glass was shaved so thin that a small noorestone placed inside made them glow like dark lamps.

Every time Mother visited, she left with new ideas for how to redecorate our entire home—until Father talked her out of it. I wondered what she thought of the Red Hall's beauty and elegance now that she was a captive.

A small sign pointed toward the stairs. True to the porter's word, several servants were stationed around the entrance hall, some offering glasses of wine as they greeted guests, while others watched us with judgment plain on their faces. All of them were dressed in the same flame-blue livery, almost like they were guards, and as one shifted his weight, I caught the bulge of a dagger hilt under his jacket.

Fear prickled through me, and I could feel Aaru's tension at my side. He was doing his best not to stare around the room in awe; all of this was *so* different from his home on Idris.

We took to the rug-cushioned grand stairs, climbing higher and higher as we listened to the guests ahead of us complain about the imposition without actually complaining.

"My knees do not like stairs." The man did his best to sound pleasant. "Of course, to be invited to the Red Hall is such an honor. I'm happy for the pain. It makes me think of the high magistrate and all he endures to keep us safe."

The woman with him nodded in emphatic agreement, even as she clutched the banister so tightly her knuckles paled.

After five flights of stairs, we were ushered through a large glass door that led to the rooftop garden. It was a space big enough for a hundred people, though only sixty or so had arrived. Many held flutes of wine or plates of bread and soft cheese, taken from one of the long tables that sat on either side of the door. A house servant was stationed near each, ready with small paper napkins, and trays for empty plates and glasses.

The hum of soft conversation surrounded us as Aaru and I paused next to one of the potted palm trees that lorded over the garden, and both of us studied this first battleground.

1. *Seventeen boxes—of orchids, lala flowers, bitter dawn trumpets, and other flowers I couldn't identify—spilled riots of color across the garden. They were carefully pruned and maintained with the meticulousness of a proud Hartan gardener, but all I could see was how trapped they were.*

2. *An entire wing of dragons graced the tiled floor, bright and colorful mosaics against the dusky red background. Drakontos sol, rex, ignitus—if I looked, I'd probably find every species represented here.*

3. *When I looked up, I caught a spectacular view of the late-afternoon city, the buildings lit red with the hot glow from the sun. From this high, people on the streets seemed so small, and the ships in the harbor were toys.*

4. *Guards—five of them—stood watch from the walls. They carried swords and daggers, and their eyes were narrowed as they scanned the garden for trouble. Hoping for trouble, perhaps.*

5. *There was but one exit: the same glass door we'd come through.*

6. *Noorestones. The power of a dozen crystals brushed against my soul, welcoming.*

7. *So far, the only people here looked like Anaheran aristocracy, or upper-class society visiting from other islands. I saw a few familiar people, but no one seemed to recognize me; their eyes slid right across my fully exposed face because, although I was in the right context, they didn't expect the tattoos and scar and harsh cosmetics.*

8. *If Nine was here, they weren't obvious about being an imperial spy.*

Aaru's jaw was tight as he studied the other mourners, and abruptly, I saw what he saw.

No Idrisi.

No men (because women never left Idris) in simple, tunic-style clothes that stood out in this display of color and excess. No men lingering off to the side, trying to force space between themselves and the others. No men actually mourning at this memorial.

This was merely a spectacle of compassion.

I pushed aside my uncertainties about Aaru's deal with Altan as I slipped my hand into his, then tapped against his knuckles. ::**Are you all right?**::

The tension in his jaw eased, and he brushed his

thumb against the inside of my wrist before he replied, ::I
will be. Did you see him?::

At first, I thought he meant Nine (no), or the high
magistrate (he wasn't here yet), or Ilina's father (still no),
but when I followed his gaze westward, toward the cliffs
and water, I saw who he meant.

Idris.

The god of silence loomed on the far side of the sea,
golden sunlight spilling around him like honey. Hunched
over in thought, Aaru's god sat there while his people suffered. While ships like the *Chance Encounter* searched for
survivors. While refugees washed up on foreign shores,
isolated and scared.

I stared at Idris over there, just sitting, and I hated him
a little. I hated all of the gods, willing to leave us like this.
::Who do you think is next?:: I asked Aaru, not thinking
about how insensitive the question was until it escaped.

::Could be anyone. I had never dreamed Idris might be
first. Could be—:: Aaru's head snapped up, and he stared
toward the door. ::Mother.::

His warning almost came too late. A small cry bubbled
up inside my chest, but I bit it down as my mother strode
through the doorway, surveying the garden as though
considering whether she might purchase it.

She looked good, dressed in a long Daminan gown
of clover green that whispered around her ankles. Her
hair had been straightened and pinned back, revealing
her strong cheekbones. Gold bangles chimed around her

wrists, though they might as well have been cuffs. She was in the high magistrate's custody, after all.

Mother's cool gaze lit across the garden, coming toward me.

Quickly, I turned away and stepped behind one of the slender palms—not to hide, but to obscure myself. ::Warn her,:: I tapped to Aaru, and then slipped toward the edge of the roof like I wanted to look across the city.

The pressure of Aaru's presence eased as he walked toward my mother.

Then her voice carried through the garden. "You're—"

Though it must have been painful for him to not only speak aloud but *interrupt* as well, Aaru did. The drone of conversation eclipsed his voice, but I could feel it deep within my spirit. Like a skipped heartbeat, or shift of the earth, he affected me in unseeable ways.

Mother's voice came again, a curl at the end like a question, but the words were lost to distance. Several moments later, Aaru returned to my side, and his finger tapped against the railing, next to mine. ::She will not come to you.::

"Good." It hurt, though. I wanted to see her. I wanted to talk with her. But if anyone saw us together, they would know. If anyone even saw us *looking* at each other, they would know who I was. "Is she all right? Is she safe? Did you tell her we still have Zara?"

He nodded. ::Yes to all.::

"Thank you." I wished I could rest my head against his shoulder, but even if that was who we were—people who casually showed affection—Chenda had warned me against letting anything touch the false tattoos. That probably included Aaru.

His hand slipped on the railing, toward mine. The quiet code came fast. ::I asked about your father.::

My breath caught.

::I'm sorry.::

I choked on a sob I wouldn't release. I'd known, hadn't I? If Father wasn't here, then he'd died back there.

Still, the confirmation burned, and I almost wished Aaru hadn't said anything, but then I would have spent all night wondering. ::Hristo's father?:: Because my protector needed answers, too.

Aaru shook his head. ::Gone.::

I let out a long breath. One, two, three, four, five: those were the heartbeats it took for me to exhale. Both fathers deserved my grief, but I couldn't let it show here. Instead, I pushed it aside, smothering those feelings to address later.

Behind us, the buzz of activity intensified, and we turned to find the Hartan matriarchs arriving in a swirl of soft robes, and then a trio of warriors just behind them. As the island governments spread throughout the crowd, I watched to see if anyone recognized me. But no one spared me a second look, except for Dara Soun of Bopha; when she saw my false tattoos on one cheek, my scar on the other, I could see her making a note to introduce herself later.

I turned to Aaru. "We'll have to start talking to people

soon. Before anyone who knows me decides to walk over."

A pained look crossed his face, but he nodded. This, too, was something we'd discussed: there would be dozens of people here who knew me, and we would need to make it difficult for them to ask personal questions. Besides, we had to find Nine, and there was only one way to do that.

Soft clinks sounded as someone tapped their glass to gather attention, and then the Fire Ministry emerged onto the roof, High Magistrate Paorah in the lead. The guests quieted as they all turned to look.

The high magistrate had a softer face than most people expected, with small eyes and a weak jaw, but keen intelligence in his gaze. He always looked as though he was weighing, measuring, calculating the motives of the people around him. He had the kind of stare that prodded people for their weaknesses and waited patiently for the best moment to expose them. As he looked over the crowd of island elite he'd assembled, I forced my expression into anything that the Hopebearer would not wear: haughty, judgmental, expectant. It didn't matter what he thought of me, as long as he didn't think I might be Mira Minkoba.

Aaru's hand slipped into mine. ::Breathe.::

I breathed.

"Thank you for coming." Paorah looked over the crowd; his voice was deceptively soft, too, yet still commanded people to listen. "While this is an unhappy occasion, I'm pleased to see you all here. This gathering signals our devotion to ensuring the survival of our people. What happened to Idris will not happen on another island."

Aaru's hand tightened around mine, and I let him even though it hurt, because it meant he still needed me.

The high magistrate glanced westward, where the sun was easing toward Idris. "We've lost a proud nation," he said. "Idris was an island filled with kind, hardworking people. I knew several of the Silent Brothers personally, and I respected them deeply for their fair rule, the warmth they inspired in their people, and the culture of cooperation they fostered. I will miss them, not only as leaders, but as friends, too."

Everyone was quiet, just listening to him. He had a compelling way of speaking, almost like a song.

"This loss affects us all. Friends, islanders, trading partners, allies: they are gone now, and so is the long history and culture of the Idrisi people. We're here this evening to mourn their passing, and hope—*pray*—that the ships we've sent out will find survivors. If the Idrisi ways are to live on, it will be through them."

All around the quiet garden, people nodded. Some were crying, their tears shimmering in the evening light.

"In a few minutes, when the sun sets behind Idris, we will observe a moment of silence in honor of our fallen friends. Pray, if you like. Mourn. Then we will go downstairs to celebrate this time together, and tomorrow, all the governments and representatives of the Fallen Isles will get to work. Together, we will ensure the Great Abandonment goes no further. Together, we will ensure the survival of our people."

A polite applause followed, and while we waited for the sun to drop, a few ministers took the chance to talk about their memories of Idris and the generous ways they were treated during their visits to the island.

While they spoke, I scanned the crowd for Mother. She stood surrounded by Hartan matriarchs, her chin lifted and her gaze firmly on the speaker of the moment. If she felt anything about the words they spoke—or the words they did not speak about the Luminary Council— she didn't show it.

A man was droning on about the quality of Idrisi cotton, bemoaning the future absence of such fine cloth, when the high magistrate stepped forward. The minister shut his mouth without needing to be told.

"The sun is behind the god of silence," said Paorah. "Please remain quiet until it is fully set."

An immediate hush wove through the garden, broken only by sniffs and soft coughs as everyone turned to look west. It wasn't true silence—no one here could give that to the Idrisi people, except for Aaru—but somehow this seemed more potent. This was grief silence. Shock silence. Dozens of people who could never understand Idris's silence all trying to give him what he valued most. Even the traffic below seemed softer, muted, like a held breath as the god shadow swung over Flamecrest, darkening the city into an early twilight.

A chill passed through me, and then I looked at Aaru.

It was good that we were in front of the crowd, because if anyone else had seen the naked longing in his eyes, we'd have been caught. He'd have been identified as Idrisi, and questions would have come from all directions.

But when I checked around, everyone who might be able to see was staring west, or looking at the nearest flower box.

The sun was sinking behind Idris, its rays growing longer and warmer. I lifted my hand so my knuckles brushed his, soft little bumps of contact. *Take my hand*, I wanted to say, but it had to be his decision.

Then his fingers twitched, stretched out, and threaded with mine.

::You are not alone,:: I tapped. ::You are not alone. You are not alone. You are not alone.:: Again and again I told him, until the sun disappeared beneath the horizon, and the city let out its breath. Life rumbled again, and the high magistrate beckoned people toward the ballroom for the rest of the night's activities.

All around us, people began to move, but Aaru stayed put, slowly erasing the anguish from his face.

I hated myself for saying it, but . . . ::We have to go. We need to get lost in the middle of the crowd.::

Aaru sighed. Nodded. And together, we slipped around the passionflowers and dragon tongues and went back into the Red Hall.

Now to find Nine.

The *Drakontos celestus*

THE FIRST DRAGON WAS BORN DURING AN ECLIPSE.

Two moons passed over the sun, one after the other, and in those moments of held-breath darkness, with dawn hovering on all horizons, the first dragon burst through the crust of the still-molten land. It was a triumphant moment for the Fallen Gods—their first and most favored child—and they painted her with gold and silver stars, a reminder of the sky on the day she came forth.

One by one, the seven gods blessed her with all their gifts.

She was fierce and fiery, yet loving and warm. She could fly across the world as a silent shadow, and from her, all other dragons would be born.

Then, as the gods finished bestowing all their love upon her, the light returned, and the eclipse was over.

CHAPTER NINE

THE BALLROOM WAS ALL COPPER AND RED, LIKE WALK-ing into a fire, and far too loud, filled with voices, footfalls, rustling fabric, and music.

I glanced over just in time to see Aaru's expression crumple under the onslaught of Too Much. It was subtle—just his eyebrows drawing inward, the corners of his mouth dropping, and a tightening around his jaw—but if I saw it, others would, too.

There couldn't have been fewer than two hundred guests inside, far more than had come to the memorial. Several were already dancing to the music of a small orchestra, even more had descended upon the buffet tables, and the rest were prowling the floor like predators looking for prey.

My hand was already resting on the crook of Aaru's arm. ::Put on a mask.:: I tapped quickly, hoping no one would notice.

Immediately, the discomfort flew from his features. I could still feel the tension in his muscles, and see it in the way he walked, but I doubted anyone else could; they didn't know him well enough.

I shoved away the nagging feeling that maybe *I* didn't know him well enough.

::I'm sorry,:: I said, guiding him toward the food, which seemed the safest route for now. ::I wish you could mourn. If you want to leave, you can.:: After all, he'd come for one reason: the memorial. If he needed to go, I could do the rest on my own.

Besides, I wasn't completely on my own, was I? Mother was here, and while that fact usually did nothing to comfort me, tonight it helped. For once, I believed she was on my side.

Aaru shook his head. ::Staying.::

"Thank you." I smiled at him. ::We need to talk aloud. They'll notice if we don't.::

"Of course." His voice was soft and gentle, warming me like a song. ::Who will notice?::

::Everyone.::

His eyes widened for a fraction of a second, but then he smoothed away the alarm and gazed around the room, searching.

When Zara and I had been young, she'd complained

that everyone at school looked at her differently—treated her differently—because she was my sister. She said they were always waiting for her to do something wrong so they could pounce and mock, so every day she went to school terrified to be herself.

Mother had taken her aside for a short talk, which I'd overheard because I had my ear pressed to the door. Mother had said that at school, all the other students felt just as awkward and out of place as she did. They all had the same sense of being watched and judged, but it was a false feeling born from insecurity. All the other students, she'd said, were too busy worrying about themselves to bother noticing Zara. Mother said she shouldn't over-think it.

Even at eleven years old, I had thought Mother was underestimating the other students, but by that time, Zara had already stopped talking to me, so I didn't offer her my views.

Later, Mother had come to me and given the complete opposite talk. *"They are watching you,"* she'd said. *"At every party, council meeting, and public appearance, they're waiting for you to make a mistake. You must never show them the true parts of you—the weakest parts—because they'll find a way to turn them into a weapon."*

After that, I'd begun to notice the eyes. They followed me, yes, but they also watched Mother and Father, and everyone else in the world. I couldn't imagine how anyone had the energy to guard themselves *and* look for flaws in others, but clearly they felt it was worth their time. The predators existed at every party, council meeting, and public appearance on every island, just as Mother had said.

They probably existed at Zara's school, too.

Aaru and I arrived at the nearest buffet table, and he nudged me to go first—probably part Idrisi sensibilities, but mostly so he could watch to see how I interacted with people. In the Pit, so out of place, I'd imagined myself as a *Drakontos mimikus*. I'd observed Gerel and learned how to survive by copying her. Now I saw the mimic dragon in Aaru, too.

When it was my turn, I pointed to a few items—cuts of spiced cloudfish, honey-glazed pineapple, and chunks of butter-drenched crabmeat on tiny crackers—and then thanked the house servant who filled my plate. Aaru followed my lead exactly, and together we wended our way around the outside of the floor, watching the dancers, until we paused beside a large column.

Aaru studied the arrangement of his plate with a soft frown. "It's so pretty."

I smiled. "Anaherans consider cooking an art."

"But it's to eat."

"Yes. That doesn't prevent it from being art as well."

He touched one of the pineapples with his fork. "The only time I've ever worried about how food looks was when checking that it wasn't spoiled or filled with bugs. I've always been too hungry to worry otherwise."

And then, in the Pit, it hadn't mattered if there were a few bugs. "This is a different world for you."

"Very." He gazed around the room, eyes lingering on the brightly dressed dancers, the intricate wall carvings, and the painted ceiling; for him, this world was as strange and unknowable as the bottom of the ocean. "But food. It's for eating, not for looking."

I thought back to what I'd learned during my previous visits. "It fits Anahera's tenet of benevolent destruction in two ways: the destructive process of cooking can be made into something beautiful. Art. When you eat it, you're given life. Eat everything you took, though. Destruction without purpose is an affront to Anahera."

He gave me a look that said he had never in his life let food go to waste.

"See the walls?" I nodded across the room, where an immense panel showed a laughing figure dancing through a raging fire. She was beautiful, all long limbs and fluid motion. Panels were mounted all around the ballroom; in one set, she was cutting down trees—and building a house in the next. In another set, she killed a goat, but then offered a meal to children.

"Anahera."

I nodded. "You can't build something without first destroying something else; you can't sustain life without death. The rule is that it must be purposeful. Meaningful. That's why they call it benevolent destruction."

"Benevolent destruction," he murmured. "Strange."

I tapped my fingernail on the edge of my plate. ::Strength through silence is strange to others.::

He bowed his head in acceptance, and in the aching sobriety of that motion, guilt needled me again. He shouldn't have to be here, enduring this, talking about other islands' beliefs. He'd just lost his home. His family. His everything.

While I nibbled on a cracker, I pretended to watch the dancers. Aaru and I weren't the only people standing on the outskirts of the floor, looking around at the other guests. Across the room, I caught Mother's eye—and quickly looked away before anyone noticed an energy between us. Still, I wished I could speak with her. Ask her questions about what happened in Crescent Prominence. Hug her.

Maybe there was a way to free her.

I pulled myself up straight, putting on the expression of this Bophan woman who Chenda had painted onto me, not letting it slide for even a heartbeat as I looked for other familiar faces.

There was Dara Soun and several senators, the matriarchs, and the tribunal. Everyone who'd been brought here by ship was standing together, eating and talking among themselves. Not dancing. The only officials who were dancing belonged to the Fire Ministry. But the "guests" all looked healthy. Fed, clothed, and probably given everything they could want. That was the high magistrate's way: flattery and bribery.

Notably absent: Elbena and Tirta.

I had no doubts that Paorah had taken them from Altan's safe house the other night, but if he'd wanted to use them, shouldn't they be here? Maybe they'd make an entrance later, although no one would believe that the Hopebearer would have voluntarily missed the memorial earlier.

I put that worry aside, scanning the room for Ilina's father. He wasn't here, but that wasn't a surprise. I did spot the twenty-five Anaheran guards who stood along the perimeter of the room, but if I hadn't been looking for them, I probably wouldn't have noticed. Not with all the surrounding splendor, meant to dazzle and distract.

"Do you see our friend?" I leaned toward Aaru so that my elbow brushed his sleeve.

He shook his head. "I don't know what to look for."

That was the problem, wasn't it? Nine might be willing to talk to me, but they didn't know we were looking for them. And we didn't know what they looked like—besides like a normal person—so we would have to do this the hard way. Mother always said that people made room for beautiful ladies, and if there was one thing I knew about myself, it was that even scarred, even sharp, even haunted, I was beautiful.

Aaru and I finished our food and handed the plates to a passing servant. Then, with my hand on Aaru's arm again, I guided him toward the nearest cluster of people I didn't know. By their dress, most were Daminan, which felt a little dangerous. But when one of the women looked up and waved Aaru and me toward them, no recognition sparked in her eyes, just interest. Introductions went around, and the conversation—about the state of trade now that Idris was gone—resumed with ease.

"Cotton and sugar are what you want to watch." Thoman was a Daminan businessman, the kind who owned a fleet of cargo ships and sent his captains to command better and better deals for him. "Without Idris, demands on those crops will go up. It's rare now. Impossible to get more of the Idrisi quality we're all used to. In Golden Cove"—that was a city on the western side of Damyan—"seamstresses and tailors are already buying all the cotton they can afford. I raised my prices three hundred percent, and I've made a small fortune in the last decan."

Aaru's breath caught, but he said nothing.

"Of course, without Idris and the farmers there, once your supply is out, that's it. No more fortune." The woman—Lilana, if I remembered correctly—shrugged. "If you ask me, the smartest bet is to keep your remaining stock hidden. Sell it in ten years: the last of the Idrisi cotton. *There's* your profit."

Thoman bowed his head. "Fine advice. I may have taken it already. The challenge, at that point, will be convincing anyone of its authenticity, but I'm working on that."

A second man spoke up: "I was just in Val fa Merce, where I heard they've started planting new fields on Harta to make up for the loss. With their gifts, the crops could be ready within a month. It won't be the Idrisi quality, but with cotton in such a demand, I doubt anyone will mind."

"Do you think it will matter?" I tilted my head, making sure the false tattoos caught the light of a nearby noorestone. "The Great Abandonment has already begun. In these uncertain times, shouldn't we focus on ensuring the continuation of the Fallen Isles, rather than our bank accounts?"

"In these uncertain times," said Thoman, "we must prepare for all possibilities. We don't know when another island will rise up, or *if* another one will. Perhaps only Idris will rise, and the rest of us are safe."

The muscles in Aaru's arm tensed.

A third man—Balmer—leaned in conspiratorially. "Some say they earned it. Did it to themselves."

"What do you mean?" Lilana stepped closer toward the group, a gleam of scandal in her eye.

"I mean," he said, "that a few people on Idris got loud."

Aaru stiffened. I squeezed him and fought to keep my voice even. "The Great Abandonment isn't the fault of a few—"

But I wasn't the Hopebearer today, so Balmer spoke over me. "This may not be the Great Abandonment at all. It's just as likely that Idris's people rebelled against his ways, and he decided to have no more of it. Truly, it's a shame, but our world is what we make it."

Disgust ripped through me, but before I could say

anything, Thoman spoke up again:

"Idris always refused to work with the rest of us. The tariffs were too high, they abhorred travel on and off the island, and the Silent Brothers drove the entire society into abject poverty. It was a sorry state of affairs, and if you ask me, they were punished for it."

"All the people?" Darkness clouded Aaru's voice. "For the sins of their leaders?"

Thoman nodded. "They were complicit in the system of corruption, allowing it to continue like that. And, as my father used to say, sin in moderation from the government— well, that leads to sin in excess from the masses. If the Silent Brothers did all those things—making rules against girls working, stealing boys from their families, forbidding marriage between two men or two women—then imagine what their community leaders and men did. All that, but in excess." He shook his head, as though he had actual pity for the people he'd just condemned.

Aaru was as still as a held breath, or the wind before a storm. "Have you ever been to Idris?" He spoke softly, carefully, but no one could ignore him. Not with the fierce look on his face, and the way his fingers curled toward fists.

"Of course not." Thoman shrugged, as if to ask how travel to Idris would even have been possible. "I hear the weather there was horrible before, and it's worse now." He chuckled, and the others joined in, ugly titters and covered mouths, like they all understood it was inappropriate to laugh, but they couldn't help themselves.

And then.

It happened so fast.

Aaru pushed Thoman.

Not hard, but the businessman staggered back a couple of steps. Others caught him. And then Balmer shoved Aaru.

It could have stopped there—Aaru didn't act again—but by that time, Thoman was in front of Aaru, and he shoved Aaru, too. "What's wrong with you?" The businessman's shout drew eyes. Around us, the dancing stopped and even the musicians seemed uncertain whether to continue playing. "We were having a laugh."

"At the expense of the dead." Aaru's fists shook, but he didn't move as several things happened at once:

1. *A pair of guards rushed toward us.*
2. *Thoman and Balmer lurched forward to push Aaru.*
3. *Seventy-three noorestones flared white hot, gleaming off the mirrors so brightly that people covered their eyes and cried out in alarm.*

The men stopped short of Aaru, their hands over their faces. I grabbed Aaru's arm, dragged him toward me—out of the way of the men—and let all the noorestones go back to normal.

By the time the light eased and everyone was blinking their vision clear, the guards had arrived. Though they, too, seemed disoriented by the sudden glare, they listened while the group of Daminan men and women explained it had all been a misunderstanding.

"Are you all right?" I asked Aaru.

He nodded. "Fine. Not hurt." And then, against my hand, ::Sorry. That was stupid.::

I squeezed his hand as the guards came toward us—a man and a small woman, both with tight grips on their daggers.

"Tell us what happened," said the female guard.

"Misunderstanding." Aaru's voice was monotone. "We disagreed and overreacted."

The guard raised an eyebrow, glanced at me, but didn't give me time to offer my version of events. I wasn't the Hopebearer here; no one cared what I thought. "All right," she said. "We'll call it a disagreement for now. But if I see the two of you causing disagreements again, you'll both spend the night in jail."

Aaru swallowed hard and nodded. "I'm very sorry."

She scoffed, delivered the same warning to Thoman and Balmer, and then walked back to her station on the edge of the room. Her eyes—and those of her partner—never left us.

As the music began again, and people shifted like they might resume dancing, Thoman, Balmer, and the others came toward Aaru and me. "Sorry if you were upset,"

Thoman said, like it wasn't obvious that Aaru was upset. "We were just joking around. People do that when something horrible happens."

My stomach turned over with revulsion. "You're a disgrace," I hissed. "Cruel. Careless. You show none of Damyan's love. None of Darina's compassion."

Thoman sneered. "How would you know anything about love, Bophan? You care more for shadows."

"People *died* on Idris." My voice hitched. "We were just at the memorial for the hundreds of thousands of people who perished when Idris rose. You say they deserved it, but you don't know the people of Idris—and now you never will. They did *not* deserve to die. Even if their leaders were corrupt, they were no more corrupt than the people of any other island. Look at the Luminary Council. Worshiping the god and goddess of love didn't prevent them from hurting the Daminan people, and now they're dead. Murdered. Answer this: Since you think it's right to punish people for the actions of their leaders, do you think you deserve the same fate, *Daminan*?"

The businessman and his friends were quiet a moment, and then Lilana sneered. "You think you know so much about the world, but you're a child. A naïve child."

Her words hit me with fears I'd only recently begun to understand—that I didn't know enough about the world, that I couldn't possibly make a difference, that my experiences didn't matter—but she was wrong. I knew, even if I didn't always feel it, that she was *wrong*. "Maybe I don't know exactly how the world works, but I know how it *should* work, and I know that people like you are the reason it's broken. Enjoy trading on the works of our dead brothers and sisters. It's the only thing you have left."

I turned and strode away, Aaru at my side, and we went straight through the dancers as we made our way to the main door, but an older woman stopped me. "Please don't leave," she said. "This ball was just getting interesting, thanks to you and your friend."

Aaru and I glanced at each other, and finally I nodded. I hadn't intended to be quite so *interesting*, but we still had to find Nine. We still needed to get into the summit in the morning.

And I still needed to know more about the empire. The eclipse. The bones.

"Good," said the woman. "My name is Valmae. Let's introduce you to some people who aren't complete dolts."

Moments later, I came face-to-face with Mother.

CHAPTER TEN

"ALLOW ME TO INTRODUCE MY NEW FRIEND," VALMAE said to my mother. "This is Caseye—"

I couldn't stop staring. My mother. Right in front of me.

Part of me was *so happy* to see her as we clasped hands in greeting, but I couldn't help but notice the way she glanced at my scar, like she couldn't believe it hadn't worn off yet. Even as Paorah's captive, she still had the energy to judge me.

Valmae kept talking, completely oblivious to the uncomfortable way Mother and I looked at each other. "And this, I'm sure you know," Valmae said, "is Mira Minkoba's own mother. The Hopebearer's mother."

Was it possible to break in half from cringing so hard?

"Caseye," Mother said, my false name strange on her

tongue. "It's so lovely to meet you."

For the first time ever, because this certainly wasn't an awkward reunion between two people who rarely got along.

"Of course." My voice turned rough, and Aaru's hand pressed harder against the small of my back. "And where is your daughter tonight? I'm surprised she wasn't invited to speak at the memorial earlier, or the summit in the morning."

Mother's eyebrows rose, but she shouldn't have been surprised. No doubt she'd already been asked that question three or four times within the last hour. If I didn't ask, I would risk compromising my disguise.

Then, Mother's expression settled and she said, "My daughter is traveling with Elbena Krasteba. Safe, thank Damyan and Darina. I'm just glad she wasn't home when the council house was attacked. The entire ordeal was horrendous enough without worrying about her."

So the Hopebearer—fake Hopebearer—would not be making an appearance tonight or tomorrow. Paorah was hiding her, either because she was too injured to be seen in public, or because he had other plans.

My heart thundered so loudly I could barely hear myself speak. "There have been so many stories about what happened that day. I'm curious to know the truth. How did you come to Anahera?"

Her expression twisted into grief. Real grief, not the careful mask she wore when she knew predators were about. "My husband had gone to the council house in the morning, but came home shortly after because he'd forgotten something. I'm afraid our younger daughter had a small meltdown—school or clothes or something—and he stayed to help her, and that's when we heard the explosion."

A sour taste clogged my throat, and I fought to keep my expression a careful blend of sympathy, concern, and warm support.

"After that, we all made our way down the escape route, but warriors had broken through. The line of people was moving too slowly, and I needed to make sure my daughter reached safety, so I tried to distract them." Mother's voice cracked, and at once I wished I hadn't asked. The others standing around us shifted uncomfortably, unused to this reveal of true emotion, but Mother continued the story. "The warriors spared my life, but not my husband's. He was killed right in front of me. So was the rest of my staff; they were practically family."

Grief surged up from the deepest parts of me, making me sway. My father—

I forced it back down. This was the worst place of all to expose feelings. "I'm so sorry." I should have stayed. I should have found a way to help them. There were noorestones all around the cliffs; if I'd thought about it, I could have *done* something instead of flee down the stairs to safety.

"I don't know why they let me live," she said. "They'd

already slaughtered so many people in Crescent Prominence. They'd already destroyed the council house. But they allowed me to live."

"Oh, my dear." Valmae took Mother's hands and squeezed. "You were so brave."

I had to agree, but I knew why they'd let her live. It was her charm. On the spectrum of strength of divine gifts, she was among the most powerful. Even from the line to go down the cliff stairs, I'd nearly been lured toward her like a dragon to noorestones. Doctor Chilikoba had stopped me, though, and ushered me down the stairs.

Doctor Chilikoba. Another casualty of that fight.

"A few days later," Mother went on, "after the earthquake, the Anaheran ship appeared. Their soldiers killed the warriors, freed me, and said that High Magistrate Paorah had summoned the collective governments of the Fallen Isles to Flamecrest for a summit. In the absence of the Luminary Council or any other Daminan authority, they declared I'd join them here. I've been the high magistrate's guest ever since."

"You're being treated well?" The question was tight in my throat.

She nodded. "He's been keeping all of us very secure. With the explosions the night of our arrival, it hasn't been safe for us to leave the Red Hall, but we've been assured the culprits for that crime are nearly in custody. Then we'll be able to safely move around."

I doubted that. "So you're here as a representative of Damyan and Darina?"

Again, she nodded. "With the Luminary Council gone, and Elbena and my daughter away, I'm afraid I'm the only one who's even somewhat qualified to represent Damina, although I must admit I don't feel up to the task. My husband was the political mind; he would have been of more use."

"I'm very sorry for all your losses. Please, if there's anything I can do for you—if there's anything you need—don't hesitate to ask. I'd like to help, if I can." The words didn't feel adequate, but I was supposed to have just met her. Already, Valmae and the others standing with us were watching our exchange with eyebrows quirked.

"That's so kind of you," Mother said. "But no. I'd rather hear about you. Have you tried the cloudfish?"

With the subject shifted to the ball—to the dancing and the food—everyone found it easier to join in, and I tapped a grateful thanks to Aaru when he spoke about the music and the carvings along the walls.

It was strange to hear him speak so much, especially after decans of silence. The others had no idea what a gift this was, but they seemed delighted by his quiet, captivating voice and gentle humor. Even Mother warmed to him, and when she finally waved us away, it was with a smile.

"My dear Valmae, we're keeping these two from their time together." Mother looked at Aaru and me. "Go dance. Enjoy the ball tonight, and I promise that tomorrow, we will ensure that our world continues for young people like you."

Valmae thanked us for spending time with her, and

thus dismissed, Aaru and I wandered around the outskirts of the dancers as the music shifted faster, and a dozen more people threw themselves onto the floor, hips swaying and arms outstretched.

Aaru and I kept our eyes on them, walking companionably—we weren't the only ones—but where his hand covered mine, we held a secret conversation.

::Everyone is more concerned with dancing and having fun than the summit in the morning,:: Aaru said. ::All of this is meant to impress, to show off power and wealth, but where is the intention to do something useful?::

I sighed, at the last moment turning it into something happy and admiring, rather than the truly frustrated exhale that it was.

::The memorial was a charade,:: he went on. ::Most of these people didn't even go. They care more about seeing and being seen. How can anyone here claim to care?:: Aaru swept me around to face him. "Dance with me."

My breath caught as I looked up at him—at the curve of his lips, the intensity in his eyes—and I nodded. The music had slowed, and we weren't the only couple here, but when others began a long, complicated dance, Aaru and I didn't separate. We stayed on the outer edge of the floor and faced each other, my arms looped around his shoulders, and his hands resting on my hips.

::I'm sorry.:: I tapped quickly against the back of his neck.

He raised an eyebrow.

::About those people earlier. They were from Damina.::

::That doesn't make you responsible for them.::

::No, but I don't want it to change how you see Daminans.::

::It doesn't change how I see you.::

My heart squeezed.

::I've been so angry.:: His words came as fast as rain pattering on a window, or a lightning strike. ::It makes my chest burn. Every time I think about the Silent Brothers, my family, my community: How can they be gone? How could Idris abandon them?:: His hands curled and his fingernails scraped along my gown. ::How could he abandon me?::

I touched his face, both of my palms cupping his cheeks, but there was nothing to say.

::My home wasn't perfect. Even before I was sent away, I knew we had problems. But still, Idris was my home, and now it's nothing.:: His breath turned ragged, as though he was saying all this aloud. ::When Thoman started talking about how horrible Idris was, I couldn't think. I was so angry already, and everything he said was everything I feared.::

Aaru's skin was warm and smooth beneath my hands.

::I shouldn't have pushed him. It was wrong, and it risked what we're trying to do here. I'm sorry.::

::It can be easy to lose control. Back in the Pit, I stabbed Altan with a noorestone.:: The words were out before I could stop them. I cringed. ::Sorry. I wasn't going to bring him up unless you did.::

Aaru let out a long sigh. "They won't find him," he murmured finally. "He's already gone."

"Where?"

"It's only worth saying if it works out." Aaru bit his lip, then shook himself out of whatever thought had captured him.

I wanted to push—didn't I deserve answers?—but I'd just gotten Aaru back. Trusting someone, trusting *him*, meant waiting until he was ready to tell me.

::He wasn't doing us any good in the closet, only making us miserable. We had to see him every day. Hear him every day.:: Aaru looked exasperated. ::I wanted to mourn, but felt like I couldn't. Not with him there.::

::I'm sorry.:: I should have thought of that.

He offered a small shrug. ::It will be better without him.::

::The others won't understand.:: I didn't really understand, except that I knew Aaru would never intentionally put us in danger. ::I wish you had told me.::

::I should have. I'm sorry.::

::If we don't work together, then we can only work against one another.:: The music shifted into a faster tempo, but not so fast that we looked strange just swaying together. ::We have to talk to each other,:: I said, stepping closer so that I could feel the heat of his body. ::Out loud. Quiet code. It doesn't make a difference to me.::

His expression began to crumple. ::After Idris—::

I shook my head. ::I understood that. It makes sense. Grief is different for all of us, and you lost so much.::

Again, his fingertips curled over my hips, pulling me a breath closer.

::But then you spoke aloud again—for the first time since the noorestones—and I wanted to talk to you.::

His lips parted. ::It hurt you that I talked to Altan instead.::

"Yes." A lump of ugly jealousy lodged in my throat. ::I was sad when you stopped talking. Out loud, I mean. After the noorestones. After Altan.::

He lowered his eyes.

::I felt guilty, like I should have been able to prevent it. Like you lost something important because I wasn't strong enough.::

::That wasn't it.:: He stopped swaying. Stood still. Gazed down at me. ::I don't know why it went away, or why it came back. There are so many things I don't understand, and I wish I had answers, but I don't. I just hurt now. All the time.::

My hands slid down his shoulders, his arms, his wrists. My fingers tangled with his. ::I love you, Aaru. Whether you speak aloud, in quiet code, or not at all, I love you. And I wish I could take the pain for you, carry some of the burden, but we both know grief doesn't work like that.:: I slid my thumb across his knuckles and took a small step backward. ::It's selfish, I know, but I thought when you finally got your voice back, you'd share it with me. Instead, you shared it with him. Our enemy. The man who tortured it away from you in the first place.::

His breath came with a soft shudder, and my heart squeezed with wanting as I watched his face, the lines of his cheeks and chin, the furrow of his brow, the softness of his gaze. I'd never realized it was possible to want such closeness with another person—only to realize they might not be able to give it.

::I know it's selfish,:: I said again. ::And I know what you've lost, even if I can't fully comprehend it.::

He bowed his head and drew me close again. ::I'm not the only one who's experienced loss. You have, too.::

My throat went tight.

::I heard you in the parlor. I should have come to see you, but I wasn't sure how to talk about it yet. My anger. Grief. Voice.::

::Damina's book says we aren't owed the inner workings of anyone else's heart.::

::But it does say love leans on others for strength, and to embrace those who need support.::

I couldn't stop my surprised stare.

::Hristo let me read his copy.:: A faint smile touched the corner of his mouth. ::He thought it might help.::

::Has it?:: Reading *The Book of Love* always helped me feel better, but I was from Damina. The words were burned into my blood.

He nodded. ::I didn't think it would, but it has.::

"You're not alone," I whispered. "No matter what it feels like, you're not alone. You have me."

"Thank you," he said. "You have me, too."

PEOPLE CONTINUED TO move around the ballroom in tight clumps, watching one another, whispering, studying. Though a significant number of the guests had been taken from their islands—perhaps against their wills, like Mother—their behavior was normal.

::Maybe Nine isn't here,:: Aaru said. ::Maybe Seven was wrong.::

I twisted my fingers with his as we wandered around the ballroom, watching people without *watching* people. Was anyone paying us unusual attention? We'd made a scene earlier. If Nine was here, that alone probably made them want to avoid us.

::The guard is staring.:: Aaru glanced up and flashed a placating smile in her direction. ::I think she's still angry. She's probably waiting for us to start another fight.::

Or . . .

"I think it's time to go," I murmured. "But first, we have an apology to make."

Aaru shot me a curious look, but he followed when I walked toward the female guard from earlier.

There was no humor in her eyes as she watched our approach. "What?"

My heart was pounding, but I steadied my voice and said, "We wanted to apologize for our behavior earlier. It was unbecoming. Inappropriate."

The guard glared at me. "Just don't do it again."

I offered a winning smile. "Seven out of nine times,

we're really well behaved. Promise."

Her glare narrowed into suspicious slits. "You need to leave here. Now."

"But—"

Nine—surely she had to be Nine—glanced at the next guard over. "I'm escorting these two out."

The other guard nodded, and before I could protest again, Nine was marching us toward the door. We drew a few curious eyes, and heat crawled up my face. If I'd been here as myself, the humiliation of being asked to leave the ball might have killed me. Even in disguise, I could feel Mother's judgment.

But instead of taking us outside, Nine led us to a small room—away from servants or guards. Chairs, tables, and other furniture crowded the space, but we all squeezed in, and finally Nine whispered, "Who are you?" Her hand rested on the dagger at her hip, and I had no doubt she was more than capable of using it. But I could feel the buzz of noorestones nearby—three inside the room, and fifteen more just outside.

"We have a mutual acquaintance." It was a risk, revealing anything, but if she really was Nine, then someone needed to take the first step. "He goes by Seven."

A quick, indrawn breath: that was the only hint she gave that she knew him, but it was enough.

"He sent us here to find you," I said.

"Who are you?" Her tone was all caution.

I glanced at Aaru, and he gave a faint, encouraging

nod. ::Her heart is pounding. She's nervous, but I don't think she means harm.:: His tap came against the small of my back, hidden from Nine's view.

I turned back to her. "You know who I am. I am Mira Minkoba. Hopebearer. Dragonhearted."

She gave only a soft grunt. "Where is Seven?"

I hesitated. "Dead."

Her eyebrows drew inward as she let out an unfamiliar curse. "How?" She held up a hand. "Wait, not now. I need to get back, and you need to get out. Paorah already has the false Hopebearer; he can't get his hands on you, too."

I'd known it, but the confirmation hit me in the chest. Still, I was glad she'd changed her mind about discussing Seven. I wasn't ready to admit that his death was my fault. "Wait, before we go, do you have a way into the summit tomorrow?"

She gestured at her uniform. "Obviously."

"We need to get in, too." Not to mention I had a thousand questions for her. What about the dragon bones?

Her lip curled in annoyance. "I'm not your friend, Hopebearer. I'm not your ally. And I'm certainly not your servant. Find your own way in."

"Seven said you would help."

"He's dead, and you could be lying." She shouldered past me toward the door, but as her hand curled around the knob, I drew a breath of noorestone fire into me. It twined around my fingers like smoke. Nine stared at me. "What are you?"

"I already told you." The blue-white light shone brighter, dancing down my hand and wrist and arm. "Now, please, I want your help."

Nine looked me over again, reevaluating. "That was you in the ballroom."

With a flick of my fingers, I made the light vanish—back to the noorestones. "That was me."

"All right, Hopebearer." She shifted her weight to one leg. "You want to get into the summit in the morning."

I nodded.

"Both of us," Aaru said.

I raised an eyebrow his way. He'd come to this for the memorial. That was his right. He didn't need to go to the summit.

"Both of us," he said to me. ::**Please. I should have been helping you since we got here. Let me do this now.**::

"All right." I turned back to Nine. "Both of us."

She studied us for a few moments, then nodded and produced a piece of paper and pencil. Quickly, she scribbled an address. "Very well. Meet me here at dawn. The summit begins three hours after that. I won't wait for you."

CHAPTER ELEVEN

THREE TIMES, OUR HORSECARRE WAS STOPPED FOR inspection, thanks to the curfew, but the memorial invitations worked as waivers, and we continued through the quiet streets of Flamecrest. By the time we returned to the hotel, it was nearly midnight.

Tanhe waited up for us, like an anxious parent, and we answered a few of his questions—if the driver had been polite, what kind of food had been served at the Red Hall, and whether anyone noticed his emblem on the horsecarre and inquired about his business. Then we headed up to our suite, exhausted but giddy with the success of finding Nine.

I wasn't even a step inside when LaLa launched herself in my direction with a happy screech, and Ilina scrambled to catch her.

"Wait until she gets changed," my friend scolded. "We talked about this. The shop said we could sell the gown back if it's in good condition, and sweet dragon weasels ruin nice things."

LaLa let out an indignant squawk and puff of smoke.

"I don't think she cares." I smiled. There was something so *good* about seeing LaLa and Crystal every day, even though we were constantly cleaning up after them. Before LaLa exploded with the need to snuggle, I found one of the hotel robes and—with my gown safe beneath the heavy cotton—stretched out my arms for my dragon.

She shot toward me and gripped the robe while I petted her and admired all her scales.

Chenda ambled toward me, glancing at my right cheek to make sure her work had stayed in place. "Well," she said, "how was it?"

"Not as fun as dragons." I kissed LaLa's nose.

"We found Nine," Aaru said. "She's mean."

Zara half fell out of her chair. "You *can* talk!"

He cocked his head. "I did the other day."

"But then you stopped again." She turned her attention on me. "Did you see Mother? Did you talk to her? How is she? Does she look all right? Does she miss me?"

"Wait"—Chenda stood—"let's hear about Nine first."

"Or how you're getting into the summit in the morning," Gerel said.

When the questions faded, I perched on the arm of the sofa and recounted the highlights of the evening. LaLa continued clinging to my robe like some kind of affectionate burr, while Aaru stood just behind me, one hand resting on my shoulder in a warm declaration of support—and quick quiet code whenever I missed a detail someone would want, or put events out of order.

Zara sank deep in her chair when I confirmed that our father was dead, while Hristo grew still and quiet when I gave him the news about his. I pushed my own sadness aside again; there was no time to indulge my grief.

"Nothing on my father?" Ilina was hesitant. It must have felt so uncomfortable for her to ask for hope when she knew there was none for others.

"I didn't see him," I said, "and Mother didn't say anything about him. I'm sure he's here, but I have no idea where. Maybe tomorrow I'll learn something."

She gave a faint nod. "Thank you."

Finally, we got to our encounter with Nine, and the meeting we'd arranged for dawn.

"Are you sure you can trust her?" Gerel asked. "Aaru doesn't seem to like her."

Aaru offered a one-shouldered shrug. "I don't distrust her. Just don't like her."

"She *is* an imperial spy," I added. "We should trust her as far as LaLa could carry her. But she'll help us get into the summit."

"She didn't lie when she told us where to meet." Aaru's voice was soft. "She meant what she said."

"How do you know?" Zara asked.

"Heard her heartbeat."

"Oh." Zara glanced around the room, clearly searching for someone to exchange an exasperated look with, but everyone just nodded to themselves like that was a normal thing to say.

"So you both intend to meet Nine in the morning?" Gerel crossed her arms and frowned. "Don't you think Chenda and I should go? She knows about politics. I know about fighting enemies."

I shook my head. "Nine may not like us, but she's expecting us. If we send other people, she could change her mind. We can't risk it."

Gerel sighed, but she didn't argue.

"All right." Ilina stood and shooed everyone out of the parlor. "To bed. At least two people have to get out the door in a few hours."

"I miss sleep." I slid off the arm of the sofa and turned to look at Aaru. Part of me wanted to thank him for coming with me tonight—and promising to come tomorrow—but it seemed inappropriate. The memorial, his entire reason for going, was a cloud over everything.

So I just squeezed his hand and said good night, and then headed for my room.

Ilina blocked the door. "Wrong way. You're in there, remember?" She pointed to the boys' room. "I told you I was going to switch everyone around. I'm sharing with your sister. Hristo took my room. I've already moved all your things. You're *welcome*."

Her tone was enough to make my whole face burn, but what could I say? Swapping rooms back would take time, and already I could feel my thoughts fogging over. Plus, I wasn't sure what insisting on changing our rooms back would signal to . . . anyone.

I slinked into the bedroom she'd sent me to. Aaru was already there, studying the floor like it was the most fascinating thing he'd ever seen.

"Sorry," I said. "I didn't think she'd actually do it. I can sleep in the parlor."

He shook his head. ::**Sleep in the bed. I can sleep on the floor.**::

"Will that make you more comfortable?" I glanced at the bed. It was big enough for him and Hristo to share; it was big enough for him and me to share, too. We could both sprawl out and not even touch.

He pressed his mouth into a line, and then: ::**Will it make you more comfortable?**::

"I would be worried about you sleeping on the hard floor." I pried off the robe—and therefore LaLa—and placed them on the bottom corner of the bed. She wiggled deeper into the fabric until she sat in it like a bird in a nest.

::**When I was young,**:: Aaru tapped, ::**I slept on the floor all the time. Before I built a bed in the basement.**::

My chest felt heavy with pressure. "Sleep in the bed." Before he could respond, I hurried into the washroom to wash my face and change clothes, careful to put the gown

147

into its protective bag. By the time I came back, LaLa was asleep and Aaru had covered all but one of the noorestones. He stood awkwardly on the opposite side of the bed, wearing soft trousers and a long buttoned shirt. He looked . . . cozy. He'd looked incredible earlier, yes, but clad only in his loose nightclothes he was Aaru, but even softer. I couldn't decide whether to hate or thank Ilina for doing this.

"Have you . . ." He shifted his weight. It was difficult to avoid acknowledging the reason Ilina and the others had moved our rooms around, but clearly he intended to make an attempt. He switched to quiet code, just quick tapping against the headboard. ::**Have you still been having those dreams?**::

I nearly sagged in relief, then tried to cover it by sitting on my side of the bed, on top of the covers, pretending like I was completely fine. Like my heart wasn't thrumming. Like we weren't avoiding anything. Like this was a normal conversation. "Yes. Every night."

He sat, too, a mirror of me. "Will you tell me?"

"It's hard to explain." But if I didn't try, we'd be forced to confront the sleeping situation. The bed situation. We'd slept close together before, but on different sides of the wall between our cells, or in separate hammocks. Nothing like a nice bed in a beautiful hotel after attending a ball together.

His voice gentled even more. "Do you want to go to sleep?"

I wanted to talk to him. It had been so long, and I didn't want it to end, but . . . I got up and covered the last noorestone. When I came back to the bed, he was already between the covers. I slipped in, too, careful of my feet around LaLa's nest, and faced Aaru. "Can I have your hand?" I whispered into the darkness.

He shifted—I didn't hear it, but I could feel his movements—and a moment later his fingers touched mine.

::There are lots of different dreams. In the ones with the empire, I see bones. Great dragon bones so big I—:: I sighed and drew his hand closer to me. ::I've never seen anything like it, but in my dream, I know they're the bones of the first dragon.::

::The first?::

::The biggest. The most powerful. And in my dream, I know that I need the bones before—before something.::

::Eclipse?::

"Yes." I tucked our tangled fingers under my chin. "Before the eclipse."

"But the bones are in the empire."

"Maybe," I whispered. "It's just a dream. Maybe they're not real."

"Maybe they are." He scooted closer. "Ask Nine."

I snorted. "That won't be strange. *Hello, Nine, I know we just met and you don't like me, but I've been having dreams about enormous dragon bones located somewhere in your vast and ever-growing empire. Can you confirm whether that's true?*"

The bed shook a little, and his breath hitched. He was *laughing*.

I grinned into the darkness. I couldn't remember the last time he'd laughed.

After a moment, he pulled his hand free of mine and cupped my cheek. When the heel of his palm brushed my lips, we both went still. Didn't move. Didn't breathe. Then he whispered, "Thank you."

I didn't ask why, because we both knew. And I didn't remind him that I'd been here this whole time, because that wouldn't solve anything. Instead, I closed my eyes and kissed his fingertips one at a time. Then: "Let's go to sleep."

"Will you dream of dragons?"

"Listen and find out."

The *Drakontos celestus*

EVEN FOR DRAGONS, FLYING WAS INCREDIBLE.

The sensation of wind under wings, the feel of fire burning inside, and the absolute defiance of gravity: it was a new joy every time. Even the way shadows fell, like grounded echoes of clouds. Or dragons. These wings stretched wide, casting darkness over the world, one piece at a time.

And from above, everything looked small, like toys. The waves, ships, and even the islands themselves, if one could only get high enough. The whole world spread below, a map of everything that mattered.

A map of everything that would soon disappear.

CHAPTER TWELVE

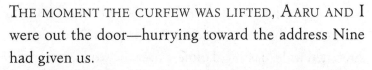

THE MOMENT THE CURFEW WAS LIFTED, AARU AND I were out the door—hurrying toward the address Nine had given us.

Dawn hovered just below the horizon, purple and deep blue. Only a few people moved through the streets—fishers, bakers, cart vendors—but if they noticed Aaru and me, they showed no interest. They trudged on with heavy, downcast eyes, looking as wrung out as we felt. They probably hadn't been up half the night looking for an imperial spy, but the need—real or manufactured—for martial law was taking a toll on everyone.

Nine had sent us to a shoe shop, one I'd passed by several times during my market visits, and even glanced into during the gown-shopping excursion with Ilina and

Zara. It seemed like a strange place to meet a spy, but then again, what did I know about spies? Maybe this was perfectly normal.

Before I could try the door, Nine let us in. She wore regular clothes, rather than the guard uniform from last night. Eerie how easy it was for them to move among us, unnoticed.

"Are you living here?" I glanced around, but it was just a typical shop: shoes on display, shoes packed onto shelves, and a small polishing station to help protect against the red dust that touched every part of Flamecrest.

"Where I live is none of your concern." She waved us into the back room, which was cramped with stores of leather and cotton and all manner of equipment. There was nowhere to sit, aside from a single stool, so we all remained standing. "I'll get you into the summit," she said, "but I need to hear everything about how Seven died."

"No." It was too uncomfortable of a topic, partly because it was my fault Seven had died, and partly because the events revealed too much about my connection with dragons. She was a *spy*, after all. She worked for the *Algotti Empire*. Information about Seven's death was one of the few things I had to bargain with. "I'll tell you after the summit."

Her gaze was steady. Dark. But at last she nodded. "Very well. But I must know what he told you regarding events in the Fallen Isles. How much do you know about our purpose here?"

We glared at each other for a moment while I

considered what she could use against me later, and finally I conceded. "I thought you'd come to see what your empress had bought with the Mira Treaty," I said, "but Seven claimed you came to investigate the disasters."

"That's right." She began rifling through a box sitting on one of the tables. "Our empress wanted to know how your problems would affect us. We may be far from you, but waves originating from the Fallen Isles have touched our shores." She frowned, as though we'd personally done that to her. "But instead of mere geological activity, we've found evidence of a civil war brewing."

"Anahera," I murmured.

She pulled a pair of trousers from the box. There seemed nothing special about them, but she nodded to herself. "Here." She tossed them at Aaru. "Put these on."

Aaru paled, but Nine didn't look ready to offer him another place to change to protect his delicate sensibilities, so he edged around a pile of crates, and I turned my back.

"It seems," Nine said, digging through the box again, "the high magistrate intends to keep this island planted firmly in the sea by collecting all the dragons he can find."

"That's my theory as well." I caught the trousers she sent flying my way. "Our holy books tell us that the dragons are the children of the gods, and that they entreat the gods on our behalf. The Great Abandonment is because of a broken covenant: we haven't taken care of the dragons, and so there are too few to speak for us."

"I know." She threw a shirt at Aaru. "I've read all of your holy books."

"You have?"

She scoffed. "Of course. You don't expect me to come here, knowing nothing about your culture or society, and try to remain invisible, do you?" She found another shirt for me. "So he gathered all those dragons to the ruins, believing their presence would save Anahera."

And then my friends and I had not only freed the dragons, but destroyed the ruins as well.

"How do you think their disappearance affects his plans?" she asked.

"I don't know." I began switching my clothes for the ones she'd given me. "Dragons have no quarrel with the goddess of destruction, only the man ruling the island, so they could still be here." My heart ached at the memory of all those dragons lying there, sick and trapped in their own minds.

"He won't rely on that."

"No," I agreed. "He won't. I didn't want to believe that one island could betray the others, even after everything Seven said. But the evidence is too strong. The dragons, the new fleet, bringing what's left of the governments here."

Nine shot me a look that might have been described as sympathetic, but she didn't seem like the kind of person to express such feelings. "I believe he intends to establish his rule here and hold out as long as possible."

"I suppose, but what if the Great Abandonment doesn't work like he thinks?" I finished changing into the clothes she'd given me. "What if it doesn't matter whether he has dragons here? Anahera might still rise."

"He has ships." Aaru appeared from behind the crates. The clothes didn't look like much—just shapeless and gray, the same sort that I was wearing now. On both of us, the sleeves and trousers were too short, as if Nine had given us her own clothes.

Nine nodded at him. "Perhaps the high magistrate intends to find another place to bring his chosen few, once the time is right. There are other islands in this ocean, you know. And other oceans. Other continents across the horizon. There's an entire world out there, beyond these shores."

I knew that. Mostly. I'd just . . . never thought anyone from the Fallen Isles would ever want to leave. This was our home. The seat of our power. The place where our gods rested beneath our feet.

We were destroying it.

I plucked at the sad, gray clothes. "What is this? How will this help us get into the summit?"

"We'll walk right in."

"In this?" I gestured at the too-short sleeves and how silly everything looked on Aaru.

Nine smiled. Really smiled, not just the smirk she'd used on us before. "Your island magic is interesting. I know people back home who'd love to study it. Our empress finds it fascinating, in fact. But let me give you a taste of the empire's power."

Then she took a small metal device from the box and pressed her fingers against the flat side that faced her. She murmured something under her breath, too soft for me to hear—and when I glanced at Aaru, he just shook his head. When she finished whispering, Nine drew a short metal rod from inside the device and tapped it against my sleeve.

My shirt transformed into the flame-blue top of an Anaheran guard uniform.

I jumped and, embarrassingly, squeaked out a panicked yelp. Nine laughed and tapped my trousers, and they, too, transformed. Miraculously—magically—they were even long enough now.

"What did you do?" Alarm filled Aaru's voice as he backed away from Nine. "What is that?"

"This"—she lifted the device—"is magic. Real magic." She tapped the rod onto Aaru's clothes and grinned while the gray fabric rearranged itself into the uniform of the high magistrate's guards. Then she changed hers, too. "Bring your own clothes. We'll stash them away for later."

My heart finally slowed to a normal rate while Aaru and I pressed our things into a small knapsack Nine lent us. The magic device went back into its box—it was probably far too dangerous to bring *that* with us—and Nine pulled out a sheet of paper with a hasty sketch of the Red Hall and the chamber where the summit would be held.

"Now," she said, "here's how this is going to happen."

CHAPTER THIRTEEN

WHEN I WAS YOUNGER, VISITING THE LUMINARY Council's chamber felt like something between a punishment and a treat. I hated politics, but I loved the marble columns and gold inlay, the brilliant noorestones, and the light and open airy feeling. I'd always thought that room, designed by the First Masters, was the height of architectural beauty.

But now, I saw the Fire Ministry's chambers, and I understood what true power and wealth could offer.

It was all polished bloodwood, with seven tiers that descended toward the main floor and the high magistrate's bench. Public and private galleries stood above, providing a space for carefully chosen citizens to come see their government at work. The furniture—long rows of desks—and even the staircases were painstakingly carved with decorative swirls and, on the bigger pieces, detailed etchings of their goddess's great works.

Even though the fifty noorestones shone their usual white-blue, the room looked red. Rich. Forbidding.

Nine had given us strict instructions on how to move, where to stand, and the need for us to do exactly as she ordered. *"I've worked too hard to earn the trust of the high magistrate and his guard,"* she'd explained. *"I don't need the two of you ruining everything in a day."*

I couldn't imagine how she'd managed to get herself inserted into the high magistrate's personal guard, let alone the two of us, but when I asked, she simply said she wasn't going to tell *islanders* her secrets. We were, after all, supposed to be enemies.

So when we arrived in the chambers, we took our positions and waited while the rest of the Red Hall security escorted the dignitaries to their seats.

The chairs filled up quickly, first with the thirty members of the Fire Ministry. Nine had said they usually took up the entire chamber, with seats next to them for their aides, but now all the ministers sat to the western side to leave room for the rest. There were no aides today.

The Twilight Senate came next, followed by all the Hartan matriarchs, then the Warrior Tribunal. Last, Mother entered, the sole representative of Damyan and Darina.

No one came to represent Idris.

I was stationed near the grand double doors at the back of the room, which meant that everyone had to walk past me, yet no one actually noticed. From here, I had a wide view of the chamber, and also Aaru—and his hands. We'd be able to communicate by quiet code.

Meanwhile, Nine was positioned near the high magistrate's bench, her posture straight and waiting. Anyone could see her there, but that was her best way of blending in. After all, who expected an imperial spy in the Fallen Isles? And in the high magistrate's personal guard? Nine had the perfect disguise, and though she was small, no one could mistake her for anything but deadly. She and Gerel would probably get along as well as sisters.

Movement sounded in the galleries above. Thirty or so people began to file in—some I'd seen last night, or during my previous visits to Anahera. They were all high-end merchants, bankers, or traders: Anaheran elite with a connection to the high magistrate.

Where were the regular people?

Well, I knew that answer. Regular people hadn't been invited. Otherwise, we wouldn't have needed Nine's help to get in. Only Paorah's friends were allowed to watch today. Maybe every day.

As everyone began to settle into their seats, the hum of voices echoed off the polished wood and obscured any single voice, but from what I could tell of people's profiles, they mostly wore curious, expectant expressions—and as the door near the high magistrate's bench opened, everyone grew quiet.

Paorah stepped into the room, robed in deep gold and red, and flanked by a pair of guards. He went to the floor, rather than his bench, and there he studied everyone he'd brought here—by force or by invitation.

"Welcome, friends." He gazed around the chamber as the last of the murmurs died, and then said, "Thank you all for coming."

As though they'd been given a choice.

"Last night, we attended a memorial for our brothers and sisters on Idris," he went on, "but let us take another moment to remember the Silent Brothers, who are forever silenced, and the Luminary Council, who were murdered by rogue warriors just a decan ago."

Everyone bowed their heads. One of the matriarchs who'd been seated near Mother reached out and offered a hand to hold.

A moment passed.

Then another.

I met Aaru's eyes—briefly, before anyone could see— and we, too, shared a moment. Of understanding. Of grief. Of longing for a world that didn't exist anymore.

Then the high magistrate cleared his throat and looked up, and so did everyone else.

"Seventeen years ago, all the governments of the Fallen Isles came together in an unprecedented way: we signed the Mira Treaty. In it, we united ourselves against our enemies on the mainland. We enacted safeguards to protect the dragons of our islands. And we declared that all of us are equal in the eyes of our gods, and that no island should be held below others. We bow only to the light of Noore."

I could not help but notice the gold-inlaid flame carved into the front of the bench behind him. The Great Flame: Anahera's fire.

"Some of you may remember," he said, "that I campaigned against the Mira Treaty."

The way he spoke the name struck a shiver down my back. I fought to stay collected, training my gaze on the wall straight ahead of me while I counted noorestones; I couldn't look at them, not without drawing attention to myself, so I touched them with my gift—not enough to make them do anything, but enough that their inner fire ran through me, warming me beneath the strange, magical clothes. With every mental touch to a noorestone, the anxiety eased.

"People often ask why I was so adamantly against the treaty. After all, its goals were noble. It was the first effort within living memory of all the islands working together. But I'll admit: I didn't think we could do it. I didn't believe that the people of the Fallen Isles could put aside their differences long enough to *make* a difference. But I was not high magistrate at that time, so I was overruled.

"For years," he went on, "it's been an unpopular stance to admit. The first time I ran for high magistrate, my opposition reminded everyone at every opportunity. It haunted me all through my first term, but by then I could not deny the good the treaty had done. I am proud to see Hartans independent. I am proud of what we've accomplished with our sanctuaries. And I am proud that—for years—we were six nations united.

"Yet, for all our effort, good intentions, and hard-fought accomplishments, the Great Abandonment is upon us. This we cannot deny. Not while the god shadow swings across the islands every evening. Not while Hartan-born are still being discriminated against. Not while council-house attacks slaughter hundreds of innocent people. Not while—as you've all seen firsthand—even my own streets here in Flamecrest require martial law to keep the peace."

My breath caught, and fifty noorestones flickered—just for a heartbeat, and I let them go as soon as I realized, but it was enough. Everyone looked around and mur-mured: How strange, was it the gods? But when it didn't happen again, they went back to looking at the high mag-istrate.

Aaru caught my eye, his worry clear.

I glanced down and I tapped against my sword hilt. ::We know he set the explosions for the night the others arrived. Could he be behind the deportation decree as well? And the council house?::

::And Idris?:: Aaru gave me a look that made it clear he thought that was unlikely.

::He didn't try to save any islands by spreading out the dragons. He tried to take them all. Maybe he didn't target Idris, but he did nothing to prevent a god from rising.::

Aaru's expression darkened.

The high magistrate was still talking, but it was hard

to hear him over the buzzing in my ears. I reached again for a noorestone, just one this time, and let its hum work through me; the panic eased into something manageable, something I could endure even without my calming pills.

"With that in mind," the high magistrate said, "I believe it's time for all of us—the surviving representatives of the Fallen Isles—to take another look at the Mira Treaty. Let us decide, here and today, about its future, and in turn, the future of our people."

All around the room, people nodded, and a sick feeling coiled up inside of me. Wasn't this supposed to be about the Great Abandonment? Wasn't this supposed to be about how we'd prevent more islands from rising up out of their seabeds and sending hundreds of thousands of innocent people into the unforgiving ocean?

I breathed deeply. One. Two. Three.

The high magistrate found Mother and beckoned her forward. "Please," he said. "I think it's only right that we hear from you first. Wife of the architect of the Mira Treaty. Mother of the Hopebearer herself. Without the Luminary Council here, you are the natural choice to tell us whether Damina still supports the Mira Treaty."

Others nodded, and again, I felt the absence of Elbena and Tirta. He had them—Nine had confirmed it—so where were they?

My heart thundered as Mother slipped from her seat and sidled into the aisle. One, two, three, four: she took the stairs down to the main floor and stood next to the high magistrate while he introduced her more fully to the other representatives, as if they didn't already know her.

Then, instead of going to his bench, like I thought he might—he was arrogant enough—he took an empty seat on the first tier to listen to Mother speak.

She looked beautiful today, her hair pressed straight how she liked it, and a light touch of cosmetics around her eyes and cheeks and lips. The soft blue dress was of Anaheran style—provided by the high magistrate, no doubt—but it hung nicely on her, emphasizing the proud way she held herself in spite of everything.

Her eyes swept the chamber, and though she was facing me now, she didn't notice me. Not in the guard uniform. Not where she didn't expect me. Even if she'd noticed a guard, she wouldn't have been able to see my scar; I stood in the shadow beneath a noorestone sconce, which threw light away from my face.

"My daughter is the Hopebearer," Mother began. "And it *is* a burden, hope. In the darkest of times, it's easy to sink into despair: to believe the world has never been worse off than this, to fear we can never recover. Therefore, hope is a light against the oppressive darkness of misery, one that must be vigilantly maintained.

"I have seen that struggle in my oldest daughter. In my Mira." Mother's voice cracked. "From the time she was born, she has endured hate-filled attacks from those who wish to move backward. While I've done my best to protect her from the ugliness of the world, it's impossible to ignore. It seeps in. It corrupts. But Mira still sees what the world ought to be, and she fights for it. Every day. Every breath. She did not ask to bear the burden of our hope, nor did she offer. But nevertheless, it is what she does.

"As long as my daughter—who's somehow endured this hope all her life—still supports the Mira Treaty, then so do I. So do Damyan and Darina."

My heart was an endless knot of shock and joy and love and anguish, and it rushed against my chest so hard I thought I might burst. How long had she felt this way? Why hadn't she ever talked to me like that? I'd always thought I wasn't good enough for her.

From his position along the wall, Aaru offered a faint, fleeting smile.

As Mother returned to her seat, several of the matriarchs reached toward her, taking her hands or brushing fingertips in reassurance. I couldn't hear their whispered words from here, but as Eka Delro stood to take her turn, she grasped Mother's shoulder and smiled kindly.

Eka was the First Matriarch of Harta, tall and regal, with warm brown skin and gentle eyes. I'd always liked her—at least until I'd seen her introducing Tirta as the Hopebearer.

She moved to the front of the room and drew a deep breath. "Before I was the First Matriarch, I was a farm worker on Idris. I went from field to field, using my muted god gift on another island's crops. I went voluntarily, because working for the Idrisi government paid better than working at home, and because I could not bear the thought of either of my young sisters going. I sent back every chip I earned, save what I needed to keep myself sheltered and fed.

"The day the Mira Treaty was signed, I almost didn't go home. I almost stayed to continue working on the island where I'd lived most of my life. But I returned, because I knew my people would need everyone willing to help make the transition from an occupied territory to an independent nation. I brought back the wisdom I had gained from my time on Idris, the good and the bad, and though I was surprised to be elected one of Harta's matriarchs, I have embraced this new duty to help my people grow.

"Hartan freedom was a long, difficult journey, but it taught me the most important lesson of my life: equality elevates us all.

"I support the Mira Treaty," she finished, "as do all the matriarchs of Harta, and all the people of Harta. We will not give up our independence. And finally, I find it not just irregular, but *alarming*, that we are having this discussion at all, without proposing anything to replace the treaty."

Murmurs bubbled around the room as people nodded. She had good points, and while everyone knew her story, it was still compelling.

Dara Soun went next, speaking in support of the Mira Treaty like the others, but her words about embracing equality rang hollow because she—and the rest of the Twilight Senate—had pushed to send Hartans away from

Bopha. If anyone here was angered by her hypocrisy, however, they didn't show it.

Then it was the Warrior Tribunal, and while the three were the same rank, they'd chosen one to speak on behalf of all. His speech went much like the others, but he said nothing about how they disregarded the Mira Treaty's requirement to disband the Drakon Warriors. Nor did he speak of *their* rogue warrior, who'd launched an attack on the Luminary Council.

Every speech earned polite applause, although a few members of the Fire Ministry seemed more focused on the notes they were taking. Above, those in the galleries leaned toward one another, discussing each of the speakers.

The chamber was quiet, with only the shuffling of papers, faint coughs, and other small noises echoing across the gleaming space. Then Paorah rose from the chair where he'd been watching the proceedings and returned to the main floor. The crest of Anahera's fire stood sharp and golden behind him.

"Thank you," he said. "I appreciate your candid responses. Your support of the Mira Treaty is noted. As for the concern that we're discussing repealing the treaty with nothing better to replace it"—he nodded at Eka—"I can assure you that I would not have brought you here without an alternative proposal."

I held my breath. All throughout the chamber, representatives shifted in their chairs and leaned forward.

"Discussions within the Fire Ministry have been heated, you might say." He smiled a little at his joke, but no one responded. "Is the Mira Treaty fulfilling its core functions? Can we restore the Fallen Isles to completeness once more? Or do we need to look at other options?"

Whispers slithered through the chamber, sharp and worried. I glanced at Aaru.

::Don't like the way this sounds.:: It was all he needed to say. I felt the same way. Even Nine watched Paorah intently.

"In the decan since Idris rose, it's become clear that the Great Abandonment is upon us. The other islands *will* rise. More of our people *will* perish. But we have the opportunity to do something. Here. Today."

My heart pounded at the sound of those words—the deepest fears of everyone in this room.

"I'll be honest," he said, walking toward Nine. My chest seized, but he moved past her, took the stair up, and went behind his bench, where he could preside over the entire chamber. "I have seen this coming for some time now. And I've been doing what I can to prepare for the inevitable day when the Mira Treaty fails and a new treaty is needed."

"What?" someone murmured. *"What is this about?"*

And: *"This is most irregular."*

And also: *"If you had these concerns, why didn't you come to us before? Why wait?"*

The high magistrate looked down from his bench and

frowned at that final comment. "I did. I voiced my concerns seventeen years ago, when discussions about the treaty were first under way. I said I doubted that it would be enough, that we could change enough. . . ." He shook his head and sighed. "We all hoped it would work. We gave the Mira Treaty seventeen years to make a difference, but has it?"

A knot of dread grew in my stomach, tightening with every breath. Seven had said Anahera was behind the Mira Treaty.

Paorah had made—was still making—a show of opposing it to disguise its true purpose. He had also engineered it to fail.

Anahera's major aspect was the destroyer—life and death and life again—but she was also a trickster, the asker of answers, known for being exceedingly clever. She painted a picture too complex for anyone to see until it was already unfolded, and the high magistrate was her devoted apprentice.

He'd twisted it, though. Like the Luminary Council made love a weakness, and the Silent Brothers made silence a weapon, and all the others perverted their gods' commandments in some way: the high magistrate turned his divine gifts into a trap, and all the Fallen Isles were caught in this fire.

Voices buzzed around the chamber, tight with questions and uncertainties, but when the high magistrate lifted a hand, everyone went quiet.

"The Great Abandonment is inevitable," he said. "We all know that. We will lose our gods. We will lose most of our people."

My stomach twisted with hot anxiety, but I didn't dare reach for a noorestone for comfort.

"But I have secured other measures of safety. I'm here to offer you a chance to join me."

"Just say it." Mother's tone was knife sharp, one that would have caused me to wither away, but Paorah just smiled and bowed his head.

"Very well." A smug smile tightened his face as he gazed over the chamber. "I have entered into a"—he paused, as though searching for the right word—"partnership, shall we say, in which we will be granted passage to a new haven. To a new home."

"Where?" someone shouted.

"Who is this partnership with?" asked another.

The angry buzz felt like walking too close to a bee's nest, tense and filled with danger. A few guards rested their hands on their swords, ready to draw, but it wasn't until Paorah said the words that a few of them actually did.

"The Algotti Empire."

CHAPTER FOURTEEN

Blood rushed through my ears, drowning everything but shock. The cacophony of protests, chairs scraping hardwood, and other guards freeing their swords: it was all lost under the thrum of my own heartbeat and the screaming in my head.

Seven had lied to us.

Nine had lied to us.

Every time I thought I understood our situation, every time I thought I had a grasp on the truth, a dangerous new facet turned up—and this was worse than I had imagined: the empire and Anahera working *together*.

The chamber rang with movement as people lurched for the doors and guards sidestepped to block them. But they were right. We had to leave.

I found Aaru's eyes right away, but before I could get him to escape with me, he looked at Nine.

The color had drained from her face as she shook her head, like she somehow didn't know about this. Like she wasn't an *imperial spy*.

I felt sick, and I wanted to leave, but all the guards were moving inward and blocking the door, ready to quell the outrage in here as quickly as they had on the streets after the explosions.

"How could you do this?" one of the matriarchs shouted above the din.

"We will not stand for a *partnership* with the empire!" cried one of the warriors. "They are our enemies."

Panic was contagious. I felt it rising in my chest, twisting and growing, blackening the corners of my vision. It sent shivers through my blood, and my hands trembled on the sword where I'd clasped my fingers.

One.

Two.

Three.

On the far side of the room, the Anaheran ministers sat calmly in their chairs, watching the chaos. They knew. They expected this. They *wanted* this. And on his bench, the high magistrate observed the unraveling of civility below, and the way his guards moved in like they might begin slaughtering government officials right here.

I looked at Aaru to find that he'd broken his post and was coming toward me. Other guards were moving around, so he didn't stand out, except for the fact that he wasn't threatening senators or matriarchs.

::Calming pills?:: he asked.

I shook my head—they were in the hotel room, safe with all our belongings—but he was right. The panic attack was coming, and all the counting in the world wouldn't stop it. And if I had a meltdown here and now, everyone would know I wasn't a guard. My scar wouldn't be able to hide me.

I did the only thing I could.

I touched the noorestones.

Fifty of them.

Light flickered, and the room filled with a new height of noise, but inside my chest, the tangle of panic eased. My hands stilled. My heartbeat steadied. All it took was a light touch, like a reassuring brush of fingertips against a comforting blanket.

Aaru took my elbow. ::What did you do?::

I shook my head. "Not now." Beyond him, I could see Nine coming toward us, determination in her expression.

As the general panic reached new heights, Paorah raised his voice for the first time. "Sit!" He slammed his palm on the bench, loud enough to be heard over the chaos. "Everyone sit and be quiet, or my guards will make you quiet."

Half the guards raised their swords, the metal blades gleaming wickedly in the noorestone light.

Everyone drew a breath at the same time, or so it

seemed. People looked at one another, stricken expressions marring their faces, and one at a time, they began to sit. Their protests died. The knifelike curses were swallowed back.

"Thank you." Paorah hadn't risen from his seat, and even now, he stayed where he was. A veil of calm fell over him. "Now, shouting and swearing has done you no good. Try listening for once."

"You're out of your mind," said one of the senators. "We will not join the empire. We will not lower ourselves to become another territory."

Paorah sighed, and he nodded toward the nearest guard.

Without warning, the guard slit open the senator's throat.

Blood sprayed.

People jumped away.

The senator slumped over the desk. Dead.

But no one dared speak. Not even a shout or a cry. Nothing.

I could feel a sob welling up in my throat, and I couldn't stop it, but it made no sound when it came out. Aaru's fingers were tight around my arm.

Nine had reached us, but she didn't speak. She just watched the muffled horror of everyone in the chamber.

"All right." Paorah drummed his fingers over the desk. "Now again, I ask you all to listen. Anyone else speaking out of turn will be dealt with similarly." He waved the guards back, and all the blue-jacketed men and women began moving toward their posts, leaving the body where it had fallen. As a reminder. "My deal with the Algotti Empire is simple," he said at last. "We all know the Great Abandonment will not stop with Idris. I don't know which island will be next, but it *is* inevitable. Sooner or later, it will be Anahera, and I have a duty to my people. I must protect them."

The room was quiet.

"I brought you all here in my new ships. The Red Fleet. This will be how we reach the Algotti Empire. However, space is limited, and we'll all have choices to make: Who do you want to bring? There will be room for seven hundred and fifty people on each ship. One ship for each island."

Dark dread poured through me. Choosing. How could anyone choose who to save? How could anyone decide between children and doctors? Or inventors or historians? It was cruel.

Movement from the gallery drew my attention, and I realized at once how naïve I'd been: the high magistrate had already made his choices, and he'd chosen his friends. The wealthy. The corrupt.

"The empress has graciously agreed to take in a number of us," he said. "We would not be her subjects, but honored guests, held in the highest esteem."

Several people looked as though they wanted to protest, but the body was still slumped over the desk, blood leaking in small rivers across the polished wood until it dripped onto the floor.

No one said a word.

"Now," the high magistrate continued, "I suggest you choose your people wisely. Look for those with skills and wealth. Social usefulness. Use families as a bargaining tool if you must, but get the people we *need* in order to make a clean transition from our islands to the empire.

"I know you're all wondering what we will be giving up by aligning ourselves with the empire." He pressed his hands against the surface of his desk. "As a gesture of goodwill, I have given the empress seven dragons, for which she is very grateful."

Dragons.

My head spun, and I swayed, but Aaru's grip remained tight on my arm. Still, I couldn't help but imagine seven children of the gods sedated and sent away, awakening in a strange land. How frightened they must have been. How angry.

"Why send the dragons away?" Eka Delro stood, and though one of the guards approached her, the high magistrate didn't give the order. "We should fight to preserve our islands, and that means we need every dragon to appeal to the gods on our behalf. If we send them away, we're inviting trouble."

"We had our chance for that, First Matriarch. We had our chance, and we squandered it away. We cannot turn back the days and nights and set our nations on a different path. The Great Abandonment is coming, and we must be prepared to save as much of ourselves as possible: our people, our culture, our values."

177

"Our people are our families," she said, emboldened now. "How can we choose who to leave behind?"

"Don't think of it as leaving anyone behind," he said. "You'll be deciding who to save."

"And who's not worth saving," someone else muttered, but that was the only dissent. Everyone, the dissenter included, was already accepting this new direction for the Fallen Isles, and now they were thinking more of the mechanics of the move and what—if anything— they would tell people. Worth saving. Not worth saving. Whether Damina would be allotted one ship or two.

My chest squeezed with the need to act, but they'd already made their decisions. They would go. They would select a few people, and leave everyone else here to die.

It was incredible how little time it had taken for them to surrender.

I tried to tell myself that it made sense; he'd just killed one of them, and survival instincts were hard to overcome. And he was going to do it regardless of their cooperation. If they resisted, that left another spot on the ship for some- one else. They saw no other options.

But they hadn't even attempted to resist, save the one senator. They outnumbered the guards. Three were *warriors*—not just any warriors, but the tribunal. I didn't know much about the selection process for the tribunal, but everyone understood that it involved combat, so the tribunal was always composed of the most powerful war- riors on all of Khulan.

I could do something, a small voice whispered in the back of my head. No, not a small voice. It was enormous. Powerful. Winged. There was something huge inside me, something straining to get out and loose white-hot fire upon my enemies.

But if I released it, I couldn't be sure what would happen, only that the last two times I did—

I sucked in a cooling breath and shook away the memories of debris raining down inside the Pit, and molten wings boiling the theater floor. Yes, I was better at controlling my ability over noorestones now, but I still needed to be careful. I couldn't risk killing everyone in here.

Still, if only one matriarch had made a move. One senator. One warrior. If only one had said *no,* Aaru and I could have helped. And I could have believed they hadn't completely abandoned the people of the Fallen Isles already.

As the tones grew more resigned and people began to discuss which inventor they'd bring, or which banker was the best option, the high magistrate kept nodding to himself, a pleased smile curling the corners of his mouth.

The hum carried through the chamber, both on the floor and in the galleries above. He let it go on for a few minutes, and then he cleared his throat. "I'm glad we're all agreed. It is not an easy decision, yet it is the right decision, the only decision we can, in good conscience, make. Now, you may be wondering what the remaining ships will be carrying."

Everyone stilled, because they *had* been wondering,

but by now they knew better than to ask too many questions.

"The remaining ships," Paorah said, "will carry our armies."

Shock pulsed through the chamber, and I looked at Nine, finding only masked fury.

If the high magistrate had indeed made a deal with the empress, he had lied to her.

He had ten giant noorestones.

He'd almost had dozens of large dragons.

And somewhere—maybe here, maybe Khulan—he had armies?

"This is madness," said one of the tribunal. "A true warrior does not seek conflict."

"But," said the high magistrate, "is always prepared for it." He smiled cruelly. "I know your book as well as mine. And let us not pretend that the empress is taking us in out of the goodness of her heart. Even skilled and wealthy, we will be refugees. No, she will take something from us, and it will be our independence. We must be prepared to fight for it."

He wasn't looking out for our independence. He intended to attack the empire and seize it for himself.

It was a bold plan. An arrogant plan. Paorah would take select people of the Fallen Isles from the certain death of the Great Abandonment . . . to the certain death of war.

No one spoke, though. No one *could* speak.

My mind whirled. The idea of chasing a war with the very empire the Mira Treaty had been meant to protect us against . . . It was unthinkable.

"Now"—Paorah's shoulders rose with a sharp, indrawn breath—"I've provided lunch. My chefs have prepared sweet cloudfish rolls, which I'm sure you will all enjoy. But first, there's one more thing we must take care of."

People shifted in their seats, as though they could sense something terrible about to happen, but they didn't know the true lengths he was willing to go to in order to achieve his goals. They didn't know what a monster he was.

He looked at the First Matriarch and smiled. "Eka, you were concerned that we had nothing concrete to replace the Mira Treaty. Fear not: another document has been drawn up, and I'd like to go over the details with you all this afternoon. But before we can sign a new document, we must put aside the old one." He nodded toward a pair of guards stationed at the door he'd come through earlier.

As the door opened, everyone quieted and stretched to see what was coming through.

Aaru and I were at the back of the room, on the far side from the door, so I caught only flashes of red. Then, when those in the front finally began to sit, I could see a fuller view of the floor—but my mind refused to accept the facts.

It was the gown that struck me first: ruby-red silk, which slid across a young woman's body like scales. I knew that gown. It was mine. The last time I'd seen it, I'd been trying to kill the person wearing it.

She was still wearing it.

But the girl inside the soft embrace of the Fallen Isles' finest silk was different now. No longer straight and tall, bright with cosmetics and focused lighting. No, here she was bound and gagged, her shoulders slumped and her head hanging toward the floor. Her skin looked gray, and if she was aware of the crowd of government officials staring at her, she gave no indication. She appeared like an empty vessel, all the life of her poured out.

Another woman came behind her, older, and just as wrung out. The bindings had cut into her wrists, leaving the skin there red and raw. Her gown was simpler than the other, but just as elegant and expensive—or rather, it had been once. Now, it was torn and stained from everything that had happened to them since Val fa Merce.

Soft gasps fluttered throughout the room as senators and matriarchs and Mother recognized Elbena, the last surviving Luminary Councilor.

And the girl with her . . . Tirta looked enough like me to fool some people, especially from afar. But here, she just looked like herself, dressed up in someone else's clothes. No one here would confuse us.

The guards marched them to the center of the floor, where the high magistrate and the speakers had stood before. They faced the crowd, and Tirta looked up just long enough to find the space everyone had made around the dead senator. Just long enough to see the blood seeping off the front of the desk and onto the chair on the tier below.

Tirta made a small, strangled noise. She tried to run, but the guard near her clamped down on her shoulders and held her there, and she had no more strength to fight.

"Oh, seven gods," someone muttered.

Another person reached to clasp my mother's hands.

Someone whispered a prayer.

"What have you done?" a matriarch asked.

::We need to go,:: Aaru tapped. ::You can't stay here.::

But I couldn't move, either. If I drew attention to myself, someone might look up here and see me—the *actual* Hopebearer.

"Before you stands Elbena Krasteba," the high magistrate announced, "and the Hopebearer: Mira Minkoba."

No one here could believe she was me, but as I gazed around the room, I saw people's hands fly to their chests and more prayers fall off tongues. They did believe, or they were playing along.

Mother was. She pressed her hands over her nose and mouth, and her shoulders trembled. She was a good actress, my mother, but part of me wondered if this was all acting. Because there was a girl who looked like me, wearing my clothes, bound up and held under guard. There was a girl who *wasn't* me, but could have been. Would have been, if I'd given that speech in Bopha.

I swayed a little, reaching for a noorestone to help steady me. But the lights didn't flicker; not this time. I was too numb now, too caught up in shock to feel anything else.

They were traitors, both of them. One who'd scarred me, one who'd become me. They'd tried to make the Hopebearer speak words she could never—not without being untrue to the Mira Treaty—and they'd both fooled me into thinking they were my friends.

They were my enemies.

And yet, seeing them here, I couldn't hate them. I couldn't celebrate that they were now in the high magistrate's hands. I could only wish that they weren't, because neither of them deserved what he would do to them.

"This is an insult," one of the matriarchs said. "Elbena is one of us. She should be up here." She gestured toward the seats left open.

"Mira is just a child," someone else said. "What have you been doing with her? Why is she being treated like this?"

I stared at that last speaker. I hadn't felt like a child in a long time. Maybe ever. I'd been treated like a doll or a puppet, useful as nothing more than a face and a mouthpiece.

"She is no child." The high magistrate's expression was cool and impassive, as though the two standing below him meant nothing. As though they *were* nothing. "She is a relic of an old and dying world. She has no place in the new world we are creating."

Tirta's eyes went wide, and my heart jumped. She didn't deserve this.

Aaru squeezed my arm.

Paorah gazed over the room, conviction lighting his eyes. "We cannot destroy the document of the Mira Treaty. That opportunity was already taken when rogue warriors attacked Crescent Prominence. But here we have the living symbol of the treaty. The Hopebearer."

"What are you saying?" a man asked.

"We are putting aside the Mira Treaty." The high magistrate stood, looming over the chamber as dark and frightening as Idris on the horizon. "We are embracing our new future."

My heartbeat thundered in my ears, and I wanted to look away, but the scene below was a magnet, drawing me back every time I tried to pull free.

High Magistrate Paorah lifted an arm.

"Stop this!" cried one of the matriarchs. "Stop this at once!"

He called out, "Now!"

It all happened too quickly.

1. *The pair of guards flanking Tirta and Elbena drew their knives.*
2. *My mother screamed.*
3. *Three warriors leaped over the desks, toward the floor, but they were too late.*
4. *The knives plunged into two soft throats.*
5. *Blood.*
6. *Someone grabbed Mother to hold her, but the screams kept coming.*

7. *The warriors met the guards on the floor,*
   killing them with their bare hands, but more
   guards swarmed in.
8. *And Tirta and Elbena dropped to the floor,*
   lifeless.

The whole world tilted as my double died. A girl I'd thought was a friend. A girl I wanted to hate but couldn't.

Paorah raised his voice over the cacophony of footfalls and screams. "You have a choice to make. Resist and die, or join me and live. But either way, know this:

"The Mira Treaty is dead."

PART THREE

NO DISHONOR IN FEAR

CHAPTER FIFTEEN

THEY'D KILLED ME.

No, they'd killed Tirta, the false Hopebearer. But they'd intended to kill me. They *thought* they had.

And now the Mira Treaty was dead.

The tenets that defined my life: dead.

Everything I'd worked for: dead.

For a heartbeat, my whole world shifted off center, and a rupture spread throughout my soul. A distant roar sounded in my head, and stars rained down their fury. I wanted to scream. I wanted to breathe fire. I wanted to ruin them the way they'd tried to ruin me.

Fiery muscles stretched along my back and shoulders. Heat poured into me as a gigantic roar gathered in my throat—

Everything went silent.

Screams.

Toppling chairs.

My own heartbeat.

The spark growing in my chest cooled, and I could see straight once more, but what I saw was no comfort.

Chaos bloomed bright below, made worse by the sudden silence: people threw themselves over desks, trying to reach one of the aisles. It was a futile attempt, though; guards blocked the way, their swords drawn.

The screams, awful before, seemed somehow louder now that their voices had been crushed under the unrelenting silence. But even as I turned toward Aaru to beg him to bring back the sound, it returned. Not all at once. But in blinks. Lightning flashes.

My mind felt whiplashed from the silence and noise and that spark of fury fading in my heart. I could hardly comprehend what I was seeing as my gaze fell again to the bodies on the floor, my view of them fractured as people rushed in front of them. But I saw the red of my gown.

They'd killed me.

Her.

Aaru grabbed my hands and pulled me around to meet his wide, worried eyes. ::**We have to go.**::

By now, sound had fully returned, and the shouts and scrapes and outright begging for mercy were oppressively loud. Dizzying movement wrenched around the chamber as people fought to escape, but—aside from

High Magistrate Paorah surveying the destruction he'd caused—there was one bubble of stillness.

People parted around Mother like she was a rock in a stream. She stood, with her hands pressed to her chest, staring at the bodies on the floor, the picture of a woman who'd just lost a child and didn't care about anything happening around her.

Aaru was right: we needed to go, before the rest of the guards either took control or killed everyone. But— "I can't leave my mother."

Heartache crossed Aaru's expression. He started to turn, but behind him, Nine changed course. "Go," she said. "I'll get her."

I didn't have time to respond. Aaru dragged me toward the nearest door, and though I didn't think the guards blocking that exit would let us out, they saw our uniforms and moved aside.

My heart was drumbeat heavy as we strode through the ornate corridors of the Red Hall. I wanted to run, but running would draw attention, and already I was waiting for the thud of boots behind us—waiting for someone to realize we weren't who we'd claimed.

Aaru and I paused just long enough to grab our bag from the room where we'd stashed it, and then we walked out of the building with as much confidence as we could muster.

No one stopped us.

Outside, the air was sticky and still, and clouds dipped

low over the city, ready to spill open. My head spun with worry and sickness and cut-short rage as we marched off the Red Hall grounds and dove into the city, scattering civilians who didn't want to be anywhere near two of the high magistrate's guards.

Wet heat clung to us, and sweat prickled down my chest and spine. It was a drowning sort of heat, growing worse as we walked.

We couldn't go far like this, not if we wanted to go unnoticed. So I ducked down an empty alley and found a small alcove, and there I stood watch while Aaru changed into his regular clothes behind me. When he touched my shoulder, I swapped places with him.

With shaking hands, I switched Nine's shirt for my hunting dress, managing to do it without ever being fully uncovered. Then I shoved off her trousers and pulled on my leggings, and then my boots. Nine's clothes went into the sack.

Aaru turned around, framed by sandstone and cloud-diffused sunlight. "Mira—"

"Why did you silence everything?" My heart thrummed ten thousand times. "Why did you silence *me*?"

His face twisted with shame. "Everyone would have seen you."

"They would have seen the other"—I moved my hands around my shoulders, indicating wings—"me. They'd never have known. They'd have been dead before they could even wonder."

He swallowed hard. "Then you would have *killed* people."

That stopped me.

I didn't actually want to kill anyone.

"And the high magistrate would have realized that the real Hopebearer was within his grasp, and he'd kill *you* this time." Aaru's voice went raw with feeling, and anguish tightened his expression. "He'd just *murdered* someone who looked like you. What do you think he'd have done if he found you, too?"

"I don't know," I whispered. But I did know. He'd have locked me away. He'd have exploited my ability over noorestones, using my mother as leverage. That was, if he didn't kill me outright.

Aaru's hand trembled as his fingertips brushed my cheek. "I've already lost everyone else. I can't lose you, too."

I knew Aaru; I knew he'd never use his gift to hurt other people, least of all me.

"Mira, I—"

The sky flashed white, and a clap of thunder was all the warning we had before rain streamed into the city, a soaking downpour loud enough to dull the noise of everything nearby.

Aaru squeezed into the alcove with me. It was a tight fit, but we didn't need much space. He touched my cheek again, his eyebrows pushed together in worry. "Are you still angry with me?"

No.

Yes.

How could I tell?

All of my emotions were a knot in my chest, growing tighter and tighter, and soon it would strangle my heart. The speech my mother had given. Anahera's partnership with the Algotti Empire. Tirta—in my dress and gagged so she couldn't tell anyone the truth—dead on the floor.

I wanted to scream. I wanted to explode.

But Aaru was right. Neither of those were smart options, and I'd promised him that he still had me. I'd *promised*.

My anger unknotted, leaving behind a burning need. I closed the small space between us, and I kissed him.

It wasn't like before. That evening on the ship had been bright and hesitant and glowing relief, before either of us had realized how terrible our situation could really become. Before his god had risen.

Now a spark ignited inside of me, and we were so close that I thought he might run. But he didn't even flinch; his arms went around my waist and he pulled, drawing me near until our chests and stomachs and hips were tight together. A soft shiver worked through him, and his fingertips dug against my rain-damp clothes. His lips made the shape of my name; I slid my fingers against the line of his jaw, keeping his mouth open against mine.

My body felt electric next to his, as charged as the lightning that slashed open the sky. I kissed him harder, with a desperation he returned in every touch and shift and ragged breath.

The world narrowed to this space. Him. Me. Three walls and the rain. I could feel his heart pounding against mine, faster as one hand slid from my hip to my leg and back up again. A question.

"Yes." I kissed his jaw, his throat, anywhere he would let me, while he explored the shape of my body with strong and careful hands. Everywhere he touched felt hot and bright, like he'd pressed stars into my skin.

I loved it, the way he made me feel, like I was seen and wanted and *needed*. I loved the way he nudged my hips back in suggestion, and when I took a shaking step, he guided me backward until my spine touched the cool wall. And I loved the gentle way he cupped my face in his hands and kissed me. First my lips, then my chin, and down to the hollow of my throat. His breath was hot and fast against my skin, and I could almost feel him trying to decide whether he should keep going; the way his fingertips traveled down my shoulders suggested he wanted to. I wanted him to.

With a heavy breath, I lifted toward him, and he gave in. Carefully, he kissed my collarbone, then my breastbone, and my whole self shifted as he knelt and pressed his lips to my stomach. He poured fire into me, and I couldn't get enough.

His hands caressed my hips, drawing me forward as he kissed a map of stars across my abdomen. A wonderful ache spread through me, but it was there that Aaru paused, gasping before he looked up at me. Dark eyes. Sharp jaw. Soft lips. I could have melted into him.

"I think . . ." His voice was deep. Husky. "I think we—"

"I know." I took his hands and pulled him up. He stood very close—he had to—and though the fire still rushed through us, I took long breaths until it became a manageable spark once more.

His eyes were closed as he, too, breathed. Beyond him, the rain drilled into the street, darkening the world beyond our small space.

My voice seemed faint under the steady clatter. "Are you . . ."

"Flying." His gaze dropped to my mouth, and his expression warmed. "Flying too high for a moment."

I could still feel the ghosts of his hands, like fire even through the fabric of my hunting dress. No one had ever touched me like that, reverent and wanting at the same time.

He looked uncertain. ::**And you?**:: The quiet code tapped against the wall next to us.

"Yes." I stepped into his arms and rested my cheek on his shoulder. "Thank you."

He hugged me close to him, gently now. "For what?"

"For—" For helping me avoid a mistake. For letting me forget for a moment. For giving me something good when everything else was so bad. "For understanding."

CHAPTER SIXTEEN

FINALLY, THE RAIN BEGAN TO SLACKEN.

Aaru and I had been standing in the alcove for less than an hour, just holding each other as the temperature dropped and the water began to settle into our clothes. "We should go back to the hotel," I said, mostly because someone needed to. I didn't want to leave this small space where nothing else existed. Not betrayals or murders or the end of the world.

But Aaru followed my gaze and nodded. "I think the rain is finished."

Reluctantly, I stepped into the last mists of storm. Aaru grabbed Nine's bag and together we walked toward the hotel.

Other people were out now, putting lids on rain barrels

197

and sweeping muck away from their stoops. As the clouds parted and the sun shone full on the city, the rain-glazed sandstone gleamed like true flame, so bright Aaru had to shield his eyes.

It didn't bother me.

Like the sun. Like water steaming off my skin. Like the way I could feel the sister dragons inside the hotel, both of them careening around the ceiling, their spark glands still tingling from the storm. So many things about me were different now.

When we reached the hotel, Nine was standing outside, still wearing the guard uniform—or the magic-made version of it, anyway. She was mostly dry, but frowning. "The owner let me wait inside during the storm, but he kicked me out as soon as it was over. Even when I said I knew you."

"He's very protective."

"So I've discovered."

I nodded for Aaru to give the sack of clothes to her. "How did you know where we're staying?"

Her mouth twitched. "I'm a spy, remember? Also, last night you left in the hotel's horsecarre."

Well, Tanhe would be pleased to know that *someone* had noticed the Fire Rose crest. "What about my mother? Is she inside?"

Nine hesitated, then shook her head. "She wouldn't come."

My heart crept up into my throat. "What do you mean?"

"I mean she refused." Nine adjusted the bag over her shoulder. "I told her that you'd asked me to get her, and she said no. Even when I said I knew the dead girl wasn't you, and that you were heading to safety, she refused."

"Why?" The word came out pale. Raspy.

"She said if she didn't stay to speak for the people of Damina, then they would have no one." Nine gave me a pitying look. "If she doesn't choose Daminan people to take the assigned ship, then the ship will go to another island or more fighters."

A chill worked through me. "But the guards," I whispered. "They were slaughtering people in there."

Nine shook her head and kept her voice low. "No. A few were killed, but only the ones who attacked first. No one else. The other officials tried to escape, so the guards were only scaring them into submission."

That wasn't much comfort. We'd been so close to helping Mother. So close to getting her out of that room. And she'd *refused*. Zara would be furious. *I* was furious enough. "I should have gone to get her."

Aaru touched my shoulder, gentle. "It was her decision. She chose to help her people. Isn't that what you'd have done? Ensured a few survived, even if you couldn't save them all?"

The words shamed me. Maybe I should have announced myself. Maybe I could have stopped all of that before it started. If I'd only *acted* instead of observed. But I didn't have that kind of bravery in me. Not when I needed it.

Nine glanced over the busy street; people were walking

past slowly, clearly curious about one of the high magistrate's personal guards speaking to two people in foreign clothes. "I need to go," Nine said. "If I don't get back to my post, I'll lose my credibility there."

She didn't move, though.

"You didn't know about the deal between Paorah and your empress?" I'd seen her face earlier; her reaction had appeared genuine, but some people were convincing actors, and she *was* a spy.

"I didn't know." She frowned deeply. "This is . . . concerning."

Aaru touched my arm, tapping where she couldn't see. ::She's telling the truth.::

"Perhaps he was lying," I suggested. "About the agreement."

"Perhaps." Her eyes went flat with anger. "But he wasn't lying about his intention to attack."

No. I didn't think he was lying about that, either.

"I'll try to get some answers," she said after a moment. "About the true nature of the relationship between Anahera and the empire. I'll find you when I have something."

If she and I had been friends, I'd have taken her hands, hugged her, or done *something* to show empathy. But instead, I just said, "Every single one of my friends and I understand how you feel. You're one of us now."

A frown worked around the corners of her mouth. "I'd rather not be."

Rude.

"Before I write my report." She looked at Aaru. "That strange silence. You?"

"Why do you think I did it?"

She rolled her eyes. "You come from the Isle of Silence, don't you? I haven't met anyone else from Idris, but there are rumors about what people from the Fallen Isles can do. Our empress is very interested in those abilities."

"I'm sure she is." An unusual note of hostility entered his tone. "Our abilities are gifts from our gods—"

"Even with"—she motioned westward, toward Idris on the horizon—"him no longer an island?"

"Apparently." Aaru frowned. "He's still *there*. He's just not— When they go, I think, the gifts will, too. But as I was saying, our gifts are not to be used to harm others."

"What about Khulan's?" she asked. "God of warriors. That sounds dangerous."

"Dangerous, yes. But strength can be used to help, too. Gifts like ours have many aspects."

Nine turned to me. "What about yours? I thought you were from Damina."

"I am."

"The Daminan gift is what I felt when I listened to your mother speak. Charm. Persuasion. I should be falling in love with you, not wondering what else you can do with noorestones."

She and I stared at each other for a moment, and finally I said, "I can make you fall in love with noorestones."

Nine gave a soft snort. "If I find myself composing

romantic poems to them, I'll know who to blame." She glanced over her shoulder. Passersby were still eyeing us. "Well. Get some rest. Talk with your friends. Decide if there's anything you want to do about"—she gestured toward the Red Hall—"all that. I may help. I may not. I do as our empress commands."

"Even if it means deals with Paorah?"

She held my gaze, sighed, and then left.

My friends reacted to the news about as well as I predicted:

1. *Zara hated everyone and everything, because we hadn't been able to rescue Mother. Had we even* tried?
2. *Gerel and Hristo glowered and muttered about the unnecessary danger Aaru and I had put ourselves in.*
3. *Chenda looked deeply distraught at the political upheaval and murders of her fellow elected—or appointed—officials.*
4. *The dragons hunched on my shoulders, trying to steal bites of the lunch the others had saved for me. In spite of Ilina's annoyed glances, I gave in and shared.*

"Did you hear anything about my father?" Ilina asked.

"He might be in the empire." Aaru looked up from the bread he'd been shredding into small chunks. "I heard someone talk about sending people to the Algotti Empire. After Paorah said he sent dragons."

Ilina's expression darkened. "So you think Paorah sent my father to the empire along with those dragons?"

"After, probably." Aaru shrugged helplessly. "It sounded like the dragons were sent months ago, and the people recently. But if the empire needed help with the dragons, wouldn't your father be the best person to send?"

Ilina was already nodding. "That's where he is, then. The empire. I . . . I don't know whether to be scared or relieved."

I reached for her hand and squeezed. If he was in the empire, then he was in danger from the empress and everything there. But if he was in the empire, he wouldn't be here when the islands rose up and cast us all into the sea.

"What are we going to do?" Chenda stood and began pacing the room, her steps clipped. "How can we use what you learned from the summit? All our remaining governments believe the Great Abandonment is inevitable. They all believe there is no putting the world back right. If they saw any other way, they wouldn't have agreed to Paorah's plan."

"They didn't have a choice but to agree," I said. "Paorah had his guards kill the first person to protest."

A frown pinched her mouth. "All right. So we don't know what they truly believe, but they are going along with his plan anyway."

On my shoulder, LaLa gave a small whine and stretched her head for a bite of shrimp. When Ilina wasn't looking, I broke one in half and gave a bite to each dragon; they flew off in a flurry of muffled squawks and satisfied grunts.

"Surely there's a way to set this right," Chenda said. "Surely there's a way to appease the gods and make them stay."

Hristo gave a hollow, mirthless laugh. "They don't care about us anymore. We broke the covenant with the dragons."

Those were not words I'd ever thought I'd hear from Hristo. He was usually so positive, but now he was losing hope. . . .

While the others were distracted, Aaru touched my hand. ::Are you going to tell them about your dreams?::

::Do you think I should?::

He gave a small shrug. ::Do you think they're real?::

Did I?

They *felt* real.

"I just don't know what we're trying to do," Hristo said. "The most powerful people in the Fallen Isles are planning their escape. Maybe when the *Chance Encounter* comes back to Flamecrest, we should consider—"

"Consider what?" Ilina asked. "Boarding the ship and just sailing away? To go where? The empire? Should we focus on saving ourselves?"

"Our governments have."

"We won't leave behind the less fortunate." I looked up. "That isn't who we are."

"But there's no way to save everyone." Zara rose from her seat. "I don't want anyone else to die. I don't. But we're all here. Mother will get on one of Paorah's ships. And Ilina's father is already in the empire. Everyone we care about—everyone left alive—can reach safety. Maybe that has to be enough."

Hristo nodded. "It's not the best outcome, but maybe it's the best *realistic* outcome."

I wanted to be horrified by this discussion, but I understood the fears—the feeling that if there were something to do, they'd do it, but there was *nothing*. No way to stop this.

Unless.

"I—I have a strange question," I said. "It may seem unrelated, but . . ."

"Ask." Chenda sat back in her chair. "It would be a nice distraction from the conversation about whether or not to abandon hundreds of thousands of people with no access to ships."

"Stop. This is no time to debate between morality and practicality. You can both be right. And wrong." I let my gaze drift toward Crystal and LaLa, who'd hopped onto the noorestone sconces. "My question is . . ." This was silly. But still, I had to ask. "Do any of you know when the next eclipse is?"

Most shook their heads, but then Ilina said, "I do. The second of Lesya."

That was just over two decans from now.

Gerel shot a raised eyebrow Ilina's way. "And how do you know that?"

Ilina gestured toward the dragons, who were hunched over the sconces like they were part of the room's decor. "They all get a little wild during eclipses, and some dragons need more space, or they need to go inside one of the buildings for the duration."

A shiver crept through me. "One moon or both?"

Single-moon eclipses were fairly common. Both moons passing before the sun—that was far more unusual.

She frowned. "Both, I think."

"You think?" I leaned forward, my heart pounding. "Are you sure?"

"My parents told me months ago, but the talk was focused on making sure we were prepared to accommodate the dragons' needs. Not about anything else. But I think it was both moons. I think I remember them saying we'd have to wait for both eclipses to pass."

Blood rushed through my head, and I swayed. No, not blood. A roar. Wings catching on the air. Wind rushing past.

If the eclipse was true, what else might be? The bones? The answers in the empire?

"Why?" Ilina asked. "What does the eclipse have to do with anything?"

"I think . . ." The words hardly felt real. "I think there may be a way to save the Fallen Isles."

Everyone jerked straight.

"What?" Gerel's tone was incredulous.

"Why are you mentioning this only now?" Chenda asked.

It was so much to explain. I couldn't even make it fit right in my own head, because it was too big. Too wild. But finally I said, "I've been having these dreams—"

A knock thudded against the door, startling everyone, and without waiting for us to answer, Tanhe burst into the parlor. Panic shook his voice. "You have to hide. The high magistrate's guards are coming through, and they're taking people."

The *Drakontos celestus*

ALL ACROSS THE ISLANDS, PEOPLE MOVED TOWARD the water.

Most cities sat along the coast already, but a few had risen up inland, and there were plenty of farms and factories and mines and elegant country homes that had been built there simply because more space was available.

Now, the poor from those inner-island communities traveled outward in rickety carts, on horses, but mostly on their own feet. They took only what they could carry, what they couldn't bear to leave behind, and whatever was the most practical: a change of clothes, small trinkets from their ancestors, and food and water and noorestones.

The wealthy traveled in carriages and horsecarres, or boats down the nearest river. They brought money, and lots of it, making plans to buy their way onto bigger ships and sell the smaller vessels to someone desperate.

And there were plenty of desperate people.

CHAPTER SEVENTEEN

THEY WERE SEARCHING FOR AARU AND ME.

My heart jolted painfully as I lurched up and said, "Get your things. We're going now."

"Going?" Confusion twisted Tanhe's voice. "You don't have to go. Just hide." Without being invited, he moved deeper into the parlor and stared as Ilina grabbed LaLa and Crystal from the sconces and pressed them into their basket on the table. "Are those dragons? Have you been keeping dragons in here?"

No one bothered to answer. He'd have been horrified to learn that—until a couple of days ago—we'd been keeping a prisoner in here, too.

I hurried into the room Aaru and I now shared. My bag was under the bed, already half packed; none of us had truly believed this refuge would last.

Quickly, Aaru and I shoved the remainder of our belongings into our bags—no folding, no thinking, just moving—and within minutes, the seven of us were in the parlor and thanking the owner for his hospitality.

Ilina pressed a few more lumes into the man's hands. "For your discretion."

He frowned but pocketed the money. "Why are you leaving?"

I shook my head. Even if I'd wanted to tell him anything, there was no time. "Thank you for everything. Really." Then I shouldered my bag and pushed out the door. It was painful to keep from checking the suite once more, to make sure nothing was left behind, but I was already moving down the stairs as quickly as I could, Aaru right behind me, and the others after him.

"Where are we going?" Zara's breath came short as we hurried down the stairs.

"Fancy?" Gerel asked.

I didn't know exactly where I was going. *Away. Fast.* That was all that mattered right now. "I nearly lost control in the council chamber," I said. "Aaru silenced everything. Now that the real guards have finished restraining the officials, they have time to search the city for us."

My boots rang against the tiled floor of the lobby as I headed for the door.

"Everyone keep your head down." Hristo hurried to my side.

Outside, the air was hot and dry, as though the storm never happened. Puddles had evaporated, and now heat made the air shimmer.

"There," Gerel murmured, just as a pair of the high magistrate's guards were walking into the building next door. We'd left the Fire Rose just in time.

The seven of us—plus two dragons in their basket—hurried past the building the guards had gone into; hopefully, they wouldn't search where they'd already been.

We moved quickly through the crowd, catching snatches of discussion as we passed.

"They have a lead on whoever caused the explosions last decan," someone said.

"That's not what I heard. I heard there was a fire in the Red Hall and they're looking for whoever set it."

There were more wild rumors, but in our rush, we didn't catch them all. No matter what, it was bad news for us.

"Where are we going?" Chenda asked.

I'd led them around several corners, staying clear of the guards swarming through the city. Sweat gleamed on all of us, and my bag weighed painfully across my body, but I didn't slow. "Nine."

Gerel shot a heavy glare at me. "We're avoiding one enemy by going to another?"

"She's been hiding in this city for gods know how long. She can hide us, too." I didn't actually know that was true, but we were out of options. The *Chance Encounter* was gone, and we had no other allies—or even potential allies—in the city. Not ones with the ability to help us.

And—I didn't know how to mention it to the others without sounding crazy—I felt a strange and uncomfortable pull toward the empire. Not like I belonged there. No, I belonged *here* in the Fallen Isles. But like I needed to go there. Find something.

The first dragon.

It wasn't long before we ducked into the shoe shop where Aaru and I had met Nine that morning. An older woman looked up, startled to see so many people entering, and all of us carrying bags. Hristo and Gerel both had weapons.

"I don't want any trouble." Her voice was low, gravelly. She pulled out a leather envelope that rattled with coins. "Take it. This is all I have."

Hristo's mouth dropped open. "We're not here to rob you."

"We're looking for someone." I glanced around the shop; it was the same as it had been earlier—quiet, meticulously clean, with a single narrow walking space—but no imperial spy.

The shopkeeper twisted her hands together and gazed around. "I'm afraid I can't help you. There's no one else here. Unless you think shoes have personalities. Some people do, you know."

I started toward the back room. "No one's staying here?"

"No." A note of alarm filled her voice, and she came bustling out from behind the counter. "Why?"

::Nine isn't here.:: Aaru's tap came against one of the shelves displaying the shoes.

I stopped in the middle of the shop and sighed. "Sorry. We shouldn't have bothered you." If Nine wasn't here, then she was probably at the Red Hall again. And in that case, I was out of ideas.

We couldn't go back to the hotel. If the high magistrate knew about the Voice of Idris, then he'd look for someone visiting Anahera—an Idrisi—so hotels would be the first place his guards searched.

The old woman came toward me and whispered, "Are they after you?"

My shoulders stiffened. How did *she* know? Maybe *she* was Nine; maybe changing her appearance was something else her magical device allowed her to do. "What do you mean?"

"I mean," she said, "they're rounding up a lot of people. No one really knows why, but everyone can't be suspects for the explosions. Why, they took my friend Hemi. She owns half of the shops on Revis Avenue, but she's afraid of fire. She had an accident as a child, you see, and . . ."

The shopkeeper was still talking, but my thoughts shifted inward. I'd assumed Paorah was after Aaru and me. And maybe he was. But if he was taking other people—people who allegedly owned *half the shops* on Revis Avenue—then he must be moving forward with his evacuation. Before gossip had time to spread. Before people had a chance to warn others. Before those taken could even get their belongings—but perhaps soldiers could be sent for those later.

"Do you think they finished their planning today?" the old lady asked. "I'm sure the high magistrate will put things back to rights, but I can't imagine how. That's why I'm not high magistrate, I suppose."

My voice was hollow. "He's not going to save anyone but himself. Everyone else needs to start thinking about how to make things right with the gods."

I didn't wait for her to respond. I left the shop, the others close on my heels.

"What do we do?" Zara asked. "Can we go back to the hotel?" She sounded hopeful.

"I don't think that would be wise." But it wasn't wise to stand out here, holding all our belongings. The dragons would grow restless soon. They'd want to fly and play, and then . . . I turned to Ilina. "We let the dragons help."

"What?"

"Regardless where Nine is at the moment, we can find her ship. It isn't in the port—or we would have seen it when we were first looking for her—but it must be somewhere. We should wait for her at her ship."

"Maybe she doesn't have one," Hristo said. "Someone could have brought her here and left with the ship so she wasn't spotted."

I shook my head. "Maybe, but if you were a spy in a

214

hostile land, in a place where islands are starting to get up, would you want to be left here without a means of escape?"

Hristo frowned. "Isn't that exactly our situation now?"

"Yes!" I cringed and lowered my voice. "But imagine us with more resources."

"I'd have a ship," Zara said. "And a second ship just in case someone discovered the first. And a third in case someone discovered the second."

Gerel snorted. "Very thorough, Little Fancy."

"So you want the dragons to look for the ship." Ilina gazed down at the basket where, already, I could feel the two *raptuses* shifting with eagerness. They *wanted* to get out. They *wanted* to work. "How will we know what the ship looks like? How will they tell us if they've found it?"

"I'll show them," I said. "And they'll show me."

Her expression was unreadable, but she nodded. "Then let's do it somewhere everyone won't see us."

Aaru reached for my bag. "We'll wait here. I'll watch for Nine in case she comes back."

I nodded and went after Ilina, ducking into a small fenced-off garden that didn't seem to be growing much of anything. "All right, little dragon flower. Careful on your way out. We don't want anyone to see you."

Ilina pulled open the lid, and both dragons shot into our arms. I stroked down LaLa's spine as she curled up against my breastbone with a throaty purr. On the other side of the basket, Ilina was kissing Crystal's nose.

"I think the best thing about these two is"—she paused—"everything, I guess. But one of the many best things is how they're always so happy to see us, even though we were just holding them an hour ago."

"Their excitement is so good for our egos." I grinned and turned to LaLa. "We need your help, sweet lizard. We need you to look for something for us. And tell us when you find it."

LaLa and Crystal were hunting dragons, and we'd been working with them for years. They were good at finding prey and leading us to it, but this was bigger. A ship. A spy. A hunt without a vole on the other end.

But as I described the black ship aloud, I held the image in my mind and tried to send it along the connection LaLa and I shared.

The dragons hadn't stopped nuzzling us—they were mindful of their sharp scales, of course—but before I was finished describing the ship, LaLa leaped out of my arms. Crystal shot up behind her.

They flew quickly—they were *Drakontos raptuses*, one of the fastest species in the Fallen Isles—but probably not so quick that someone didn't notice them. So Ilina and I hurried out of the garden and returned to our friends, moving everyone away from the shoe shop.

"Do you think they understood what you wanted?" Hristo asked as we walked.

"They didn't seem to be paying attention." Ilina sighed and looked up, but the dragons were no longer in sight.

216

But just as I was about to voice my agreement, an image flashed in my mind:

A small black ship. Sharp rocks. Steep red cliffs. And the path I would take to get there, if only I could fly.

Chenda touched my shoulder; I'd stopped walking. "Are you all right?" Concern laced her tone as she gazed down at me. "You didn't eat much. . . ."

"I'm fine," I breathed. "Better than fine. I know where the ship is."

IT WAS A long walk from the city to the small cove where Nine had moored her ship. By the time we arrived, the sun was dipping deep into the western sky, and the god shadow swung heavy over the cliffs. A faint chill followed.

Aaru stepped close to me and twisted our fingers together. Warmth rushed off his body, curling around mine. My shiver of excitement felt wholly inappropriate for the moment, but I couldn't forget the way he'd touched me earlier. Maybe he couldn't, either, because his throat jumped and he glanced at me to see if I'd noticed.

I squeezed his hand and wanted to say something reassuring, but then our narrow path led us around a pillar of red rock and we caught sight of the black ship.

It was a single-masted thing, bobbing gently as the tide moved out, and it gleamed like oil against the sea and stone. For a moment, I wondered if it was safe with the low tide, but it was *so* small that maybe it wouldn't matter.

The cabin window was dark, which probably meant

Nine wasn't here yet, and we had a long, boring wait ahead of us.

As the sun finished its descent, a few seagulls cried above, squawking irritably. Below, piles of white feathers were scattered beneath the red rocks where Crystal and LaLa perched, their stomachs round after an enormous meal.

"Well." Ilina leaned her weight on one hip. "I see two dragons who won't need treats for at least a decan."

The dragons looked at each other and chattered quietly.

The piles of seagull feathers made me think of Kelsine. We hadn't seen her since Altan found us in the dishonored camp outside Lorn-tah, but before he'd arrived, the young dragon had been playing in a rain of white feathers while LaLa and Crystal hunted for the people who lived in that camp.

Aaru was watching my face. ::I'm sorry.:: His soft quiet code came against my knuckles. ::I should have found out where he sent her.::

Before he could slip his hand from mine, I squeezed. I wanted Kelsine with me, but it wasn't Aaru's fault that Altan had been an uncooperative prisoner. If we were going to have a contest of taking blame for her absence, then I would win: in the tunnels, I should have made sure she was with our friends, not trying to fight on my behalf.

I clicked for LaLa, and she flew to sit on my shoulder as we rounded a bend and came along the black ship's starboard. There was no gangplank to climb, and no other way to get onto the ship without wings. "She's not in there, is she?" I asked Aaru.

He cocked his head and listened. Then nodded. "Cooking."

"Oh, good." Hristo pressed his palm to his stomach. "I'm hungry."

I nudged LaLa. "Go make noise she can't ignore."

She pushed off, Crystal on her tail, and the pair began screeching and clawing at the cabin door and window, while the rest of us sat on the rocks to rest our legs. But several minutes later, Nine finally emerged onto the main deck, dodging two small dragons, and glared around.

"Some spy," I said above the crash of water on rocks. "We could have been anyone."

"What are you doing here?" She propped her fists on her hips. "I told you that I'd come find you when I had something."

"We had something first. Let us on."

She sighed and touched the railing, and a long ramp slid out from the side of the ship and settled onto the rocks. We boarded one at a time and followed her into the small cabin, then down the hatch into the lower deck.

Lights glowed along the dark walls, but they weren't noorestones. Instead, sharp, slashing symbols carved into the metal danced orange-white, like fire. It was strange, getting used to the flickering light, but the lower deck had enough of the symbols to fully illuminate the space. It was split into three different sections: a cargo hold, a brig, and a clear area in between; the mast drove through its center and into the ship's hull.

"Sorry there's not much space." Nine gestured around the lower deck, then motioned for us to sit. "These skimmers aren't meant for hosting parties, but I don't want you all on the main deck in case someone else happens to find me here."

LaLa and Crystal fluttered around, inspecting barrels and crates until they found the glowing symbols. Together, they flew to a porthole close to a symbol and balanced on the bolts of metal while they sniffed the source of the light.

LaLa bumped it with her nose and the light went out.

She turned to Crystal in alarm, and the silver dragon nosed the symbol as though to check if it was dead.

The light came back.

Both dragons chittered excitedly, and then they turned the light off again.

Then on.

Then off.

"Great." Gerel covered her face with her hands. "I have never been happier to have dragons around."

"The fate of the Fallen Isles depends on them, you know," muttered Chenda. "These majestic creatures."

LaLa pecked at the markings excitedly, then looked around to see if anyone had witnessed her domination of light.

"Pretend like you don't notice." I dragged my hands down my face. "If you ignore their bad behavior, they'll get bored. Eventually. But if you reward them with attention, they'll think it's a game."

Nine just rubbed her forehead. "Who are all of you?"

I introduced Nine to my sister and the rest of my friends, and then we took turns telling her how the high magistrate's soldiers were moving through the streets to take people.

Nine sighed. "All right. I'll add it to my report. But what do you want from me? Why do you have all your worldly possessions with you?"

"We can't go back to the Fire Rose. It's only a matter of time before Paorah starts looking for Aaru and me."

"All right." Nine crossed her arms. "And?"

I clicked for LaLa and held her steady with the tips of my fingers. "And," I said, "we're in trouble. We have few allies, and even fewer friends. Our governments are against us, and our gods are ready to abandon us. We need options—better options than a few people getting saved and the rest being left to die."

"We aren't friends," Nine said. "Not even allies."

"I know." My breath shivered on its way in. "But I need to ask for your help anyway."

Her eyes narrowed. "Spit it out."

I should have talked to the others first. I should have given them a chance to offer other options, but back in Harta, Chenda had insisted that I needed to take charge.

She was right: I was the Hopebearer, the Dragonhearted, and the living symbol of the Mira Treaty, even if Elbena had tried to bleed it out of me, and Paorah had killed another girl to destroy it.

We couldn't stay in Flamecrest. I knew that now. And the dragon dreams had been telling me what to do—where to go—ever since the Great Abandonment began. This whole time, some immense and fiery part of my soul had been telling me how to save everyone, but I hadn't understood.

Not until now.

So I just said it:

"I want you to take me to the Algotti Empire. I want to meet with your empress."

CHAPTER EIGHTEEN

THE PROTESTS ERUPTED IMMEDIATELY:

"What is wrong with you, Fancy?" Gerel surged to her feet and glared down at me. "We don't meet our enemies on their own land. Not if we can help it."

And from Hristo: "You know I'd follow you anywhere, but this is beyond reasonable."

"I'm not going!" Zara was already on her feet and marching toward the hatch, but Hristo stood in the way. "You can't make me. I'll tell Mother."

LaLa stared at me, and a warmth spread through my chest. *She* knew what we had to do.

"I'm glad everyone else hates that plan," Nine said after a minute. "Because it's not happening. I'm not taking you anywhere. You can stay here tonight, but then it's

223

over. I'm not doing anything else for you."

"Please think about it." I looked around at everyone. They were all standing now, though Chenda and Hristo had their heads ducked thanks to the low ceiling. "Paorah isn't just gathering up the skilled or wealthy people; he's putting armies on these ships. He's not going to the empire to make friends with the empress. He intends to take her land, and he has the giant noorestones to do it. With ten of them—that we know of—he can devastate a city and still have some to threaten her with if she tries to resist."

Nine crossed her arms and frowned. "All right, he has ten giant noorestones. Perhaps a few more, if he has control over the *Star-Touched* and the *Great Mace*, but that's still a limited number, and our empress can count. When he's out of your deadly noorestones, she'll return with a bigger army and crush him."

"At the cost of a city?" I asked. "Two cities? Armies?"

"Our empress has many cities. The temporary loss of one or two will be but an annoyance. Although," she allowed, "Sunder is her favorite, and where the high magistrate is most likely to land."

"I have power over noorestones." I held my hands in front of me, palms up. "You've seen only a small example of what I am capable of, but if I wanted, I could prevent the high magistrate from using any of the noorestones against the Algotti Empire."

Gerel's mouth dropped open. Chenda stared at me,

disgusted. The others, too, looked confused. Even Aaru.

"I know how it sounds." I straightened my shoulders. "I'm offering to help our enemies—to protect them from our own people. I know it sounds wrong.

"The world has seen enough destruction, hasn't it? Our people have done so much to hurt one another, but what if we took all that effort and put it into helping? Maybe then we could be proud of the world we live in, not scared of it. But someone has to end the old cycle and begin a new one. That can be us.

"We can make peace with the empire by warning them of a betrayal. We can learn the truth about who they are, not just believe everything our ancestors told us. And we can try to find a temporary place for our people to stay until we reach a new home. Our gods are abandoning us. Do we really want to go to war with the Algotti Empire on top of that?"

My friends shook their heads.

"We don't want to belong to the empire, either, Mira." Hristo spoke softly. "And if we go there—if we try to take over whatever deal the high magistrate made with the empress—then we risk selling ourselves to them, and I can't be part of that."

"I know." I touched his arm. "I'm not willing to bargain away our sovereignty. Still, we must consider our survival. Not just us. Not just those wealthy enough to buy their way onto one of the high magistrate's ships. But everyone. Farmers, weavers, bakers, maids, tailors, cooks—"

"Repair people," Aaru said quietly, "and girls forbidden to work."

Hristo closed his eyes. "Gardeners."

"Doctors." Zara bit her lip and stared at the floor.

"Revolutionaries," Chenda murmured.

"Dragon trainers," Ilina said.

"Dishonored." Gerel took a long breath and glanced westward. "All right. It's wonderful that we all agree that people deserve to live, but how do we do that without swearing ourselves to an empress we don't want? We have information about the high magistrate, which Nine is already going to impart, and we have two people"—she nodded at Aaru and me—"who can prevent a noorestone attack, but as Nine already said, it's one or two cities out of many—an acceptable loss to someone as powerful as the empress."

"You're assuming she even wants you." Nine studied everyone's faces as she spoke. "Besides, what gives any of you the authority to strike a deal with our empress? What makes you more acceptable than Paorah?"

No one spoke for a long moment, and then Ilina said, "You think your empress would rather work with Paorah than Mira?"

Nine narrowed her eyes. "I am but our empress's eyes and ears. It isn't my place to judge who she forms partnerships with."

I looked at her askance. "You were judging her earlier. In the chamber."

"I was surprised."

226

"You were horrified." I kept my tone gentle. "And you were right to be. We've all felt that way about those who were elected or appointed. They're people we thought we could trust. Every single one of us has been betrayed like that."

Her frown eased, and she sighed. "Your argument is compelling, but I can only ask that you be allowed to speak with our empress. I cannot take you from the Fallen Isles without permission from my superiors."

"We don't have a lot of time." I motioned west, where the sun had already set behind the folded figure of Idris.

"You can wait an hour." She sighed and started toward the hatch. "But before I do yet another favor for you, you need to tell me how Seven died."

I glanced at Gerel and Chenda, and the latter said only, "Friendships are not forged by keeping secrets." Her frown belied the encouraging words.

I agreed, but the truth didn't make us look good. Even so, I told Nine about seeing the black ship outside Val fa Merce, noticing Seven in the First Harta Dragon Sanctuary.

"His jacket was too small," I said. "But you have those devices. . . ."

Nine shrugged. "Our weavers can hold only a few patterns. He probably thought it was easier to borrow a uniform, rather than make an imprint of it, if he didn't plan to go back there."

"All right." I told her the rest of the story of capturing Seven, and then: "When we saw the skimmer from a distance, we didn't know it was friendly. Hush sensed my fear and decided to protect me."

"You named a dragon Hush?" Nine's lip curled.

"I personally didn't name her Hush, but I can only assume the name was chosen as some sort of plea."

"I can confirm that," Ilina said. "She loves to roar, especially first thing in the morning."

Nine snorted. "Fine. So Hush set fire to the skimmer and then . . ."

"Gerel rescued Chenda, then Seven, but by then it was too late. He'd been badly burned and was unconscious in our infirmary for hours. He awakened long enough to pass on the truth about Anahera, and then he was gone."

Nine closed her eyes and sighed. "That isn't how any of us expect to go."

"How . . . ," Aaru started, then thought better of it.

"Poisoned in our sleep," she said. "By a rival seeking our positions."

"Oh."

"If we're not good enough to prevent it, then we're not good enough to keep our position." She waved away more questions and started up the ladder.

"You're not mad?" I would have been furious if someone had taken a friend from me like that.

"What good does anger do at this point? Your dragon defended you. Seven sent you to me. Now I'm going to ask if it's worth bringing all of you to the empire. I'll come back down in an hour, so make yourselves comfortable, but not too comfortable. I'm still hoping you'll go away." When she was up, she closed the hatch after her.

Chenda faced me, glowering. "How could you make that kind of decision for all of us?"

I closed my eyes and breathed out. "I'm sorry. I meant to say something before. I was trying, but we had to leave the hotel. . . ."

Ilina slumped down to the floor. "Is that why you were asking about eclipses?"

I nodded. "Ever since the earthquake, I've been having these dreams where I'm flying. I look down and I see my shadow on the water, or over the land, and it's a huge dragon. I feel"—I dragged my palms down my ribs and stomach and hips—"separate from myself. Like Mira, but more."

"That doesn't make sense," Hristo said.

Maybe not, but that didn't change what I felt. "There's an eclipse—or one coming—and I know I have to do something by then, but I don't know what. Only that it's important."

The others—except Aaru—just looked at me, uncertainty written clearly all over their expressions.

"I know how it sounds, and I'm sorry I didn't tell you all sooner, but I had my doubts, too, until Ilina confirmed the eclipse." My heart pounded with the words. "I don't know what else is true—if anything is—but I need to follow these instincts."

"And they're telling you to go to the empire?" Chenda

229

looked dubious. "I thought you were against leaving everyone in the Fallen Isles to die."

"I am." I pressed my fist against my heart, like I could crush its pounding into submission. "But I think to save the Fallen Isles, I need to leave. For now. I'll return."

"When?" Zara asked.

"Before the eclipse." I closed my eyes. "If I can find something and bring it back, then I think we might have a chance. The Fallen Gods might be appeased. They might stay."

Everyone was quiet a moment.

"What about Idris?" Aaru asked softly.

"I wish I knew." My dreams were only dreams. They didn't tell me if the islands would return to normal, or if the Great Abandonment would just stop, with the evidence of our near extinction looming on the horizon. The god shadow. Maybe *shadows* by then, if I didn't move quickly enough.

"What do you think you need to get?" Hristo asked. "What could the empire have that's so important to us?"

I glanced upward, as though I might be able to see Nine through the solid metal of the ship.

::I have silence around us,:: Aaru tapped. ::She can't hear you.::

"Bones." I swallowed hard. "Dragon bones. From the first dragon."

No one said a word.

Haltingly, I told them my dream about the Fall, and

how the first dragon burst from the bones of the gods, and led the war for the Fallen Isles. With the exception of Zara, they all knew the story of the Celestial Warriors, who'd gone to the mainland to burn away the strongholds of our enemies, but they hadn't known—couldn't have known—that the first dragon had led them.

And she was the one we needed to bring home.

"That's—" Ilina stopped. Blew out a breath. Frowned. "I've never heard of the first dragon before. Are you sure?"

"No." It was the honest answer. "But you're the one who said there's an eclipse coming. If the eclipse with both moons is real, why can't the bones of the first dragon be real, too?"

"We're talking about going to the Algotti Empire based on your dream." Zara looked exasperated. "Didn't you dream that you were a fish once? And you couldn't find your skirt, so it started to storm?"

"I was ten," I said. "And everyone has strange dreams like that. Right?"

Everyone was suddenly very interested in the dragons, who'd gone back to playing with the light symbols. Light. Dark. Light. Dark.

"All right," I said. "But I know the difference between those dreams. I know that one is silly and forgettable to everyone but Zara, because she loves holding things over my head for seven years, and that one feels like fire in my soul. Like wings. Like stars." No, they couldn't understand that. I tried again: "Like a memory."

Light. Dark. Light. Dark. LaLa and Crystal continued their game while the others absorbed everything I said. It was hard to blame them for doubting.

"None of you have to come along," I said after a few minutes. "None of you are obligated."

"Well," Gerel said. "That's a dumb thing to say. Obviously, I can't let you go off to the empire alone."

"We all already said we'd go." Ilina clicked for Crystal, then petted her dragon's nose. "If Nine says yes. But you know I'll go anywhere with you, wingsister."

"Do you really think you can do it?" Hristo asked. "Save the Fallen Isles, I mean."

"I think," I said slowly, "if we are all together, we have a chance."

"'Hate cannot abide where many stand in love,'" Chenda murmured.

"Who are we, though?" Ilina asked. "Why should we have more authority than Paorah when it comes to making deals with other lands? Even if it wasn't a fair election, people voted for him. No one chose us."

No one spoke for a few minutes, that thought weighing us down.

"I was chosen," I said. "It was a fluke. I happened to be born on the right day to get a treaty named after me. But no one chose any of you."

A pout formed on Ilina's mouth.

"You chose yourselves." I met their eyes one at a time: Chenda and Gerel, leaning against the metal bars of the brig and holding hands; Ilina, twisting a braid around her finger; Zara, cleaning under her fingernails like she didn't care about any of this; Hristo, half sitting on one of the barrels; and Aaru, tilting his head while he looked at me. "Every one of you chose to stand up for something greater than greed or hatred. You made a choice to protect other people at the cost of your own freedom or happiness. Some of you went to prison for it." I swallowed hard, thinking about all the things my friends had given up.

Families.

Freedom.

Comfort.

Safety.

"And yet," I said, "you chose to be chosen."

"I didn't do anything." Zara glanced up. "I didn't choose myself. I'm only here because you're supposed to protect me, which so far has put me in more danger than I've ever been in."

"Sorry."

My sister shrugged and tapped the side of her head. "I'm keeping it all in here so I can tell Mother later, assuming we don't die."

I sighed but went back to the point I was trying to make. "Look at us." I gestured around at everyone. "There are seven islands, and seven of us. And look at your gifts. You're powerful, all of you. Surely you've noticed that your gifts are strong even away from your home islands. We've seen the way Chenda wields shadow even so far from

Bopha, and how Aaru manipulates silence on the other side of the Fallen Isles from Idris. The way Ilina and Zara talked people in Flamecrest into giving us bargains was nothing short of divine. Gerel, you fought all of Altan's warriors when they boarded the *Chance Encounter*. And Hristo—"

Hristo was amazing. Invaluable. And charming, from all his time on Damina. But if he had a Hartan gift, I didn't know about it.

"Hristo made all of the gardens in the dishonored camp grow." Aaru looked at my protector. "When we were running to the tunnels, all the gardens we passed started to grow. I could hear the roots moving."

No one spoke, and the only sound was water rushing against the metal hull.

"Oh." Hristo lowered his face, but he couldn't quite hide the pleased smile. "Well, that's . . ." He didn't finish, taking the thought inward instead.

"Have any of you ever seen that before?" I looked around. "People's god gifts being that strong, even away from their gods?"

Everyone shook their head.

"And not only are you the most powerfully gifted people I've ever seen, but there's a representative here from every island," I said, but Ilina held up a hand.

"Excuse me, I do not represent Anahera. I was born on Darina, same as you. And I'm *charming*, not conniving."

I smiled. "You are charming, wingsister. But you're

234

cunning as well. Unless you disagree that you come up with excellent plans and know how to make twenty lumes stretch into one hundred?"

Her mouth dropped open. "All right, those things are true. I am exceedingly clever. But it doesn't change where I was born."

Hristo looked at her, his expression gentle and deep with understanding. "You can have both, if you want."

"I don't want," she snapped. But then she closed her eyes and softened. A heartbeat passed while she took in Hristo's meaning. "Sorry. I guess I just never thought of it that way—claiming both. I just listened to everything my parents said about Anahera. I didn't think that not everyone there was like the high magistrate. I mean, Father came from Anahera and he's a good person. It stands to reason there would be others. I didn't think about it, though. Not until we got here."

Hristo crossed the small space and sat next to her, putting his arm around her shoulders. "You get to choose."

She leaned her head on him.

"If we represent the islands," Zara said to me, "then what about you?"

"I'm from Damina," I said. "Like you."

"But you're not charming."

Aaru frowned. "I think Mira is charming."

I smiled at him. "I'm not like Mother or Zara, though. And this"—I pulled noorestone fire from the dragons' basket—"isn't a Daminan gift. It isn't a gift from any god."

235

The white-blue glow flickered around my hands before I released it, letting it flow back into the crystals.

"Maybe it's not from any one god," Ilina said. "Maybe it's from every god."

Before she had a chance to elaborate, however, Nine came back down the hatch, wearing an annoyed look. "All right. You've been invited to the Algotti Empire as a special guest of Her Imperial Majesty Apolla. We leave first thing in the morning."

The *Drakontos celestus*

AN ISLAND TREMBLED WITH ANGER, THREATENING TO rise with every moment that passed. The ground lurched, the waters crashed, and the structures erected by humans a thousand years ago began to crumble under the constant tremors.

Hundreds of warrior-born worked to add new sections of the God Shackle, even as the current links groaned with strain.

They thought they could contain a god.

But in a corner of that island, in a camp that used to be rocky cliffs and seagull perches, another group chopped and sawed and sanded a forest of newly grown trees, fashioning them into small ships. They were crude vessels, meant merely to float when the God Shackle inevitably snapped.

Some humans tended gardens, which had grown up out of nowhere. Eagerly, they packed jars of preserves, packets of dried fruits, and barrels full of vegetables. These were people who'd learned to live with nothing, and they knew the danger of waste.

When the dragon shadow passed overhead, they looked up, but they didn't pause their work.

All across the Fallen Isles, they prepared.

They planned.

They prayed.

It would do no good.

CHAPTER NINETEEN

IN THE MORNING, NINE UNMOORED THE SKIMMER and climbed up to the quarterdeck, where she took the wheel. Using some sort of magic, she manipulated the sails, and the skimmer carried us out of the cove.

The rest of us stood on the main deck, careful to stay out of the way of the rigging as we leaned to watch the red sandstone cliffs grow smaller in the distance.

"This ship is fast," I said. Good thing, too. The eclipse was only two decans from now.

Gerel nodded. "It took Chenda and me almost no time to catch up with you on the *Chance Encounter*. The wheel has all these sigils carved into it, some for speed, some for the sail, some not immediately obvious." She shrugged. "Seven told us a couple of them, mostly because he didn't want me to crash his ship, but I think I would have figured it out eventually. Besides, the ship is metal. It probably would have done more damage to the rocks."

"I don't understand how it doesn't sink from the weight." Hristo ran his fingers along the rail.

"More of their magic," Chenda said. "There are sigils for buoyancy and speed carved all over the hull."

That must have been how Nine communicated with her superiors so efficiently, then: magic. More and more of it.

"Do you think all their magic works away from home?" I asked. "Like these ships and the weaver device?"

"I don't know," Gerel said. "Their magic is different from our god gifts."

"Imagine how quickly they could conquer the Fallen Isles," Zara murmured. "If they wanted."

Gerel shot my sister a *look*. "I said their magic is different, not better. What they have is impressive, but our gods give us strength. They would never have defeated us, had they come here looking to conquer."

Or maybe we were just so small and out of the way that no one cared about us as much as we thought. We had god gifts, which made us dangerous to keep on the islands but useless away from home. We had noorestones, but clearly the empire had other forms of illumination that worked just as well. And we had dragons; they were probably the most tempting resource of the Fallen Isles, but difficult to capture.

I didn't trust the empire, or the empress, or even Nine. I'd meant what I said about looking for more options, but trust needed to be earned.

That went both ways. If I wanted the bones of the first dragon, I needed to figure out how to ask her about them. And after two thousand years, they could be buried. Broken. Lost to time.

I still had to find them.

Ahead of us, Crystal and LaLa were flying off all the seagulls they'd eaten the day before. Gold and silver flashed and vanished and shimmered in the morning sun as the skimmer carried us farther east than any of us had ever been.

Two or three at a time, we abandoned the main deck and climbed to the quarterdeck, all of us gazing off the aft of the skimmer, where mist sprayed in our wake.

Fingers twisted around mine: Ilina's on my left, and Aaru's on my right. Slowly, the horizon ate up the scrape of land that was Darina's northern edge, and then the tall red cliffs of Anahera, and finally towering Idris all the way on the far side of the Fallen Isles.

They were gone. Out of sight.

My heart twisted, pounding painfully as we all stared westward. Homeward.

Just then, when it seemed like we'd be able to pull away and talk about things that didn't matter, LaLa and Crystal jerked straight up and screamed.

Their little wings pumped as they threw themselves

into the sky, shrieking mournfully, and a huge wave of desolation crashed against me. The force was so strong that I staggered back a few steps before catching myself.

"What?" Ilina touched my arm. "Is it—"

I let out a choked sob. "It is."

Another god was about to rise.

SEVERAL HOURS AFTER we lost sight of the Fallen Isles, the dragons calmed and returned to us. It could only mean that the earthquake was over and the god had risen, but I was so relieved to have LaLa back in my arms that I could almost put the horrible truth out of mind.

Almost.

"Who do you think it was?" Tearstains marked Zara's cheeks. "Does it even make a difference?"

Ilina looked up. "What do you mean 'does it even make a difference'?"

"It's terrible no matter who," my sister whispered. "No matter who it was, people died, and—" Her voice caught and she couldn't finish.

Cautiously, I put my arm around her shoulders. "I know what you mean."

My sister sniffed and leaned against me.

We stood together in silence, all of us grieving people we knew and people we didn't, and what a horrible, unfair world this could be.

Later, Nine shouted for us to look ahead. Something new had come into view.

"Is that the empire?" Zara wandered toward the bow and leaned forward.

Nine snorted. "No. The empire is much larger, but I think you'll be pleased anyway. We'll be able to get off this skimmer. And just in time, too. It won't be long before a wave reaches us. We want to be on something more solid when that comes through."

The rest of us drifted after my sister as a dark smudge grew on the horizon. Its size made it look like land at first—it was easy to understand Zara's mistake—but as we drew closer and the sun pulled higher, I began to see the glare of light against metal, and that what might have been hills was actually the decks of an enormous ship.

"Welcome to the skimmer den." Nine looked up as we approached the massive ten-masted vessel, deep black metal with gold detailing along the hull. All the sails were furled and its two anchors dropped.

I gathered LaLa into my arms, while Ilina took Crystal. Both of the dragons wore their hunting gear now, and we kept our grips tight as the new ship loomed over us.

Nine was still talking. "The proper name for this class is *skimmer carrier*, but it's practically a rabbit warren inside. Quarters, mess halls, infirmaries. Even a library. One den can carry fifteen skimmers. More if you don't want other cargo, but for long missions like these, people like to eat."

The skimmer had felt small to begin with, and as we sailed toward the den, it seemed like the larger ship might stomp on us and drown us in the watery depths. It blocked the whole horizon as we drew alongside it, and—to everyone's horror—it began to break open with a terrible screech and rush of water.

LaLa shrieked and flapped her wings, but I held her tight against my chest and wrapped an arm around her body. Her head swung up at me, and she chittered worriedly.

"Seven gods!" Zara clapped her hands to her chest and backed away from the carrier. "Turn around, Nine! It'll sink and take us with it!"

Nine just smirked, not worried at all as a huge sheet of metal lowered into the water. Lowered, though. Not fell.

It was a door.

A panicked laugh escaped me as the skimmer entered, and the door began to close behind us.

At first, the area seemed dark after the midday sun, but as my eyes began to adjust to the flickering light of the sigils, I took in our new surroundings.

We were in a chamber big enough to hold three skimmers—there were three wooden docks just the perfect size. Men and women bustled about, their voices and footfalls echoing on the platforms that loomed above and around us.

LaLa's chirrup echoed through the room, drawing curious looks. I gripped her jesses tighter and curled my shoulders around her. "Stay with me, little lizard. I'll protect you."

I hoped.

"Our engineers limited these spaces to only a few

skimmers," Nine said, "in case the section is breached. The bulkheads between will prevent water from flooding into other compartments. Go get your things, and then we'll find your quarters."

"I don't want to be impressed," Ilina said as we grabbed our belongings from the lower deck, "but this is incredible."

"How long do you think it's been out here?" Hristo asked.

Gerel shook her head in wonder. "Decans, most likely. As long as the spies have been in the Fallen Isles. I'd say the den serves as a port of sorts, where the spies could come and go as needed. The supplies they must have on this thing. . . ."

"It's eerie." I looped my bag over my shoulder and readjusted LaLa. We could have put the dragons in their basket, but I wanted LaLa by my side; she made me brave. "Thinking about it being just a few hours off the eastern end of Anahera. All this time."

"A few hours by skimmer," Ilina corrected. "Even with our fastest ships, it would take longer to reach it. I'd be surprised if the *Star-Touched* or the *Great Mace* ever come out this far."

"If the den is as fast as the skimmers, it won't take us long to reach the mainland." Aaru held tight to Doctor Chilikoba's medical bag, which he'd taken charge of, as well as his own small bag of clothes we'd bought for him in Val fa Merce.

"I can't believe we're doing this." Ilina licked her lips.

"Getting into this ship. Visiting the empire. Meeting the empress."

"That's if Nine is being honest," Gerel said. "If her people don't attack us the moment we go back up."

"Do you think the imperials would?" Zara's eyes went round.

"If they'd wanted to do that," Hristo said, "they would have already."

"I don't trust them." Gerel frowned.

"Good." I started to climb the ladder through the hatch. "Stay wary. But this is our chance to make a difference for the Fallen Isles."

"What's left of them," Ilina murmured.

She had a point, but I didn't agree out loud. Two gods had already risen.

Five to go.

CHAPTER TWENTY

Nine didn't bother to introduce us to any of the workers before guiding us out of the docking compartment. They weren't important enough, she said once we were out of earshot.

But we'd looked at them, and they'd looked at us, and it seemed like we were all thinking the same thing: *they are so normal.*

Along the way, the dragons chirped and clicked, listening to their own voices bounce along the vast walls. As we passed, most eyes dropped to the tiny gold and silver sisters, like moons in our hands. A young woman smiled at them and made kissing noises, as one might make to get a cat's attention.

The dragons would have loved to explore the docking

compartment—and introduce themselves to everyone in it—but Ilina and I held firmly to their leashes and didn't give them so much as a breath of slack as we climbed the stairs. Through a door, we came into a long corridor wide enough for three people to walk abreast.

Nine beckoned us to stay behind her so that people walking the opposite way didn't have to press against the wall while waiting for us to pass.

"There's a lot of ship," she said. "And a lot of rules about where to walk and when to stand. I can't give you a full tour now—you won't be permitted to wander about, regardless—but after you get settled in your quarters, I'll show you the mess and a few other places you'll be allowed to go."

"We aren't prisoners, are we?" A challenge rose in Gerel's voice.

"Of course not. You're guests." Nine glanced over her shoulder. "When you're in someone else's home, do you roam about and peek in all their closets?"

Gerel scowled. "I think you and I both do that."

Nine let out a soft snort. "Well, that's fair. But don't do it here. I can only protect you so much. Try to behave."

By and large, the corridors all looked the same—with that strange black metal and light sigils—but stairwells and intersections did have signs, which helped. Sort of. While the letters looked familiar, they were long and slanted in strange ways, as though we'd once shared an alphabet, but time and distance had squished ours, or stretched theirs, or maybe both. Spellings were different, too, but similar enough that we probably wouldn't get completely lost. And, whether I wanted to or not, I was counting steps and turns and stairs, so I was confident that, if nothing else, I could get us back to the docking compartment.

"Unfortunately," Nine was saying, "you'll have to share quarters. Somewhere around a thousand people work aboard this ship, so everyone has to share, aside from the captain. Lower-ranked crew usually have ten to a cabin, but the higher-ups get two." She motioned us faster down the corridor. "As honored guests, you'll have two to a cabin, with one group of three, unless one of you wants to share with me. My usual bunkmate won't be here."

"It wasn't Seven, was it?" I asked hesitantly.

"No." She pressed her mouth into a line. "Not that it's any of your business."

That was fair; I was curious how close she and Seven had been, because everything she'd told us about being an imperial spy (not much) was so strange. But curiosity didn't mean I deserved answers.

"So we'll pick who we share with." Ilina glanced mean-ingfully at me. How, even *now*, even *here*, was she still thinking about making sure Aaru and I had time alone? There was more of the trickster in her than she liked to admit.

"A thousand people on one ship," Chenda breathed. "Not even our biggest, most advanced ships can hold so many."

Gerel nudged her, as if to say stop giving the enemy

information, as though Nine didn't know all about our capabilities.

"The skimmer den could hold more," Nine said. "If it weren't for all the skimmers and the supplies needed to repair them when they break down. And maintaining a population this size requires a lot of food."

"And water," I said.

She nodded. "We have a system for extracting salt from seawater, so that, at least, isn't as much of a concern." She paused in front of a line of doors. "Here are your quarters. Drop off your things. I'll wait out here."

A few minutes later, Ilina had everyone sorted into cabins, and I trailed after Aaru into the one she'd assigned to us.

In spite of the size of the ship, there wasn't much space: just two narrow beds, two closets with shelves on the bottoms, two nightstands, and one lavatory. The last was behind a partition, and it had a sink and commode. Nowhere to fully bathe, but hopefully Nine would show us somewhere later.

There was no porthole, either; we must have been deep inside the ship.

Aaru looked between the beds. "Which one do you want?"

I let LaLa off her leash and put my bag on the left-hand bed. "This isn't so bad, although it isn't much bigger than our cells in the Pit. I wouldn't want to live here for decans at a time."

"They probably don't do much living in here." Aaru dropped his bag on the second bed and offered a hand to LaLa. She trilled and tumbled to him, landing with a thump. "It's probably sleep and work. If there's time for recreation, I bet they do it somewhere else." Carefully, he stroked down LaLa's spine, a faint smile tugging at his lips.

"Do you mind this?" The words were out before I could think better of them. "Sharing a room, I mean. Ilina didn't exactly ask."

He looked up, face dark with embarrassment. "I heard what they said. Before the memorial. I know what they meant—why they wanted us to share."

"I—"

A sharp knock on the door saved me from having to finish that conversation just yet. I put LaLa back on her tether and found an impatient Nine in the corridor, accompanied by three large sun-darkened men. I didn't know much about imperial fashion, so from their dress—loose cotton shirts and trousers, and brown boots that went up to the middle of their calves—I couldn't tell if they were important people Nine wanted to introduce us to, or . . .

"Hello," I said, but they didn't respond.

"These gentlemen are here for your protection," Nine said. "Don't worry about them."

Guards.

I wanted to be angry, but we'd have done no different to her, had our positions been reversed.

Finally, the others emerged from their cabins, and Nine imparted more rules—mostly ordering us to stay out of the way. Then she showed us how to find the mess hall, the infirmary, a communal washroom, and a small library stuffed with books.

"Are these novels?" I trailed my fingertips over stories from another world. It hadn't occurred to me that such a thing would exist, but it made sense: humans were creative creatures, and everyone had some sort of story to tell.

"I found histories," Ilina murmured. "This will be useful. We can get to know the empire and its many conquests." Her tone was pleasant, but I didn't miss the bite.

"I think you'll be impressed." Nine was leaning in the doorway, one hand on her hip. "The peace our empress has brought to so many warring kingdoms is truly remarkable."

Reading about the empire's steady expansion over the years—its steady destruction of individual nations—wasn't something that exactly thrilled me, but these histories would be the best place to look for information about the first dragon, her bones, and where I might find them.

Surely, in all these books, there must be mention of a dragon somewhere.

On the far side of the library, Aaru stood with a small book in his open palm. *The Book of Silence,*" he said when he caught me looking.

"We have all of your holy books," Nine said. "The

others and I read them before our mission, along with copies of all your important documents and records. We have our own interpretations of your history, of course, but if I wanted to fit in, I needed to know what your people believe."

"That's . . ." I frowned and straightened.

"You don't have to like it," she said. "I do my job."

"How long until we leave for the empire?" Zara asked.

"Half a decan."

I exchanged glances with some of the others. The eclipse wasn't so far away that we had time to just sit here in the middle of the ocean reading books. "Why must we wait? We're in a hurry."

Nine rolled her eyes. "You think we're going to move a thousand people just to convenience you? Try to remember that you're guests. If you want to find one of your own ships to sail to the Algotti Empire immediately, feel free. But the skimmer den is faster than any vessel from the Fallen Isles, so even with this half-decan delay, we'll still be there before you. Try to be patient."

I scowled. Our islands were rising out of the sea, and she had the nerve to lecture us about manners. "How long?" I asked. "Once we leave, how long will it take to get there?"

"Just a few days."

"So fast." Even so, that didn't leave us much time to find the bones of the first dragon before we needed to return to the Fallen Isles.

Nine gave a pointed nod. "As I said, we'll reach Sunder long before any Fallen Isles ship. For now, I suggest you enjoy the library and learn what you can before you meet our empress, and your new friends will help you find your quarters when you're finished. If there's anything you need, they will get it for you. And now, I'm going to change into proper attire." Without another word, she pushed off the wall and left.

LATER, AFTER OUR "new friends" guided us back from the library to our quarters, Aaru returned to our earlier, aborted conversation.

"Are you all right with this?" He swept his hand around the room, indicating our situation, I thought, and not the small, confined space.

"Yes," I said. "And no. And very much yes." My whole body felt warm when I thought of the previous day in the rain, the way he'd kissed me and touched me, and the fire he'd sparked that made us both feel like we were flying.

Aaru offered an awkward little smile. "All right. Me too."

"Ilina's from Darina. Chenda doesn't take anything slowly. But we don't— I mean— That doesn't have to be us. We don't have to—"

With any luck, the embarrassment would just set me on fire and put me out of my misery.

Aaru studied me while I stammered my way through a few simple words. "Is that what happens next?" His voice was soft. Curious. "I've been reading *The Book of Love*, but it doesn't say what happens when."

My heart squeezed around my ribs. "*The Book of Love* isn't like that. It's about emotions. Compassion. Good works."

He nodded.

"I suppose it's people who decide what they do. When they're ready." My voice trembled a little. "But there aren't rules. We don't need to do anything we aren't ready for. It's up to us to make that choice."

Tension slipped out of his shoulders. "All right. Good."

That yearning, wanting feeling coiled up inside me, wonderful but too big for me to fully explore. Still, it was tempered by the knowledge of what my friends assumed and expected. I wished they'd asked before moving me into the Fire Rose room with him, but I couldn't deny that the idea of being so close to Aaru—no walls between us, no hard ground, no gap between hammocks—sent thrills into the deepest parts of me. And now, in here, with the beds bolted to the floor, I was both disappointed and relieved.

It was a peculiar feeling: the desire for him and the desire to wait, all at once.

How could I *sleep* like this?

Across the room, Aaru sat in a mirror of me. In the low light of a single sigil, his eyes were dilated wide, as soft and black as the spaces between stars.

"I think," I ventured, "that on Damina, people sometimes

forget about the other things. The in-between things."

He tilted his head in curiosity.

"I think people get into a rush." When I glanced down, I realized I'd been weaving my fingers around the top of my blanket. I pressed my palms to my knees to stop fidgeting. "They want everything right now, no waiting. But that's not what I want. Not with you. I'd rather take our time getting there, if we decide we want to."

He nodded. Closed his eyes. Nodded again. "Have you ever—"

"No." I bit my lip and lowered my voice. "No. I never have. Partly because Mother would have killed me. She thought I needed to be *pure*—her word—and untouchable." Although Mother had sent us off to go dance the other night. Maybe she liked him. Or maybe she didn't see him—a quiet Idrisi boy—as a threat to my virtue. I cleared my throat. "But mostly, there was no one I'd have wanted to be with anyway. Not like that."

A question grew in his gaze, but he didn't ask, and I wasn't going to answer. Finally, he drew in a heavy breath. "I want to take our time. We decide together. We decide for us."

I smiled. "I like that."

It was a small thing. A huge thing. All my life, other people had made decisions for me: who could touch me, when, for what purposes. I'd been permitted to kiss a few people—only those Mother deemed acceptable—and later instructed how to break off relationships before they could take root. But even on an island that touted free-dom, control over my own body had only ever been an illusion.

And here, across the room from me, was a boy from Idris—a place where girls and women had historically been stripped of their choices, control over their own lives—and he, better than anyone I'd grown up with, understood the value of those simple words: we decide together; we decide for us.

Not society. Not expectations. Not friends. Not family. Us.

The knot of nervous energy faded from inside my body. I stood and tapped off the last light sigil, and when I slipped between the cool sheets, I reached across the space between our beds and found him already reaching back for me.

CHAPTER TWENTY-ONE

OVER THE NEXT FEW DAYS, WE MOVED PRIMARILY between our cabins, the mess hall, and the library. We took our meals quickly, eating the strangely spiced food without comment, and tried to ignore the curious stares of the crew. One of Nine's many rules had been to limit our interaction with the people on board this ship—for our protection, she'd insisted—and for the most part, the guards she'd assigned discouraged confrontation.

Once, though, a wiry old man stalked toward us wearing a scowl, and carrying a knife taken from his table. "You're the islanders, aren't you? You think you're everything because of those gods of yours. Well, where are they now?"

I'd barely had time to comprehend his words before Gerel and Hristo—who'd just stopped wearing his sling—were on their feet, standing between the man and the rest of us. The whole mess grew quiet, turning to watch. Hundreds of eyes, like ours, but not, just staring and waiting to see if we'd fight with one of their men. *How* we'd fight.

But it didn't come to that. Our guards stepped in, and the wiry man stepped back. They didn't even need to say anything. With some sort of gesture with his fist and little finger—probably meant to be rude—he slinked back to his friends.

Otherwise, we went about our days unhindered.

On our fifth day aboard the skimmer den, the seven of us sat around the table in the library, surrounded by piles of books, when one of the guards spoke up.

"We've just started to move," he said from the doorway where the trio always positioned themselves. "We'll reach Sunder in three days."

I glanced at my friends, but if they'd felt the ship begin to move, they said nothing. There'd been no jerk, no strange sway. Even as it was, I could barely feel the motion of the ship—as though we'd been living aboard a small island the last five days, rather than a ship. It was eerie, the way I could barely feel the ocean beneath us.

"Thank you," Chenda said, and we all turned back to our books. "Three days. It seems wrong to be able to move anywhere so quickly."

"Imagine going back to the Fallen Isles with a fleet of

ships like this." Ilina looked up. "We could save so many people."

"And then what? Float on the ocean for a thousand years?" Chenda shook her head. "Sorry. It just seems so impossible to believe there will be anything to go back to."

Gerel touched Chenda's hand, and the Dawn Lady's shoulders relaxed a little. Then Gerel lowered her voice, addressing everyone around the table. "Anything yet?"

It was difficult to speak freely with our new "friends" over there, but Aaru had built up a wall of soft silence, so that our voices were muffled but not completely muted. It might have been a little suspicious, but they hadn't said anything about it. Yet.

I shook my head. "Their spelling and the shapes of their letters makes it hard to read."

Chenda took the library's copy of *The Book of Shadow* and flipped through it, sighing wistfully. "At least these are right."

"What if we can't find anything?" Zara propped her elbows on the table and hunched forward. "I mean, all the histories of the Fallen Isles, and all the books we have about dragons, and there's nothing about the first dragon in any of them, right?"

Everyone looked at Ilina. "I haven't read anything about it, but if Mira thinks it exists . . ."

LaLa and Crystal chittered from their perches atop one of the table lamps—*lamps* being a generous term for simple arcs of black metal with light sigils carved into them. They made excellent dragon stands, at any rate, and it was nice to have light directly over the books.

"The dragons think it exists," I said, mostly teasing, but it was true.

"Even if we do find something," Zara said, "who's to say we'll be able to get it in time? The empire is immense."

"The city we're visiting is called Sunder," Hristo rumbled. "It can't be a coincidence."

Gerel shook her head. "The Sundering took place all up and down the coast of the mainland. There are probably half a dozen cities and towns with some variation of sunder in their name. And Little Fancy is right: the empire is immense, and just because the first dragon's bones *might* have been here two thousand years ago doesn't mean they still are. Empires aren't good about leaving things the way they were. Things get moved around. That's the whole point of conquering: changing things to suit one group's preferences."

"I know," I said. "And it's just as possible that the bones were never discovered, and now they're buried under a thousand layers of rock."

"Even if they do know where the bones are, how do we get them?" Zara scratched her nose. "Assuming the bones are real, and assuming they're not lost or broken or stolen by bandits, and assuming they're somewhere we can reach and still get back home in time for the eclipse—"

"This is far too much assuming to be healthy," Gerel muttered.

"Then the empire—or the land they've taken over—has had the bones longer than the Fallen Isles did. Why should we expect anyone to give us the bones because we ask nicely?"

That was a fair question. Zara and Ilina were both *very* persuasive people, but Damina's charm wouldn't change someone's mind about something they weren't already willing to do; it only made it easier to say yes. Any other method of obtaining the bones involved violence, theft, or bargaining away something valuable. Like our sovereignty.

"I suppose," I said softly, "that's a conversation to have when we get more information. There's no point in making a hundred plans for a hundred different scenarios."

Aaru pulled *The Book of Silence* toward him and flipped through the soft papers; they barely made a sound. "'The greatest calamity,'" he read, "'comes in the night, when the people are not listening.'"

Hristo closed his book, marking the page with his thumb. "Is that about the Great Abandonment?"

Aaru nodded solemnly. "I've thought about Idris's words a lot since the earthquake. I wished I could read them again. To find answers." His voice was rough with unshed tears. "I read from my family's copy every day at home. I didn't think I'd see one again. Least of all here."

Under the table, I pressed my foot against his.

A beat of quiet lingered in the small library before Gerel said, "That's a good idea. Seven gods know I haven't been a good follower of Khulan. Maybe I could learn something."

Chenda frowned and touched Gerel's chin. "Khulan saw fit to grant you incredible strength, even away from him. You're a truer follower than most."

Gerel looked dubious, but also like she didn't want to risk being comforted in public anymore, so she just shrugged. Still, she pulled *The Book of Warriors* to her and opened it on top of the history she'd been reading.

On the other side of the table, Ilina and Zara put *The Book of Love* between them, while the others moved the books of their gods closer, too.

The Book of Destruction lay at the end of the table, untouched. Feeling bad for it, I dragged the volume to me. I'd read it before—I'd read all of them before—but the lessons on other gods had been cursory, and long ago. My religious studies had focused mainly on Darina and Damyan, although I had asked why, as the Hopebearer, I wasn't more thoroughly instructed on others' beliefs. Mother had only said they weren't as important as our own.

Still, those lessons had given me just enough to remember that *The Book of Destruction* had several long passages devoted to the Great Abandonment. Of course. As the goddess of destruction, Anahera would have a lot to say on the subject of our ultimate end.

As we lost ourselves in the words of our Fallen Gods, a quiet fell over the table: the rustle of paper, the occasional sigh where words twisted with emotion, and then a small gasp.

Chenda pressed her finger against the page. "Bopha says the rending of her shadow from ours will take place on the darkest day. Could that be—"

"The eclipse." Gerel shivered and looked at me. "You were right. The gods confirm it."

Chills marched up and down my arms. That was only fifteen days away. If we didn't return to the Fallen Isles with the bones of the first dragon, then there would be nothing left.

No one else said anything. There was no need. We just studied until the day began to wane, and finally my eyes caught on a passage:

> *Where there is light, there must also be darkness.*
> *Where there is hope, there must also be fear.*
> *Where there is life, there must also be death.*
> *Every first is paired with a last.*
> *There can be no beginnings without endings.*
> *But do not despair. Instead, have hope, because what lives falls to dust, and from dust comes new life. It is sacrifice that enables change.*
> *The Great Abandonment is an ending, yet it is also a beginning. The shadow soul of the dragon, the fellowship of the Fallen, and the rending of earth: these are the signs of the end and the beginning.*
> *In the moment when the day and the night are the same, when the first and the last become one, and when hope and despair meet on the field of battle: then the Great Abandonment will be done.*
> *Remember: fire cannot exist without something to burn.*

I read the passage aloud, forcing my voice steady even as waves of *knowing* rushed in and out of my heart. The words were like a waking dream.

"'The shadow soul of the dragon.' I just saw that." Chenda turned a few pages in her book and read aloud. "'The brightest lights yield the blackest shadows, but even during the darkest day, the shadow soul of the dragon reigns.'"

"What does that mean?" Ilina asked.

"I don't know about the Anaheran passage," Chenda said, "but the Bophan one has always been thought of as a warning and a blessing. To us, shadows are often interchangeable with souls, but some interpretations believe there is a subtle difference. Shadows are"—she paused to consider—"texture. They add depth. If an object does not cast a shadow, is it really there? Shadows are the shapes of us, the details unseen, and if even our souls have shadows—"

"Perhaps someone's soul casts the shadow of a dragon." Ilina glanced at me, something between worry and awe in her eyes. "When you were telling us about your dreams, you said when you looked down, your shadow was the shape of a dragon."

Slowly, everyone else looked at me, too.

"You have this connection with dragons," Ilina went on. "I used to be jealous of it, but then I saw what it did to you when we found the dragons in the ruins. That cured that." She offered a tight smile, as though needing forgiveness for her feelings.

"I'd have been jealous if it had been you." My voice was hoarse. "I was already plenty jealous that you got to spend so much time with dragons."

Her shoulders relaxed a little.

"So"—Zara spoke slowly—"does this mean the passage is talking about Mira? Is it saying that Mira has a dragon soul?"

A dragon soul.

Foreboding weighed over the group as we all turned back to the books, but just then, Nine came in, clad in the same type of loose cotton clothes everyone else aboard the skimmer den wore.

"Have you prepared your statement for Empress Apolla?" she asked.

My heart was still pounding from the words I'd just read, but I'd had a lifetime of speaking around my anxiety. I managed to keep my voice level as I said, "Of course. We want safe harbor. We want ships to rescue our people. In exchange, I will help her with the problem of the high magistrate."

She frowned, like she didn't really believe that would be enough for her empress. "You want to take over the deal she and he made."

"Yes." Because I couldn't tell her that I wanted to scour the empire for dragon bones.

"All right." She nodded at the piles of books on our table, all the histories and holy words, and the pages and pages of poetry. "Have you learned anything interesting?"

Only this:

1. *I knew how to save the Fallen Isles.*
2. *Because endings made way for beginnings.*
3. *And sacrifices enabled that change.*

I'd been dreaming of the first dragon, because I was the last. And when I found her bones and took her home, I would entreat the gods on behalf of the humans. I would take her place. My shadow soul—my *dragon* soul—would reign.

But I'd have to sacrifice something dear. For my dragon self to complete its ascension, I'd have to leave my human self behind.

PART FOUR

LOVE SURVIVES DEATH

CHAPTER TWENTY-TWO

EVERY MORNING FOR THE NEXT THREE DAYS, WE returned to the library and searched the books of our gods, as well as the histories of the Algotti Empire, but we discovered nothing new.

At least, *they* didn't. The more I read, the more I was convinced that the sacrifice described would save the Fallen Isles, but I didn't tell them. I couldn't.

Guilt needled me whenever we came back to those passages, and the truth almost spilled out a few times, but I knew how that conversation would go. Hristo and Ilina would drag me into the ocean and swim me back to the Fallen Isles themselves if it meant they didn't lose the human part of me. They would prevent me from finding the bones of the first dragon and entreating the gods, because they'd rather have me as me than have the rest of our world.

Ours was a powerful love, built over time and trials, and I had no doubts that they'd try to save me above anything else, because I would do the same for them.

And then there was Gerel, who'd say I made the worst plans, and Chenda, who'd quietly agree, and Zara, who couldn't lose more family than she already had, and Aaru . . .

Aaru, who slept across the small cabin from me every night, who reached for my hand and held on like he needed me, who talked with me until we both mumbled and lost track of our thoughts and fell asleep. I'd promised he wouldn't be alone. I hadn't meant to break that promise so soon.

So I made it my secret, and hated myself for keeping it, but if this was the only way to ensure the Fallen Gods remained on Noore—

I started looking for alternatives. Other interpretations. And in the back of my mind, I prepared to keep track of my lasts, because by the final day of our journey east, I'd found nothing else that would save the Fallen Isles.

My dragon soul would consume all the human parts of me, giving everyone else—even the people who'd hurt us—a new chance to live. I'd always wanted to be a dragon, hadn't I? And come the eclipse, I'd get that wish, but now I had so many reasons to want to stay human.

It seemed vastly unfair.

• • •

"WHAT ARE YOU thinking?"

It was the night before we were supposed to reach the empire, and I wasn't doing a good job hiding my fear. Not from Aaru. And not from LaLa, though she tried to reassure me by showing me how fun it was to be a dragon. She kept bringing me her noorestone—the other was in Ilina's room with Crystal—and various other toys.

"It's time to go to sleep, little lizard." I handed the noorestone back to her. "Put this in your basket and get ready for bed."

She gave me an annoyed chitter, but clutched the noorestone between her teeth and flapped into her basket again. Rustling sounded as I tapped off all but one of the light sigils and climbed into my bed, facing Aaru. He faced me, too. The shadows were deep and cool, jumping as though a candle flickered on the far side of the room. Aaru looked soft. Sweet. Worried.

"You seem preoccupied," he said. "Are you afraid about what will happen tomorrow?"

A shiver crept through me. "A little." A lot. In just a few hours, we'd disembark the skimmer den, and step foot on imperial land. On the mainland. That alone would have been terrifying enough. But for me, it meant another move toward the sacrifice.

If we could find the dragon bones.

"I never imagined leaving the Fallen Isles," I said, because I needed to say something. "I never imagined being so far from home."

Aaru made a soft noise of understanding.

"Are you afraid?" I asked.

"Yes." No hesitation. No shame. He just admitted it. "But I never thought I'd leave Idris, and when I did, I survived."

In more ways than one.

"We'll come through this," he murmured. "You'll persuade the empress to give us ships and safe harbor. You'll persuade her to let us find the bones of the first dragon. We'll save the Fallen Isles, and everything will be right again."

I wished I could agree with him. "Do you really believe we have a chance? It's such a short amount of time."

He smiled softly. "I believe in you."

There was no adequate reply—nothing gracious or witty enough—to accept or deflect such a soul-warming statement. And heartbreaking. Even if we saved the Fallen Isles, I wouldn't be there to experience it with him. Not in the same way as I was now.

"It's all right if you don't believe in yourself yet." Aaru sat up in bed, the blankets sliding down his side. "It's harder to believe in yourself than it is to believe in others. But you have a lot of people putting faith in you. Ilina and Hristo would die for you. Gerel and Chenda both think you're worthy of following. Even your sister looks up to you in a way she didn't before."

"She's just doing what Mother told her."

"No." Aaru shook his head. "She respects you. I think

274

she finally understands you now."

I swallowed hard. "I wish it hadn't taken the end of the world for my sister to decide to put up with me."

A small, quiet laugh came from him, and his finger-tips drummed against his knee. "You should have seen the way my sisters fought. They loved one another, of course, but some nights they would beat on the tables in quiet code—yelling—until Mother came in and gave them a *look*. Once, I saw them blinking quiet code at each other. Hard, angry blinking so they didn't get in trouble for yelling. I almost—"

His smile fell into a broken sob.

I pushed up and crossed the floor to sit beside him.

"It feels like waves." His voice was low, rough. "One moment, I feel peaceful. Happy. And then I remember something small, like the way my sisters argued, or how Father helped me pin curtains over the basement windows so I could sleep during the day. And then I'm caught. It sucks me in and it hurts to breathe. I miss them."

I leaned my cheek on his shoulder and slipped his hands in with mine. His were warm and trembling. "'Love survives death.'"

"*The Book of Love*?" he asked.

I nodded. "It means that nothing—not even death—can hinder love. Your souls are tied together, so that even in death, your family can feel the way you love them. It means you can feel their love, too. Can't you feel it?"

Aaru stilled. Closed his eyes. Breathed. His head tilted

the way it did when he was listening for something almost impossible to hear.

One heartbeat. Two. Three.

"Yes," he whispered. "I feel it."

"Good." I wiped the tear trails off his cheeks; stubble scraped my fingers, sending a shiver through me. "You're not alone," I reminded him, pushing down the guilt of my own inevitable abandonment. I told myself he had other people who cared about him, too. "Not if you don't want to be."

He twisted and rested his forehead against mine. "I don't want to be."

A question pulsed between us. Soft. Hopeful. Hesitant. That kiss in the alley remained in my memory, a fire that wouldn't stop burning. I wanted to talk to him about it, to ask if he wanted to kiss like that again. But other than a few gentle touches and one soft kiss good night, there'd been nothing.

Then the moment passed, because neither of us was brave enough to give the question voice. Not when everything felt weighed down with expectations and unreadiness. Instead, I said, "You've been speaking aloud a lot more."

He pulled back, brow wrinkling. "Have I?"

I let out a soft breath of a laugh. A couple of decans ago, he wouldn't have even asked that in quiet code. He'd have let his expression—or lack of one, rather—do all the communication.

"Is it funny?" He took my hand again. ::Is it wrong?::

Another laugh bubbled up, and I tapped against his palm. ::I like it. You have a nice voice.::

He ducked his face. "It's just like any other."

"No." I leaned close again, until I could feel his breath against my lips. "It's special. It's yours."

His mouth curled into the sweetest smile, and I couldn't help myself anymore. I kissed him.

It was just soft. Brief. But he gasped, and then gently his arms slipped around my body, while I braced myself against the bed with one hand and let the other explore the lines of his neck and shoulder and ribs.

"Mira," he whispered against my lips.

"Yes."

He smiled. "You didn't even let me ask the question."

"Ask, then. But the answer will be yes."

He touched my cheek. "Do you want to share tonight? Bed, I mean. Not to— Not for anything except sleeping. But I want to be close to you. If that's all right."

My heart squeezed up at his nervousness, his sweetness. "We'll have to be really close. These beds are tiny."

"If it's too much—"

"But my answer is still yes."

Tension flowed out of his shoulders, and then wound back up again as though reality had just caught up with him. We'd be squeezed together all night—or what there was left of the night.

I was about to offer to let him take the question back,

but he reached across the space and grabbed my pillow and settled it beside his. Then, carefully, we scooted next to each other and turned onto our sides, his chest to my back. His breath came rapid against my temple as he slipped his arm around my waist and pulled me tight against him.

"You're warm," he whispered.

"It's about to get warmer," I said, listening to the rustling that came from LaLa's basket. Then her head popped out and she peered at us, eyes wide. "Get the light first, lizard."

She chirruped and flew to the last light sigil, bumped it with her nose, and came to settle in the curve of my shoulder and neck, careful of her sharp scales against my skin.

"Two of my favorite people," Aaru whispered.

My heart swelled, and I smiled, but I couldn't sleep. I was too aware of the way he felt behind me, the cadence of his breathing, and the gentle way he rested his hand on my hip. He wasn't sleeping, either, and I wished I knew what he was thinking. Not about anything like that day in the rain; that would have been evident.

But neither of us spoke, both of us hoping the other would be able to fall asleep before dawn. And now that we weren't talking anymore, my mind shifted back to my short future as a human, and my long future as a dragon.

LaLa nuzzled my cheek, in comfort, but also as a reminder. When I became a dragon, we'd be together forever, and that would be good, wouldn't it?

It would be.

Months ago, before all of this started, I'd been right: I *was* born for being with dragons.

Several minutes or an hour later, a horn blasted somewhere on the upper decks of the ship, and footfalls crashed through the corridors outside our room.

"Is it morning already?" My voice felt raw with exhaustion. "I wish we had a window." Like everyone who lived deep inside the ship, we had to go by the complex system of horns and bells to tell the time. This one didn't sound like the morning combination, but I had only a few days of pattern to draw from.

"No." Aaru sat up and scooped a sleeping LaLa off me so I could move. With one hand, he curled her against his chest, and then tapped the nearest light sigil with the other. The flickering orange glow touched his face and the soft way he gazed down at LaLa.

I sat up and turned toward him, knees bumping knees on the narrow bed. "What was it?"

"I can hear—" He shook his head. "I'm not sure. This ship is so loud. It's muddled."

Another blast sounded, and he winced.

"We've arrived." He looked up at me. "We're in the Algotti Empire now."

CHAPTER TWENTY-THREE

Strange as it was, I hadn't considered what my first glimpse of the Algotti Empire would look like. Part of me had thought we'd simply appear in the empress's throne room—or wherever she received people—and then . . . and then I didn't know. The empress, for all that Nine loved to talk about how grand and impressive she was, remained a shadowy mystery. Altan had believed her people worshiped her, as they might a god, and the imperial subjects we'd met so far had done nothing to challenge that.

When Nine fetched us and said it was time to get our first look at the empire, I thought we'd probably see a port, same as arriving at any other city, with bustling docks and yelling and seagulls stealing food. But either the empire had very different ports than we did, or Nine had made special arrangements.

With LaLa and Crystal on their leashes, we were escorted to a viewing deck—three levels above the main deck, railed in tight to keep anyone from falling. It was close with the seven of us, plus Nine, plus the three guards, but there wasn't much in the way of frivolous space on any ship, not even one this big. From here, we could see the vast swath of the main deck, the layers of the other upper decks, and all ten of the great masts as the crew worked to furl the sails and let the harbor boats tug the skimmer den in.

That was when I saw them.

Dragons.

A pair of immense obsidian *Drakontos titanus* statues bracketed the mouth of a river ahead, their wings arched back and their talons raised up. Sunlight gleamed in the black depths, beautiful and deadly. They were even bigger than real *titanuses*, at least by half again.

"Welcome to the city of Sunder." Nine stretched one arm out before us, and pride shone bright on her face.

"Seven gods." Ilina dropped her head back as we began to pass between the dragons. Crystal and LaLa agreed, flapping their wings and letting out spurts of fire. "They're magnificent."

"I've never seen anything like them." I couldn't help the awe in my tone, or the way my chest tightened at the sight of those carved dragons. It was masterful work, making my soul crave the Fallen Isles. I hoped Hush and all the dragons she'd helped free were still safe.

Beyond the twin *titanuses*, pale buildings rose on either side of the wide river, with immaculate lawns that ran down to retaining walls just ahead of the sandy banks.

Wait, no. There were multiple buildings on the western bank of the river—separated by small yards—but the eastern side held a single, long building that moved upward along with the land. White marble, swirled with pink and blue and flecks of gold, dominated this face, with elegant columns and patios that shaded small clusters of people in colorful dress. Dozens—hundreds—of windows winked in the midmorning sun.

"What is that building?" I asked as numbers ticked in the back of my head: windows, people, buildings. There was too much to keep track of.

"The imperial palace," Nine said. "The main entrance is on the other side, but we wanted to get you here quickly, with as little fuss getting through the city as possible."

I'd have liked to see the rest of the city, but perhaps she was right. We were all tired and rough from travel, and I didn't want to embarrass the Fallen Isles by coming through looking so wrung out.

Then again, this arrival felt like all the times I'd traveled as the Hopebearer, my escorts ensuring I saw only the parts of cities they wanted me to see: the wealthy districts, the acceptable masses, and the poor only from a distance, and only when someone was actually helping them. Prosperity like this usually masked hardship for others.

"This is the River Akron; it runs from the Sunken Mountains, far to the north. It's the main artery of the Sundered Lands, this province. There are hundreds of cities growing along the river and its tributaries."

Now that she said it, I recognized some of the names from the map we'd seen in the ship library. The empire was huge, but not unknowable—though I didn't plan to be here long enough to learn it better. I'd talk to the empress. Find the bones. And get home.

Twelve days before the eclipse.

Twelve days before I became a dragon.

The skimmer den slowed as we approached a raised platform that protruded from the eastern wall. When the ship came to a stop, two uniformed people standing on the platform drew signs in the air, and a ledge moved outward and met with the viewing deck right in front of us, like a bridge. One tall, dark woman in copper-colored armor stood at the rear of the platform, chin high and hands behind her back.

Aaru touched my arm. ::Do you think she's the empress?::

I smiled and started to shake my head, but what did I know about the empire? I pressed my hand on top of his. ::Maybe, but probably a guard.::

::She looks fierce.::

I gave a faint nod while the others gave the bridge a dubious eye.

"Is that safe?" Zara crossed her arms and hunched her

283

shoulders inward. "There's not much holding it up."

"Our empress employs only the best mages in the Algotti Empire. It will hold." As though to prove it, Nine stepped onto the bridge. "You'll be escorted to your quarters and given time to settle in."

"Settle in before what?" Since no one else seemed willing to go first, I hiked up my bag, doubled my grip on LaLa's leash, and followed Nine onto the bridge. It didn't so much as dip under my weight.

"I don't know." She glanced over her shoulder. "There will be schedules in your rooms."

"You won't be there?" She was the only person in this whole strange place we knew. I didn't like the idea of separating from her.

"I have work to do, Hopebearer. I'm not your minder." Her tone softened. "I'll check on you, though. To make sure your little dragons haven't started any fires."

We reached the platform before I had to form any sort of response. The two men—mages, Nine had called them—wore stiff linen uniforms the color of seafoam, bright against their sun-darkened skin. The didn't speak as I stepped onto the platform, but their eyes followed LaLa as I carried her after Nine toward the armored woman at the other end.

When Ilina and the others came up behind me, Nine introduced the other woman. "This is Alusha. She will be your escort throughout the palace." Nine met our eyes one by one. "She is responsible for your safety. If something should happen to one of you, she will offer her life to our empress as penance. So please, take no risks, because you, in turn, are responsible for her life."

I chanced a smile at Alusha. "We'll be good."

Her mouth pulled into a frown. "This way." Without waiting to see if we were coming, she turned on her heels and marched down the stairs. At the bottom, a flagstone path led to a covered patio and a wide double door, guarded by two dark men in steel armor and pale green tabards, emblazoned with the imperial insignia. It must have been hot inside all that metal and linen, but if they minded, their expressions didn't betray them at all.

"You'd better go," Nine said. "She won't wait while you gawk."

No one had offered to carry our bags, but that was probably for the best; none of us would have been willing to give up any part of our homeland, even temporarily.

"Thank you for all your help, Nine."

After the others made hasty good-byes, we hurried after Alusha, Ilina and I holding tight to our dragons as they strained to look around.

Then, it happened so fast I hardly realized—

My foot landed on Algotti ground.

There was no rush of feeling, no thrum of my heart speeding faster, nothing to mark the enormity of the moment of not only leaving the Fallen Isles, but stepping onto enemy land for the first time.

Instead, we just strode down the flagstone path after

Alusha, and the guards pulled open the doors to grant us admittance into the imperial palace.

One last look at the obsidian dragons that marked the mouth of the River Akron. One more prayer—*give me peace, give me grace, give me enough love in my heart*—and then, at last, I stepped inside.

LIKE EVERYTHING ELSE in the palace, our apartments were extravagant.

1. *One grand entrance hall, bright with gold drapes and glass mirrors, and small obsidian dragon figurines—not as detailed as the pair on the river, but impressive nonetheless.*

2. *One public parlor with a domed ceiling, twenty marbled columns, and a fountain set into the very center of the mosaic floor. Its splash filled the room, loud enough to mask our footfalls—or anyone else's.*

3. *One formal dining room, large enough to seat thirty, with gold and blue silk tapestries hung along the walls. A small doorway on the far side led to a kitchen, but we weren't permitted back there.*

4. *Ten "smaller" guest suites, each with their own private parlors, bedroom, dining room, washrooms, and servant rooms. One had been assigned to each of us—except for Chenda*

and Gerel, who insisted on sharing—along
with a wardrobe full of clothes and an
attendant to keep our rooms clean and help
us dress.

Alusha said we'd been given apartments reserved for the empress's most esteemed guests, but it felt like a grand house, big enough that anyone who lived here didn't have to see another human for days if they didn't want to bother.

"You could get lost in here." Ilina stood in the public parlor, gazing at the fountain where LaLa and Crystal zipped between streams of water, chasing and splashing each other. "And we'll never get them out of that."

I dropped my head back to look into the dome. A spiral of light sigils shone brightly against the engraved marble and gold. At the point, a skylight revealed a shock of blue and brilliant sun. "Do you think Paorah came here? Do you think she gave him these rooms?"

Ilina sank onto one of the sofas that stood around the fountain. "If he came here, surely he would have realized he could not win a battle against the empire's might. Not away from our gods. Not without a thousand giant noorestones. I've never seen anything like this place. I've never *imagined* anything like it. Don't tell your mother, but it makes your house look like a cute summer cottage."

"What does that make your house?"

"A hovel." She shook her head in amazement.

"Compared to this, my house is that cabin we stayed in after the Pit."

"Ah, yes. The one that blew apart in the storm."

"Exactly."

I sat next to her, feeling so tiny in this huge space. The others were in their own rooms, unpacking or looking at the treasures that filled every surface. If this was where the empress kept her favored guests, what did *her* rooms look like?

"Paorah is desperate," I said at last. "And desperate people take desperate risks."

"Like us." She rested her cheek on my shoulder. "I can't believe we're here. In the Algotti Empire. In the imperial palace."

In the fountain, LaLa splashed in the pool of water while Crystal stalked her from one of the spouts. The moment LaLa ducked her face underwater and blew a burst of fire—making steam rise above her—Crystal dove and they tumbled around the wet tile with tiny shrieks of joy.

"Be careful," Ilina warned. "We won't come in after you if you drown."

A lie, and the little beasts knew it.

"I suppose it makes sense that you'd be here," Ilina murmured. "You're the Hopebearer. You're important. Everyone knows who you are. Even the empress, apparently. But the rest of us? We don't belong here."

"None of us belong here. We belong in the Fallen

Isles, surrounded by dragons, the sea, and our gods. But all that's in trouble, and if none of the people appointed to the continuation of the Fallen Isles are going to help it, then we must. Dragon trainer. Personal guard. Annoying little sister. Disgraced warrior. Unseated Lady of Eternal Dawn."

"And Aaru?"

My heart fluttered at his name. "He had a lot of jobs on Idris. The last was to oversee men who sorted trash."

Ilina cringed. "I bet your mother will love that."

"She does seem to like him, actually. Or maybe she just didn't see him as anything more than an escort. Most people underestimate him."

"They shouldn't," she murmured. "Not after what happened at the ruins."

She meant the pulse of his grief, that surge of silence that smothered every sound for leagues around us. It was the Voice of Idris, able to silence any sound, even the deep note of noorestones that made them glow.

"I'm glad you're all here with me," I said after a moment. "I wouldn't want to be here by myself."

And what I didn't say: it was hard enough, knowing exactly how many days I had left as a human. I didn't want to spend a single one of them without the people I loved most.

"I think you would do all right if you had to be here alone." She bumped against me. "You've been managing your anxiety a lot better recently."

"It's because you're here." I said it teasingly, but it was true. Having my best friends helped more than I could tell her.

"You make me blush."

"And noorestones, I think. Their fire burns those buzzy feelings away, at least for a little while." I frowned at the floor. "It would have been nice if I'd had this years ago."

"It was inconsiderate of them to wait so long to be this helpful." Ilina pulled herself straight and clicked for the dragons. "When do we speak with Empress Apolla?" She held up a hand as Crystal flapped over, spraying water everywhere. "There was a schedule in my room, but it only had tours of the palace and meals with strangers. How long do they think we're going to be here?"

"My schedule says this evening, before I join her for dinner." I looked toward the other rooms. "Surely every-one is going."

Ilina shook her head. "I don't think the rest of us are invited."

"Maybe I can ask Alusha—"

"No." Ilina brushed water off Crystal. "I think we should follow our schedules. Be the best guests we pos-sibly can. We want them to have every reason to help us, right? So let's be agreeable and easy. If we need to fight something, we want to be in a strong position to argue."

"You think that's better than showing spine first thing? We don't want them to push us around."

She tapped her chin. "Hristo and Gerel would say

to insist, but I think we want to be diplomatic. Chenda would agree."

I nodded.

"Talk to the empress tonight. The rest of us will go to the events scheduled." She nodded toward one of the ten thousand decorative tables in the parlor, covered with dragon figurines. "Clearly, they like dragons around here, and so do we. Between all of us, we should be able to learn about any legends regarding the first dragon. That's our priority, right?"

Was it? Getting the bones felt like a priority, but I had to be practical, too. Ships and safe harbor could save so many people—and we *knew* that. There was no doubt.

The dragon bones . . .

"I think you should take a noorestone with you tonight, though. Just in case."

I nodded, although Nine would no doubt have told her superiors about my control over the noorestones. I just hoped that the empress's guards didn't view a small crystal as a weapon.

"LaLa isn't invited to dinner," I said. "If you can believe it."

At the sound of her name, my little dragon looked up and sent a questioning spurt of fire.

"Rude," Ilina agreed, and together we got up to take another look around the apartments, noting the differences between our rooms and the wardrobes full of clothes someone had chosen for us. All the dresses were cut in what

I assumed was the imperial style, with long, loose sleeves, tight bodices, and flowing skirts. And for those who wore shirts and trousers, those were of similar cuts, elegant and expensive. Aaru, for his part, opened his wardrobe and closed it right away—even though everything inside was suitably subdued. It was all just so *expensive*. Meanwhile, Chenda had already changed into one of the dresses.

"Nine must have given them our measurements." Chenda smoothed the green brocade down her ribs. "If I didn't like this dress so much, I'd be unsettled."

Gerel didn't say anything. She just sat on the sofa in their private parlor, admiring Chenda as she turned to get a better look in the mirror.

Lunch came, and we were all summoned to the big dining room, where Alusha stood at the head of the table. "Tonight, you will all attend dinners with different officials. I will explain the proper way to take a meal with such esteemed company. Pay attention, because your performance reflects on me. If you make fools of yourselves, you make a fool of me. Furthermore, I do not care what customs are similar or different. I'm not here to learn about your vanishing islands."

She wasn't here to be the least bit tactful, either.

Still, I didn't want to embarrass myself, so I paid close attention as she went over the multitude of rules: who took the first bite, what order to eat the food, and even the proper (by imperial standards) way to wipe one's mouth.

The level of protocol made the most formal state

dinners at home seem casual, but I, at least, had some background in eating while obeying dozens of unspoken rules. Chenda and Zara, too. The others struggled a little more, but everyone tried.

Once lunch was finished, attendants whisked me back to my rooms to dress for my meeting with the empress, filling my head with more protocol and advice as they worked. They washed and combed my hair, brushed creams and powders onto my face, and scrubbed and painted my nails. Then, at last, they said I was ready.

I emerged from my suite, glittering in the uneven light of a hundred sigils. The gown was possibly the finest thing I'd ever worn, though I wouldn't dream of telling my old seamstress. The fitted bodice was gold and blue silk, a topaz-beaded sun burning on my abdomen, with spiraling rays of light emanating outward. The skirt—the deep blue of a sea at midnight—flared off my hips and swirled around my ankles. The stiffer brocade of my bodice descended down the back, all the way to the floor, to create the illusion of a heavy golden cloak over the lighter silk.

They'd left my hair long and loose, except for the front, which they'd swept back with a comb, gold and studded with topaz sunbursts. As for my face, the attendants had decided to keep the cosmetics simple, darkening only my eyelids and lashes, and coloring my lips a deep red. My scar showed, highlighted with my hair pulled back, but I didn't mind; looking in the mirror wasn't a shock anymore.

At my entrance, the others turned and stared. Aaru's breath caught as he stepped forward, then stopped. Still, his expression was soft and admiring, making my heart flutter with warmth. I'd liked his surprise before—in Anahera, when we'd left for the ball—but the way he looked at me *now* was different. His gaze said that he thought I was beautiful, and his step closer said I was approachable: a Mira he knew and loved and trusted.

"You look amazing." Ilina smiled. "Ready to meet an empress."

I flushed. "You too." They were all dressed for dinner, looking finer than I'd ever seen them. But there was no time to pay more compliments; Alusha scowled and gestured for me to go with her, and with Nine's warnings in mind, I followed.

Just as I was about to step out of the suite, tapping drew my attention. Aaru. The quiet code. He said, ::Careful what you say. They have listening magic.::

CHAPTER TWENTY-FOUR

AARU'S WARNING HAUNTED ME THROUGH THE GREAT halls of the imperial palace, but even with the knowledge that none of our conversations would be secret, I couldn't help but admire the glorious archways, the detailed murals, and the masterfully cut statues we passed. It was almost enough to make me lose track of my numbers, but even here, in a faraway land with strange magic, my mind counted away.

As we walked, Alusha gave more and more instructions—how to stand, where to look, how often to breathe—and I put it all in my head, the same way I memorized speeches or Mother's directions before an event. Occasionally, other people traversing the halls would look over, but if anyone realized I was from the Fallen Isles, they didn't show it. Or maybe they simply didn't care. What were we to them but a mere curiosity?

At last, we paused in front of huge, gold-embossed doors, waiting as the pair of guards hauled them open.

I felt it before I saw it, like a fire in my chest, and a rushing in my ears, and a *knowing* in my soul.

Power.

Recognition.

My heart thundered as I lifted my eyes into the chamber beyond the doors. At first, all I saw was gold and white marble: columns and banners and fourteen statues of the Upper Gods; I noted Suna and Theofania and Zabel, among others, and wondered if they called the Upper Gods by the same names we did, and if they acknowledged the Fallen Gods at all, and who—if anyone—they really worshiped.

At the far end of the chamber, a young woman clad in gold and white sat on a heavy throne, but it was what rested next to her that captured my whole attention.

A dragon skull.

It was enormous, as big as a house, with dozens of still-sharp teeth and empty eye sockets that seemed to stare straight into my soul.

The neck and spine extended beyond it, behind the throne, curving upward toward the gargantuan wings; the bones of the left wing stretched into an arc over the empress's throne, framing her. Strangely, as light glimmered over the curves, I thought I saw scales. Faint, iridescent, and maybe my imagination. But the effect was beautiful.

The skeleton took up an entire chamber beyond the throne, lit with those eerie, flickering sigils. Against these massive bones, the light was all wrong. It should have been steady, cool blue-white, and sharp. It should have come from noorestones, the light of the Fallen Isles.

Nevertheless, we were here. Together.

The rushing in my ears became a roar, washing through my entire body. Muscles in my back ached, trying to stretch wings I wasn't wearing. My throat tingled with the echoes of sparks. Fire. Smoke.

Standing there, dwarfed in the shadow of these colossal bones, I could feel those first dreams—of great wings and burning stars, of fire and screams, of power untold—and I knew I'd reached the one I'd traveled across an ocean to find.

The first dragon.

Fire and death and sky incarnate.

My twin across time.

"At last." The words tasted like smoke.

The *Drakontos celestus*

FOR TWO THOUSAND YEARS, I WAITED.

From the moment the arrow pierced me. From the moment my body crashed to this strange land. From the moment I closed my eyes and the earth began its long burial. From the moment people dug up my bones.

I waited for the one who would bring me home. I waited for the one who would make me whole.

While I waited, I watched everything, letting my mind slip in and out of the clouds, using starlight as my vessel. I watched my birthplace change and grow and begin to eat itself. And now I watched her.

She was a small creature, human and breakable, but a fire burned at her center. She carried the soul of a dragon. She was everything I needed.

AT LAST.

CHAPTER TWENTY-FIVE

From the corner of my eye, I saw Alusha give me a sidelong look. "What's wrong with you?"

My mind wheeled, still trying to make sense of what I was seeing:

The bones of the first dragon—the Fallen Gods' first and most beloved child—trapped here, displayed for Empress Apolla's pleasure. To make *her* look powerful.

"Hopebearer?" A note of concern entered Alusha's tone. I couldn't imagine what I looked like now, just standing here and staring not at the empress, but the skeleton of an ancient and powerful and dead dragon.

"I'm fine." I wrenched my eyes away from the skull. "I'm ready."

Alusha cast me another dubious look, but then she

gave my name to a young man standing on the inside of the door. He, too, shot me a sidelong glance filled with curiosity before he turned back to the empress's throne room and lifted his voice. "Mira Minkoba of the Fallen Isles, Your Eminence. The Hopebearer, the Dragonhearted."

At the far end of the chamber, framed by brilliant light and a great dragon's skeletal wing, the young woman lifted her hand, and Alusha nudged me into the room.

"Do not embarrass me," she muttered. "I have to fetch your friends now, but I'll know how you did. Remember to bow when you reach Her Eminence."

Somehow, I remained on my feet. I registered her words. I remembered how to be the Hopebearer, in spite of the first dragon staring at me.

I moved forward, my shoulders thrown back and my head high. My shoes sank into the soft rug that ran from the door to the empress. As if the great dragon skeleton at her side were nothing but decoration.

But I knew.

With every step, I could feel the first dragon's presence thrumming through the floor, pounding into my heart, sending pieces of me into the wide-open sky.

She was ancient.

She was power.

She was everything.

But I couldn't let myself get lost in her now. I had to focus. Be in this moment.

I pulled myself together, piece by piece—out of the

sky, out of her eyes, out of her all-consuming presence—until I was just Mira again. Just a girl who loved dragons. Just a girl who'd come here to help her people.

It took all my effort, but I focused my attention on Empress Apolla to find her studying me: my movements, my manners, my preoccupation with the dragon skeleton.

Aside from twenty or so guards stationed around the room, she and I were alone. No court. No secretaries. No servants. She and I just gazed at each other; I would not be the one to look away first.

She was younger than I'd expected, perhaps only a few years my senior, but her hazel eyes held a weight belonging to someone three times her age. Otherwise, her brown skin was smooth and unblemished, brushed with dark powder around her eyes and in the hollows of her cheekbones. She wore white brocade silk, with gold embellishments emblazoned across every stitch of fabric. A thin circlet rested on her brow, and jeweled bands were clasped around her forearms. Her posture, stiff and straight, did not change as I approached.

Ten steps. Twenty.

I reached the dais and stopped, keeping my expression neutral as I met her eyes. "Your Eminence. I'm glad to meet you."

Her head tilted slightly. "You will not bow?"

"I offer you my respect," I said. "And my thanks for your hospitality and consideration. But I cannot bow to you, or to anyone else."

One heavy eyebrow lifted. "I could force you."

"I hope that you will not." My heart pounded, but I let my mind touch the noorestone in the satchel at my hip. Its fire singed the edges off my anxiety.

She glanced beyond me—at the grand hall occupied by only her guards—and then nodded. "I am glad I arranged to meet you without an audience." She stood, her gown rippling around her as she moved. Slowly, like a careful dancer, she came down the steps. One. Two. Three. "Otherwise, I would have had to make an example, and that is not what I want."

We stood face-to-face, the Algotti empress and me. We were of similar height, but where I was lean from Mother's constant fretting over my food, followed by decans in the Pit and fleeing across the Fallen Isles, the empress had a softer figure, filling out her gown in a way I would have described as pleasant if she hadn't been the most powerful, and therefore dangerous, person in the empire.

"You're younger than I thought you'd be." She had the same accent as everyone else I'd met here—with longer and sharper syllables—although she spoke with a gravity the others didn't possess.

No, she probably didn't have the accent. Not here. In the empire, I had the accent.

She looked at my scar. "What happened?"

"Someone tried to bleed the Hopebearer out of me."

"That is not a thing that can be taken unless you allow it." A faint smile eased the weight in her eyes. "It becomes you."

I resisted the impulse to touch the ridge of scar tissue. Instead, I nodded, and for a moment more, we just looked at each other, evaluating. What the other wanted. How hard she would fight for it. Our chances of success if neither of us was willing to bow to the other.

Then the empress turned and inclined her head. "Walk with me."

I fell into step with her. She had a slow, stately rhythm, as though nothing could entice her to walk at a normal pace. But it gave me a chance to see the room, the beautiful galleries and gods and marble floor, and I stored away the details to tell the others later. They would like it, and if anyone was truly listening to our conversations, they'd quickly grow bored.

Then I would tell them about the first dragon, whose presence followed me throughout the wide chamber, twisting into the back of my mind.

Light sigils flickered as we glided by. What about listening sigils?

"Nine reports that your high magistrate intends to betray me," Empress Apolla said at last. There was no accusation in her tone, no hint that she blamed all of the Fallen Isles for his duplicity, but I could still hear a question of *my* authenticity in there. Would *I* betray her if we struck a bargain? I hadn't bowed, after all.

"He intends to bring armies to your shores."

She looked straight ahead as we walked past a guard. "Perhaps he seeks only to defend himself. The Algotti Empire is vast, and he must be frightened of us."

I couldn't imagine Paorah frightened, and I didn't think she believed that, either. "Your Eminence, the high magistrate is a proud and ambitious man. Perhaps he does fear you, but he won't be content simply defending himself. He must solidify his power over the remains of the Fallen Isles, and that will require more action than taking a handful of people to safety. No, he must destroy in order to build something new. He sees it as his duty to his goddess—a duty that just so happens to benefit him."

"He would not be content to settle here?"

"He worships the goddess of destruction, the trickster." I looked at her, a sharp, dark profile against the pale room. "In the Fallen Isles, we have a saying: Anahera asks answers. She's always several steps ahead of the rest of us. Her people tend to be clever. Some would say they tend to be schemers. High Magistrate Paorah is smart, manipulative, and a devout believer in destruction. Though Anahera cautions her people to carefully consider the consequences, Paorah will destroy whatever he must to further his own goals."

Now she did look at me, a hint of curiosity in her eyes. "Anahera teaches the eternal cycle."

"Benevolent destruction is what they call it." My thoughts tried to flicker back to the passage in *The Book of Destruction* I'd read on the skimmer den—*It is sacrifice that enables change*—but I pushed aside my own fears. I needed to focus on *this. Here. Now.*

"Ah." She kept walking, and I had the sense that she

was thinking deeply, weighing every word she spoke, every tone she took. We reached the double doors and the boy who'd announced me, then turned to walk up the other side of the chamber. The guards watched us without watching us, standing as still as the statues. Maybe they *were* statues, and they were yet another example of imperial power.

Questions teetered on the edge of my tongue. I wanted to ask about their magic, the images of the Upper Gods lining her grand hall, why she'd arranged for this meeting without an audience, and how she'd come to possess the bones of the first dragon, but everyone had warned me against voicing too much curiosity, and—even if I wouldn't bow to the empress—that was one of Alusha's many rules I could follow. Besides, I didn't want to accidentally reveal anything secret through my questions.

The first dragon grew in the back of my thoughts, ever more present.

"Nine also reports that you possess the ability to forestall High Magistrate Paorah's attack." It was said without question, but hinted at one nonetheless.

"As long as his attack comes by noorestone. I have no armies of my own."

The empress looked at me, her expression inscrutable. "Do you not?"

"Not as far as I'm aware." My thoughts fluttered back to my dreams, filled with images of the dishonored, great wings of dragons, and young girls floating in the middle of the ocean. "Even if I did have anything that could be called an army, yours is more than adequate to defend this coast from any army Paorah could muster. As Nine said, it would be little more than an inconvenience for you to retake Sunder or any other coastal city. And he doesn't have the strength to take them from you to begin with—not without those noorestones."

She gave a single nod. "Tell me of your noorestones."

"Surely you already know all about them," I said. "From your spies."

"Certainly. But they can only tell me so much. You, on the other hand, grew up with these crystals. Tell me about them."

As I reached for the satchel on my hip, a guard came to life—moving toward me—but the empress held up a hand and he fell back into position. I removed the small noorestone and cupped it in the palm of my hand.

We'd stopped walking, and now she looked into the bright crystal. "It is beautiful."

I flattened my hand and held it toward her. "Hold it, if you want. It's not hot."

With her same careful movements, she plucked the noorestone from my palm and turned it in her fingers. "We have no need for these," she murmured. "Our magic is more than sufficient. But still, such light pulled from the very bones of Noore . . ."

"Noorestones have an inner fire," I said. "In stable noorestones like this, energy trapped within is released as light. They're perfectly safe." It seemed unwise to tell her about the strange substance Altan's people had poured onto regular noorestones to make the energy transfer into Aaru. It wasn't her business, and I didn't know what they'd used, anyway. "Most people can't hear it, but there's a soft hum that comes from within the crystals. It vibrates, imperceptible to most of us, but its frequency causes the energy to release as radiant light."

She offered the noorestone back to me. "And that is how you manipulate it? By changing the frequency at which the stone vibrates?"

That sounded a lot more technical than what I felt when I connected with noorestones, but I nodded, because it was as good an explanation as any.

"Show me."

I glanced at the guards nearby.

"They will not interfere," she said.

With a nod, I opened myself to the noorestone. Immediately, a knot of anxiety loosened and fluttered away; my shoulders relaxed; I breathed in and hushed the stone so that it dimmed and went nearly dark. Only the faintest light glimmered from the cool blue depths. Then I urged it bright—so bright that even when I squeezed my hand into a fist, the light blazed out from between my fingers.

The empress looked away, blinking to clear her vision. "That is sufficient."

I released the noorestone, and it returned to its normal luminosity. The crystal was cool and smooth under my fingers as I placed it in the satchel, my demonstration complete. "It isn't a trick meant to impress others, Your Eminence. I know of no one else who can affect noorestones the same way. The gods saw fit to give me such an incredible gift—to help my people, not to entertain them."

A hint of a frown tugged at her mouth. "I understand. My apologies for imposing."

I was actually glad she'd wanted a demonstration. It had given me the perfect opportunity to show *my* power, and that I wasn't helpless while I was here.

And—perhaps—that *she* needed *my* help, just as I needed hers.

"The noorestones Paorah is bringing here are huge. Unstable. The explosive potential is devastating, and if he were to place these noorestones where they will cause secondary explosions . . ." I didn't need to finish the thought. She already understood.

"But you would be able to prevent that," she said, "using this ability you possess."

I nodded.

"That is one possible solution to the threat he poses," she murmured. "Another, simpler solution, is to ensure his noorestones never make land. If they detonate, then they do so aboard his own ships."

"Then innocent people will die."

"But they are not my people." She turned and strode toward the dais and the giant skull next to it, moving at a faster pace than before. "Besides, can't you prevent them from detonating on the ships? Your task is just as easily accomplished away from my shores."

I stared at her, aghast.

"Hopebearer, you've said nothing to persuade me that I need your aid, and nothing to persuade me to come to yours." She glanced over her shoulder. "Yes, I know why you came here. You want me to give you ships. You want to assume command over the arrangement I made with High Magistrate Paorah. It's sweet that you want to help, but you've given me nothing my own spies haven't. There is no bargain we could make that would outweigh the one I've made with him, and if he attempts to betray me, I will simply destroy him."

What? That was it?

The empress reached her throne, adjusted her gown, and sat. "You are dismissed now, Mira Minkoba. Stay in the palace as my guest for a few more days. Enjoy Sunder. But we have nothing further to discuss."

Fury filled me, but I kept it locked deep inside of me where she—and her guards—wouldn't see it. How could anyone be so callous? The people of the Fallen Isles needed help, and she had so much. Couldn't she spare just a little?

No. She hadn't become an empress by being generous. For all her shows of magnanimity, it was just that: a show. It was a display of her wealth and power. Even her decision to take this meeting without an audience was part of that pretense of friendliness, of intimacy. There was nothing real in her except her desire to take from those of us who would soon have nothing. Our information. Our lives. Our dragons.

Dragons.

The first dragon's skull stared at me, evaluating, commanding me to be worthy. If I was to be like her, able to entreat the gods on behalf of my people, I needed to be stronger.

"The dragons the high magistrate sent you—how are they? Healthy?"

Interest flashed in her pale eyes, but she said nothing.

"At the summit recently, he told everyone that he'd sent seven dragons to you—as a gesture of goodwill. But you should know that he also plundered the sanctuaries of the Fallen Isles, stealing dragons in the night. When people asked questions, he led them to believe that *you* were the one behind those thefts. He painted *you* as the villain of the Fallen Isles." I glided forward now, my steps long and even. "He kept dozens of stolen dragons in first-century ruins above Flamecrest. I found them. I intended to free them. But what I discovered was sick, dying dragons."

A storm passed across the empress's face.

"How are the dragons the high magistrate sent to you?" I asked again. "Are they well?"

"They've taken ill." Her voice was soft.

I shivered. I could feel them in the distance, faint threads of connection stretching and spinning between us. In them, I sensed the walls of their illness—the same

310

thing that had weighed down the dragons in the ruins above Flamecrest. "I can heal them."

"That is unnecessary."

"Are you that proud?" I stood before her throne again, no longer the Hopebearer in this discussion, but the Dragonhearted. So close to the first dragon's bones, I could feel the ancient power rippling off them—into me. "Or did Paorah send people to heal them?"

"Yes."

"And have they been successful?"

She said nothing.

"I healed the dragons in the ruins," I said, stepping up the dais until I stood over her. "I felt their agony, just as I can feel that of the dragons placed in your care. They won't recover. The people sent to heal them will be unsuccessful. They're dying, Apolla, and if you turn me away, you'll be turning away the only benefit of all this business with the Fallen Isles."

"But *you* can heal them?" Now, a note of hope entered her voice, and for the first time it wasn't a carefully planted display of emotion. Now that I heard the difference, I'd never miss it again.

Suddenly, she was just a young woman who'd grown up listening to tales of dragons, who saw the *Drakontos titanuses* at the mouth of the River Akron every day, and who sat on a throne guarded by the bones of a dead dragon. Now, finally, she'd been given the opportunity to have living dragons—only for them to wither under her care.

311

In her, I saw a shadowy mirror of myself, raised in a political world though her heart belonged elsewhere. But she'd never seen living dragons as a child, never held a baby *Drakontos raptus* and fallen deeply in love, and maybe she'd never needed them in the same way. She didn't have a dragon soul inside her, after all, straining to get out. The sanctuary for dragons had been a sanctuary for me, too, the only place I'd never felt trapped and tangled in anxiety. But Apolla had accepted her role as empress—perhaps too soon—and here she was: a conqueror with dying dragons.

Perhaps she would decorate her throne room with their bones, too.

"Yes." Part of me hated her; she had everything, and still she couldn't find it within herself to help someone without some kind of benefit to her reign. "I can heal them."

"And in exchange, you desire ships to rescue your people." That cool tone was back, a lifetime of polish placed over the real girl.

I *wanted* the bones gracing the wide, sigil-lit chamber behind her. I *wanted* to appease the Fallen Gods and beg them back to sleep. I *wanted* my world to be made whole. And I *wanted* to grow old with all my friends and my dragon—but as a human.

But if she put up so much of a fight over a few *ships*, then she would never give me those dragon bones.

That didn't change the fact that I needed the ships.

An ugly sensation crept up inside me.

I could heal the dragons, of that I was certain, but they would still be here in the empire. Away from their rising gods. Locked away for the empress's menagerie.

What if they grew sick again?

Or what if they lived out the rest of their lives as her pets?

If I healed the dragons, I was choosing people over them.

If I didn't heal the dragons, my people died, and so did the dragons.

Either way, the dragons lost.

"The high magistrate sent you dead dragons." I made my voice into steel. "But I will heal them if you send ships. The gods are rising, and my people don't have much time."

"Neither do my dragons."

I wanted to argue that they weren't *her* dragons, because dragons belonged to no one but themselves, but I just nodded. Even now, the connections between them and me grew stronger; visions danced behind my eyes, faint suggestions of broad sky and jagged mountains, and a great link of an iron shackle. Bile burned up my throat; the dragons were chained down, strapped to the hard earth.

"Take me to them tomorrow." I breathed around the dragons' pain, reaching for my noorestone to soften the edges of their agony. It seemed unfair that I had the luxury of doing so, but I needed to focus, and I couldn't—not with them in the back of my head. It was hard enough with the first dragon here. "But there is one thing you can do now."

"What?" she asked.

"Have the keepers remove the chains."

Her eyes widened with true surprise, but it was covered quickly. "How could you know about the chains? Did someone tell you?"

"The dragons showed me." I drew a heavy breath. "I will need noorestones to heal them—the giant ones from the high magistrate's ships should suffice—but they will be more comfortable without the chains, and perhaps I can help them in the meantime."

"I'll take you there," she said. "First thing in the morning."

"You'll want my friend Ilina, as well. She's incredible with dragons." And, hopefully, her father would be there. She deserved to see him.

Empress Apolla nodded. "And your little dragons? Will you bring them, too?" There she was again—the real Apolla. "Perhaps they could bring the others comfort."

"Perhaps," I agreed. "We'll bring them."

"Good." The empress nodded, and her gaze flickered beyond me. "Back to your stations."

I glanced behind me and found all twenty of the guards with their swords drawn, points toward my back.

Because I'd stepped onto the empress's dais, disrespecting her.

They'd only been waiting for her order.

"Let's go to dinner," she suggested, sweeping one arm toward the main floor.

I paused, considering what I'd just learned of her. And to allow myself to stand beside the first dragon just a moment longer.

But then we stepped down together, and she said, "I'm glad you didn't bow earlier, when you came in."

"Oh?"

"You should have seen the way Paorah prostrated himself. It was pitiful, and obviously false. I hated him."

"You're far from alone in that feeling."

She smiled, and there was a moment of each of us wondering if we'd won the other to our side.

But I needed her help more than she needed mine, and she knew that.

There were listening sigils planted somewhere in our suite.

And she had the bones of the first dragon. Here. Displayed.

No matter how she felt about dragons, she'd been willing to let the Fallen Isles die without so much as lifting a finger to help. Empress Apolla was not my friend.

This was no triumph.

CHAPTER TWENTY-SIX

A SENSE OF WRONGNESS FILLED THE SUITE WHEN I
returned from dinner.

The dragons were perched on the fountain spouts,
bouncing quietly as they looked up through the skylight,
while my friends and sister had pulled several of the
benches close together. They'd all changed out of dinner
clothes and into one of the other outfits provided, but no
one looked comfortable.

I paused in the entryway, drawing glances and raised
eyebrows, but that was the only greeting offered.

"Is everything all right?" I asked.

"Perfect." Ilina flashed a dazzling smile from where
she sat beside Hristo.

"What Feisty said." Gerel lounged next to Chenda,

who wore an expression of practiced pleasantness.

Only Aaru and Zara seemed normal—one quiet, and the other pouting.

"That's good. How were your dinners?" I stood there awkwardly as they told me about their engagements for the evening, the people they'd met, and all the wonders of the imperial palace. Their hosts had found them charming or sweet or impressive—all that applied to each person—and every word they spoke was filled with flattery and praise.

And then I understood.

They knew they were being spied on.

Well, good.

I excused myself to change into something less expensive, and when I came back, Aaru found my eyes and patted the seat beside him. I slipped my hand into his. ::You told them?::

He kissed my temple, as though in greeting. ::Yes. Careful.::

My skin tingled where he'd kissed. How . . . strange. Not that I minded, but Aaru barely kissed me in private.

Which meant something *else* was wrong. Something besides the fact that we were being listened to.

I stilled, then asked, ::Can they see us, too?::

::Not sure.::

Which made obvious quiet code hazardous, and writing impossible.

It was a devious plan on the imperials' part: make us assume that we were always being observed, and we'd

317

keep our conversations pleasant and neutral. The benefit to them was, of course, if we didn't figure it out, they might catch us conspiring against them. Or, even if they didn't assume the worst of us, they'd know ahead of time what we planned to use in negotiations; they'd be able to prepare a response for anything we came up with.

There was no benefit for us at all.

Unless . . .

We could misdirect them.

But that depended on whether they knew *we* knew they were observing us. What a mess.

"How was your meeting with the empress?" Ilina asked.

"Productive." I weighed my words carefully. "We came to an arrangement that benefits both the Fallen Isles and the Algotti Empire. First, Empress Apolla has committed ten ships to our cause, all as big as the skimmer den, but equipped with only half the skimmers. They'll have more space for living quarters, but still allow for search and rescue. She's also generously agreed to stock them with food and other supplies."

Everyone's shoulders dropped as a small measure of tension left them. It wasn't enough—it wouldn't save everyone—but this would help a few more people find safety.

"The ships are scheduled to depart in three days. I need to stay here, as I've sworn to help defend against Paorah's noorestones, and I assume Hristo will insist on staying, too—"

"Yes."

"But anyone who wants to help with rescue efforts in the Fallen Isles is free to go."

They just nodded, putting that option away for later. I doubted anyone would go—*maybe* Chenda and Gerel—but they needed to know I wouldn't be upset.

"What is Empress Apolla getting out of this?" Chenda's tone was neutral, but there was real worry in her eyes. "Are we taking over the agreement High Magistrate Paorah made?"

"I don't know all of the details of the agreement they made, but I told her I could offer something he could not."

"What is that?" Hristo frowned.

"In addition to helping stop any noorestone attacks, I can heal the dragons Paorah sent here."

"Mira." Ilina's expression twisted. "Those dragons belong in the Fallen Isles."

"I know." And there was no harm in Apolla hearing that, because she knew, too. "But we must be realistic about what's happening in the Fallen Isles. Even if she were willing to void her entire agreement with Paorah and return the dragons to us, what would they go home to?"

Ilina slumped a little. "You think they have a better chance of survival here."

"I think neither of us can guess where all the other Fallen Isles dragons are going. We can't promise safety for these. If Her Eminence follows our advice tomorrow, and I'm able to heal them once the giant noorestones get here, then perhaps they'll be able to live out their full lives."

No one looked comforted.

"We may end up here, too." I hated to remind them that being stranded in the empire was a real possibility. "The people of the Fallen Isles may have nowhere else to go. When the Great Abandonment is complete, we can't just live on ships. We'll have to go *somewhere*."

It was such a sobering thought. And it was also the truth. The eclipse was real, the bones of the first dragon were real, and it seemed I would lose my humanity to the effort of keeping the Fallen Gods from leaving. But just because I asked didn't mean they would oblige.

Which meant we needed Empress Apolla to like us. We needed her to be willing to take in thousands—potentially tens of thousands—of refugees.

"You have a point." Ilina leaned on Hristo's shoulder and sighed. "But I don't like it."

"I'm sorry. But I do have good news. You and I"—I nodded to Ilina—"are going to the dragon park tomorrow morning to see if we can help make the dragons there more comfortable until Paorah's ships arrive."

Ilina closed her eyes and exhaled. Her father was with the dragons Paorah had sent. She'd get to see him, at last.

"You might enjoy Empress Apolla," I told Ilina. "She's . . ." I considered all the ways one might describe the empress, and which ways she might not mind over-hearing. Where the high magistrate ruled through fear, Apolla ruled through a careful display of power, promised security, and fear disguised as awe. "She is formidable," I said at last. "And I know it won't make much of a differ-ence in your feelings about where dragons belong, but she does seem to like them."

"Clearly." Gerel motioned around the public parlor. "All these little dragons, that pair of obsidian *titanuses* out-side—none of us thought she put those up for our arrival."

Finally, an opening. I leaned forward. "Those are the least of her dragons. You should have seen her throne room. She has dragon bones."

Everyone went still. Then breathed, as though remem-bering all at once they were being observed. Aaru squeezed my hand. ::First dragon?::

::Yes.::

"What kind of dragon bones?" Zara asked. "Do we need to worry about those two?" She pointed at LaLa and Crystal, swaying together as they gazed at the sky, though the light sigils must have obscured all the stars.

"It was one of the biggest dragons I've ever seen." That was a lie. She'd been *the* biggest dragon I'd ever seen. "Truly, it was an impressive display of Empress Apolla's power."

"And now what?" Gerel yawned. "You want a huge dragon skeleton, too? Imagine how Paorah would tremble."

"Exactly."

"I'd like to see that skeleton," Ilina said. "If someone found those bones here, they must be very, very old, prob-ably from the Sundering itself."

"That sounds likely." Chenda looked at me. "Could we

arrange a viewing? I think we'd all like to see it, if possible."

"We should ask." I put on my best Hopebearer smile. "Empress Apolla seemed quite accommodating, and perhaps she'd like to know more about the skeleton, too."

Ilina raised an eyebrow—did I mean to say I wanted the empress to know about the first dragon?—and said, "You know I'm happy to talk about dragons until ears fall off. Don't tempt me to bore anyone, though. I wouldn't want to get kicked out of the empire because people don't want seven-hour lectures on the correlation between wingspan and the number of vertebrae."

"Anyone should feel honored to hear you speak." I grinned. "All right. That's our plan. Tomorrow, Ilina and I will visit the dragon park, and we'll ask about everyone viewing the dragon skeleton before the ships leave. We have another decan before we should start expecting Paorah to get here, so everyone who remains here should use that time to make allies among Empress Apolla's court. We'll need all the friends we can get, if we can't find anywhere to take our people."

Zara shook her head and frowned. "This seems too big for us."

"I know." I wished I had something reassuring to tell her, but I didn't want to lie. "The Mira Treaty should have taken care of all of this, but it didn't. Our parents' generation, and their parents' generation, should have done something, but they didn't. So it falls to us."

"That doesn't make me feel any better, and when Mother gets here, I'm going to tell her." A smile pulled at the corner of her mouth.

I grinned at her.

As the others went back to discussing schedules and all the people they needed to impress, I leaned back on the bench Aaru and I shared and watched LaLa and Crystal. They were still gazing up, crooning softly at the sky.

::**Are you all right?**:: Aaru's question came against the palm of my hand.

I wasn't. Even with the walls and rooms and vast hallways between us, I could feel the first dragon in the back of my thoughts, waiting for me to take her home. Even with roads and city and sky between us, I could feel the captive dragons as they suffered silently in their sickness. And here, in this chamber, I could feel LaLa and Crystal—entranced by this new place with new things for them to destroy, but missing the Fallen Isles so fiercely it hurt.

It was impossible to explain. It was bigger than mere words, and yet, more personal, too.

The first dragon was a child of the gods, born in the fires of their Fall. She'd fought conquerors until her final moments.

And now, seeing her arranged behind Apolla, as a symbol of *imperial* power—Aaru would have to see it for himself to understand.

Hristo would already understand; all his life, he'd known this feeling I was just discovering.

323

::Mira?:: Aaru looked down at me. "Mira?"

Abruptly, the sense of wrongness I'd felt earlier intensified. On the water spouts, both dragons stiffened and began low, anguished keening.

Everyone lurched to their feet, staring. Slowly, slowly, the dragons started flapping their wings, and their cries grew more frantic.

Aaru went completely still. Ilina and Hristo rushed for the dragons. Chenda and Gerel hugged each other. And Zara looked at me. "What is it?" she asked. "Why are they making that noise?"

"Earthquake." The word came out monotone. "At best, it's an earthquake."

My sister's face drained of color. "And at worst?"

"A third god is rising."

CHAPTER TWENTY-SEVEN

THE NEXT MORNING, A PALL HUNG OVER OUR SUITE
as we prepared for the day. Everyone kept asking which
island it might have been, or if the people might have
had a chance to get to safety. And then, suddenly, we'd
all go quiet, like talking about it made it real.

But it was already real.

Soberly, Ilina and I dressed in our dragon clothes—her
in a sanctuary uniform, and me in a hunting dress and
leggings—and put LaLa and Crystal in their gear. The
dragons resented the restraints, but after last night, they
needed the supervision. The last thing any of us wanted
was to cause some sort of incident because of a grieving
Drakontos raptus.

In spite of the tremor—which we didn't feel here, but

we were told there might be waves—Aaru, Gerel, and Chenda continued their scheduled activities, touring the palace and meeting with various members of the empress's court.

It was dawn when Ilina, Hristo, and I climbed into a large white and gold carriage with the empress, two of her guards, and an older woman who introduced herself as Mekka. She was an imperial historian and would be acting as our guide during the drive to the dragon park.

"The park is on the river, so we could take the imperial barge," the empress said, "but I thought you might like to see the city."

One of her guards pressed his shoulders down and didn't quite hide a scowl, and I got the sense there was an old argument in there: he wanted to keep her as safe as possible, while she was strong-willed and the one who made the rules anyway.

But surely she would be safe in her own city. Even if she wasn't, a cadre of mounted guards surrounded the carriage as we moved down the long flagstone drive, passing fountains and statues and huge monuments to imperial heroes and accomplishments. Our guide enthusiastically described battles and conquests, filling the interior of the carriage with stories of lives and adventures I'd never even considered.

How strange to think of history marching along here, at the same rate it had in the Fallen Isles, but so different from ours. And all this time, we'd been unaware. Not that people lived here—of course we'd known that—but of their lives and struggles and triumphs. Still, it didn't affect us, at least not that we could discern, so most of us had never paused to consider all these lives lived and lost parallel to ours.

I listened to the guide speaking, my gaze fixed out the large window nearest me. Sigils were scratched into the glass, allowing us to see outside. But, when viewed from the other side, the glass seemed darker, almost opaque.

Not only did their history move along a different path than ours, intersecting only now, but even their magic was different. It was a wonder that our languages and writing had remained so similar after two thousand years.

Unless we hadn't been all that separate.

As the carriage sped down the main avenue that ran out of the city, LaLa stayed perched on my knee, preening. Her teeth clicked against hard, smooth scales, drawing glances from the empress and her guards.

The way Apolla looked at LaLa, I could tell she wanted to hold her, but she was too polite to ask. And I wasn't about to offer. Paorah had already sold seven dragons to the Algotti Empire, and I wouldn't give them another, even for a moment.

I stroked down the ridge of scales along LaLa's spine, earning a soft purr, and looked at the buildings we drove by. Close to the palace, everything was big and opulent, dripping wealth like raindrops suspended on a spiderweb. As we moved farther out, the buildings were not as lavish, but still impressive. Everything had a uniform style that suggested a city planned well in advance and built to last centuries.

"Why is the city called Sunder?"

Mekka stopped midsentence—I'd barely realized she'd been talking—and peered at me, as though she'd *known* I'd slipped into my own thoughts but she'd kept speaking because she didn't want the empress to see her frustration. "The name of the city?" The guide frowned. "Well, that's the eternal cycle. Beginnings and endings and beginnings again. Sunder is named for an ending. Stories of the actual events are vague, lost to time and poor record keeping." She said the last part with a tone that suggested she felt personally slighted.

"We know dragons were involved," said Apolla.

"Because of the skeleton in your throne room?" I lifted an eyebrow with practiced curiosity—not too much, but enough to seem genuine.

"Yes, most likely." Mekka picked up the story, happy to have an interested audience at last. "Several other fragments were found along the coast, at least according to records inherited from the Sundered Lands' previous occupants."

"Where are those bones?" Ilina asked.

"In reliquaries and museums throughout the region, close to where they were first discovered. All Algotti emperors and empresses have understood the importance of territories retaining their history."

Who was she trying to convince? Us? Or was she placating Apolla?

"And the obsidian dragons?" I asked. "The pair at the mouth of the river."

Mekka nodded. "They, too, were present long before the empire came to the Sundered Lands."

"Gods willing," Apolla said, "they'll be there long after."

Now there was an interesting revelation. She didn't think the empire would last forever.

I must have shown my surprise, because Apolla just smiled. "I'm no fool, Hopebearer. I know empires end. I can only hope the Algotti Empire endures beyond my reign, and that nothing I do causes it to fall." Her gaze shifted to the street outside. "The eternal cycle gathers up everything in its path. Even, one day, my land."

Sunder. The split between the old and the new world. I closed my eyes and remembered the dreams—the first dragon sweeping down over the land, shooting fire so hot the cliffs ran like liquid.

How interesting to learn the truths of the Sundering had been lost here. Then again, they had largely been lost in the Fallen Isles, too. Time eroded everything.

Apolla's voice turned gentle. "Perhaps it's insensitive to wonder aloud at the Algotti Empire's unknown ending, considering everything you're going through. Please forgive me."

"It's only natural to think about now," I murmured, "when we are here because our world is ending. Of course you'll think about yours, too."

"Is there anything you can do to prevent it?" she asked. "Surely you must be able to find some way to appease your gods, persuade them to stay."

My heart twisted, but I pushed aside my worries about the sacrifice; I couldn't let them distract me here. "Dragons were meant to entreat the gods on our behalf. But our ancestors didn't take care to ensure their survival, and so . . ."

Empress Apolla frowned thoughtfully, but she didn't offer to let us take these dragons back to the Fallen Isles. Perhaps she knew these few would make no difference, or perhaps she simply didn't want to let them go.

We drove the rest of the way in easier conversation. The empress inquired about Crystal's body language, and Ilina answered gladly—it was easier than discussing the end of either of our worlds.

While they talked, I petted LaLa and let my mind wander down the threads already formed with the dragons waiting in the park. Now that we were getting closer, the shapeless horror of their illness grew stronger. I could feel the darkness of their thoughts, the empty weight of their limbs, the undefined boundaries of their bodies and minds.

It felt the same as the dragons back in the ruins above Flamecrest, but lonelier, if that was even possible.

The distance. It had to be the vast distance between this *park* the empress's people had devised, and the dragons' gods. Their families.

"I'd love to hear about the sanctuaries you built in the Fallen Isles," Apolla was saying. "How do you persuade the dragons to come to them? How do you make them stay?"

"We don't make them stay." Somehow, Ilina managed to keep her tone light, but I could almost hear her internal scream. "They know they're safe there. That is why they stay."

Apolla nodded to herself. "I see."

At last, we drove past the last of the fine, orderly buildings, and fields opened up, offering a view of a depthless blue sky and a wide, lazy stretch of the River Akron. Mountains stood sharp in the distance.

Then we arrived.

The dragon park was similar to the sanctuaries at home, but with a decorative wall rather than the imposing structure that stood between public and sanctuary lands. These low walls wouldn't keep even children out.

We took a path into the park, driving by yet more imperial guards, and finally the carriage stopped. When the guards ensured the area was clear, we were allowed to exit.

I couldn't imagine where anyone thought attackers would hide. The park was all flatland with only a few unfamiliar trees pushing up through the ground. The river splashed in the distance, and aside from that, the only interesting features were a small (guarded, obviously) building and the path of glowing white flagstones.

And the dragons.

The seven of them were tangled together, their bodies twisted and lying on top of one another, as though they'd pulled close for comfort and then just never had the energy to move apart. If not for the different colors of their scales, it would have been impossible to tell where one dragon ended and the other began.

"Oh, seven gods," Ilina breathed.

"Can you help them?" The empress looked from Ilina to me. "Others have tried, but without success. I did send a message to ensure their chains were removed."

"They were chained?" Horror tinged Ilina's tone black, but she'd known already; I'd told her last night. "How long have they been like this?"

The empress shook her head. "Decans. They were carried aboard one of our own ships, fast enough to bring them here with minimal time in a closed space. The Anaherans said the dragons had been sedated and would awaken within a few days, so my people took them up the river to this park, which was prepared solely for them. True to the Anaherans' word, the dragons awakened, but they were wild. They breathed fire and nearly killed a man; they were chained down for safety."

My stomach turned over. I wanted to be sick.

Had Paorah explained nothing to her? Had she believed these dragons—living dragons—would be as docile as the skeleton in her throne room?

"They did calm after that, but they crawled into a heap and refused to move."

Ilina reached for me, and I took her hand. On our shoulders, LaLa and Crystal clucked and worried, but they didn't try to lift off. Maybe they'd understood the part about chains.

"I'll—" I shook my head. "I'll try to comfort them a little." I looked at Ilina. "Perhaps you should speak with the keepers."

Faint hope filled her eyes as she passed Crystal's leash to me. "Good idea. Hristo?"

"I'll stay here," he said. "Where I can see both of you."

Ilina walked toward the building, both hands pressed against her stomach. She hesitated in front of the opening door and then rushed to meet her father, who appeared in the doorway. I watched for a moment, allowing myself a breath of relief and happiness for her.

Then I turned toward the pile of dragons.

The rise and fall of breathing was almost imperceptible; I could feel it through our connection more than I could see it. Scales ground against scales, horrible and painful in the back of my head; LaLa whined and shifted from side to side.

I looked at the empress. "It isn't normal for big dragons to form piles like this. It isn't normal for them to want to be anywhere near one another. Dragons this size are lone predators, and territorial. With the exception of visiting mates, they rarely meet. That's why sanctuaries are so big—to allow them to avoid seeing another dragon for decans at a time."

"Then why . . ." The empress didn't finish her question. She already knew the answer.

I shifted both leashes into one hand as Crystal perched on my arm, while LaLa lorded over her from my shoulder. "You should wait here," I told the empress.

A surprised frown crossed her face, but it vanished quickly. She wanted an explanation, but I wasn't going to offer one. Hristo could, if he wanted.

I headed toward the dragons; they needed my care more than anyone else here.

My boots crushed soft grass, then scorched soil. LaLa clucked by my ear, and when I followed her gaze, I saw tracks of bent grass where the chains had been dragged away. Sickness writhed in my stomach.

Finally, I reached the nearest dragon: a *Drakontos mimikus*, colored blue like the softest of skies. I walked around the mound, finding two *ignituses*, a *maior*, a *maximus*, and a *rex*.

Only six.

Then I found the seventh, completely covered by the others: *Drakontos titanus*. Like they'd come to him—the biggest of all—for protection.

My heart broke to see their scales dulled, missing in some places where the shackles had rubbed those first days, before the dragons had stopped moving. Their talons were yellowed and cracked, and—when I held my palm toward the closest dragon—their bodies felt cool.

Along the threads that connected me to them, I felt

334

only an expanding darkness. Silence. Nothing.

My throat closed up and tears stung my eyes. They were so, so sick. Worse than the dragons in the ruins. That darkness in their minds was death, and they were only a breath away from it.

"What is Mira doing?" The voice belonged to Ilina's father, Viktor. "It isn't safe so close to the dragons."

"Trust her," Ilina said. "She can help them."

I pressed my free hand against the *maior*'s left flank. She might have been a statue.

"I've done everything I can," Viktor said. "But no medicine or magic will help them. They're going to die."

They were going to die.

The words turned over in my head, sickening. The high magistrate had not only *given away* seven dragons, but he was killing them, too. Murdering them. Hastening the Great Abandonment.

Had these poor dragons even felt Idris rise? What about the second? Or the island last night?

Did they know their world was falling apart?

I listed toward the dragons until the front of my body pressed against cool scales; the edge of a scale scraped over my scar. Crystal and LaLa readjusted themselves, clicking as they rubbed their noses on the bigger dragons' sides, doing their best to offer comfort.

"Aren't you worried about Crystal and LaLa?" Ilina's father asked. "What if they catch the same illness as the others?"

"They won't," Ilina said. "It hasn't spread to the smaller species yet, although . . ." She didn't have to finish the sentence. It was worrying to see the *mimikus* and *ignituses* in here, just as sick as the larger species. How long before the smaller species were vulnerable, too? "They won't catch it." Ilina's voice was hard. "Being with Mira protects them."

Oh, how I hoped that was true.

I pressed my palms against the big dragon's side and whispered a prayer. "Give them peace. Give them grace. Give them enough hope in their hearts." Here, so far away from Darina and Damyan, the words didn't bring a rush of warmth or comfort. They were just words, spoken to gods who couldn't hear me.

Haltingly, I pulled back, giving LaLa and Crystal time to readjust themselves. Then I reached into the satchel at my hip and pulled out the two noorestones we'd been keeping in the *raptuses'* basket.

The little dragons poked and nudged at the noorestones in my hand, whining faintly like they wanted to play.

"They're not much," I murmured, "but maybe they'll help."

LaLa looked up at me questioningly.

"These dragons need the noorestone fire more than we do."

My tiny dragon trilled and turned her golden gaze to the larger dragons, and warm agreement flickered through me. She knew what I intended to do, and she agreed.

It was hard to say how long before the giant noorestones

arrived. A decan, at least. Impossible to say if these dragons would live until then.

I moved Crystal to my free shoulder, then clipped her and LaLa's leashes to my belt. With a deep breath, I let myself sink into the noorestones.

A hot calm passed through me, like standing under the noonday sun while waves crashed around my feet. I held on to it for a heartbeat, letting it burn through the dark buzz of anxiety, and then I released the fire into the closest dragon.

Just a trickle.

A breath.

A gossamer thread of relief.

These dragons were so big, and their pain so deep, I didn't want to risk not having enough for everyone.

I moved around the mound of dragons, letting my hands slide across their cool, still bodies. Scales rasped against my skin, and someone—an *ignitus*—drew a shuddering breath. It was the most they'd moved since I'd come.

When I shifted sideways into the connection already spun with these seven dragons, I saw darkness—pure, uncompromising darkness. But when the noorestone fire brushed past them, stars appeared. Suggestions of stars that might have been imagination, but even if they weren't real, it was more than there'd been before. It was hope.

"It's working," someone muttered behind me. "Seven gods, they're moving."

The dragons groaned under my fingers; I could feel their voices more than hear them. Still, it was beyond anything I had dared hope for.

"May I go see them now?" The empress kept her voice soft.

"That's not a good idea," Ilina said. "If they do wake, they'll be . . . *unhappy* probably isn't strong enough."

Now the empress's voice was small, but I could still hear it, amplified by the power racing through my veins. "Will they hate me?"

Ilina was silent a moment, weighing the wisdom of confirming that to an empress. These dragons would never love her: she was their captor. But at last, Ilina said, "These keepers Paorah sent have done everything in their power to care for these dragons, given the facilities here. But they need more. I hope you'll allow us to offer some advice on building a proper sanctuary—away from the city, away from public traffic. The mountains, perhaps."

"Of course. Whatever they need, it will be done."

Noorestone fire spun through me, out my hands, and worked through the dragons—filling them up like water. LaLa and Crystal clicked and chirped, bouncing on my shoulders as the bigger dragons gasped and rolled off the *titanus*, leaving me space to reach in and press fire back into him, too.

Their relief was yawning, desperate, depthless. The fire from these two noorestones was but a mere spark of what the dragons needed, but it burned through them, awakening—

The last of the fire slipped through my fingers, like strands of silk falling away.

I shuddered and stepped back, touching LaLa and Crystal to reorient myself.

"Mira, are you all right?" Hristo was at my side, one hand on my back.

"Fine." Mostly. Not really. I pulled the noorestones from my pouch. They were dark. Slowly, I unclipped the *raptuses'* leashes from my belt and handed them to Hristo. Both dragons sprang toward him with eager squawks, and I returned to where the empress, Ilina, and her father stood. Two guards and the guide waited in the background.

"You helped them." A note of awe touched the empress's voice.

I dropped the darkened noorestones into her hands. "These bought the dragons a few more days of life. They're still trapped in endless misery. They're still going to die, unless—"

Dissonant buzzing ripped through me. My heartbeat stumbled, my teeth itched, and my thoughts spiraled with hope and fear and shock. I knew that noise in the back of my head, that black harmony that grated rather than sang. Noorestones. Giant noorestones.

Thirteen of them.

"Mira?" Ilina asked. "What's wrong?"

I gasped, struggling to get the words around the knot tightening inside my throat. "Paorah is here."

CHAPTER TWENTY-EIGHT

QUESTIONS SPIRALED THROUGH ME, UNSTOPPABLE without the noorestones. I fumbled for my calming pills.

1. *How had Paorah gotten here so quickly?*
2. *Where had the other three giant noorestones come from?*
3. *Could we get any of those noorestones here fast enough to help these dragons?*

But at my declaration—*"Paorah is here"*—the empress and her guards pushed into motion.

"Return me to the palace," she said. "Send this ahead: I want the high magistrate arrested and brought before my throne. In chains. Assemble the harbor guard to surround his fleet. As for the people with him"—she glanced at me— "try not to hurt them, but if they attack, respond in kind."

I tried to tell myself anyone from the Fallen Isles would make the same decision, but all I could think was that my mother was on one of those ships, and if an imperial killed her . . .

"Your will is ours," a guard said, nodding, and pulled a small metal device from his jacket, turning toward the carriage while he sent the empress's message.

"It's time to go, Your Eminence," said the other guard. "The park isn't defendable enough."

The empress gave a firm nod, but I didn't believe for a moment that she was worried for her own safety. The high magistrate had sworn to attack the Algotti Empire, and here he was, early and with a promise he intended to keep. Her people were in danger. She turned to me. "Come along, or stay. Whichever you prefer. If you remain, a carriage will return for you in a few hours."

Hristo stood at my side, his jaw clenched tight. "We should go."

Ilina looked up at her father, her wish clear enough on her face.

"Your Eminence," said the guard, not quite impatient, but Apolla held up her hand, and he went quiet.

I touched my friend's arm. "Ilina, we'll come back—" The dark hum in the back of my head sharpened. Widened. Became a shriek.

My knees buckled. LaLa screamed and dove for me, but Hristo held fast to her leash, while Ilina and her father caught me just before my hands and knees struck the flag-stone.

I must have looked out of my mind, clutching my head and groaning, but the noise was so loud. It was impossible to think around, impossible to *breathe* around. My whole body began to shudder as the shrieking crescendoed. It was just one noorestone, but it was overwhelming. Couldn't everyone else hear it, too?

"Mira?" The empress's voice was distant. "What is it?" Her guards urged her to leave, but—

"It's too late," I gasped. "Seven gods."

The heels of my palms dug against my temples, so hard my bones felt bruised, but it wasn't a sound that existed outside my head; I couldn't block it like this. I couldn't block it at all. No matter how I stretched to suppress it, the noise grew worse.

"What is it?" Hristo held me up; he must have passed the dragons to Ilina or Viktor, because both his arms wrapped around me now. "Mira, what's happening?"

"Run!" The keening rose higher. The noorestone moved, propelled into the air, and I didn't think. I reacted. I lurched away from everyone else, and I *pulled*.

Power crackled toward me. Into me. So fast it cut the air and thunder broke all around.

Excruciating fire slammed into my body. I staggered back, leaving patches of scorched grass where I stepped.

Guards leaped in front of the empress. Ilina's father jerked her away from me. Hristo stepped toward me, like he wanted to do *something*, but there was no help to

342

offer. No way to make this right.

Noorestone fire screamed through my veins, twisting sideways with the instability that made these crystals so dangerous. In the back of my mind, all I saw was the *Infinity*, exploding into a million fragments. That was going to be me, because I couldn't contain this. I couldn't *control* this.

But still, I pulled faster and faster, because it was me or my friends, and none of them would be able to survive this.

It was too much.

Even now, I was separating from myself. I could see my body shuddering violently under the onslaught of power. I could see fire and wind whipping around me in a deadly storm. And I could see the others pulling away— the empress's guards dragging her bodily to the carriage.

Screams tore from my throat, deep and wild, and nothing at all like a girl. Plasmic wings ripped from my back and stretched wide against the world. And angry noorestone fire sizzled along my skin like scales.

Someone shouted my name.

I couldn't hear it, not really, over the wretched keen, and the horror of everything I could see but couldn't say.

Beyond the others, above them, I saw an object flying high above the city of Sunder.

It was the size of a small house. On its own, a rock that large would have done incredible damage, shattering buildings and cracking open streets, crushing anyone who happened to be in its path.

But this was a noorestone: giant, deadly, and unstable. A blue-white inferno stormed around it, splintering apart where I grabbed at the power and pulled. Ropes of fire sailed across the sky, drawing stares from people across the city—those who hadn't yet noticed the noorestone. But then their gazes traced the fire from end to end, and there they saw it.

Death.

Panic flared. People fled on foot, as though they could outrun what was coming. They had no idea how bad it was going to be. A conflagration. Consuming. Complete. True destruction, down to the dirt.

I opened myself wider, drawing in noorestone fire. Faster. Hotter. It choked me, clogging in my throat, in my pores, in my fingernails. It was too much, and still it wasn't nearly enough.

And then—

The noorestone hit.

It crashed into a building. A temple to Suna, the Judge, with delicate spires and decorative arches carved from rose marble, some pieces shaved so thin that sunlight shone through the smoky stone. It was a masterpiece of architecture, awe-inspiring and imposing, and now it shattered apart.

"No!" The roar spilled from my wide-open jaws, but it was too late.

The noorestone exploded as it slammed into marble and limestone and metal framework, and drove into the earth below. Shards of glittering fire shot out in a thousand directions. Into the sky. Into surrounding buildings. Into carriages. Into orderly rows of trees. Into people.

The ground quaked with the impact, and the unconscious dragons groaned fitfully. The humans with me stumbled—some toward me, but most toward the uncertain safety of the carriage.

I couldn't blame them; I was terrible to behold: wreathed in blue-white fire, skin shining with dark, unearthly light, and those wings. Not the wings from before, when I'd gripped noorestones in the theater or Pit, but wings that buzzed and flickered and *hurt*. They weren't right. They weren't natural. And they were going to kill me if I couldn't do something with all this power.

But that was secondary. There was no space to worry about what was happening to me, because in the city, a firestorm rained on buildings and parks and people, incinerating everything in an instant. I saw their faces, terrified and blackening as they died and disappeared; the intensity of the noorestone fire took even their bones.

That was just the first few moments: twenty-three buildings demolished, three hundred and eleven people dead and evaporated, four—no, five—thousand running as though they had any hope of survival.

The numbers grew worse from there.

Ash mixed with falling fire—all the shards that had flown up and out after the first strike were now dropping back to the tender earth—and terrible dry heat rushed through streets and windows, heralding the flames hot enough to melt stone, which ran liquid and black over the charred earth. It was a Sundering of a different sort.

"Stop!" I screamed for the noorestone shards, drawing their fires deeper into me. Thousands upon thousands of threads spun off the fragments, reaching toward me, but I was too late. Too slow. Too unprepared.

Over the palace, silence bloomed.

It spread like a bubble, rising and stretching toward the shattered noorestone, enveloping gardens and courtyards and temples in pure silence as it rolled outward. But even that wouldn't be enough. It would quiet the noorestone fragments, but it could not quell the fires that blazed through the streets of Sunder, or ease the heat that sucked moisture from everything, even stone, or prevent the stampede of people fleeing in every direction.

I let out a furious cry. My wings flexed wide, scorching crescent moons into the ground around me. I pulled more and more of the noorestone's shattering power into me, making every piece of my body buzz with dissonance, with unstable harmony, with *burning*. I wanted to fly into that plume of silence and let it cool the agony of this inferno, but the noorestone shards still rained on Sunder, exploding anew and killing more and more.

Too much unsteady power. Too much ill-fitting fire. My grip on it grew soft and insubstantial as my fragile human body gave in to flame, but there was nothing to *do* with everything I took in. I was filled up, overflowing, bloated with the unwanted energy. Even if I could have steadied myself long enough to go to the dragons, this was not healing fire. This would rip all of us apart.

Desperate, I slammed my palms against the ground. Thunder cracked and the planet shook as I pushed power deep, deep into the earth. Through dust and dirt and thin crust, far into the liquid fire that fueled the world.

Silence touched the edges of my awareness. Over the city, it had reached the first remains of the noorestone, smothering the sharp ringing in my head, shard after angry shard. The violent tide of power eased as fragments went silent.

I pushed noorestone fire into the ground.

Silent.

Chaos in the city spread, but new explosions slowed.

Silent.

Tethers of fire snapped, and that was all. There was nothing left as the silence rolled across the city, allowing the last of the noorestone fragments to fall harmlessly to the blackened pit that marked the place where Suna's temple once stood.

People still ran, and fires still spread, but emergency teams came in with hoses of water siphoned straight from the river. There were medical stations for some, and black mercy for the rest.

I heaved the last of the noorestone fire from my body. Staggered. And dropped to the ground.

At last, I knew darkness.

PART FIVE

SOMETHING TO BURN

CHAPTER TWENTY-NINE

THE FIRST DRAGON PEERED DOWN AT ME, ECLIPSING the whole sky as she nosed my chest and breathed a puff of smoke into my face.

Wake up.

She was huge and black and speckled with stars, with graceful horns that curled at the points. Never had I seen scales like this, bigger than both my hands splayed wide, and light shining from within. When I peered deeper, strands of pink and blue and orange darkdust glimmered in the blackness. An illusion. A trick of the eye.

Wake up.

No, the stars and darkdust and galaxies were real. Each scale showed a different sky, and if I could only step through one, I'd find another world.

Wake up.

The dragon pulled back, and that was when sunlight caught it: a long, puckered scar down the left side of her face.

Not the first dragon.

The last.

THEN HRISTO WAS there, Ilina in the background—hazy, though.

Fractured movement.

Everything hurt. Every breath became a scream. Every scream became thunder.

A stranger leaned over me and drew invisible lines in the air above my face and body. They shimmered, flickering in and out of existence. I tried to grab them, make them stay so I could get a better look, but my arms were too heavy.

I closed my eyes.

I AWAKENED IN my bed in the palace, darkness and silence all around me.

My body ached. Skin and muscles and bones. It all felt raw and ready to fall off. Even the soft silk of my sheets hurt, scraping places that felt like they should have scales. The muscles in my back felt clipped short, broken, pulled tight and snapped.

Everything felt wrong.

A groan squeezed out as my mind slipped from

confusion to sharp understanding of what had happened.

The high magistrate had attacked Sunder.

Aaru and I had fought back.

It hadn't been enough.

Even now, after, I could still feel the giant noorestones—twelve of them. They buzzed in the back of my head, terrible, but nothing compared to the nightmare of the attack. Of the crystal crashing into the city. Of the fire burning through my body. Of the shriek of something in that noorestone *changing* just before it was launched at thousands of unsuspecting people.

No. This harsh humming was nothing compared to that.

"The strangest thing happened in the park." Ilina's voice came from across the room. A sigil lit just above her head, illuminating the way she'd half vanished into the giant cushions of a chair. Her legs were tucked against her chest, and she wore a long nightgown of creamy cotton with embroidery stitched along the hem.

I opened my mouth, but only another groan fell out. Still, she understood the question, and unfolded herself to rise.

"You tried to absorb all that noorestone fire. I knew you could do that." She sat on the bed next to me. "Hristo told us all about what happened at the theater. What he saw. What he thought he saw. So even though it was a shock to actually see you like that, I wasn't *that* surprised. But there was something else."

I just looked at her.

"Scorch marks," she said. "In the shape of a huge dragon."

"What?" That hadn't been what I'd thought she was going to say at all.

"All across the grass, the flagstones, even under the dragons. It was incredible. And you were at the heart of it." She touched my shoulder, casually like a friend, but then— ::Everyone saw. There have been questions.::

My wingsister's quiet code was slow, cautious, but it was a relief to know she was able to communicate like this. And the light was low enough that anyone watching wouldn't be able to tell—unless they could see in the dark.

Which was possible, I supposed. Imperial magic was a mystery of possibilities.

I took her arm and tapped slowly. ::What questions?::

::About the wings. The scorch mark. What dragon it was. Then someone asked if it was the same kind as the bones.::

I groaned.

::When I told them I hadn't seen the skeleton, they took me into the throne room. I got a good look.::

She didn't need to say that the scorch mark and the bones were the same species. *Drakontos celestus.* The first and the last. Although she probably didn't know what to call it yet.

::I said no, but I think they knew I was lying.::

The imperials didn't have *all* the answers—how could

they when *I* didn't even understand?—but it was still far more information than I'd wanted them to have.

::They heard us talking about the first dragon that first day,:: I tapped. ::By the fountain.::

Ilina nodded. ::They already knew we were interested. Now they think they know why.::

::Because of me. What I am.::

My wingsister just squeezed my shoulder. "Can you sit?"

"Maybe." I pushed myself up, letting Ilina help steady me. My whole body ached, like I'd been taken apart and put back together, but there was no more time for resting. If anyone even thought they knew what I could do, what I was—I couldn't trust anyone with that kind of information. No one outside my friends. I had to take care of this. "What happened after—" My voice cracked.

Ilina stood and went to a small table to pour a glass of water.

The drink helped soothe my raw throat, and I asked again, "What happened after I fainted?"

"Aaru held the silence as long as he could; no one was sure what would happen when he let it go. Gerel and Chenda have been out there helping every day, sending Chenda's shadow to look for survivors. It's hard, she said, because lots of the light sigils are broken, but usually there's enough for her to look around. When they find someone, Gerel digs them out. And, if you can believe it, Zara has been helping in the medical tents, mostly talking to people to distract them from the pain. They really like her."

"Of course they do. She's like Mother." I frowned as the rest of what she said caught up with me. "How long have I been asleep?"

"Four days," Ilina said.

"Four days?" We didn't *have* four days to waste with pointless sleep. I drained my water and stood, the coral-orange nightgown slipping straight across my body. Someone had changed my clothes while I'd been unconscious. "You let me sleep four days?"

"We tried to wake you." Ilina stood, too. "The empress's personal healers and doctors have been in and out. We've all taken turns sitting with you, hoping you'd wake up. But whatever you did must have cost you. Even Crystal and LaLa came to sleep next to you at night. And before you ask, they're with Hristo right now. They're fine."

"Good." I wrenched open the wardrobe door and tapped the interior light sigil. "What's happened? Was the high magistrate arrested? Is my mother here? What about the people in the city?"

Ilina blew out a long breath. "A lot happened. First, the death toll would have been much higher without your and Aaru's intervention. As it was . . ."

A chill poured through me as I faced her. "How many?"

"At least three thousand." Shadows muted the grief in her eyes, but the tightness in her voice made her feelings clear. "It's difficult to say for sure, because there aren't"—she swallowed hard—"remains around the impact area. There's nothing to count. Just ash."

"Just ash," I whispered. "Seven gods."

"At least five thousand more were injured, but most of them should make it. Healers have been working day and night to treat burns and injuries from collapsed buildings. And again, it would have been much worse without you and Aaru."

The numbers swarmed around my thoughts. So many people dead because of one man. "And Paorah?"

"He wasn't on the ships."

I swore.

"I know."

"And neither was your mother, I'm afraid."

My throat went dry. I wanted to ask more questions—like if anyone from the islands knew where Mother was—but I didn't dare. If she was dead, I didn't want to know yet. If she was alive but Paorah had her . . . I didn't want to know yet.

"I'm sure she's fine," Ilina said.

"She always is." The words felt wispy and uncertain, though.

My wingsister joined me at the wardrobe and pulled out the first thing she saw. "It sounds like they intended to catapult one noorestone into the city, then send their demands to the empress, with the threat of another attack. But Aaru silenced the rest of the noorestones on their ships, and the harbor guard subdued them quickly. There were mutinies and arrests, and it turns out Paorah is still on Anahera because he's an absolute coward who won't fight his own battles if he can talk someone else into doing it." She thrust a dress at me. "Put this on."

I shimmied out of my nightgown and stepped into the dress, half wishing I had time for a bath. But I had to speak with Apolla. Now. About the dragons, what she'd seen me do, and what she intended to do with the people who'd come from the Fallen Isles.

What if she planned to punish everyone on behalf of Paorah?

"Empress Apolla sent the ships she'd promised," Ilina continued. "Even with the attack, she made sure to keep her end of the bargain, and she expects you to keep yours as well."

Heal the dragons with the giant noorestones? Impossible. But I put that worry aside for now. "When will her ships reach the Fallen Isles?"

"They should arrive along the eastern shores of Darina any day now. From there, they'll spread out among the islands and search for survivors. But I have no idea how they'll persuade everyone to come aboard when we've always hated the empire, or how they'll choose who gets to come on and who doesn't." She shivered. "I can't believe that we're here, surrounded by all this, and everyone at home is just waiting to be next."

"They must feel so alone." I closed my eyes, wanting to pray, but not sure how to do it around the fear that Darina or Damyan might have been the last one to rise.

Ilina hesitated. "There's more."

I didn't think I could take any more, but I nodded for her to say it.

"The islands after Idris were Bopha and Harta."

My heart sank. "Do Chenda and Hristo know?"

"They were present when the news came. They know."

I didn't ask if they were all right.

Ilina motioned toward the washroom. "I'll tell Alusha you want a meeting with Empress Apolla, and you take care of yourself in there. You may have needed four days to recover from that noorestone, but it didn't do your breath any favors."

I winced, but she was right. My mouth tasted disgusting.

After following Ilina's orders, I headed into the public parlor, where Aaru and Hristo sat on a bench, both dragons playing between them. In the entry hall, Ilina spoke with someone in low, urgent tones.

At my entrance, Hristo and Aaru stood. My guard hugged me first.

"I'm sorry," I whispered. "I just heard about Harta."

He gave me a squeeze and nodded, and then Aaru's arms were around me.

"I heard it coming." He drew a heavy breath. "The noorestone."

Of course he had.

"I should have silenced it right away."

Oh.

"You couldn't have known what would happen."

"I did know. I just couldn't. It was so loud I couldn't—" His face twisted with pain.

I understood. And I couldn't reassure him, because three thousand lives had been lost. It didn't matter that they belonged to the Algotti Empire, that they were supposedly our oldest enemy, or that we'd recently thought they'd quietly conquered the Fallen Isles. They were people, like us. They'd been attacked. And we hadn't been able to save them.

Reassurance would only feel like saying that the ones who died didn't matter, and they deserved more than lies we told ourselves to feel better.

"How did you finally do it?" I asked.

"You." He licked his lips. "I knew what you were doing. I knew if I didn't help, you might not survive."

"Thank you." The words were inadequate, but I didn't know what else to say.

"Mira?" Ilina started in from the entry hall. "Empress Apolla is ready to see you."

Before I could go, though, Aaru took my hand and squeezed. He didn't speak aloud; his warning came quickly against my fingers: ::Careful. I overheard what she said while you were unconscious. She knows about your dragon soul.::

CHAPTER THIRTY

EMPRESS APOLLA WASN'T IN HER THRONE ROOM.

Instead, I was escorted onto the imperial barge, surrounded by a small army of the empress's personal guards,
and taken up the River Akron. It was faster than the
carriage had been and offered a different view of the man-
sions and courtyards of Sunder. It had no view whatsoever
of the damage done by the giant noorestone.

From here, Sunder was still the portrait of beauty,
wealth, and elegance. Even after the attack, Apolla wanted
to impress me.

Or remind me of her power.

While I waited to arrive, I was given a lavish breakfast
of sausage, eggs, orange slices, and tea thick with honey.
I ate everything, hungry after sleeping for four days, but
tasted very little. No matter how Apolla tried to win me,

I couldn't forget that she was an empress first. She commanded armies and conquered kingdoms. If she knew about my dragon soul, as Aaru believed, then surely she would seek to use my ability the same way the Luminary Council had used my voice.

I would not be her weapon.

On the western horizon, black clouds rolled over the ocean. Lightning shot through the sky, illuminating the shapes of the billowing, boiling storm. With every flash of light, the back of my throat tingled, and a thread of excitement skittered through me. Dragons loved storms, and this one promised to be incredible. Though still hours off, it would be a drenching downpour when it arrived—a deluge that the city of Sunder did not need right now.

"We're almost there," said the lead guard as the barge servants cleared away my tray. "Just a few more minutes."

I thanked him, but I could already feel the dragons' proximity.

And the noorestone.

It was a grating, scratching noise in the back of my head, hot with unstoppable power. When we reached the dragon park, it was the first thing I saw. Even though I was prepared for the size—I'd seen them before—it still shocked me.

It was huge—as big as a small house—and its glow rivaled a summer sun. Fourteen imperial soldiers stood at attention around it, though they kept their backs to its impossibly bright shine.

In the cool blue-white light, the scorch mark that covered the ground was perfectly black. I followed the shadow of the *Drakontos celestus* from the noorestone to the keepers' building, then to the river where one wing extended, and then on past the mound of unconscious dragons.

And there, waiting by the dragons, stood Apolla. As always, she was resplendent in gold and white, with a stiff brocade cape that trailed after her. Boots peeked out beneath her gown—white, of course—but perhaps mages had woven sigils of repelling into all her clothes, because the fabric was spotless.

I approached, flanked by the guards she'd sent along with me.

"Mira." Her tone was cordial, pleasant. "You've awakened."

As though this meeting were a surprise. As though her people hadn't been listening to every word uttered in the suite she'd *generously* given us.

"Yes." The dragons—their slow breathing, their walledup minds, their slide into death—made me keep my own tone level. No matter my anger, my fear, I needed to keep it separate from them. They didn't deserve to feel any more negativity than they were already suffering. "I've been told your personal doctors and healers saw to my recovery. You have my gratitude."

She smiled—a polite, practiced expression. "You and your friends are the most valuable guests I've ever had the honor of hosting in the imperial palace."

Her words sent a shiver through me. *Valuable*. The Algotti Empire had listening sigils, healing magic, the power to make ships cross the ocean in mere days—but they didn't have someone whose shadow separated from her to search for survivors; they didn't have someone who could make crops grow with only a thought; they didn't have someone who could *silence* entire cities to allow only one voice to be heard.

We were *valuable*. And Nine had warned us when she'd said Apolla found our gifts fascinating.

Of course, after the Great Abandonment finished, those gifts might be gone forever.

"So valuable I needed an escort this large." I motioned toward the men and women who'd come with me on the barge. They'd stayed a respectable distance away, allowing Apolla and me to talk in relative privacy, but I had no doubt they were straining to hear every single word.

"Yes." She stepped close, as though imparting a secret. "In difficult times, such as those following unprovoked attacks, otherwise civilized people can become violent. Would that I could vouch for every one of my citizens, but I'm afraid there may be some who will see you no differently than they see those islanders who attacked the city. Protecting you is among my highest priorities."

A slow ache pounded through my head, but it wasn't mine; it belonged to one of the dragons lying nearby. "I was not told that I would be leaving the palace today," I said, keeping my tone neutral. "Otherwise, I would have asked my personal guard to accompany me."

It wasn't that I needed Hristo immediately. With the giant noorestone buzzing darkly in the back of my mind, I was more than capable of defending myself. Where there were noorestones, I was powerful.

That was why neither Hristo nor I had been informed of the location of this meeting. It was a show of control. A reminder that I needed her.

Apolla simply nodded. "My apologies," she said, without a trace of sincerity.

I smiled, as though I accepted, and moved on. "What of the people who came aboard all those ships? Are they being guarded as well?"

"Yes." Apolla motioned for me to walk with her around the mound of dragons. They didn't notice our presence, and the burned ground crunched under our shoes. "My harbor guard is protecting the island fleet from anyone who would unduly harm the people residing there. Many of them seem to be merchants or bankers, tradespeople with no ability to defend themselves."

"Paorah wanted to bring wealth and skills of the Fallen Isles."

"In the coming days, we will determine who was complicit in the attacks on Sunder. Already, several arrests have been made—those of notable rank aboard the ship that fired the noorestone into the city. They're being questioned and awaiting trial."

"Trial?" I raised an eyebrow. "They're citizens of the Fallen Isles."

"They're refugees seeking shelter in the Algotti Empire,

per the agreement I made with High Magistrate Paorah."

"Which he violated."

"Shall I have the violation clauses brought up?" Her words were clipped. "I assure you, the results would not be pretty."

"The agreement you and I made supersedes the one you made with him."

"We haven't signed anything."

"Nevertheless," I said, "you agreed to it. And no part of our agreement gives you authority over my people."

She shook her head slowly, continuing to glide around the dragons as though we were taking a leisurely stroll together. Her tone turned gentler. "And how will you impose your authority? Will you take them back to the Fallen Isles for judgment?" She looked at me askance. "I know you wish to maintain your independence, but you're already dealing with significant problems. These people hurt my city. My people. Allow me to take the burden of pursuing the truth and meting out suitable punishment. You would, of course, be consulted."

"I cannot give you the *burden* of judging my people." My words came sharper than I intended. "You are correct in that the Fallen Isles already have heavy troubles, and that it will be difficult to bring the attackers to justice, but they are still my people. If you want to pursue an agreement between the Fallen Isles and the Algotti Empire regarding this matter, Chenda would be delighted to begin that process. But I'm afraid I cannot allow you to move forward with a trial until an extradition agreement is formalized."

"I don't understand this hostility," Apolla said. "I thought we were friends."

"You and I don't have the luxury of being friends." I smiled, for real this time, though it was a sad sort of expression. "I think we could be, if not for our titles."

She just nodded. "I'll have an extradition agreement drawn up and sent to Chenda this afternoon."

I relaxed—only slightly. It wasn't that I even disagreed with her—not really. The crime had been against her people, and on her land. And we had gods rising and people evacuating. The Fallen Isles were in no position to hold a trial.

But.

If we let her do *favors* like that. If we let her take the *burden* of governing. If we let her *help* without formal agreements.

She may as well have conquered us already.

She knew it.

I knew it.

Neither of us needed say it out loud.

"What of High Magistrate Paorah?" Apolla asked, a little more cautiously than before. "He committed crimes against both the empire and the islands. He violated the agreement we made in good faith."

"He's still on Anahera." I turned my eyes to the dragons, barely moving as the sun reached upward. "He will be tried and punished for what he's done to the Fallen Isles, and if our agreement is approved then you'll have a chance with him, too."

"You could leave him on Anahera and let him die as his god rises."

My gaze cut to her. That was cruel, albeit no crueler than what he'd done to the rest of the Fallen Isles and the dragons he'd captured. "It isn't my place to cast judgment, so I won't speculate, but when the people learn of what he did—creating a lie out of the Mira Treaty—there will be backlash. When they find that his actions may have *hastened* the Great Abandonment . . ."

"He will be lucky to survive until his trial," she agreed. "Such betrayals from those entrusted with power bring out the worst in people."

Together, we completed one transit around the unconscious dragons. They were breathing, but when I let my mind drift around theirs, the starless walls had returned. Anything I'd managed to give them four days ago was gone, and they once again balanced on the edge of death.

"I appreciate you, Mira. You stand your ground without attempting to take what isn't yours."

Unlike her?

"Now, as I'm sure you realize, I wanted to meet you here for this." She motioned to the great noorestone, not averting her gaze, but unable to keep from squinting at its radiance.

I gazed into the blue-white depths as easily as I looked

at the sun. The noorestone buzzed louder in the back of my mind, now that I was actively aware of it again, but I pushed past the din as I stared into the center of the stone at the bright spark that was the fire of Noore. It flickered and crackled, bending in a way that smaller noorestones didn't.

That was the instability. That flicker.

I tore my eyes from the noorestone to find Apolla watching me. "I had it brought over last night."

Then it had been casting its unstable shine on these poor dragons for hours. Washing out starlight. Ringing in their ears.

Apolla didn't notice my concern. "Originally, the ship we took it from had three of these. One landed in my city. I thought it only right to take this one to heal my dragons."

Her dragons.

My chest went tight, but I bit my tongue. We were already at odds, and she already knew too much about me, and she already had all the leverage. Besides, I was going to have to disappoint her again, and I needed to measure my words carefully.

"Are you ready to heal them?" Apolla's face was gentle as she gazed up at the noorestone-lit dragons. "I've been told they don't have much time."

A telltale knot of anxiety tightened around my heart, but I had to tell her. "Your Eminence, I'm afraid I cannot heal them with this noorestone."

Her eyebrows raised. "I can have a second brought

immediately, if that's what you need."

I shook my head. "That's not it. The problem is the giant noorestones themselves. They're too unstable. That's why Paorah wanted to use them as weapons: he's already destroyed one of our own ocean-crossing ships in a test of their destructive potential. One of your spies told me that."

"You said you needed to wait for the giant noorestones to get here before you could heal the dragons. Now you say the giant noorestones will not work."

"I thought they would." I closed my eyes and exhaled. "Until the other day, I believed a noorestone was a noorestone, unstable or not. But these *are* different. They're noorestones, but wrong."

"How?"

How could I explain the not-quite dissonance to her? The way I'd *known* the moment I felt the fire that they would never heal the dragons? The sight of that flicker deep within the heart of the crystal? "Imagine you needed water, but the only water available was salt water. Ocean water. Would you drink it?"

She pressed her lips into a line. "We have magic that removes salt from water."

"If you have magic that can make this noorestone stable, then I will heal the dragons with it. But right now, it would be toxic to them. It would kill them even more quickly."

"You're saying this stone is like salt water."

"Yes." I let the mask of Hopebearer drop. Let her see the truth in my eyes. "Dragons hoard noorestones in their dens. In my home sanctuary, the smaller species play around the ancient ruins that have still-lit noorestones embedded within the walls and spires. That's why we brought the noorestones for Crystal and LaLa—because dragons need them. They help dragons heal and, I think, live longer lives."

She nodded.

"But this one"—I motioned toward the giant crystal—"is damaging. Even leaving it here overnight, when these dragons are so weak, might have hastened their illness."

Her pale eyes narrowed as she weighed my words for truth. "I can have it removed immediately, but what do you need to heal the dragons? If you don't do it today, they'll die."

"I am aware of that." I placed my palm against one of the dragons' flanks—the *Drakontos maior*—and again felt how unnaturally cool the scales were. How rough and dull. "Have the other noorestones brought here. The regular ones."

"Will it be enough?"

"I can't say." I dropped my hand back to my side. "When I healed the dragons in Anahera, we were in first-century ruins. The noorestones there had been lit for more than two thousand years, because they were still connected to the gods. They were stronger than anything I'd ever felt, and by the time the dragons were healed, all two thousand

and thirteen of them were dark. Dead."

Empress Apolla turned to the dragons and touched the *maior*, as I had. I fought the urge to bat her away; it would help nothing.

"This day is not going how I thought it would," she said at last.

I couldn't disagree. "If you know anything about me, you know I care about these dragons. All dragons. I would do anything for them. You know I'd rather these children of my gods live here—*live* here—than die in the Great Abandonment."

It was true.

If the dragons survived this illness.

If they stood a chance of surviving the Great Abandonment, even from afar.

Empress Apolla sucked in a sharp breath. "Every noorestone aboard every island ship will be here within the hour."

"And then I will do everything in my power to save these dragons."

CHAPTER THIRTY-ONE

TRUE TO APOLLA'S WORD, THE GIANT NOORESTONE was removed immediately.

After one terse conversation with her guard, a team of fifty men and women arrived and maneuvered the house-sized crystal onto a wheeled platform, reinforced with strength and agility sigils, and rolled it out of the park.

"Where are they taking it?" I asked, watching as the noorestone went down the road.

"To a facility for study." Apolla motioned me toward the keepers' building. "Perhaps one day we'll be able to understand its instability and fix it, and it can do some good in the world."

I sighed, and when she looked at me, we both knew what I was going to say.

"Certainly we can work out an agreement." She motioned for me to enter the building first as a guard opened the door. "We do seem to be considering lots of agreements today. What's one more?"

The interior of the building was much cooler than outside, boasting a moderately sized common room with a heavy wooden table, and several closed doors that might have led to individual quarters. If there were medical facilities for the dragons, I couldn't guess where they would go.

"Noorestones that size are extremely valuable to us." I took a seat at the table; Alusha would have been scandalized, but I didn't care about protocol anymore. "They are our sole means of traveling outside the Fallen Isles. They're incredibly rare. The fact that so many are here in one place—that's something I've never seen before."

Empress Apolla lowered herself into the seat across from me, adjusting her gown as she did. Somehow, even in these rugged surroundings, she managed to look regal. "I see. Would you be interested in some sort of trade, perhaps? Something equally rare and valuable?"

The bones of the first dragon.

I would give her all the noorestones for the dragon bones.

But I couldn't say that. Not without consulting with the others. The noorestones weren't mine to give.

"I think my people would be open to a trade," I said slowly. "But let's save that discussion for another day."

Let her think I wasn't in a rush for the bones.

I *was* in a rush, though. Idris, Harta, and Bopha had already risen. There were only seven days until the eclipse, and we still had to sail there. Even taking a skimmer den would require three days. That didn't leave us much time to barter.

"One thing I do wonder," I mused aloud, "is how Paorah's ships reached the mainland so quickly. They possessed only one noorestone each—except for the one you said had three. Usually, they do boast three, and it would still take them nearly two decans to get here."

Apolla was nodding. "I was curious about this as well. It seems there was a substance used to torture prisoners in a place called the Pit."

My heart tumbled over itself with knowing. With disgust. All I could think of was Aaru in the interrogation room, the chair with straps to hold him down, and the basins with noorestones against his bare feet.

His screaming.

His silence.

Darkness. Terror. Voicelessness.

He hadn't even known who I was then—not my full name or title—and he had no idea why he was being tortured.

Apolla, if she noticed my distress, didn't comment. "It's a combination of dragon root, dragon blood, and several other minor ingredients that, when it contacts noorestones, changes the way the inner fire is expelled. I'm told that when applied correctly, this substance will transfer the energy into another object—like a person—or it can push a ship faster across the sea." She frowned to herself. "They say they were unsure whether it would work. Some believed it had just as much of a chance to explode the ship as it did to speed the journey."

"That's why Paorah didn't come himself," I murmured. "He couldn't face the empire, and he couldn't even face the chance of dying on his own ship."

He could have killed everyone he'd intended to save.

"I'm sure he told everyone that the goddess of destruction would protect them." Apolla shook her head, disgusted. "Do you think he will follow them? Should we expect another attack?"

"The ten with single noorestones are the entirety of the Red Fleet," I said. "What is the name of the eleventh ship?"

"The *Star-Touched*, I believe."

"It's likely he has the *Great Mace*—a Khulani ship. He may follow, but if I've learned anything about him, it's that I shouldn't try to guess what he's going to do."

She offered a faint smile. "Shall I have refreshments brought in?"

Apparently, Paorah wasn't the only one who liked being unpredictable. I nodded, and a short time later, her personal servants arrived from the palace, bearing trays of fruit tarts and sweet drinks. We kept the remainder of our conversation to small, trivial things, though it hardly eased the tension. It was only a matter of time before everything fell apart.

Things I knew for sure:

1. *I was no politician.*
2. *I really didn't want to be.*
3. *Apolla was born for this.*

From the small window, we watched workers bring cart after glittering cart of regular noorestones to the park. The crystals were dumped right onto the scorched grass, in the depression carved by the giant noorestone. The gentle, safe hum of these noorestones surrounded my thoughts, cushioning me from the crush of anxiety that threatened every time I wondered if I really could heal these dragons. We were so far from home, and if this didn't work . . . nothing would.

Three hundred noorestones.

Five hundred.

Seven hundred.

As the noorestones piled up in a ring around the dragons, I imagined holds going dark, and cabins lit only by ambient light through the portholes. Hundreds upon hundreds of people confined to darkness aboard the ships they'd hoped would carry them to safety.

Apolla must have caught my look, because as the last cart was wheeled away, she said, "I know it's not the same, but I've ordered mages to carve light sigils into the walls of the ships. It's difficult to say how long trials and treaties will take."

"Thank you." It was an unexpected kindness.

Of course, it was also possible it was an excuse for her mages to board the ships and carve listening sigils—or something even less desirable.

We finished the last of our treats and went outside, where the hot glare of the afternoon sun had eased with the first edges of the coming storm. The air was cooler, and a few early droplets of rain pinged off the guards' armor and darkened the white silk of Apolla's dress, but if she was annoyed about being out in the rain, she didn't show it.

"These don't hurt to look at," the empress said as we approached the ring of noorestones, and the small path left as an opening for us. Raindrops bounced and dripped off the faceted edges of the crystals, shining beautifully. "Why?"

"The stability." I picked up one of the crystals as we passed, letting my thumb slide across the smooth, damp facets. "I'm going to try my best," I said. "I'll give the dragons every bit of energy these noorestones have, but I can't promise they'll be completely healed. You need a proper sanctuary."

She nodded. "I've spoken to Ilina and Viktor extensively, and plans are being drawn up today."

"Good." I closed my eyes and touched the first noorestone to one of the *ignituses*. "You may want to step back. I don't know how they'll react when they wake."

I didn't open my eyes, but I felt her move away—through the space in the noorestone ring and to the safety of the line of her guards. Metal creaked and fabric caught air: the palace servants had opened up a small tent for Apolla to stand beneath.

That was probably a good idea. Already rain dropped faster and faster, running down dragon scales and dotting my face, where they sizzled and steamed off my skin.

I squeezed the small noorestone in my hand, then drew upon its energy.

The fire of Noore flowed through me, smooth like silk or oil, and this time, it felt *right*. Power rushed in, filling up the cracks and soothing the raw places where the giant noorestone had scraped, but I pushed it away before the wounds could finish healing; the dragons needed everything.

The light of two thousand five hundred and thirty-three noorestones bent toward me, droplets of radiance sliding up to my heart like beads of water on silk threads. The crystals themselves dimmed, but the whole arc above the dragons must have been blindingly bright as I slowly let the power slip into an *ignitus*.

It was like pouring water into sand.

Noorestone fire fell in and vanished, and nothing happened with the dragon. He just lay there, unmoving, his flame-red scales dulled to a dusty ember.

Cautiously, I opened the stream of fire a little wider.

The dragons were *so* sick, *so* close to death. Maybe they just needed more pressure.

But still, the fire drained into them and went nowhere. Did nothing.

Doubt crept into me. What if I was too late? What if they were too far gone?

Thunder sounded above, rumbling through the sky as though inviting the dragons to come enjoy the storm. But they didn't—couldn't—move.

I had to keep trying. Warily, I slipped around to the next dragon, the *mimikus*, to let the power slide directly into her. "Wake up." My voice was hoarse, thick with hope and fear. "It's time to wake up and fly."

But the same thing happened as before: nothing. Noorestone fire went in and in and in, hot blue-white beads of energy that could save this dragon's life—that *should* save her life—but her heart merely continued its weak flutter.

This wasn't going to work.

The giant noorestone had done too much harm. They'd already been sick. Dying. Drifting toward whatever waited for dragons. The giant noorestone, with its dark harmony and stuttering inner fire, had been too much.

The empress, in her urgency to have the dragons healed, had only hastened their deaths.

Or maybe it was my fault, because I hadn't awakened in time to tell her that the giant noorestones wouldn't work.

My heart broke a thousand times as I pressed more fire into the *mimikus*. "Please," I whispered under the rain and thunder. "Please move. Breathe. Fly. *Something*."

But she was as still as death.

With terror filling up my veins, I moved to the *rex* and urged noorestone fire to flood through this dragon, to pour through her hollow bones, to make her membrane-thin wings glow like she'd flown in front of the sun. A lit-within silhouette.

The *Drakontos rex* didn't move. Hardly breathed.

The *maximus* was next, and there I felt it: the first noorestone went dark.

It was hard to say how long I'd been working, but I'd opened myself to every single one of the noorestones, and over two thousand strings of light arced toward me, power spiraling in soft, bright waves. And now, the first noorestone, the smallest noorestone, was dead without having saved a dragon—without having even stirred one child of the gods from this deathlike sleep.

A sob wrenched out of me as I opened myself wide and pushed the fire into the dragons with renewed desperation.

Please, Darina. Please, Damyan. If you care for your children at all.

But the gods were so far away, in a different part of the ocean. If they could hear me, they weren't listening.

I was on my own, and the only chance these dragons had of surviving the day. The hour.

Faster, I drew on the noorestones and let the fire flood into the dragons like there was no limit. More crystals winked dark, but no one else would be able to tell—not with the blue-white light stretching from the noorestones to me to the dragons. I pushed the fire of Noore into the *titanus*, urging him to awaken, to heal, to *live*.

And then it happened.

Just as the first sheet of rain slammed down on the park—

Just as lightning sliced open the sky—

Just as thunder wrenched the ground underneath us—

In the walls of darkness that surrounded the *titanus's* mind, a star flickered to life. Under the force of so much energy, the walls began to strain and crack, and light flooded in.

I sobbed in open relief, and with both hands pressed hard against the dragon's throat, I could feel his pulse quicken under my fingers. Strength surged in as his heart began to beat a steady rhythm, and warmth glowed across the chipped scales.

The healing fire spread from the *titanus* into the other dragons, through the connection they shared. The same way they'd fallen ill, they were now coming back to life.

Slowly, they began to take deeper, more even breaths. They shifted their bodies around, off one another, as even the ragged, damaged scales glimmered like starlight as noorestone fire rushed through. Water slid down the groaning dragons, making them soft and sharp at once as they gathered themselves.

A wing fluttered.

Spark glands tingled.

Seven heads untangled from the mound and gazed around the park, their eyes gold and green and noorestone blue. They were confused and lost, but awake for the first time in decans.

Behind me, someone gasped. Another person cried out. A servant, perhaps, or a keeper, because I couldn't imagine the empress or her guards expressing their emotion so openly.

The *rex* lowered her eyes to me, blinking as though seeing something strange. But I didn't know this dragon. She didn't know me.

Except . . .

Wings. Mine.

They were great, plasmic wings that stretched around me—and around the dragons as well. They were blue-white, like noorestone light, and crackling with energy. They were foreign and familiar at once, like a dream that felt like memory.

The last dragon.

Thunder rolled across the sky. The ground trembled. One at a time, the other dragons looked at me.

One thousand noorestones had darkened by now, but power still poured into them, giving more and more life.

Tails lashed, knocking noorestones out of the way, and talons dug into the dark, muddying ground. The whole park smelled like smoke as they tested their spark glands and let out small breaths of fire.

"Should she move away now?" someone asked, and at once, I remembered the crowd gathered near the keepers' building, and rain drumming on the tent, and eyes locked onto the beautiful draconic wings extending from my back.

"I don't think we need to worry about her." That was Apolla, her voice confident in spite of the seven—eight, maybe—dragons before her.

Another three hundred noorestones went dark.

The dragons rolled their bodies in long, serpentine movements, like cats stretching. The *mimikus*'s scales shifted to black—same as the scorched ground beneath him—and the *ignituses* shimmered with ghosts of fire around their brilliant red bodies.

They were beautiful. Majestic. *Powerful.*

They were alive.

Fire roared through me, into the dragons, and as lightning flared and thunder pealed above us, the *titanus* lowered his head directly in front of me.

Then the *maior*, the *rex*, the *maximus*, the *mimikus*, and the pair of *ignitsuses*.

All of them pressed their chins to the ground at my feet, their forelegs carefully bent, and wings stretched in neat arcs.

"Are they—"

"They're *bowing* to her," someone whispered.

Four hundred noorestones darkened as the dragons held their positions before me.

"How can they do that?"

"Look at her."

"Why does she have wings?"

"Didn't you hear about this scorch mark? That was her."

"Stop. Both of you, stop." Apolla's voice was crisp with confusion and anger. And . . . jealousy. "She is the dragon soul. That is why they bow."

My heart pounded, and the remaining two hundred noorestones pulsed in answer.

One hundred noorestones.

Seventy-five.

Thirty-three.

The dragons waited, soaking in the last of the fire as rain drummed across their bodies and smoke and steam poured through the clearing.

Two noorestones.

One.

When the last noorestone flickered dark, my wings dissolved into ghosts of light, and then nothing at all.

"Is that it?" someone asked.

The dragons all lifted their heads. Beautiful. Sharp. Wild and powerful and unknowable, just as the gods.

I lifted my hand before me, and an *ignitus* bumped my palm before twisting away and launching into the rain-soaked sky. Then the *maior*, and the rest and the rest until only the *titanus* remained. He pressed his nose into my hand, so gentle for something so big, and then he, too, flew.

Cheers rose behind me, but I couldn't look away from the dragons as they spiraled through the air, circling into a small tower like the dragons at the ruins had. Colors flashed. Fire spouted. Roars made the whole world tremble.

It was a fierce and joyous sight, making my heart tangle up with gladness and relief and awe.

I'd saved them. In spite of the distance from our gods, and the illness that had ravaged their minds and bodies, and the toxic leech of the giant noorestone, I'd healed these dragons. They were alive. Happy.

They were incredible.

Then . . .

Through our connection . . .

I felt the change the moment they did.

Far to the west, in the middle of an ocean with nothing else around, seven Fallen Gods waited. Three had risen. The other four were still pressed against the bottom of the sea.

But imperceptibly to everyone but the gods' most beloved children, one of the Fallen Gods began to shift.

And the dragons began to scream in horror.

CHAPTER THIRTY-TWO

THE RUSH OF FEELING CAME IN GREAT, UNFORGIVING waves.

First, the horror.

Together, we screamed at the knowledge of another god preparing to leave and tens of thousands of lives about to be lost. It was a nightmare, the kind of dread that should have disappeared at dawn, but there was no waking from this. No respite. No certainty that everything would be well in the end.

Second, the pain.

It was a deep, soul-wrenching agony I'd never experienced before—not in my darkest moments. It felt like ripping, like fire, and scream after scream ground out of me as I grasped for something—anything—to hold myself together with. My fingers dug into the brittle, scorched grass, and the muddy dirt beneath, but that was too insubstantial. I was falling apart. We were all falling apart.

Third, the grief.

Nothing had happened yet, but that didn't ease the onslaught of emotion. It was like hearing a death sentence: inevitable, final, and completely devastating. And, because this was merely a warning, there were hours and hours of this to live through, and when the god—Khulan, my dragon soul told me—finally rose, it would still somehow be a shock.

The change was terrible. One moment, the dragons had been soaring over the park, rapture in their hearts, wings snapping with the rolling thunder.

And now: horror, pain, grief. The emotions ripped through them and surged into me before I had a chance to break off my connection.

I staggered backward. My feet skidded over a darkened noorestone, and I tripped. I fell. Dull, lightless crystals gouged at me through my clothes, but I barely felt it. I shifted around to all fours, then lifted my head to scream at the sky, still caught up in the dragons' fury.

Soon, Khulan would rise.

The god of warriors would abandon his people.

Another nation would be lost.

It was unthinkable, but it was happening. Again and again until there were no more Fallen Isles left. And I was here in another part of the world, safe with our ancient enemies, instead of *helping*. I needed the bones of the first dragon. I needed to go home. I needed to renew the bargain with the Fallen Gods.

But what if they were all risen by the time I made it back?

The possibility of that made a roar rip from my throat, aching and polyphonic—not human at all. It was another part of myself, the shadow soul of the dragon, and as the dragons above grew frenzied with fear and loss, the draconic side of my heart wanted to join them.

I surged to my feet and reached for the sky, roaring with every piece of both my souls. And then, even without the fire of noorestones, my wings flared and scales rippled down my body like armor. A too-big sensation filled my chest, like if I breathed just right, I could inhale into a second set of lungs.

Like I could breathe fire.

I inhaled sharply, sort of sideways, and the back of my throat tingled with possibility.

Stop.

Not the dragon me, but the other me. The girl me.

Stop.

I looked up to find the other dragons still screaming, circling, waiting for me to join them. And I could do it. I could lift my wings—

Stop.

Reason cut through the grief at last. If anyone saw me like this . . . if *Apolla* saw me like this, using my dragon powers . . .

I had to protect myself, and my dragon soul, from

anyone who might want to use me for their own gain. I'd already spent most of my life in that position. My face, my opinions, my voice. I couldn't let it happen again.

"Go," I told the dragons, and then I wrenched my soul back from them, damming the threads between us.

The dragons screeched, their talons ripping at the rain-drenched sky. Flame arced overhead, higher than before. At last, they peeled away from me, flapping and spitting fire as they twisted through the drenching sheets of rain, flying toward the mountains as fast as they could.

Or maybe they were flying *away* from the city and the empress.

I watched them, heart whole and shattered all at once. They were healed. Their world was broken.

Then the dragons were gone.

I dropped to my knees as the wings and scales and fire disappeared. My skin itched and my chest felt shrunken, but even though I was only a girl again, rain sizzled where it hit my body, and steam rushed up around me.

Khulan was leaving.

Idris, Bopha, Harta, and now Khulan.

For several minutes, there was only the sound of rain pounding on the field, plinking off the darkened noore-stones, and hissing off my face and shoulders and arms. There was only shock and terror and thunder rolling through the sky.

And there was anger.

Maybe it was surprise that had delayed her rage—I

couldn't imagine that it had been fear of the dragons or me—but all at once, Apolla left the protection of her tent and rushed at me in a storm of her own making. Guards and servants followed, but she was faster.

"What did you do?" The empress reached me, her hazel eyes hot with fury. "Tell me what you did."

"I healed them." The words came out with little puffs of smoke. "Like you asked."

"I asked you to heal them," she growled. "I had their chains removed because you told me to. I had your crystals moved from the harbor, let you have whatever you needed, and now you've sent them away. *My* dragons."

"No." I climbed to my feet, and mud and rain sluiced down the front of my dress. "I didn't send the dragons anywhere. They felt a tremor coming in the Fallen Isles."

Her expression said that was no real answer.

"They always feel it first. Sense it. Even from so far away, the dragons are connected to the Fallen Isles because they were born from that land—from the very bodies of our gods. And now the earthquakes aren't just—" My voice caught. "They aren't just earthquakes anymore."

Empress Apolla just glared at me as her guards and servants and all the keepers came to stand behind her. Some looked at me as a challenge, while others seemed wary. Even those from the Fallen Isles watched me with uncertain gazes, as though I might breathe fire on them here and now. Even Ilina's father.

"These earthquakes make the dragons act . . ." How?

As though their parents were leaving them? As though they were being abandoned, too?

It was true.

And I could try to explain all that to Apolla, but the fury in her eyes was starting to shift to something else—something darker and harder to soothe.

"I gave you the means to heal the dragons," she hissed over the rush of rain. "I gave you everything I could offer to someone of your station. And this is how you repay me: telling them to go."

"I didn't—" I had, though. I had told them to go, but I'd meant to go without me, go blow fire somewhere else—away from the people and city.

Apolla's gaze was steady and sharp. "You planned this, didn't you?"

"How would I have planned an earthquake? *Why* would I plan for one of my gods to abandon my people?"

She just shook her head. "You tricked them somehow. You've betrayed me."

Lightning flared and thunder clapped, the only break in the endless drone of rain. I tried to keep Apolla's gaze, like a dragon refusing to submit, but the memory of their grief and horror was so strong, and my own knowledge of another god rising—it was too much. It was overwhelming.

"Guards." Apolla snapped her fingers, and a pair of uniformed men closed in. "Escort Mira and the island keepers to the barge. We're returning to the palace." She spun to address one of the servants. "Send a message ahead of us.

I want the throne room ready. Summon Mira's friends. All the other islanders who were taken off the ships. Including"—Apolla glanced at me—"her governments. Bring them to me in the throne room."

"And the court, Your Eminence?" One of the servants already had the small communication device out.

Apolla pressed her mouth into a straight line, so hard her lips lost color. Then: "Yes. Summon everyone. I wish to make an announcement."

The guards flanked me.

"Will you go without fighting?" Apolla turned her attention back on me. "Remember, I have Ilina's father right here. And all your friends are back at the palace. If you can't control yourself . . ."

"Your threats are unbecoming." I stepped around her—moving toward the barge still moored on the rain-swollen river. We both knew I wouldn't resist going back to the palace. That had never been a question. But the fact that she had felt the need to threaten me . . . That was revealing.

She was scared.

She didn't know what I would do.

She didn't know what I *could* do.

And maybe neither did I, because I'd never had wings without noorestones until now. But I knew what it meant: every day, I was becoming more of Mira the Dragon—and less of Mira the Girl.

When I reached the barge, I was deposited inside the

main cabin, where the last of the rainwater hissed off my skin and clothes, leaving my dress torn and stained with smears of dried mud. A table held a carafe of cold water and four empty glasses, a tray of refreshments, and several sheafs of paper. Drafts of the agreements we'd discussed—before the dragons had flown away.

They closed the door, leaving me alone in the dark; no one had touched the light sigils, and I didn't want to risk the guards seeing anything I did as a threat. Rain drummed on the roof, a desolate and hollow sound.

For several minutes, I stood in the center of the cabin, trying not to let my thoughts drift to the people who were about to lose a god, to the dragons who were losing another parent, or to my friends. I could only imagine what they would think when they were summoned to the throne room.

Finally, Apolla's voice sounded from the deck, and the barge lurched into motion down the river once more.

When the cabin door opened, the empress stood there, framed by stormlight: bright and beautiful and unforgiving. The clatter of rain was loud against the deck, then muted as the door swung closed behind her. She tapped the nearest light sigil, and a warm, flickering glow filled the space as she just looked at me, evaluating.

Her anger had cooled, but now she was thinking clearly again. That seemed more dangerous.

"Sit, Mira." She gestured to one of the chairs.

"I'll stand."

She only lifted an eyebrow before taking one of the chairs herself. "I know why you came to the Algotti Empire." She kept her tone conversational as she poured a glass of water—for herself—and drank deeply. "I knew it the moment you entered my throne room."

My breath caught, and instinctively I stretched out my mind for a noorestone—to burn away the anxiety—but there were none. Only the scattered piles of darkened crystals in the park, growing more distant as the barge lumbered down the river. There wasn't even a spark left in them.

Now threads of panic seeped through me like a poison. I forced myself to breathe evenly.

"You know we've been having your apartments monitored."

"Of course." My voice came thin.

"My listeners told me you'd come looking for legends about something called the first dragon, but none of us knew what that meant. But I saw your face as you came into the throne room. I saw the way you looked at the bones—the way your friends looked at them, too." She smiled and sipped her water. "I've seen awe, admiration, fear. Often shock. Those are natural reactions to seeing a huge dragon skeleton. But I've never seen *love*."

My heart pounded too hard, too fast, and everything seemed to be spinning. She'd known this whole time. Maybe not that I wanted to take the bones back to the Fallen Isles, but that I hadn't come simply to warn her of Paorah's attack, and that I hadn't come simply to take over his agreement with her. She'd known that I had come for something else entirely, and she'd been waiting for me to make some sort of move toward taking what I wanted.

She probably thought this was it.

And now she hated me.

"Tell me," Apolla said. "What good are my dragon bones to you? And when were you planning to steal them from me?"

CHAPTER THIRTY-THREE

APOLLA WAS NOT A PERSON WHO DELIGHTED IN CRU-
elty, and for that, I was grateful.

When I held my silence, she didn't threaten to hurt me,
or hurt everyone I loved. She just nibbled on the fruits and
cheeses as she flipped through documents, and when we
arrived at the palace, she declared that both of us would
need to change before we were presentable.

"I won't have anyone imagining I treat my guests
so poorly." The empress glanced derisively at the mud
streaked down my dress. "Clean her up. Put her in something beautiful."

I didn't resist as I was taken through the palace. The
halls were empty—everyone was already waiting in the
throne room—and my apartments were quiet except for

the fountain bubbling in the center of the public parlor.

In my suite, the attendants peeled off the filthy dress, and—once I'd been scrubbed clean—they approached with a soft blue gown, embroidered with silver filigree across the bodice.

I waved it away. Though it was stunning, I didn't want to go wearing an imperial-style gown. I wanted to go as the Hopebearer.

"Get one of my hunting dresses," I said. "The deep pink with white-gold trim." That, with black leggings and boots, would be more than sufficient.

The attendant holding the gown shook her head. "I'm sorry. It's not here."

"What do you mean?" I glanced around the dressing room. Now that she said it, I didn't see the bag I'd brought from the Fallen Isles. "Where are my things?"

"I'm sorry. I don't know." Her eyes were round, like she thought I might hurt her. Like she'd already heard what I'd become in the dragon park.

How quickly she'd learned to fear me.

Thunder shook the whole palace as I sighed and allowed them to dress me in their choice of gowns. Hair, shoes, nails: with the amount of care they put into my appearance, it might have been difficult to remember that Apolla hated me now. Then the guards escorted me to the throne room.

Even before I got there, I could feel the first dragon.

It was remarkable how powerful a presence she had,

even two millennia dead. When I stood before the open doors, hearing the buzz of conversation—worry and delight and speculation—the great bones drew my eyes. I looked at her, and she looked at me.

The first and the last.

No one else paid her any mind. The courtiers spoke only to one another, and if they glanced the first dragon's way, it was only to confirm that Apolla hadn't yet appeared on her throne.

Before I could scan the court for the other islanders, my guards escorted me to one of the high galleries where my friends—Ilina, Chenda, Gerel, Hristo, Zara, and Aaru—were already positioned. We'd been sectioned off from the rest of the imperial court, and from up here, we had a clear view of the entire throne room: the white columns and statues, the brightly dressed courtiers in the upper and lower galleries, and Apolla's throne.

And of course, beyond that, the bones of the first dragon, lit in the warm glow of flickering sigils. Beautiful. Deadly. Long dead.

When I'd arrived, my friends had been staring at her, hope naked on their faces, but now they turned to me and—after hugs and questions and Aaru slipping his hand into mine—I gave them the short version of everything that had happened since this morning.

"Khulan is rising?" Gerel clenched her jaw and swallowed hard, clearly trying not to cry.

"I'm sorry," I whispered.

Chenda took Gerel's hand and squeezed.

"What do you think she's going to announce?" Ilina glanced around the throne room, her face hard, and I knew she wanted to talk about Khulan, but not here.

"Nothing good," I said. "Where are LaLa and Crystal?"

"Outside." Hristo frowned. "They were already worried when they couldn't find you, and then they started behaving the same as they did the other night. The skylight above the fountain opens, it turns out. When they started breathing fire, one of the attendants opened it and the dragons got through before we could stop them."

My heart sank, but I didn't have time to worry any more, because a young man at the door announced Apolla, and she strode down the aisle, straight-backed and severe in her movements. Of course, she wore white and gold, with a long cape, a perfect and elegant contrast to her court.

As she went by, I caught the way courtiers' eyes shifted to the gallery below ours, twisted with outright frowns and offended glances.

"Who's down there?" I glanced at Aaru.

His quiet code was soft, quick against my knuckles. ::Islanders.::

The court hushed as Apolla reached her throne and turned to face everyone. She didn't speak, but it wasn't necessary. Everyone—the finely dressed courtiers, the guards, the servants—bowed low and murmured, "Your Eminence."

No one from my gallery bowed.

Rain droned against the walls of the palace, and thunder vibrated through the floor. Aaru squeezed my hand, and I wondered if storms would always remind him of Idris.

Apolla gazed around the room, pausing only a moment on the seven of us up here, not bowing, not showing submission. If she was surprised, or annoyed, she hid it behind her mask of cool superiority. "You may rise." Her voice came low and deep, more like the empress I'd first met, less like the young woman who'd revealed her love of dragons.

The people straightened.

"People of the Algotti Empire." Her voice carried through the throne room; a few members of her court listed forward, as though to catch every syllable, every nuance in her tone. Maybe they didn't worship her as a goddess, but they *did* worship her. That much was clear. She went on: "Recently, we welcomed guests from the Fallen Isles. Some of you may know already that their world is in trouble. Their gods are pulling themselves out of the sea. Several representatives from the islands have come to us for aid. The first was High Magistrate Paorah, of Anahera. After I agreed to help him, he had our city attacked.

"But we had another visitor, one who promised to help thwart the high magistrate's assault. While she was not successful in preventing the attack, she did help mitigate the damage and death toll. However, helping us—and seeking help for her people—was not the only reason she came here. That, I hope, will be revealed today." Apolla looked up at me. "Please, if you will join me."

::Hate cannot dwell where many stand in love,:: Aaru tapped.

I squeezed his hand and then followed a guard down the gallery stairs, which deposited me toward the main doors of the throne room.

Clad in the blue and silver gown chosen for me, I made my way up the aisle, toward the throne and the empress. I kept my gaze straight ahead—on the bones of the first dragon—but I heard the whispers as I walked past the imperial court on one side, and dignitaries from the Fallen Isles on the other.

"Mira," someone breathed. The voice sounded like the First Matriarch of Harta. "Seven gods. She's alive."

"Did you see that scar? How do you think she got that?"

"Oh, seven gods," Dara Soun murmured. "I saw her during the new year. She didn't have that."

"Has she been here since then? Did the empress kidnap her?"

"Who was that other girl? The one with Elbena?" asked another.

My heart twisted for Tirta, caught up in this horrible conspiracy because she looked enough like me to fool people, and then killed for it. Killed because she dared to dream a better life for herself. And none of them even knew her name.

I lifted my chin and set my eyes, following the graceful lines of the first dragon. The arc of her wings. The length of her spine. The shape of her skull. If only I could get her back to the Fallen Isles—to her home—we stood a chance of saving what remained.

When I reached Apolla, who stood before her throne, I halted.

She motioned me to stand beside her, as though we were together in this announcement she planned to make, and for a moment I felt sick—a sharp twist of disgust in my stomach. Here I was in imperial dress, standing beside the Algotti empress, with nothing to show for *my* position. I wished LaLa hadn't flown off. I wished I had my dragon on my shoulder.

I did have the first dragon behind me, but only a few knew what she meant.

"Before you," said the empress, "stands Mira Minkoba. Hopebearer. Dragonhearted. She is not dead, as some of you believed."

Muttering filled the gallery where the islanders stood.

Apolla turned to me and said softly, "Mira, I'd like to give you an opportunity to speak to your people—to tell them your truth."

I lifted an eyebrow. "Why?"

Her expression didn't change—not here, in front of all these people—but I sensed a thoughtfulness in her, a hint of the gentleness she sometimes displayed. "We are not friends, as you've said, but I cannot help but see myself in you sometimes. Were we in each other's positions, I'd appreciate the opportunity to speak truth to those who have so long been denied it."

For a moment, I'd thought she meant she wanted me to tell my side of the dragon story first, so that she could contradict me, ridicule me in front of everyone. But that wasn't it: she meant my larger truth, the one I'd been living with for months.

In her way, she was doing me a kindness. Before she made whatever announcement she'd brought everyone here to make—one we both knew I wouldn't like—she wanted to offer this last acknowledgment of the alliance we could have had.

I wished she'd believed me about the dragons.

With a long, steadying breath, I faced the people of the Fallen Isles. Twenty-three of them—Ilina's father, Dara Soun, Eka Delro, and other leaders included—stared at me, waiting.

Maybe this was as strange for them as it was for me. Whatever words came out of my mouth next, they would be *my* words, not theirs. A Hopebearer without a script must have been terrifying for them.

I'd have smiled if I wasn't so terrified myself.

While I looked over the islanders, noting who stood next to whom, and which people had cuffs around their wrists, I put my thoughts together before committing them to sound. Time was precious now, and I needed to make every word matter.

These were the people who'd forged me, who'd hurt and used me, and who'd denied me the freedom to make my own choices.

It was time to offer them a choice.

"Thank you," I said after a moment. I knew this part: the waiting, the working myself up to speaking, and the weight of expectation that clung to my words. "Although the Mira Treaty was named after me, I think it's fair to say that the treaty shaped the course of my life. For seventeen years, I believed in the treaty—the intentions behind those compassionate words, the hope for the future, and the promise that my generation would inherit a better world. That faith was never shaken until the day I was imprisoned for trying to uphold the ideals set forth in the treaty." Everyone in the room went quiet, some with confusion, some with knowing. "Allow me to explain.

"In addition to uniting the Fallen Isles and ensuring equality among our people, the treaty was meant to protect dragons, the children of our gods. But when I found evidence of corruption—someone sending dragons where they didn't belong—I was imprisoned in the Pit. Tortured. Made to see others tortured." I glanced up at Aaru, heart twisting inside my chest. "It was there, in the Pit, I first began to untangle the truths of the Mira Treaty.

"First, I was told the treaty sold the Fallen Isles to the Algotti Empire; my father, the architect of the treaty, confirmed this. But that was merely another layer of an even more complex lie. The truth is that the Mira Treaty bent

405

all the Fallen Isles to one island: Anahera.

"Years before High Magistrate Paorah was elected to his office, he worked to bring the Mira Treaty to life, even as he claimed to oppose it. He did this to lend him credit for the day he declared the treaty useless—and then slaughtered the girl who was pretending to be me."

In the gallery where the islanders stood, a few people shifted with discomfort. Many of them had witnessed that murder.

"High Magistrate Paorah manipulated everyone, without caring that it would damn hundreds of thousands of people once he got what he wanted: dragons, noorestones, ships, and desperation. That is how you all"—I gestured to the Fallen Isles gallery—"and those aboard our ships ended up here, attacking the very people who wanted to help us.

"Everyone who signed the Mira Treaty in the belief that it was the only way to avoid a long, bloody war—they were all betrayed. And in turn, they betrayed the rest of us. By accepting a lie. By creating a new lie. By not standing up for what was right when they had the chance."

Eka and Dara glanced at each other.

"We are all given a voice," I said. "Some naturally louder and stronger than others, some artificially given more weight. Like mine. You gave me this voice. You tried to deny it when I used it as *I* saw fit. But here I am. Alive. Speaking. I hope you're listening at last."

Uncertain quiet followed, and then Empress Apolla

looked at me thoughtfully. "Is that all you want to say?"

"That is what they need to hear." Behind me, the first dragon's power thrummed and rolled through me, rattling my bones and lending me courage. I wanted, as I had before, to touch her, but now was not the time. Not yet.

Soon.

"Very well." There was a look in Apolla's eyes, a mix of admiration and disappointment, but she just turned to the court. "The Algotti Empire has offered aid to the Fallen Isles in their time of need. Ten ships have been dispatched to rescue survivors of the Great Abandonment. Originally, we intended to bring the survivors here, temporarily. However, after recent events, I've come to a firm decision on how I will handle the refugees."

The low boom of thunder was the only sound.

"Though it pains me, I must turn away the refugees of the Fallen Isles."

A few people gasped, and someone let out a choked sob.

She turned to address those in the lower gallery. "I will restock your ships with food and drinkable water, enough to last for months, if necessary. The ships I sent in advance will continue to work until they're no longer needed. But I'm afraid this will be the extent of the Algotti Empire's influence in Fallen Isles affairs." She smiled, as though to say we'd done this to ourselves. Which we had. "Tonight, you will be sent back to the Fallen Isles to determine your own fates."

"What?" Eka was outraged. "How could you be so

callous? We came to you for help."

"You came at High Magistrate Paorah's behest and attacked my city. Three thousand people are dead because you came here, and I must value the lives of my own people above the lives of yours."

Sadness filled me. I understood why she felt that way, but *The Book of Love* urged us to help one another, to ensure our neighbors were cared for and welcome into our homes if needed.

It was just another reminder that she was not from the Fallen Isles, let alone Damina, and she had likely never read *The Book of Love*. Or, if she had, she thought it encouraged weakness.

"This was not an easy decision to reach," Apolla said, that same grave tone in her voice. "But I have considered all I've given to the Fallen Isles already—my finest apartments, clothes, magic, ships, everything you've asked for and more. I wanted only one thing in exchange. One thing. And I was betrayed."

I hesitated, only a moment. Confrontation rarely worked well for me, and confrontation with an audience—it was nearly unthinkable. But I gathered up my strength and spoke as the Dragonhearted. "I did not betray you. I did exactly as you asked, Apolla."

Someone gasped at my use of her given name.

"You wanted me to heal the dragons," I said. "Those dragons never should have been sent away from the Fallen Isles, but Paorah used the authorization he gave himself via the Mira Treaty and did what he wanted, heedless of the fact that his actions would hasten the Great Abandonment.

"The dragons were dying, thanks to being kept in captivity, but I lifted them out of death. I poured Noore's own fire into them and gave them new life. You saw that." The bones behind me rumbled—or maybe that was the thunder.

Her eyes narrowed. "And then, when they began to scream, you told them to leave."

"One of our gods is rising!" My shout rang across the throne room. Stunned silence rang in response. "*Khulan* is rising. The dragons would have burned everyone in that park if I hadn't told them to go. They were distressed. Frightened. Grieving. Because right now, Khulan is pulling himself out of the ocean, throwing off tens of thousands of innocent people. Right now, a way of life is ripping apart, and irreplaceable artifacts are being crushed under buildings and mountains."

In their gallery, the islanders gasped and whispered, and the warriors there stepped to the rear of the crowd to hide their emotions.

"Yet," Apolla said, "it is not my problem anymore. I want everyone to go. Now. Before I change my mind and have my ships called home. Leave the Algotti Empire and do not return; there will be no safe harbor for you here." She swept her hand toward the great doors.

"You'd condemn hundreds of thousands of people to

death." I made my voice softer. "That's what you're doing, Apolla. You know that, don't you?"

"I did not become the Algotti empress by acts of charity, Hopebearer. You know this." We glared at each other for a moment longer. "I've given you ten ships. And I'm giving you the lives of these people—some who were complicit in the attack on my city—and rations to feed them during the long journey home."

"Where they will die."

"Where they will no longer be my problem." She just shook her head. "This is the height of my generosity. There is no more after this."

At last, I bowed my head. We'd gotten ships. Our people. Our lives. "All right," I said. "We will go."

"Everyone but you." Apolla's voice was low, but the room was quiet—save the droning rain—so everyone heard. The reactions were immediate:

"No!"

"You can't have her!"

"This is outrageous!"

The noise erupted throughout the throne room, and all I could do was stand there in shocked silence.

Chaos broke out above, as Gerel and Hristo pushed their way down the stairs to the main floor, the others following in their wake. Guards rushed in to stop them, but Gerel was stronger than fifteen of them put together, and Hristo would never let anyone come between him and me. Together, they shoved a path for the others to follow, and then they were all marching up the aisle.

Even Eka, Dara, and some of the other government officials had broken free of their assigned area.

But the empress's guards were fast. They stepped in front of us, creating a human wall as they drew their swords.

Gerel and Hristo stopped short; neither was armed.

"Why?" My voice cut through the cacophony of protests.

Empress Apolla frowned at me. "You are far too valuable," she said. "I've seen what you can do. Besides, your people will not harm my city while you're here. The substance that affected your giant noorestones has been removed from your ships and destroyed, and the catapult that launched that noorestone has been appropriated for alternative use. Their removal made room for more food rations. I'm sure everyone agrees they'd rather have food than weapons."

"Then you've crippled our ships. They were only able to cross the sea because of the substance. It will take decans to return without it." And we had mere days before the last gods rose.

Apolla smiled grimly. "Then they'd better leave now."

My heart twisted. "Please reconsider."

"I've already considered. Everyone from the Fallen Isles—except you—will leave immediately. The ships are being prepared as we speak."

"Release Mira." Hristo stepped forward.

"No." Apolla sighed. "If you don't go, then I'll deem you subjects of the empire. You'll certainly be welcome to stay here, if that's the case, but you'll also be arrested and placed in prison for your attack on my person."

Gerel glanced at Hristo, to see whether he planned to rush through the guards and grab me, I supposed. And beyond them, I caught Ilina's worried gaze, and Zara hugging herself as she looked on, and Chenda making her shadow flutter beneath the guards—like she might be able to use it to help free me.

And then there was Aaru, dark-eyed and worried, but he kept himself pulled up tall as our gazes locked. ::**What do you want?**:: he tapped.

They would fight for me, I knew it. And they would lose.

A deep hum set in my soul, drawing me toward the first dragon. I needed to go to her. I needed to touch her. I needed to—

No. First I needed to defuse this situation. My heart pounded, but I made myself speak the word: "Go."

"What?" Chenda's mouth dropped open.

"You can't be serious." Zara stepped toward me, but the guards blocked her way. "Mira, you're coming with us."

"No," I said. "You need to go. Find another island to settle on for now. Search for a new home."

Ilina shook her head. "We'll never make it home in time to save anyone. And what about—" Her eyes flickered to the bones of the first dragon behind me.

"It doesn't matter anymore," I said. "I'm sorry. This is the only way."

Zara stared at me, confusion in her eyes, and for a moment, we shared the sort of sisterly connection I'd always wished for us to have. Our relationship had changed so much in the last few decans, and now that we could almost acknowledge liking each other, the empress wanted to force us apart.

I looked at Apolla. "Please allow me to say good-bye to my friends. My sister, at least."

The empress considered; I saw the way she weighed the outcomes, the chances of me somehow betraying her, and how she'd appear to her court. At last, she shook her head. "You've already wasted your time. The tide will go out soon, and if they aren't gone by nightfall, everyone here will be my prisoner."

A whispered wave spread through the imperial court: speculation, amusement, anticipation.

Maybe she was a cruel person after all.

"I'm sorry," I told Zara. Then I hugged myself and addressed the others, tapping and tapping my elbow. "I'm sorry, but you have to go."

Hristo started forward again, but Aaru put his hand on his shoulder. "We go." Aaru wasn't looking at Hristo, though; his gaze was locked on my tapping.

The others stared at Aaru, their faces twisted with confusion. How could he—who claimed to love me—be the first to say to go? How could he abandon me?

But Aaru always respected my wishes. Always.

"No." Zara clutched her fists to her chest as she met my eyes; hers were shiny with unshed tears as Ilina wrapped her arms around her. "I don't want to leave you."

"It's all right," I said softly. "Find Mother."

"Go." Apolla waved them away.

And with that, my people were escorted out of the throne room.

CHAPTER THIRTY-FOUR

FOR AN HOUR AFTER MY PEOPLE LEFT, APOLLA CON-tinued holding court.

Through the petitions and concerns, I stood beside her: a prize won in some indirect battle she believed was the war. Finally, the imperial court began to file out, their gowns sweeping and their suits shimmering in the sigil light.

When they were gone, leaving only the guards and statues and dragon bones, a team of servants hurried in to clean bits of paper and dirt off the floor. They were fast, nearly noiseless as they worked, and then Apolla and I were alone—except for the statue-like guards.

"You made the right decision." She turned to me. "I know it wasn't easy for you to send them away, but it was for the best."

"I made the only decision that ensured their freedom. It wasn't a fair choice." My back was starting to hurt from standing, but I wouldn't let down my guard, even if it was only by sitting.

"Most choices aren't fair to someone." She regarded me with a sad smile. "Tell me, Hopebearer, would you do anything for your people?"

"I came here, didn't I?" Even as the words snapped out of me, I knew that getting on a ship and sailing to the relative safety of the mainland was hardly *anything*. The presence of the first dragon pulsed in my chest, like a second heartbeat, and I couldn't help but remember the words from *The Book of Destruction*: *it is sacrifice that enables change.*

That was anything. Sacrificing my human soul so the dragon soul could reign. Sacrificing my future with my friends so they could have a home.

Would I do anything?

Anything?

"Are you afraid?" Apolla's pale eyes missed nothing. "You seem nervous."

"I'm worried my friends will drift across the ocean for months and die, because the gods will be gone and there will be nowhere for them to make land." I turned to her, but even as I spoke, I knew it was pointless. "You've sent them out to die. Thousands of people."

She clenched her jaw. "You should have thought of that before."

"I doubt it would have mattered." I strode toward the skull of the first dragon, and the throb of power intensified. "No matter what I'd done with those dragons, you'd have decided to keep me here."

Apolla watched me, not moving from her position. "I meant what I said about my city being safer with you here. If your people figure out how to hurl another noorestone at us, you'll be able to mitigate the damage the way you did last time."

The way I'd done it last time had nearly ripped me apart.

"I'm also hoping you'll bring my dragons back to me. They're more than creatures. I know you feel the same way. I want them to be my family."

That was impossible, but it didn't benefit me to deny her that dream. "Those are not the real reasons. You already prevented my people from attacking Sunder when you removed the noorestone substance and the catapult. And once the earthquake is over, it will be a simple matter to call the dragons back to the park—although I can't say what will happen during the next one."

Only three more.

"Tell me the truth," I said. "You owe me that much."

She sighed, not with annoyance, but resignation. She didn't hate me enough to toss me into the nearest prison, which meant she intended to keep me close. And it would be easier to tell me now than endure questions until one or both of us died of old age.

"I know what you are," she murmured. "They call you Hopebearer, and Dragonhearted, but you have a dragon soul. It's clear to see, and after what I witnessed in the park—both times—I have no doubt that you could be a most important asset to my rule."

The Luminary Council had seen me that way, too.

"I am a conqueror, Mira. No, I'm not interested in your islands, and I wouldn't be even if they were staying. Your magic is interesting, but powerless away from its source—aside from the gifts you and your friends possess. Your lands have nothing I value, aside from dragons. And now I have a girl who can tell dragons what to do. Imagine what we could accomplish together."

I sighed. If she believed she could ever persuade me to join her in conquering other kingdoms, then she didn't know me at all.

Seconds ticked away in the back of my head. Every one of them took my friends farther from me, but not fast enough. Not with the limited noorestones.

"Are you hungry?" Apolla asked. "Should we go to dinner?"

It hadn't been long enough—an hour would barely get them out of the harbor—but I had no more time to give them, not without risking more than we could afford.

"Mira." Apolla's tone sharpened. "I asked you a question."

"It's hard to consider whether I'm hungry when you've sent my friends and family off to die, and you're planning

418

how you'll use me to conquer your enemies." I drifted back toward the skull, and the thrum of her power pulsed through me, welcoming and eager. "You know, *The Book of Love* has a great deal to say about forgiveness, as forgiveness is an inherently loving act. It offers peace and resolution to both the person being forgiven, and the person who is forgiving. It's a love that benefits both parties."

"Why are you telling me this?" Apolla drew herself out of her throne, but she didn't approach me, even as I drifted to a stop in front of the skull. My fingers ached to touch it, to complete this connection that had been knitting itself between us since the moment I stepped foot in the throne room.

"We have many holy books in the Fallen Isles," I said. "Over the last few months, I've come to understand that all our books have more in common than I'd ever realized. We may prize our shadows or strength or silence more than someone from another island, but valuing family doesn't prevent you from valuing cleverness as well." I smiled her way. "I suppose I'm telling you this because in spite of our differences, I want you to know that I forgive you, and I think we probably have more in common than we don't."

The confusion began to evaporate from her expression. "Whatever you're doing—"

"I am sorry." I spoke quickly, because her guards were coming to life, slipping through the room as though they weren't sure whether they were needed, only that their empress was frustrated. "I'd have liked to get to know you better. One day be allies."

"Stop."

But it was too late. I pressed my palms against the skull of the first dragon, heart beating in triple time, and power flooded into me. It was different from noorestone energy, more like flying into stars, but familiar all the same. Light flared from the place my skin touched bone, and in the alcove beyond, all the sigils flickered and went dark.

"I hope you'll decide to forgive me one day." I looked at Apolla and offered a smile. "You're going to be angry, but I think you'll understand why I have to do this. You promised to protect your people; I've promised to protect mine."

Before she could protest further—before the guards could reach me—I climbed onto the skull and braced myself. Then, slowly, the first dragon lifted her head for the first time in two thousand years.

Apolla screamed, then slapped her hands over her mouth, as though she still couldn't bear to be seen as anything like human.

The guards drew their swords, but I was high above them, with a nimbus of fire rippling down my body and all along the first dragon's skeleton. Every pass of flame revealed night-black scales that shimmered with stars—echoes of the incredible creature who led the Sundering.

In the back of my head, shrieks of joy and recognition erupted, and nine living dragons hurtled toward the imperial palace as fast as they could fly—LaLa, Crystal, and the others who'd been sent here against their will.

A growl rolled out of me—or the first dragon, I couldn't tell—and every one of the guards backed away to form a circle around the empress.

I gazed down at her. "I'm going to take this dragon home," I said. "And the others as well. They're already on their way."

"How do you know?" The empress's voice seemed tiny coming from the middle of all those guards. I hadn't even threatened her, beyond the growling.

"You were right that I came here for more than I said. And I'm sorry. Perhaps I should have been more forthright from the beginning, although I think you understand my hesitation perfectly well. I've trusted the wrong people before; I'm sure you have, too."

"Mira, if you leave, we can never be friends."

"I told you that already." I smiled down at her as thunder boomed outside, and rain continued its endless drone against the roof. "We're going now, and we're going to keep the Fallen Isles in place. By the time we return your ships, I hope you will have remembered what I said about forgiveness."

"You can't do this," the empress said.

"I can," I whispered. "I told you I would do anything. This is my anything."

With that, I crouched low atop the skull, digging my fingertips against the smooth, ancient bone. The

421

first dragon wrenched her body free of its confines, and together we breathed in—sideways, into second lungs—and fire spun up and out.

Flame burst against the high ceiling, illuminating the throne room in shocks of orange and blue and white. My flame. The first dragon's flame. They were the same. *We* were the same, though I still felt my own body—two arms, two legs, one pounding heart. I felt hers, too, ancient and exhausted, but bursting with determination to go home. After two thousand years, she didn't want to wait anymore.

Fire tore at the ceiling, and the marble began to crack and crumble, crashing to the floor in clouds of white powder. As the ceiling grew thinner and a hole appeared, rain spit through, and the noise of thunder crescendoed.

The empress's guards charged the first dragon, but their blades hit bone with a loud *clang* that sent them staggering back. More soldiers flooded into the throne room, but they backed away quickly when they saw me.

And suddenly, the first dragon and I weren't alone. The other large dragons ripped open the roof, breaking off chunks of marble and glass, widening the hole as quickly as they could. The shredded parts of the building crashed to the floor, causing the guards to raise their shields around the empress—to protect her from debris—and a human part of me felt guilty for ruining her throne room so soon after Paorah's people ruined parts of her city.

But then the hole in the ceiling was big enough for us to fit through, and the first dragon stomped over the wet rubble until we could rear back and climb up.

It was awkward and uncomfortable, squeezing out of the palace through a hole in the roof, but once her wings were through, the rest followed quickly, and we crouched beside the other dragons, all of us on the storm-slick roof.

Wind grabbed at my hair and gown, but I didn't struggle to stay on, even when the smooth surface of her skull grew slippery with the lashing rain. I could feel when she was about to move, when she would turn. I compensated for her every motion before it even happened.

In the throne room below, under the rumble of rain and thunder, I could hear shouts and orders to summon archers and mages. And from the palace grounds and city, terrified screams sounded.

We had to go.

Carefully, I climbed down the first dragon's spine, until I reached the vertebrae directly between her wings.

Power pulsed through me, a thousand lightning strikes, as I bent low and *breathed*.

Fire rippled.

My back muscles flexed and grew.

Seven big dragons pushed into the air.

LaLa and Crystal floated around me, chittering with encouragement and excitement.

And when the way was clear, my wings—huge and fiery and strong—settled perfectly inside the skeletal wings of the first dragon, and together, we leaped into the sky.

CHAPTER THIRTY-FIVE

MY WINGS.

My wings.

They were fire and thunder, wind and song, strength and light as they carried me over the imperial palace. Rain sizzled through the flame, passed between the bones, but still we—the first dragon and I—stayed aloft. My wings defied the rules of the world as I'd previously understood them, and yet the fact that we were flying was undeniable. It was exhilarating, terrifying, overwhelming.

I spun through the sky, shrieking with unadulterated joy at the simple miracle of flight.

And it *was* a miracle, because though we were both dragons, neither of us was particularly suited to the task right now: one of us wore frail human skin, and the other was long dead. Yet alive. Mixed up with each other, it didn't matter.

And we were going home.

Wind tangled my hair and dress, glided around the curves of my body. I could feel both the piece of me clutching the knobs of the first dragon's spine, and the electric flickers of muscle and sinew and scales that shimmered across the skeletal expanse. The effect was fleeting, but from the corner of my eye, it almost looked as though she was struggling to become whole again.

Soon.

Very soon.

The eclipse was only seven days away.

With a sky-shattering roar, I flapped my wings, echoing thunder as I pushed myself higher and higher over the city. The sight drew memories from both sides of me, and as I looked down on the soft curves of orderly streets, the gentle turn of the River Akron, and the black crater where the noorestone had struck and its conflagration spread out, I saw the past lying atop the present: crowded, cluttered roads with crumbling houses, wild growth on the banks of the river, and everything burning under the brilliant fire blasted from all the dragons who'd come here to defend the Fallen Isles.

A city razed. A city reborn. A part of me wanted to complete my—her—mission from two thousand years ago, but these were different people, and they'd already been hurt.

I breathed in the scent of ash that boiled up from the noorestone site, making myself look at the broken buildings and medical tents before moving onward, toward the obsidian dragons that stood at the mouth of the river.

Even from flight, with the real creatures all around me, the black glass dragons were beautiful, majestic. The people of Sunder were proud of them, and they should be, but they weren't real. They were the only dragons the Algotti empress would ever own.

As all of us flew between the black dragons, one after another, lightning cracked across the sky, making the back of my throat tingle.

I lifted my head and breathed fire.

We must have looked terrifying to anyone on the ground. As far as dragons went, the *mimikus* and *ignituses* weren't big, but the former kept shifting shades of gray—to blend with the storm above—and the latter looked like a pair of flying suns. And the others—they were *big*. Their wings made windstorms, and their roars shook the whole sky.

And then there was the first dragon. Me. Us.

An immense skeletal dragon who'd been displayed in the empress's throne room for decades. Centuries. Maybe longer. With wings of fire and a cry that could rip the world asunder. I imagined anyone who looked up went inside their homes as quickly as possible.

They couldn't see me up here, a young woman in a sodden blue gown, or the pair of *raptuses* clutching to the

426

first dragon's bones, shrieking with wild abandon. Their wings were tented up, their faces turned high, and hot blue flame poured around their teeth and dragged along their tiny gold and silver bodies. It was safer for them here, where the bigger dragons wouldn't accidentally knock them around, and the first dragon welcomed her tiny wingsisters.

And she loved it. She loved all of this as much as I did. Now that she was surrounded by her own kind, a fierce, burning joy filled her. Flying together, wings pounding, and fire burning through the rain: this was everything she'd wanted for two millennia.

As we flew over the harbor, the first dragon and I dipped low, letting the tips of our wings skim across the surface. Trails of steam rose up behind us, and the *raptuses* chittered with glee.

Then: human voices called, and black ships moved into formation. Mages—men and women wearing the same kind of robes I'd seen when I'd first arrived—climbed onto the decks and lifted their hands.

Through my connection with the dragons, I could feel their curiosity, the stir of fire in their throats. I understood, too, the desire to hurt those who'd hurt them.

But now wasn't the time to pit dragon fire against imperial magic. I'd promised them we'd all go home, so I drew myself up and up and up, and the other seven followed until the ships were toys in the water.

It was from this height I realized the harbor guard and

mages weren't mobilizing against us.

The Fallen Isles fleet moved west as quickly as it could, but without the noorestone substance, they'd never be able to outrun the imperial ships. My friends had only moments before they were in range of the cannons.

I pulled down again, breathed into my second lungs, and screamed fire into the water between the two fleets.

Steam surged upward, then more and more as the other seven dragons flew after me, spitting fire into the sea.

The black ships did not slow their approach.

I turned and passed between them again, blowing fire as hot as I could manage. The others came after me, and within moments we'd created a wall of steam and boiling ocean, but still the black ships didn't slow.

Again, I turned and spit fire, hitting the same stretch of ocean as before. My heart sped as I watched the ships draw near the steam pouring upward. I didn't want them to get hurt—that was why I'd given them time to stop—but if they were going to sail straight into the steam . . .

Maybe they didn't care about crew lives. Maybe their mages would protect them. I didn't understand enough about imperial magic to know what they were capable of.

But finally, as I went back for a fourth pass between the fleets, the black ships began to slow. By the time I came around again, all the other big dragons flying in my wake, the imperial fleet had fully stopped.

Time was less meaningful to dragons, but we could

grow bored—even of breathing fire. But the storm waned and the rain thinned, and still I directed the others back again and again, blocking the way of the imperial fleet with our flames. And every time I looked toward the Fallen Isles fleet, they were farther away, although it wouldn't take much for the black ships to catch up. So we burned and burned, and finally, some communication must have been sent to the imperial ships, because they adjusted their sails and changed course—heading back to the mainland.

My dragons and I stayed for a while longer, circling until the island ships had fully vanished in the distance. Only when it seemed clear the empress wasn't going to come after us did I peel away, flying westward.

Light from the setting sun gleamed across the water, beautiful and bright. I let myself fall into the joy of flying again, wings pumping as we caught up to the Fallen Isles fleet. A cheer rose from below, people celebrating the freed dragons and, perhaps, me. My flight with the first dragon.

LaLa and Crystal chittered and let go of the first dragon at the same time, catching the great gust of wind after me. Then, together, they dove toward the ship—toward Ilina, who waited for them with open arms. Another wave of celebration greeted them, but through our connection, I knew they only cared about seeing Ilina and Hristo again, and the full bellies they'd have after receiving whatever treats she'd stashed away for them.

I flew.

My wings. My roar. My sky. My life.

I flew as the sun lowered and the sky purpled, and finally I came back to myself. Still connected, still flying, but ready to settle and change into *my* clothes—not Apolla's gift.

For a moment, I wasn't sure how I was supposed to land, or if I even could, but the dragon part of me knew what to do. I found the *Star-Touched* and set myself down, careful of the sails and lines and delicate people. I was immense, but I made myself as small as possible.

And that was all.

The burning wings vanished. The fire in my throat went out. And I was just a girl clutching the damp bones of the biggest dragon that ever lived.

I thought I'd feel weak, my human muscles trembling after the strain of clinging to the first dragon for hours. I thought I'd want nothing more than to sink into the nearest hammock and sleep for a decan. But instead, I felt strong. I felt good. I felt *hopeful*.

The imperial gown tore as I climbed down, but I didn't care. I landed on the deck with a thump, and then my friends were rushing toward me with questions and exclamations and more questions, and then Aaru wrapped his arms around me and squeezed.

"You did it." His words were soft against my cheek as he kissed me. "You made it."

I hugged him back, feeling the thump of my heart

430

echo his. "Thank you for trusting me."

He pulled back and cupped my cheek, so gentle. "I always have."

I lifted my face and touched my lips to his. Softly, quickly, because everyone else was coming toward us, but enough that he understood I intended to kiss him more thoroughly later.

"Good work, Fancy." Gerel looked up at the circling dragons, almost wistfully. Chenda took her hand.

"I can't believe . . ." Zara glanced at the first dragon and shook her head. "Mother will be *so* furious."

"I know." It was a risk, but I hugged my sister, fully expecting her to pull away. Instead, she tensed, like a cat not sure whether she should run. "I'm sorry about all of this," I murmured. She hadn't asked to come along, and she was right that she'd been in more danger than ever. But she'd been helpful, and mostly, I was glad she was here. With me.

At last, she relaxed into my embrace—"It's not your fault," she whispered—and then pulled away.

I wanted to say something else, tell her how much I really cared, but we weren't *that* close, and with the eclipse just days away, I didn't think we would ever be. I wished I'd made more of an effort earlier—taken the time to understand her and get to know her. But if one of the last things I had as a human was a sister who sort of liked me . . . that was all right.

Ilina and Hristo had the *raptuses* cradled in their arms

as they came forward. "That was incredible," Ilina said. "And I have a lot of questions."

"I'll try to answer them. But first we need to go. I don't think Apolla's ships will come after us, but I still want to get away from here as fast as possible."

"Unfortunately, we can't move that quickly." Ilina motioned downward, to the middle of the ship where the giant noorestone was housed. "The empress told the truth when she said she had the noorestone stuff removed. Without it, we won't get very far very quickly. And we certainly won't make it home before the eclipse."

"I can push the noorestones," I said. "Like I did with the *Chance Encounter*."

"All of them?" Chenda lifted an eyebrow. "The giant noorestones?"

Hristo frowned. "I don't like it. Not after what happened in the dragon park."

"We don't have a choice." Already, the sun settled beneath the horizon, and the stars began to peek out. The sister moons rose in the east—two halves, one gold and one silver.

"So when we get to the Fallen Isles," Ilina said, "where do we go?"

I lifted my hand for LaLa, and she flapped toward me with a happy squawk. "We go to the birthplace of the first dragon. The island of life and death and life again: Ana-hera."

PART SIX

THE DARKEST DAY

CHAPTER THIRTY-SIX

Damyan rose next.

Through my connection with dragons, I drowned in grief for hours, screaming and sobbing in my cabin until it was over. For all of us, it was a waking nightmare. Even when the quake passed, everyone dragged themselves through their work and cried, because we were too late for yet another island.

I pushed the giant noorestones harder, bringing us closer to our shattered and rising home.

Four times a day, I urged the stones to move the ships faster and faster. We had to time it perfectly, keeping all the ships clear of one another as we flew across the endless swells of the ocean. A collision at these speeds would mean death.

If I could have pushed the noorestones all day, I would have. But touching them, all of them together, was more awful than I'd anticipated. It felt like a slow poison to my dragon soul, sapping my strength.

The sixth morning, I could hardly pull myself out of bed. Every muscle in my body hurt, and the idea of connecting with the giant noorestones again made my stomach tie into a thousand knots. Plus, I'd been having nightmares. In them, we'd already reached the Fallen Isles, but no one realized because the islands were gone; the Great Abandonment had finished before our return.

They weren't dragon dreams. They were real nightmares, made out of fear and anxiety and overwhelming grief. Still, they haunted me as I shook myself into wakefulness.

Aaru, who'd been sitting on the bed beside me, pressed the back of his hand to my forehead. "You have a fever."

"It's just the dragon soul." My voice was scratchy, but that was because I wasn't sleeping well enough. "I can look at the sun, and water steams off my skin after baths. I'm different from what I used to be." I forced a smile, but it hurt. Everything hurt. Especially the knowledge that soon, I'd become a dragon for the rest of time, the new link between the gods and the people, and I'd never have another quiet moment with Aaru again.

This might be the last one I ever got.

"That doesn't mean you don't have a fever." He caressed my cheek and chin, so gentle in the way he touched me.

"We're almost home. If you can't push the noorestones again—"

"I can." I struggled to sit up, pretending not to notice the way he helped me balance. "If we're almost there, they should only need me a couple more times. And then . . ."

"And then?"

Then I took the first dragon to her birthplace and begged the gods for mercy. Begged them to stay. Promised that humans would take better care of dragons if I were one, too.

It is sacrifice that enables change.

It was what I'd been born for.

"Mira?" Aaru tilted my chin up. In the flickering sigil light, his features were soft and concerned. "And then what?"

"I'll know when we get there." I watched him, waiting to see if he believed me, hoping my heartbeat didn't give me away. He'd already lost so many people; surely I could protect him for a while longer.

Aaru cupped my cheek and kissed me, and I couldn't tell whether he believed me or not.

But he was kissing me, so I kissed him back, letting myself get lost in the careful way his lips touched mine, and the gentle way his fingertips traced over my face. It felt as though he was memorizing the texture of my skin, the line of my jaw, and the swell of my cheek; it felt as though he was committing me to his heart.

Maybe he did understand that if everything went

according to plan, these could be our final hours together.

Aaru let out a small, desperate moan as our kiss deepened, igniting a fire of longing inside me. I pulled closer until I sat on him, facing him. Our chests pressed tight together; our leg muscles clenched against each other. He leaned back a little, braced with one arm, and held me to him with the other. His palm was flat against my spine, smoothing lower until he found the curve of my bottom. He hesitated there, but only a moment. Then he was caressing down my thigh, exploring the shape of my body like he'd never get another chance.

I understood. I needed to touch him, needed to fit everything I felt for him into this small space of time. "I love you," I whispered, hoarse. "I've always loved you."

"Mira." He kissed my neck, my collarbone. "I want to—"

Footsteps sounded outside the small cabin, and Aaru froze, listening.

After a moment, his body softened against mine, easing away with a resigned sigh. "It's Hristo."

"Pretend like we're not here." My heart still pounded with whatever he'd been about to say before. What did he want?

Smiling a little, Aaru drew back and tucked a strand of hair away from my face. "Will you let me up?"

"If I say no, can we stay like this forever?"

He brushed his fingertips across my lips, and then the knock sounded on the door.

I sighed and twisted off him, grimacing at the pain in my muscles. For a moment, I'd forgotten how much I hurt.

Aaru picked himself up and answered the door.

"The captains are ready," Hristo said.

Biting off a groan, I bent over to lace up my boots, then heaved myself up, muscles pinching and stabbing with every motion.

Both boys watched me, but when they offered help, I waved them away. I wasn't above leaning on them, but if I arrived on the main deck looking like I felt . . .

No. I needed to appear strong, because whether I liked it or not, the Fallen Isles fleet followed my command.

We stopped by the mess long enough to get a drink of water and a bite of the rations Apolla had stowed on the ship prior to my breakout. The idea of food made my stomach flip uncomfortably, but I forced it down anyway. If I wanted to convince everyone of my wellness, I had to be seen eating; last night, Ilina had told me she'd overheard people talking about how I'd lost weight even in these last few days.

Dawn gleamed over the main deck as the three of us climbed up. Water dipped and swelled all around, and the other ten ships followed in our wake. Above, seven dragons flew in formation. They could have reached the islands already, but they'd stayed behind to escort us, even though we were supposed to be the ones protecting them. I imagined they were exhausted, flying for days like this. Two of the ships had managed to clear spaces large

439

enough for even the *titanus* to land and sleep, but it wasn't much of a break, especially with the giant noorestones all around. But like me, they took what they could get.

The first dragon, of course, had not moved from her place on the *Star-Touched*, and as we drew closer to the Fallen Isles, I could feel her power growing. One night, I'd thought I'd seen the bones glowing like noorestones, but no one else had commented on it.

"Are you ready?" Gerel asked as I reached the bow.

Wind tugged at my hair, and the scent of salt tickled my nose. Water stretched all around, brilliant and blue and serene. And not too far away, islands were being ripped up from their roots and people were dying.

"I'm ready to go home." My voice didn't sound quite as strong as I wanted, but only my friends were here to witness my weakness.

"All right," she said gently.

I gripped the rail and closed my eyes, opening my awareness to the dark harmony of eleven unstable noorestones. Their energy skittered through me, sharp and ugly, straining to escape its crystal cages. Then I grabbed the noorestones and *pushed*.

Those awful, flickering sparks of Noore's own fire flared hot, and the ships lurched forward, jerking over the water without grace. The movement made me feel sick, but I urged the ships onward, trying to ignore the seep of poison.

It was easy to lose track of time with noorestones.

With the regular ones, I usually was surprised by how much time had passed, because using them was so easy, so natural. With these stones, however, minutes seemed endless, and I forced myself to count out the seconds to keep myself from asking over and over if an hour had passed.

An hour had not passed.

Three hundred seconds.

Five hundred.

A thousand.

I bit off a scream and kept counting.

At two thousand four hundred and forty-two seconds, someone gripped my arm. "Stop!"

I didn't ask questions. I let go of the noorestones as quickly as I'd have dropped a venomous slug, and the ships all jolted back to their normal speeds.

I doubled over, the rail catching my stomach, and heaved up the breakfast I'd forced down earlier.

Hands touched my back and shoulders as I spit out the rancid taste and caught my breath. Every muscle in my body trembled, but as the crew started to shout, I pushed myself up just enough to see what happened.

Evidence of the Great Abandonment spread out before the ship: bodies on boats, driftwood, and floating wreckage.

Some were dead, their corpses bloated and sunburned. Others clung to their small rafts, waving as we approached, begging for help. And still others were harder to tell; they might have been unconscious, or they might have slipped away moments before.

All the ships lowered lifeboats, and crewmen spent hours pulling the living aboard. As far as the dead, we couldn't take bodies onto these ships, not with space so tight, so they lashed the wreckage and rafts together and pushed them away from our small fleet.

When we were sure the wind wouldn't blow smoke back at us, I followed my threads to the seven big dragons and asked them to burn it.

It was better than letting them float out here forever.

The *Star-Touched* was silent, save the rush of fire in the distance. It seemed like we ought to have said something meaningful, a eulogy of some kind, but I couldn't make myself speak as the flames consumed the pyre. The grief was too much.

And the horror.

Because new nightmares loomed on the western horizon:

1. *The now-familiar shape of Idris hunched over, waiting for the other gods to join him.*
2. *A muscular figure, standing straight up, mace lifted, and dripping with immense chains meant to bind him to the seabed.*
3. *A man, tall and graceful, reaching for something—someone—still in the water. Waiting for her to rise.*

4. *A woman, round with late pregnancy, cradling her belly in her arms.*
5. *A slice of ink blacking out the sky. Indistinct but terrifying.*

Only two gods were left in the ocean.
One day until the eclipse.

CHAPTER THIRTY-SEVEN

By late afternoon, we'd fished dozens more people out of the ocean.

They were sick and sunburned, eyes crusted over with salt. Some clutched small personal items—jewelry or bags or dolls—but most had nothing at all, beyond the ragged clothes they wore. A few didn't even have clothes; they'd given them to the children, to shield them from the unforgiving sun.

The infirmaries grew crowded with survivors, and soon all the cabins were taken over and made into sickrooms where people lay in the cool darkness, sipping coconut water as they clung to life.

Three died in there, and we consoled ourselves by saying at least they'd gone surrounded by friendly faces, not on the open ocean, alone but for the dead.

We burned their bodies, and those of the countless others we'd been too late to save, and no one talked about the gods looming taller and taller as we came within sight of Anahera's red cliffs and the brightly lit city of Flamecrest. We just looked at them, felt the weight of the shadows falling over us, and wondered if it was too late for prayer.

Give me peace. Give me grace. Give me enough love in my heart.

I stared back at Damyan, who'd wrenched himself up from the ocean, separated from Darina until she, too, made ready to abandon us.

How could our gods, these beings who'd given us life and gifts and a place to live, desert us? How could they turn their backs on their own children?

My chest tightened with grief I'd never imagined possible, and the prolonged presence of the giant noorestones. If I'd pushed them again, we'd have been in Flamecrest hours ago. But the people floating on the open ocean . . .

None of us could have passed them by—or crashed atop them—and lived with ourselves.

Now, my friends and I stood at the bow of the *Star-Touched*, the bones of the first dragon coiled up behind us.

Gerel leaned her head on Chenda's shoulder as they looked at their gods, not quite silhouetted as the sun edged lower in the sky. The chains hanging from Khulan's body—the God Shackle, warriors called it—gleamed with rust and uprooted plant life as they swung through empty air. And Bopha—she was a dark, terrifying form who cast no shadow on the water. She *was* the shadow.

Aaru and Hristo stood together, both quiet as they faced Harta, and whatever complicated feelings my protector felt toward the island of his birth—they didn't seem to matter right now. His god had risen and now he would never get to know what a life there would be like—not the way it was before.

And then there were Ilina, Zara, and me. LaLa and Crystal perched on the rail between us, chirping softly. We watched Damyan for a while, his arms open and waiting for Darina to join him. I wondered if it had hurt, that separation. They were two gods, two islands, but connected by an isthmus where his arms held her. Everyone spoke of them as one island, so much that we'd long ago combined their names, but now . . . now they were broken in two, torn apart by the Great Abandonment.

It had always been a choice, I thought. This sacrifice. This slow shift of my human soul into the dragon soul. Just because it was laid out in text didn't mean it wasn't my decision in the end.

But now, seeing them with my own eyes, and witnessing the despair that dragged at my friends, I didn't know how anyone would choose differently. I would let go of my human self. I would become a dragon. And I would do everything in my power to make the Fallen Gods stay.

Even if I was successful, though, the damage was already done. Hundreds of thousands of people were gone.

Homes. Societies. Histories.

Nothing would ever be the same, no matter how we tried.

It wasn't long before we approached the harbor, and my seven large friends flew over the ship-choked port to rest on the red cliffs. A dull noise rose up from the city, like wind.

"What's that?" Hristo asked.

"Cheering." Aaru moved to stand beside me. "They're cheering for the dragons."

"Because they think the dragons are here to protect them?" Ilina shook her head and sighed.

"I think people have been hearing that Paorah was gathering up dragons to appease the goddess of destruction. They probably think this is his doing." I slipped my hand into Aaru's as the *Star-Touched* pushed toward the port, leaving the other ten ships behind. There wasn't enough room for all of them to come in at once, but I suspected few were unhappy with the situation. Why disembark a ship when there was no guarantee of being able to get back on it when the island started to move?

The *Star-Touched* maneuvered toward a berth being cleared, and by the time we eased our way in and the crew began securing the ship, night was full upon us.

"Do you know where the birthplace is?" Hristo scanned the crowded port, searching for danger, probably. "Do you know how to get there? Anahera is a big island."

I closed my eyes, thinking back to my dreams of the

first dragon's creation, the way she'd burst from the ground in an explosion of light and molten rock, her scales glittering with stars. So much had changed in the two thousand years between my birth and hers, but Anahera's nature had not. "Ruins."

Ilina glanced at the cliffs where seven dragons waited, watching us. "Like the ruins up there? The ones we destroyed three decans ago?"

"Like those."

"That seems like something you should have thought of before you destroyed them," Zara muttered. "Will I need these ancient and powerful ruins again? Maybe? Better not rip them apart."

"Yes. These would have been easiest, but any ruins will do." I forced a smile. "There are ruins all across Anahera, more than on any other island. They are temples to her. We'll find the closest one."

Ilina looked west, where both moons were slipping behind the great shadow of Bopha. They were razor crescents now, just slices of gold and silver, and tomorrow both moons would be new. Tomorrow, they'd pass before the sun, one after the other, and the whole world would go dark.

The Great Abandonment would be complete.

And the only survivors would be those who'd managed to get on one of these ships.

"We'll go tonight. No delays. The eclipse won't happen until noon, right?"

Ilina nodded. "That still doesn't give us much time. What if Anahera rises before we get there, or—"

"The dragons will warn us."

"Or what if it really does need to be the exact site, not just the island?" She bit her lip. "And even if the dragons warn us of a tremor, we'll be too far inland to get away. Not to mention all the ships will leave as soon as they see dragons flying."

"We have a very narrow window for success," I agreed, because that was all I could say without falling into despair myself. "But that's not what I'm going to tell them."

Ilina followed my gaze as thousands of people pressed together in the port, all of them staring up at us—at the bones of the first dragon.

I couldn't imagine what the people saw in her—they didn't know about the first dragon any more than I had until the dreams started—and most people certainly didn't know about dragon bone structures, or that even a *Drakontos titanus* wasn't as big as this.

But they must have sensed *something* about her, because a hush passed over the crowd as people began to point up.

"What are you going to tell them?" Gerel asked.

"The words I was born to say." Now that we were back in the Fallen Isles, I could feel the noorestones glowing all around us. As I climbed up onto the first dragon, I let the power of several thousand noorestones trickle toward me—not enough to make their light so much as flicker, but just enough to heal the parts of my soul made tattered by their giant counterparts.

My ascent up the first dragon's spine was immediately noticed, but no one recognized me.

I was dirty, scarred, skinny, and wearing a ragged hunting dress; no one knew who I was—not until I reached the skull and stood where everyone could see me. Then my name was a whisper through the crowd, louder as LaLa abandoned the rail and came to perch on my shoulder.

As the questions and speculation grew, I glanced at Aaru. He nodded, and then the entire harbor went quiet.

Not silent. Not like the morning he'd seen Idris on the horizon. But quiet enough that I could be heard over the hum of thousands of voices.

"I'm not going to say good evening." I gazed over the assembly, forcing myself steady. LaLa rested her cheek against mine, lending me strength. "We've all seen the gods on the horizon. We've all been wondering which island is next. We've all been hoping for a miracle that would save our world. It isn't a *good* evening."

While I'd been talking, Aaru had eased the silence; more than anyone here, he knew how dangerous a weapon silence could be, and that no one should use it to strip others of their voices. So when the questions came, they were a rushed jumble of noise; I didn't have a hope of understanding individual words.

Aaru raised an eyebrow at me, but I shook my head and lifted my hand. Immediately, the port went quiet again.

"I know what you've heard," I said. "You've been told that I was killed, and that the Mira Treaty has been repealed. But that isn't true. The Mira Treaty isn't a person, and it isn't repealed until we say it is. The ideals put forward in the treaty—equality, unity, and conservation—are still ideals I believe in, and we can decide that those are the qualities we want moving forward." Again, I lifted my hand as murmurs rose up. "I can't tell you everything right now. I wish I could. What I want you to understand is this:

"In spite of High Magistrate Paorah's claims that only he can protect the people of the Fallen Isles, his actions have hastened the Great Abandonment. Nor did he plan to protect everyone; he built a fleet of ships, allowed only his chosen on board, and sent them to the Algotti Empire, where the empress had agreed to take refugees. But even in that, he proved a traitor. He left orders to attack her city, but he was not there to face the consequences when they were stopped. He stayed behind in the Fallen Isles, with another ship to take him to the empire after everything was finished."

Grumbling filled the port.

"I'm sure you're asking yourselves how you can trust that I'm telling the truth. You can't. That's fair. For years, I spoke everyone else's words, and not my own, but after everything I've experienced in the last few months, that's changed. I know better now. I know the truth. And I hope you'll believe me when I say that Paorah has never been on your side. If he's promised you salvation, he will not deliver."

"What can you promise us?" someone called, and a few people shouted in agreement.

LaLa chirped at them, scolding.

"I won't promise anything I'm not certain I can deliver," I said, touching LaLa's shoulder; it was sweet that she wanted to defend me, but unnecessary this time. "However, I have come to help. The ships sent to the Algotti Empire are waiting in the harbor, and we've been rescuing people from the ocean since we returned to Fallen Isles' waters. They will come into the port one at a time and take as many people as will fit. I urge you to consider leaving the island if possible. If you have boats or ships of your own, I hope you'll make room for others."

People stared, confused. All the speeches I'd ever made during a crisis included a promise and vague description of what was being done to solve the problem, but this wasn't any normal crisis. This was the end of our world.

And I'd just told all these people to prepare for the worst.

It wasn't very Hopebearer-like.

I took a deep breath, trying to find a balance between baseless optimism and honesty. "I can promise you this: I will do everything in my power to save what's left of the Fallen Isles. Everything. I will do anything." I swallowed hard, ignoring the crawling sensation of my friends' curious stares. "I won't claim to have miracles at my disposal, but I do have her."

People looked around, searching for a person, but I swept my arm down toward the first dragon, immobile beneath my feet. Yet her head was up, held aloft by nothing at all. For a skeleton, she seemed eerily alive.

Attention sharpened. Focused. Anyone who'd somehow missed the enormous dragon skeleton looked *hard* at her now.

I lifted my voice again; lots of these people were probably from other islands, but plenty must have been Anaheran. I hoped they'd recognize the words of their goddess. "*The Book of Destruction* says 'In the moment when the day and the night are the same, when the first and the last become one, and when hope and despair meet on the field of battle: then the Great Abandonment will be done.'

"Tomorrow, the moons will cross before the sun, one after the other, and twice, our world will darken. The eclipse will make day and night the same.

"And she"—again, I gestured at the bones—"is the first dragon, the first child of our gods. Two thousand years ago, she died protecting the Fallen Isles during the Sundering. Now I've brought her back from the Algotti Empire because I believe she can protect us once again."

"What about the last?" someone called.

I pressed my mouth in a line, and then I *pulled*. Thousands of noorestones flared, then dimmed as threads of their light spilled toward me. A corona of light formed around my body, and when I willed my wings into existence, they blazed up and out, stretching as wide as they would go.

LaLa squeaked with joy, and beneath me, the first

453

dragon rumbled in question, but I bade her back to sleep for now.

Soon. Soon we would become one.

And then . . .

I released the noorestones. The light returned to normal; my wings vanished; no one even had a chance to scream.

"I am the last," I whispered, but still, it carried across the crowd. "As I said: I cannot promise miracles, but I will do everything in my power to protect you. And in the meantime, we all need to prepare for the worst. So get on ships. Help others. And remember this:

"Without hope, we achieve nothing. Without one another, we *have* nothing."

With that, I turned and stepped down the first dragon's spine, with LaLa clucking soothingly into my ear as the crowd erupted into conversation and planning, and people pointing out the dragons perched on the cliffs.

At the lowest point of the spine, Aaru reached up to help me down to the main deck, his hand warm around mine. "That was good. Everyone was inspired."

I smiled. It wasn't my best speech, but I didn't want to dismiss the compliment. Not from him. And not when it might be one of the last times I heard his praise. "Are you ready to go? We have ruins to find."

"I'm ready to leave before Paorah finds out that you're here." He touched my face gently, and his gaze dropped to my lips. He didn't kiss me, not here, and certainly not in front of everyone, but the moment lingered as his thumb caressed the curve of my lower lip. "Do you think after this—"

I wasn't certain there would be an *after this*, but I was ready to agree to anything if he just kept touching me.

But then his gaze flickered beyond me, and he gasped. Shock went sharp over his features—shock and hope and disbelief. I followed his gaze to see what had struck him into such a clear display of emotion, there for anyone to see.

In the fore of the crowd, a girl stared up. She was maybe three or four years younger than us, with dark brown skin and a sweet round face, and black hair that floated around her head like a halo. She had both fists pressed against her mouth, as though trying to crush the sound of her squeal, but even that couldn't hide the huge grin stretching across her face as she looked back at Aaru.

My heart twisted—with jealousy, at first, as much as I hated to admit it—but then I realized who we were looking at.

Safa.

Suddenly, I remembered this girl from my dragon dreams—all those girls in boats, this one in particular—and I knew why Aaru had been so interested when I told him that part. He'd known, somehow, she might be one of those girls, and only a few days later . . .

My chest tightened as I scanned the crowd, but some people were never hard to find. I saw him immediately. Altan.

Altan was here.

Aaru had sent Altan after Safa.

And Altan had *done it*.

Then more familiar faces stuck out to me: warriors. Or, rather, the dishonored. Naran was in the lead, but several others stood behind her.

Had Altan retrieved them, too? I couldn't imagine why. Unless . . .

Aaru had told Altan everything—about the spies, the empire, the high magistrate's duplicity—in exchange for finding our friends.

I couldn't be mad, not when Aaru's face was shining with relief, and just beyond him, Gerel was noticing Naran in the crowd. And not when LaLa and Crystal shrieked with draconic joy and went diving off the ship—straight for Kelsine, the *Drakontos ignitus* who'd been separated from us back on Khulan. The dragons tumbled together, clicking and roaring with complete happiness.

After only a few minutes, Safa, Naran, Altan, and Kelsine had come aboard the *Star-Touched*, along with several other dishonored and young girls I recognized only from my dreams. Aaru and Safa embraced, while Gerel and Naran clasped hands. LaLa and Crystal were perched on Kelsine's back, chittering and preening their larger wing-sister, as though updating her on everything that had happened since they'd separated; I could almost hear the awe of such scandals in their tones. Kelsine puffed out smoke and cocked her head, listening.

Altan approached me, ignoring Hristo and Ilina at my

sides. The burns LaLa had given him were healed now, but his skin was lumpy with scars. "Nice performance, Fancy."

I ignored that. "What do you want?"

"To help." He grinned, lopsided now, thanks to the burn scar, and motioned over his shoulder to the others. "I found an army for you," he said, "and good thing, too, because I've been keeping track of Paorah, and I have some bad news."

My heart sank. Of course Altan brought bad news.

"He's convinced his people that he knew the attack on the empire would fail, and the only thing left to do, as a proper follower of Anahera, is to begin again. He's at the Archland Ruins, only a few hours' walk from here, with an army of his own, as well as some fanatics and political enemies—including your mother."

My legs felt weak, but I locked my knees and forced my voice steady. "Why?"

"*The Book of Destruction* speaks of a sacrifice, doesn't it?"

"What?" I breathed. "He can't. Surely he wouldn't."

Altan almost looked like he felt sorry for me. "He believes the sacrifice is necessary to complete the Great Abandonment and bring about a new world—one he intends to rule."

CHAPTER THIRTY-EIGHT

WASTED TIME MEANT WASTED LIVES.

While Ilina and Zara went to charm wagons and horse-carres out of local shop owners, Gerel, Naran, and forty dishonored warriors lifted the first dragon off the ship and settled her on a platform meant for moving cargo crates. I could have done it more quickly, but the last time I'd merged with her, I'd lost track of everything. If we wanted to get to the ruins, and if I wanted to appeal to the gods without getting shot out of the sky with arrows, then we needed to do this the long way. It was the only chance of success, no matter how I wanted to fly across the desert and breathe fire upon my enemies.

There was too much of a risk of hurting my allies. My mother.

Within the hour, we'd accumulated fifteen wagons, drawn by thirty horses, and another quintet of horses to pull the first dragon's platform. And then we rolled north on Revis Avenue—all one hundred and forty people who'd joined me. My army, Gerel announced.

1. *Safa. Over a dozen girls had escaped from Idris, but when people found out these were the last children of Idris, families took in the others without question. Only Safa remained with us, refusing to be separated from Aaru ever again.*
2. *One hundred and five dishonored, including Naran.*
3. *Altan, unfortunately. Some people didn't care that they weren't invited.*
4. *My friends and sister, of course.*
5. *Twenty-seven people from Flamecrest, who just wanted to help.*

Then there were the dragons, although the seven we'd taken from the empire had flown off to reunite with the others, so that left LaLa, Crystal, and Kelsine, who were only permitted to come because I couldn't bear the thought of leaving them behind.

As we rode through Flamecrest, LaLa curled up in my lap, pressing her nose into my stomach every so often, while Kelsine was resting on the floor of the wagon, her

brown body leaned against my legs like she needed constant reassurance of my presence.

Gerel and Chenda drove our wagon, while seven of
us sat in the back—Ilina, Hristo, Zara, Aaru, Safa, Altan,
and me—bouncing every time a wheel caught in a rut. It
was jarring and uncomfortable, but better than walking
through the crowded streets of Flamecrest.

Altan sat closest to the driver's bench, so that he could
give Gerel and Chenda directions when necessary, but for
now, he faced the back, answering a thousand questions.

"How did you get out of your closet that night?" Hristo
asked. "You were bound up."

The warrior shrugged, but his gaze slid over to Aaru,
whose face turned hard with resolve.

"I let him out," Aaru said, tapping his words as well.
"Mira told me she had a dream about girls in boats, and I
thought it might be Safa"—he glanced at her, sitting next
to him, and he smiled warmly—"so when I could speak
again, I gave Altan what he wanted: information about
the treaty, the spies, and Paorah. In trade, I asked him to
find Safa, if she was really out there."

"You should have told us," Ilina said.

Aaru tapped Ilina's words, too, and it was then I
noticed Safa following the quiet code, rather than listening.

"I should have," Aaru acquiesced, his eyes flickering to
me. "I'm sorry. I wasn't thinking clearly at that time."

I'd long ago forgiven him, even though I hadn't

460

understood *why* he'd released Altan. Now I did, and I forgave him once more. He had a sister again. He wasn't the only Idrisi left in the world.

"Tell me more about Paorah's plans." I turned to Altan. "You said he intends to rule a new world."

Altan nodded. "He knows his designs against the empire failed. I don't know how. Maybe he has spies of his own. But he immediately changed his mind about the will of Anahera. The Great Abandonment is as inevitable as it's ever been, but now she doesn't want them to be conquerers. Instead, if the sacrifice is made correctly, then the Great Abandonment will finish and there will be a new world in place of the Fallen Isles—one he will rule."

Ilina gaped. "So he's going to kill people to ensure that happens?"

"As soon as the eclipse begins," Altan confirmed.

The thought made me ill. I turned to Zara and made my voice strong. "I won't let anything happen to Mother. She'll be safe."

My sister gazed at me with resignation in her eyes. "You can't promise me that. But I believe you'll try."

Scouts rode out ahead of us—a pair of dishonored— while the wagon jostled over a bump in the road; I held LaLa tight against me, wishing I were riding like the scouts, or flying.

I forced my thoughts back to our plan.

We'd go in, capture Paorah, and rescue all the people he intended to sacrifice. Then I'd take the first dragon and . . . that would be it. The gods would lie back down. Paorah would be prevented from sacrificing people in his wild belief that a new land would form out of nothing.

I'd be a dragon.

While I brooded, the conversation shifted. Ilina and Zara mused whether our mothers would be real friends after this, at last, while Hristo glared knives at Altan.

Across from me, Aaru and Safa sat close together, tapping back and forth about everything that had happened since they separated. He was smiling, his whole manner soft as he gazed down at her and the quiet code she beat against her knee.

::Even before you were arrested, I was coming and going from Grace Community.:: Safa grinned up at him, her gaze flicking to his hands every so often—checking to see if he was going to say anything. ::I found other girls with the Voice of Idris, and during my visits, we taught one another how to use it—how to control it. I made sure to warn them to keep it a secret.::

A mixture of annoyance and appreciation spread across Aaru's face. ::I hope you were careful when you practiced. That was dangerous.::

::More careful than you. You got arrested.:: She smirked, but the expression didn't last. ::But yes. We were careful. And after you were arrested, I understood how dangerous it was to be a girl with the Voice of Idris. If they arrested you, a boy, for speaking in the square, what would they do to us?::

The wagon bumped over another rut, and the sand-stone buildings grew farther apart as we moved out of the city. Ahead, a long road bent around plateaus and crags, with brittle scrub the only plant life I could see. The city had grown up all the way out to the edge of the desert, and then stopped.

Above, the sky was huge and black, strung with star-light and clouds of pink and blue darkdust. Even without the moons, the heavens were bright enough to cast shad-ows across the ground.

Aaru's attention stayed on Safa. ::What then?::

She heaved a sigh. ::I told everyone to find boats and stock them with food and water, like you did with mine. We were scared, but we didn't have a choice anymore, so we agreed to meet on the river and sail to the ocean. It wasn't easy, but we were just in time. The earthquake began as we were escaping the island.::

"How—" Ilina started over in quiet code when Aaru directed Safa to look. ::How did you avoid getting caught in the undertow?::

Safa's eyebrows went up, as though she hadn't expected someone else to know the quiet code, but she went along with it. ::We used the Voice of Idris to still the water around us. We sat in our boats and waited, and when it was over, we decided to sail to Khulan. That was where we'd planned to go from the start.::

How incredible they'd managed to escape just in time. And fourteen of them, all isolated until now, with no experience with anyone who wasn't also Idrisi. That took immeasurable courage.

Safa continued. ::**We were just in sight of Khulan by the time Altan found us. He said he would take us to you::**—she looked at Aaru—::**but first, he needed to find some people in Lorn-tah.::**

Altan hadn't moved from his place at the front of the wagon, but now his head was leaned back far enough that he could stare at the sky. If he noticed anyone talking about him, or looking at him, he didn't show it.

Strange how Safa didn't seem to hate Altan. She probably didn't know how he'd tortured Aaru.

Well, Aaru would tell her if he thought she needed to know.

::**I'm proud of you for leaving. That was brave.::** Aaru squeezed Safa's shoulder, and the way he looked at her was enough to break my heart. He'd feared everyone he'd loved on Idris was dead, but here was Safa, against all the odds. ::**What about Mother? What about our sisters and Danyal?::**

Safa went still, then shook her head. Quickly, she glanced over the clattering wagon to see if Ilina and I were still watching, and she moved her quiet code to the back of Aaru's arm, where no one could see.

I looked down to where LaLa was curled in my lap, and Kelsine rearranged herself against my leg, but from the corner of my eye, I caught the way Aaru's shoulders slumped and his expression went carefully blank, as though she'd confirmed his worst fears. Whatever had happened to the rest of his family . . . they were all gone.

As our caravan continued through the desert, Aaru and Safa kept the rest of their conversation private, and I turned my thoughts inward again. To the Great Abandonment. To the Fallen Gods. To the dragons.

Would anyone even understand a new covenant with the gods? Maybe I should tell them what was going to happen, but I couldn't risk them stopping me. If it was the only way to help my people . . . I'd do anything.

I shivered, even though the air was warm.

Ilina touched my arm, her quiet code coming soft against my skin, hidden from anyone's view. ::**Are you all right?**::

I raised an eyebrow, and she inclined her head toward Aaru and Safa, who were still talking privately.

::**Fine,**:: I tapped back. ::**I'm glad she's here.**:: And I was. He was devoted to his family, and he'd always intended to go back to them. I had no idea how he'd thought the two of us might continue to be together—or if he'd even considered that it might be difficult—but after Idris had risen, it hadn't mattered anymore. There was no going back home.

But now Safa was here. She knew his history, his world, his hopes and dreams. She was a sister he'd chosen, which meant that whatever happened in the next few hours, he wouldn't be left entirely alone. I could take comfort in that.

Still, the selfish part of me wished he would pay attention to me, too. If I was about to turn into a dragon for the rest of my life . . .

It was still my choice.

I picked up a noorestone from the floor of the wagon and let its energy flow through me, burning away the knot building in my chest. With all the hope I'd passed on to others, I wished I had saved some for myself.

A FEW HOURS later, when the stars were wheeling away from midnight and the caravan was quiet with the sounds of people resting—saving their strength for whatever was to come—I began to sense the Archland Ruins. Or, rather, the noorestones embedded there.

They were one thousand two hundred and three pinpricks of light against the darkness of my thoughts, glowing brighter with every moment. Warm humming set into my bones, comforting in its harmony. There was something deeply *right* about these crystals, the fire they contained, the way they felt connected to the island itself.

In the driver's seat, Chenda and Gerel spoke in low tones to each other, though most of their conversation was lost under the clop of horse hooves on the packed-dirt road. Altan had his arms crossed, his head tilted back, and his eyes closed, but I doubted he was sleeping. Maybe he was reconsidering every move he'd made to bring him here. *I* certainly couldn't think of a good reason not to toss him out into the desert. Aside from perhaps needing another person who knew how to use a weapon.

I sighed, letting my attention drift through the wagon a little more. Zara and Ilina both leaned on Hristo's shoulders; his eyes were closed, but his breathing didn't have that slowness of sleeping; he, too, was awake and waiting. And across from me, Safa had curled onto the bench, and now she was using Aaru's lap as a pillow. Through the dimness, he looked at me and tapped, ::**Do you feel them?**::

The noorestones.

I nodded.

::**Are you afraid?**:: he asked.

Of course I was afraid. Every moment of my life was terrifying these days, but it helped to know that we had so many people who believed in this cause—who believed I could affect the decisions of the gods. People had believed in me all my life, but only because they'd been told to, never because I'd done anything to deserve it.

Now was my chance to prove that their faith in me was not misplaced.

I was the Hopebearer. I would give them hope.

But before I could figure out how to put all of that in words, or if there was even any point in telling him, an enormous *bang* rocked the road in front of us.

A thousand things happened at once:

1. *Fire bloomed from the packed sand, blindingly bright against the nighttime desert.*
2. *Horses shrieked and lurched away from the explosion, toppling wagons in their effort to escape.*

3. *Everyone threw themselves into motion, drawing weapons as they leaped free of the wagons.*
4. *New explosions burst from the ground around us, confusing everything.*
5. *LaLa and Crystal launched into the air, while Kelsine gave a long, low whine.*
6. *Hristo lunged for me, pushing me to the floor of the wagon to protect me from falling debris.*

But none of it mattered. The explosions were merely a distraction, a net meant to ensnare us. Because while we were all struggling to make sense of the noise and fire, Paorah's blue-jacketed soldiers swarmed in with darts, and one by one, we all went down.

CHAPTER THIRTY-NINE

THE DARTS MUST HAVE HELD A SEDATIVE, NOT A POI-son, because I awakened just as the sun crested the horizon, bathing the desert in a million shades of gold and red, contrasted sharply by the deep pockets of shadow that stretched from plateaus and ridges. Light shot through the delicate stone arches that stretched from rock to rock. Dragon's breath bridges, they were called, because people said *Drakontos sols* had carved them from the stone a thousand years ago.

Whether or not that was true, they were beautiful, and the effect of the sun shining through these grand windows was the first thing I noticed upon opening my eyes.

The second was that we'd been brought to the ruins.

I wasn't ready to move yet, and my hands were tied

over my head anyway. I couldn't see the shape of the structure with my eyes, but I could feel it in the noorestones humming all around me, showing me more than I'd know about this place otherwise.

Though smaller than the domed ruins where we'd freed the dragons, the Archland Ruins had an elegance all their own. Graceful spires soared into the purpling sky, glittering with bright crystals. A building stood in the center, just big enough to hold a few dozen people, but whatever its purpose was, I couldn't fathom.

Finally, I registered that I was lying on a floor, smooth after all these centuries of stinging desert wind. I'd been positioned on the eastern corner of the portico, and breathing to my right indicated at least a few people had been dumped up here with me. Were their hands tied up, too? Probably.

Voices sounded: people whispering and praying, but one rose above them all, coming from somewhere ahead of me, off to the right. The front center of the portico.

"It is Anahera's will that we make these sacrifices. The death of these individuals means new life for Anahera's chosen, and that is us, my friends. We have faithfully served our goddess of destruction since the beginning of the Fallen Isles, and we will serve her during this end, too."

My heart stuttered as I recognized the voice: High Magistrate Paorah.

He'd been waiting for us.

He'd been planning for us to come, planning to

capture us, and planning to use us as part of this sacrifice. What else would solidify his reign over a new world, but the death of the representatives of the old one? Never mind that the goal was to make the islands *stay*.

Paorah continued speaking, his voice as deceptively soft as the rest of him. "I saw the Great Abandonment coming decades ago. Before anyone else was worried about the number of dragons still living in the Fallen Isles, I began breeding programs in an effort to bolster their numbers, because I knew that we would need all the dragons to entreat the gods on our behalf. But I was dismissed. Ignored. Patronized, when people felt kind about it."

Dregs of the sedatives still slithered through my veins, but I forced myself to focus on my surroundings. Blue-jacketed guards stood watch around the ruins, scanning not just the crags and cliffs, but the people who'd gathered here.

Slowly, I turned my head to get a look at the people next to me. The movement hurt—everything hurt—but I kept my motions steady and careful; hopefully, no one would notice.

Aaru was by my side, his eyes already open. I kept my voice low, only for the two of us. "Are you all right?"

He gave a small nod. "Just woke up. We were ambushed."

I bit off a groan, trying not to wonder what had happened to those scouts. They'd been killed, probably. Or captured before they could return to warn us.

Beyond Aaru, I could see Gerel, Ilina, Chenda, Safa, Hristo, Zara, Altan, and several others I recognized from the caravan of dishonored and the port. Still more seemed to have been laid out in the wagons, not enough of an annoyance for Paorah to put on display.

He was still talking, still addressing the people gathered before him.

"I was a young man at this time, and no one listened to me." Paorah's voice tilted, like we were all supposed to empathize with him. "So I developed a new plan: I would convince the other governments of another danger—an immediate danger. The Algotti Empire. The threat of imminent invasion encouraged cooperation, but I knew that spirit would only last so long, and then the Great Abandonment would be upon us."

A shiver ran through me, because I could see it. I could understand his frustration, knowing the Great Abandonment was coming but being unable to convince anyone of the danger. But to separate oneself from everyone else, to use fear to motivate rather than hope and love . . . That was the difference between him and me.

"So I made more plans," he said, "covering every possible scenario. I struck bargains with our enemies. I arranged to destroy an empire and build one anew. I did everything within my power to fight for the survival of the Fallen Isles, but when my scholars returned from their studies of *The Book of Destruction*, they offered a different interpretation of Anahera's will—one I hadn't been

472

prepared to hear, and still shocks me. But that is why we are here today.

"The Great Flame Anahera is a goddess of life and death and life again. She is the light of Noore, the goddess of beginnings and endings." The high magistrate sounded rapturous, his words ringing across the desert like a prophecy. "Though it is counter to everything I set out to accomplish in my youth, I've embraced Anahera's will, and I urge you to do the same.

"How, you ask? How can we take actions that seem opposed to what we wanted? I answer you: If we are followers of the Great Flame, then we do it gladly. We let go of our attachment to the Fallen Isles, our *dependence* on the Fallen Gods, and forge a new land of our own. Though our time with Anahera has ended, her teachings live on through us. A new beginning waits just beyond today's eclipse, fulfilling her divine promise.

"But to earn it, we must be willing to let go of the past—to relinquish what makes us weak. That is why sacrifice is required. In the words of our holy book, 'It is sacrifice that enables change.' So that is what we will do today. When the moons begin to cross before the sun, our old world will fall away."

A huge cheer rose up from the crowd of people he'd assembled, calling for our deaths, calling for the new world.

I bent my wrists and felt around for a way to free my hands. But they were bound tight, held in place with

473

another rope tied around a column. If only I could find the knot— But my fingertips grazed over the prickly fibers, and there was no way I could get enough leverage.

My heart kicked faster as I considered my options.

1. *I was still the Hopebearer, and I wasn't gagged. If I spoke up over Paorah, surely someone would object to his treatment of me. But . . . no. They all knew who I was. They didn't care. They wanted him to do this. Or, at best, they were just going along with whoever seemed the most powerful right now.*
2. *I could summon noorestone fire, but there was no guarantee it would burn off the ropes without also hurting Aaru or the others.*
3. *Even if I tried to burn only my ropes, it might not work fast enough—before Paorah and his guards noticed.*
4. *Perhaps if I just pushed the noorestone fire into Paorah . . . But that was the same problem as before. Even if I managed to bring him to his knees—or worse—we'd still be tied up and at the mercy of all his guards. And, from what I'd seen so far, they outnumbered us.*

But I had to do *something*. We had only hours before the eclipse and slaughter began. And with two gods left in the sea, Anahera and Darina, one was sure to rise any moment now.

I took a deep breath, forcing myself to think past the sedatives making my mind like sludge. I'd come here for a reason: to merge with the first dragon.

I needed to find her. Get to her. Stop the gods from rising.

I closed my eyes and felt for her presence.

She was nearby, not even a league away, but she might as well have been across the ocean. I needed contact to merge. Which brought me back to the problem of how to get free.

Just then, someone touched my hands, fumbling around the rope. I stiffened, but as the ropes began to loosen, I forced myself to relax, even as the cool skin—no, not skin—brushed over my wrists.

Aaru shifted toward me and murmured, "Chenda says to wait until she's finished."

Her shadow.

She'd set her shadow to freeing us.

I resisted the urge to twist my head and look.

Finally, the bonds slipped, and I caught only the edges of darkness flitting away—toward the wagons and the rest of the people we'd brought with us. I forced myself to look at anything else while she worked.

I wished Chenda would hurry. And where were the dragons? In the distance, I could feel LaLa and Crystal circling in the sky, being of absolutely no help. But that was for the best; they were safe.

Kelsine . . . She was here, trapped inside the building. I could feel her fear, her worry. She might have been a dragon, but she was still a juvenile, and she'd been through a lot in her short life. I just wished we hadn't been reconnected only to bring her into more danger.

It seemed like ages slipped past as Paorah spoke on the glories of cleansing fire, but the sun hadn't moved far by the time Aaru leaned toward me.

"She said everyone is free. In one minute, our people will attack. Can you get to the first dragon?"

I flexed my fingers and wrists, my legs and feet. Lying flat on hard stone had done nothing for my circulation. But I could do it. If given the chance, I could reach her. Slowly, I turned my face back to Aaru, memorizing his features while I counted the seconds. His lips, soft and warm, so often tilted up in an expression of neutral pleasantness.

Forty-five.

Those dark eyes that saw everything.

Thirty-two.

The sharp lines of his cheekbones.

Nineteen.

Everything. Everything about him.

Five.

I wished we had more time.

Four.

I wished I'd told him sooner how I felt.

Three.

I wished there'd ever been a future for us.

Two.

But given our different lives, the world we lived in, the choices we'd have made if left alone, maybe it was a miracle we'd ever met in the first place.

One.

"I love you," I said.

He smiled, because he knew what would happen next—of course he knew—and then silence descended over the ruins, darkening every noorestone.

Soundless, chaotic motion burst all around us, with our fighters leaping out of wagons, through the ranks of Paorah's soldiers, and taking fallen weapons for themselves. Even dishonored, even far from their risen god Khulan, they were faster and stronger than Anaherans. And when Gerel hurled herself into the fray, she was a vision of perfectly practiced violence.

Without the noorestone light obscuring Chenda's shadow, it loomed darkly in the golden morning sun, holding a line between the fighting and the portico—protecting our group up here. And for Chenda's part, she was pulling Safa into the dubious safety of the building and the juvenile *Drakontos ignitus* within.

Then, almost as soon as the sound vanished, a pulse of charm rippled across the space, so strong it almost pulled me in. As I rolled to my hands and knees, I saw Ilina and Zara moving toward the front of the portico, where

Paorah held Mother at knifepoint. My wingsister and my blood sister had their hands clasped, their god gifts working together.

A gag filled Mother's mouth, and her hands had been tied with a length of ribbon, but she didn't look afraid. No, she lifted her gaze to meet mine, and there I found a mirror: determination, resignation, and—though I'd never really expected it—love. Then she lifted her chin in clear instruction: go.

In one motion, I finished shedding the ropes around my wrists and ran for the nearest break between Paorah's soldiers; most of them had left their positions when they went to quell the resistance.

Frantically, I looked around for a horse—the first dragon wasn't *nearby*—but they were all tethered and yanking wildly at the restraints.

So it would be my own two feet the whole way.

The moment I was clear of the fighting, I turned south, toward the pull of the first dragon, running as fast as I could. A stitch grabbed at my side, but I pushed through the pain. And when Aaru's silence began to lift, I seized power from the noorestones and yanked it into me.

Fire wrapped around me like armor, and now that I had wings giving me lift, I half flew across the desert— toward my destiny.

I moved faster than I'd ever moved in my life. For my friends, I ignored the pain of my body. For the people I'd promised to help, I counted every footfall. And for all those I hadn't been able to save, I prayed: *Give them peace, give them grace, give them enough love in their hearts.*

Sweat streaked down my face, evaporating as the sun lifted higher. Salt crusted on my skin, and a deep, desperate thirst rolled through me. Still, I didn't stop. And when a noise sounded behind me—like hoofbeats—I didn't dare risk looking over my shoulder. I couldn't lose my momentum, and if someone was chasing me, I needed every piece of my body focused on getting to the first dragon before they did.

Noorestone fire stretched after me, soaking into my blood and bones as deeply as possible—and then the connection snapped. The distance was too much.

But by then, I could see the first dragon. I pushed myself harder, gasping for breath as I took in the facts: the platform had been hobbled, its wheels smashed and lying on the desert floor, but the first dragon was still upright, waiting for me.

Almost there. A few hundred more strides, at most.

Then, above, a dragon screamed.

The sound sent a shiver of terror into me, and I stumbled, caught myself, and pushed onward again, but that scream could mean only one thing.

An island was about to rise.

I felt it, too. The way my heart twisted in knots, the way the earth shivered under my steps, the way my dragon soul wrenched in horror: Anahera was next.

Within an hour—faster than the others had risen once

the dragons took notice—but the moons were already making their trek toward the sun. I couldn't see them, but I could feel the weight of them on the horizon, chasing after the sun, closing in, almost there. Anahera was already preparing to rise; it wouldn't be long before Darina pulled herself up out of the sea, too.

And then our whole world would be finished.

Unless I reached the first dragon in time. Unless I begged the gods to wait. Unless I gave up everything that made me human.

It would be worth it, if the Fallen Isles could be right again.

Another draconic scream ripped through the sky. LaLa. I'd recognize her voice anywhere, and it made my heart twist to hear her like this, aching with anxious terror and grief. Months ago, it would have destroyed me. Today, I made it strengthen me, because I knew how to help her. I could do it.

Four hundred strides away from the bones of the first dragon.

Three hundred.

Ahead, the bones flickered. Glowed. Shone like noore-stones. But when I blinked, the effect was gone.

I was hot. Sweating. It must have been a mirage.

Or a greeting.

The hoofbeats behind me were gaining, heavy on the packed road. Then a horse groaned and something—its body—thumped to the ground, and all I could hear were the hard footfalls and panting of my pursuer.

I jerked faster, but it wasn't enough. Hot, blinding pain ripped down my back.

Shock made me scream, and I tried to scramble forward, but my pursuer kicked me. I dropped to the ground on all fours, rock and sand digging against my palms.

"I can't let you do this." The voice was soft, empty of emotion, but short with exertion.

Paorah.

I dug my fingertips into the ground, counting breaths—three, four, five—and then hauled myself up, even as the wound in my back tore wider, making red and white shimmer in the corners of my vision. I gasped for the breath that wouldn't fill my lungs. Fire flared over my back, centering on the spot where a blade had pushed through skin, through muscle, through something vital. That was bad. Maybe really bad. But if I could get back to the ruin noorestones, this would heal. I just had to hang on until then.

I *had* to.

My head swam as I pulled myself straight, turning to face him.

His chest was heaving with want of breath, and sweat trickled down his face in thin streams. But when he looked at me, his gaze was steady. Beyond him, a horse lay dead on the rocky ground, an arrow sticking from its leg. "I can't let you do this, Mira Minkoba," he said again.

"I don't see how you can stop me." Somehow, my voice

didn't shake. Maybe because I could *feel* the first dragon at my back, only one hundred strides away. *So* close.

But she wasn't like the noorestones; I couldn't tap into her power from here. No, we had to touch, and one hundred strides might as well have been one hundred leagues.

Paorah lifted his knife, the blade still dripping with my blood. "You know I'm not afraid to use this."

I knew. And we both knew that I was injured, barely standing. He could kill me faster than I could make a run for the first dragon.

"You must be afraid of something"—I clenched my jaw—"or you wouldn't have come all this way. You wouldn't have felt the need to stab me." My legs trembled with the effort of staying up, but I clenched my jaw and locked my knees. No matter what, I would make it back to the ruins and finish what I'd come to do.

"You'll spoil the sacrifice." His gaze was steady. Even. The knife lowered to his side, and my blood oozed down the point, into the sand. "It may already be spoiled, but I'll do what I must for the chance at saving it."

"You're going to kill a bunch of people for nothing," I said. "Their deaths will mean nothing to the Fallen Gods, beyond that we are unworthy of their presence."

He took a step forward.

I took a shaking step back.

"The gods are slaughtering more people than I ever could." His knuckles paled around the knife handle—I couldn't stop looking at the blade, waiting for him to use it against me again—but he didn't come closer. "At least this way, their deaths accomplish something. We aren't meant to stay with the Fallen Gods, Mira. They're supposed to leave us."

"What makes you such an expert?" I tried to block out the pain in my back, but it was so loud, so demanding. It was a warning, I knew; pain insisted on being felt because something was wrong, but I. Was. Aware. "Do you think that because you saw the Great Abandonment coming decades ago that you are the sole voice of what it means? You hastened this day."

He shook his head. "*The Book of Destruction* has always been clear that the Great Abandonment would happen during an eclipse, and the moons don't move differently because of our actions. Today was always the day, Hope-bearer. If I did anything, it was all in accordance with Anahera's plans. She is the trickster, after all, and we are but puppets."

"You're wrong," I hissed. My thoughts listed to one side of my mind, drifting out as the pain in my back tried again to take over, but above, LaLa screeched and blew fire, despairing over the impending tremor—the abandonment. It took everything in me not to reach out to her, to offer comfort, if I could. The last time I'd been connected with a dragon during the period before an island got up, I'd nearly lost myself to the despair, too.

Of course, the pain might get me first. I couldn't stand here and talk to him all day; we'd never agree how to set the world right, and the eclipse was close, and—I heaved my thoughts over the mountain of agony in my back—he was trying to distract me. Delay me.

"Anahera may be the trickster," I said, "but we are not puppets. We make our own choices, and you chose to serve yourself."

He looked at me like I was crazy, like he couldn't believe there was any other choice. "And what do you serve?"

"I serve hope." I pivoted and threw myself toward the first dragon.

It wasn't enough. My movements were clumsy with pain, my range of motion limited, so when Paorah surged forward, his knife plunged easily into my shoulder.

I stumbled, screaming, and when I reached around, the only thing I could feel was a sticky, hot mess of blood flowing. Everything hurt, and all my muscles trembled from the strain of running so far in the desert heat, and now this, too. Now, this man coming after me, threatening me, *attacking* me.

Three more steps. I staggered that far, reaching for the first dragon with my good arm; my bleeding shoulder hurt almost as much as my back, rendering my right arm useless.

Four steps. Five.

But that was as far as I got before Paorah grabbed me and spun me around, like he wanted me to die looking at him, the man who'd arranged for the Mira Treaty to be written and signed, only so that he could tear it apart.

The man who'd steal dragons to force them to entreat our gods, only to let them wither to the brink of death. The man who'd made a deal with the Algotti Empire, only so that he could attack them, conquer them.

He promised wonders but delivered destruction.

And then—

An earsplitting shriek rent the air as LaLa stooped, flame spilling from her jaws. Then her wings flared, and she shifted so that her talons reached forward—and my sweet little dragon gouged Paorah's eyes, blowing fire all across his face.

He ducked and tried to shield himself, but he was too late.

The knife dropped.

I didn't waste time. Gasping for breath, I hurled myself toward the first dragon. Closer, closer. A wispy part of my mind marveled at my LaLa. How incredible that she'd come to my rescue, even in the throes of her own grief. Any other time an earthquake had been nearing, she'd been inconsolable, unreachable. But when she felt my peril, she'd come straight for me. I didn't deserve such devotion, but I loved her more than ever.

Fifty strides.

Blackness curled at the corners of my vision. I pushed onward, struggling to keep my focus on the wooden platform, the bones, and the place I'd need to climb up.

Twenty strides.

My vision went gray, and my feet started to trip over each other. I fell, landing heavily on my good hand, but still the agony in my back and shoulder spiked. I cried out, vomited from the pain, and struggled to crawl forward. But now I was lost. I couldn't see, and I didn't know which direction to go. And with all the blood seeping out of my body, I didn't have time to go the wrong way.

Surely I hadn't come so far only to fail.

Then, a pinprick of light found my eyes—fire—and gusts of air fanned against my face.

LaLa.

I made a strangled noise of relief, gulping at the marginally cooler wind made from her wings, and followed the dim light of her fire. Crawling, groping over the rocks and broken wheels in front of me, but moving.

My knees banged against the debris, my blood-sticky hands stung with grit, and I could feel the consciousness draining out of me, but I had to be close.

Another spark of light urged me onward, but a faint roar of blood filled my ears, drowning all my thoughts. I couldn't move my hurt shoulder anymore, and my back—and whatever he'd punctured there—was a knot of agony, spreading outward. I couldn't do it. I couldn't—

I pushed my failing body forward once more, and that was it. I dropped. The rush in my head was so loud I couldn't even hear the clatter of wood and dirt, but something sharp dug into my sternum. I couldn't roll off it.

A faraway roar echoed in my ears. LaLa. She was still here.

For her, I summoned the last of myself and reached ahead of me. Nothing but air. Nothing but rock. Nothing but sharp teeth clamping around my fingers and pulling until finally I touched bone.

At first, it was static. A shock through my body. But it shoved me back into awareness, and when I stretched my fingers again—LaLa's teeth still firm around my knuckles—power erupted into me.

I jolted, gasped, and lurched forward to fully grasp the delicate wing bone LaLa had pulled me to. My breath caught, and for a second it seemed like I could just stop here, letting the first dragon's power wrap around me, but now that my sight and hearing were clearer, the thuds of Paorah's footfalls propelled me into motion.

Letting go of the first dragon, even for a moment, was torment, but I threw myself against her ribs and clawed my way upward, blood staining the white bone. My shoulder and back lit white hot with pain, but I wouldn't stop. I couldn't.

Then, somehow, I was up.

The moment I reached my perch between the first dragon's great wings, the moment I let my thoughts melt into hers, the burning eased and the blood clotted and it seemed like I might be able to heal after all.

LaLa was already there, waiting for me. Her golden eyes were wide and worried, filled with fathomless love and grief.

"We're going to make it, little dragon flower." I stroked down her spine, down those bright, smooth scales, sharp under my teeth-marked fingers. "We're going to make it because of you."

She chirruped and gazed north—toward the ruins.

"Don't do this!" Paorah's words came from below, garbled with the burn of LaLa's fire. His face was a mess of melting flesh, no longer soft. "You can't do this!"

"I can do anything," I murmured, but now, here, connected to the first dragon of all, my words were thunder. Wings poured out of my back, fanning into the skeleton in a blend of fire and bone. Black, galaxy-filled scales glimmered across her body, flickering in and out of view, gleaming over the hints of muscle and sinew and organs. The glow of our inferno heart brightened into a small sun. And there, in the back of her mouth, the spark gland shimmered into existence, and when we exhaled out of our second lungs, fire unfurled.

I shifted at the last moment, so the flames spilled across the sand at his feet. It must have been incredibly hot, regardless, but I couldn't—wouldn't—kill him. I never wanted to be the kind of person to destroy my enemies, even if I could breathe fire over them. Maybe *especially* if I could breathe fire over them.

I could do anything. I could be merciful.

Instead, I let the power of the first dragon thrum through my heart and mind and soul, and when LaLa was settled, we pushed into the air, fire streaming around us.

And there on the desert floor, burned and bloodied, Paorah dropped to his knees.

Maybe I wasn't that merciful after all.

CHAPTER FORTY

Screaming welcomed us as we approached the ruins.

It hadn't taken long for us to reach them, and with every wingbeat, the first dragon grew more substantial. Our shadow flickered over the hot red sands of the Anaheran desert, skeletal and strange as my power fed her, and hers fed me. A few times, the dark shadow skimming over rocks and crags looked solid.

Then there were the ruins. Tall. Ancient. Impossibly white against the red landscape, and glowing with the fire of Noore.

As we rounded one of the broken spires, light arced off and shot into us. Then another, and another, and after one circuit of the ruins, one thousand two hundred and three threads of noorestone energy bent toward us, surrounding us in a nimbus of white-blue light, filling us up. It was strength, fire, and a strange sense of coming home. As we landed on the central building with a tremendous crash, I realized something incredible.

She was whole.

For the first time in more than two thousand years, the first dragon was completely whole, with muscles and organs and arteries and scales black enough to make midnight jealous. Even her wings were complete, no longer filled in with the fire of mine. She was here. Alive. Beautiful. Fierce.

Drakontos celestus. The first dragon.

Then, slowly, she turned her head around, neck muscles flexing gracefully, and looked at me just long enough to give me a chance to notice the scar on her left cheek.

Not the first dragon.

Not *only* the first dragon.

And I understood. My heart beat in time with hers, and I could feel every muscle stretch and flex when she lifted her wings and straightened her body. Every motion echoed in me, though I didn't have wings or talons or a tail; it didn't matter, because we were the same.

We roared fire, making the desert tremble beneath us. A few people kept on fighting, determined to kill one another before the island beat them to it, but others stared up at us, dropping their weapons to the wet, red dust.

My whole body—my human body—still trembled with the blood loss and the last dregs of pain; the noorestones had finished healing the wounds, but it was much harder for the mind to recover after such trauma.

Still, I gazed down at the battle below, talons crushing the fragile stone, and soon even the people fighting surrendered.

It must have been so hard for them to look at us, what with all the white-blue light, but as I shifted LaLa to my shoulder and climbed to my feet—standing atop the *Drakontos celestus*, where everyone could see me clearly—I held everyone's attention.

"This is the day." It hardly sounded like my voice, filled with noorestone fire and dragon smoke. "When the day and the night are the same. When the first and the last become one. When hope and despair meet on the field of battle."

Shouts rose up, buried under the rush of fire.

I found my friends and met their eyes. Chenda's hands rested protectively on Safa's shoulders, while Gerel stood guard nearby. Hristo clutched at his heart as he gazed up, while Ilina and Zara stood near Mother, who was bleeding but might live. Then there was Aaru, wearing that same expression as before. A smile, all sadness and perfect understanding.

"Remember," I whispered, as the world began to rattle beneath us, "'Hate cannot abide where many stand in love.'"

Then I dropped back to the dragon, breathed in, and reached through the noorestones to the goddess of destruction herself.

It was bold. Presumptuous.

But the gods had given me this power. It was their will that I use it, that I fight for the survival of my people. So I reached, my thoughts plunging downward through pure noorestone fire—bright, hot, flawless in every way.

People had long speculated that these noorestones were still connected to the world, to the gods, and as I followed the path that blazed ahead of me, I wished I could tell them that they'd been right.

At last, I landed in a place neither light nor dark, neither loud nor quiet. A between world, burning with brilliant noorestones and images of every part of the Fallen Isles.

This was what the gods saw:

Coins exchanging hands as men and women tried to
buy their way onto ships.

People reaching out to pull strangers aboard, and
others pushing the helpless into shuddering waters.

Mothers and fathers gathering children into their arms
as the island began to tremble and they had no
way to escape.

Birds taking flight, all their feathers black against the
sun.

Ground-dwelling animals tunneling deep into their
burrows, while deer and squirrels and other
creatures ran for safety they wouldn't find.

Dragons all over screaming in anguish as yet another
god prepared to pull herself free of the ocean floor.

Two moons closing in on the sun.

Dozens of people standing in front of ruins, some in

flame-blue jackets, others in their regular clothes.
The dust around their feet shivered upward. Their
weapons littered the ground, and many wept
openly as they stared at the biggest dragon any of
them had ever seen, wreathed in noorestone fire.

I saw everything: the good and the bad and all the reasons the gods might want to leave.

The stars. The vast and perfect darkness between
them. The holes in the sky where these seven deities
used to dwell.

The Upper Gods and their longing to reunite with
their Fallen brethren.

Stay, I prayed. *Stay, stay, stay.*

With every beat of my heart, I begged her to listen. The first and the last were here, together. Wasn't that what she and the other Fallen Gods wanted?

Please, stay.

I came to the goddess of destruction as a child might a mother: yes, people had behaved poorly, and yes, we deserved to be punished, but maybe, more than anything, we needed mercy—a chance to do better.

Please.

And then, with a voice like stars colliding and oceans boiling and mountains shattering apart, the goddess of destruction said no.

No.

No.

No.

Shock and despair ripped through me. I shot straight

up, out of the in-between world, and screamed as my connection to every single one of the Archland Ruins' noorestones stretched—and snapped. Then all of them— all one thousand two hundred and three of them—went black. Not just dark, but *black*, burned out from the inside.

Shrieks of terror rent the air as red dust billowed, and people began to flee south—toward the harbor. But we were too far inland; even if there was space aboard ships for this many people, they'd never make it there in time.

The ground gave a mighty lurch, throwing dozens to their hands and knees.

This didn't make sense. I'd brought the first dragon here; I'd become her; I'd *begged* the Fallen Gods—all before the eclipse began.

I'd been willing to give up my humanity to save these people. Wasn't that enough?

Hopelessness clawed at me, beckoned me toward it—but I pushed away the temptation to sink into the spiral of fear and regret and self-blame. Anahera was rising *now*, which meant these people would die unless someone acted.

Me. I had to do something.

I clenched my jaw and *reached* for every dragon I'd ever met. Big, small, everything in between. It was hard to break through the howling grief, but first I found Kelsine, shrieking below, and then Hush. Others came more quickly, then: Lex, Siff, Tower, the seven empire dragons, and dozens of others whose names I didn't know, but whose hearts I did. Their roars reverberated through my soul, and then they were coming.

In front of me, LaLa squawked and flapped her wings, and through our connection, I could feel her urgency.

"Go," I whispered. "Find your sister and get to safety."

She bumped her nose against the tip of my finger and pushed off in a flurry of gold wings, and I—the first dragon, the last dragon, the *Drakontos celestus*—leaped off the roof of the ruins and landed with a *thud* on the trembling ground.

I found Aaru first. He wore an expression of anguish, as though fighting the urge to put his hands over his ears to block the noise of Anahera struggling to rise. But when I called for him, when I stretched out my hand, he came, climbing onto the dragon.

Thumps sounded as more big dragons arrived, bending low to accept passengers. And they weren't alone. All across the island, dragons swooped in to find families and allow people to climb onto their backs. Only a few hesitated; after all, the Mira Treaty had made riding dragons illegal, and most people had never seen one up close. But in the end, they scrambled up and held on tight as the dragons pushed into the air.

I could feel them all—every single dragon in the Fallen Isles—soaring over the mountains and plateaus and canyons and cliffs, their keen eyes searching for movement on the ground. A child. A man. A person reaching up, desperate for help.

And here, at the ruins, dragons launched into the air with four and five people clinging to their backs. Their wingbeats were heavy, strained under all the extra weight, but they rose into the brilliant blue sky.

Then, finally, when they'd all gone, I pushed off, spreading my wings wide, feeling the muscles work, the sinews stretch, the starlight blood pumping through my veins. Three more people had climbed onto my back—Safa sat behind Aaru, and then two I didn't know—and their screams were wild and terrified and euphoric. Because we were flying, and because just behind us, the island pulled herself up tall with a deafening roar and splash, and the place where we'd all been standing minutes ago surged underwater.

We'd escaped, barely.

We shouldn't have needed to.

"Seven gods." Aaru's voice was almost lost to the wind.

They stood all around us. Gods.

Bopha was a great darkness, pure shadow even in the noon sun.

Khulan kept his mace raised, while Damyan reached for his Fallen love. Harta curled her arms around her belly, and Idris remained far to the west, isolated even now. Behind us, Anahera's arms were lifted in joy, caught in a dance to music only she could hear.

Darina alone remained in the sea, all mountains and river valleys and green fields. Knots of civilization dotted even the north end, though I couldn't see any movement—not from this height, and maybe not even if I got closer.

The last Fallen God.

I bit back a horrified cry. The eclipse was close. There was no time to discuss with my friends, or read through all the holy books again. It was done. Over. I'd failed.

In the back of my mind, another great wave of despair crashed through me—through all the dragons—as Darina began to stir.

"No," I groaned. "Please no."

But I hadn't shed my human soul, and apparently I didn't know how, so there was no reason for her to listen to my prayer.

Still, I might reach the dragons.

"Be strong," I whispered. "Stay here." They couldn't lose their passengers; these were some of the last people born to the Fallen Isles, and everyone we'd failed to save was a star in a sky full of tragedies. "Please," I breathed. "Please keep them safe."

Quiet code tapped against my arm. ::**Let me onto one of the ships.**::

I flew downward, catching the crash of waves and scream of wood as the ships all strained to avoid getting caught in the wild currents. The vessels rolled over huge waves, struggling to remain afloat as the water betrayed them.

"Are you sure?" I called, my voice almost lost under the wind and roar of the sea.

::**I will silence the water, like Safa did after Idris.**::

I just nodded, wishing I understood what I'd done wrong, and how I could make it right. I wished I could talk to him about it, but even as we neared the water, a pressure of silence built up around us and expanded toward the nearest group of ships.

After the noise and cacophony of the world ending, my ears rang sharply with the sudden silence. But it was working. Waves rolled out from Anahera, breaking against the bubble of Aaru's power. It was incredible, *seeing* the edge of silence like this.

As ships began to steady, other nearby vessels moved into the space Aaru was protecting. It was slow, agonizing work for them, trying to maneuver in such nightmarish conditions, but soon, two dozen ships had gathered into this small area of relatively calm water.

Carefully, I lowered until I was even with one of the ships—the *Chance Encounter*, I realized—and started to let people off. First the two strangers, then Safa, and then Aaru.

When I didn't follow, Aaru turned around, curiosity and concern written in his expression. "Mira?" No sound came out—the world was perfectly silent.

I offered a tight, sad smile, and tapped against the first dragon's starlight scales. ::Sail toward the Algotti Empire. Maybe she'll change her mind.::

A thousand emotions passed between us—grief, sorrow, longing—but there was no more time for us.

::I love you,:: I said. ::Tell the others, too.::

Aaru's mouth opened, as though he wanted to speak through the solid silence he'd cast, but I didn't give either of us a chance to change our minds. I ducked back into my place and flew, climbing and climbing, not looking back because I couldn't bear the thought of seeing his face when he figured out why I'd said good-bye.

They needed to go—all of them—but I couldn't give up while there was still one island left.

My island. My home. My birthplace.

I had nothing to go on this time, just hope that Darina would listen to me.

I burst from the bubble of silence with a roar that could shatter stars. All the pain, fear, and despair—I screamed it away as I wheeled toward Darina, rounding Damyan as he still reached out for her. I soared over the green mountains and valleys, the farms and fields, and the pristine beaches. I flew as fast as I could, taking in the last Fallen Isle with tear-distorted yearning.

I would not—could not—give up.

Then I saw it: Crescent Prominence. My city.

The prominence itself was still there, a seven-fingered hand stretching to the ocean, and utterly still, like no one had dared return to the houses there after the evacuation. The harbor was empty: no ships, no fishing boats, no people searching the abandoned crates for supplies.

As for the main part of the city, all the smoke had long ago cleared from the air, but the evidence of the explosion was still present. Blackened buildings crumbled in the sunlight, and the streets were a mess of debris from the attack that day . . . and other tragedies, which must have occurred after I'd left. Maybe there'd been anarchy after the Luminary Council was killed. Or panicked looting and trying to escape, after Idris rose. Or rioting, after Paorah declared the Mira Treaty—and me—dead. It was impossible to say.

My heart ached to see my home this way, but it was better empty than filled with people. In the back of my mind, I could feel the island shuddering, and with my dragon eyes, it was just possible to make out debris starting to jump over the empty roads.

Soon my goddess would leave, too. Unless I could persuade her to stay.

There was no time to look at the city more closely. I flew past, pushing my body—both bodies—as hard as it would go, until finally I reached my destination: the sanctuary.

There were the facility buildings where Ilina's parents and the other keepers used to work. There was the beautiful drakarium where LaLa, Crystal, and dozens of other small dragons used to live and play. And there—not far from the main structures—were the ruins.

They looked the same as the last time I'd seen them, that day in the sanctuary when Hristo, Ilina, and I had discovered the shipping orders that started all of this. It seemed so long ago; I'd lived a lifetime since then. But as I landed, shaking the earth underneath me, a familiar hum wrapped around the back of my thoughts.

I, the human part of me, dismounted the *Drakontos*

celestus and approached the tall, broken arches. These ruins were smaller, more modest than either of the sites I'd visited on Anahera, but coming here felt like coming home. These were the first ruins I'd ever seen, ever wondered about.

Spindly arches, crumbling towers, still lit with glowing blue noorestones even after all these centuries. I'd never been allowed to explore the ruins before, because Mother worried I'd hurt myself, but now there was no one to stop me.

The *Drakontos celestus* came along, sniffing the air and stretching her—my—wings.

At last, I stood before one of the great towers, all white and glowing and studded with noorestones. An electric hum vibrated the air between my palm and the smooth stone.

Before I could touch it, another hum filled the sanctuary: crickets singing and birds settling in their nests. Strange. The air was cooler, the world dimmer, and the shadows cast by trees were lit with tiny crescents.

Heart pounding in my throat, I looked up, straight into the impossibly bright sun. I didn't need to squint or look away; my eyes didn't even water. Not since becoming a dragon.

Nevertheless, the sight made me gasp. The first moon was more than halfway across the face of the sun. The eclipse had already begun.

CHAPTER FORTY-ONE

I HAD NO TIME FOR DESPAIR.

As the ground lurched under my feet, I slapped both hands against the tower wall and screamed, *"Please, Darina!"*

I didn't know what I expected. A soft, beautiful figure to come striding out of a glowing white background, asking if I had enough love in my heart? Or a voice from nowhere and everywhere, ready to make a bargain with me? Or something else entirely?

Instead, I plunged into the white-blue between place, fire crackling around me, and came face-to-face with myself. Or, at least, she looked like me, down to the shade of her skin and the tilt of her nose and the texture of her hair. No scar, though, and she held herself differently, with a confidence that wasn't just a layer of her mask.

There were other differences, too. While I wore a tattered hunting dress, smeared with red dirt and damp with my own blood, she wore a billowy gown that might have been sewn from the night sky; it was black and strewn with stars and darkdust and faraway galaxies. And where I was filthy and sweating, my hair all windblown and wild, she looked freshly scrubbed, her black curls tight and gleaming.

We stared at each other, both evaluating, until finally I said, "Are you Darina?" It seemed presumptuous to wonder if the goddess of love might take on my appearance to talk with me, but I'd reached through the ruins to make this appeal; why wouldn't she appear to me with a face I recognized?

She laughed. "Do you really think you're worthy to look upon your goddess, in any form?"

Blood flooded up my throat and cheeks, but I didn't let the insult cow me. "The Fallen Gods gave me this task. The least they could do is have a conversation."

Her smile showed teeth.

"And you aren't me."

Now she laughed. "No. Not at all. But I'll give you a hint." Great black wings flickered into view behind her, stretching wide.

"*Drakontos celestus*," I whispered. My twin across time.

"You look like me. As a dragon, I mean." She shrugged, but now that I knew who—what—she was, I could see where her movements weren't quite human. "I thought it was only fair that I took on your appearance."

I couldn't argue with that. "The eclipse has started."

"Yes. And the Fallen Gods will rise."

"How can I stop them?" Surely, more than anyone, she could understand the need to keep the gods here. She—her bones—had been away from the Fallen Isles for so long, and now she was back. She had just as much reason to want them to stay.

"Why do you think you're supposed to stop them?" The first dragon shook her head. "I told you before: the Great Abandonment was set into motion the day I died."

"I thought—"

"You thought if there was a last dragon—a new me—then the greatest calamity would be averted?" She smiled again, all teeth. "Tell me, when Tirta took on your title, was she a true replacement?"

"No." The word came out as a growl. "But you can't compare me to her. The gods chose me."

"The gods chose you because you were in the best position to do what needed to be done. They chose you because the Luminary Council chose you, and we both know the Luminary Council chose Tirta, as well."

"That's not comforting."

"Dragons aren't meant to be comforting. Something you'd know if you paid more attention to your dragon instincts." She gave me a moment to think about the time I'd nearly blown up the Lexara Theater, or the way I'd almost lost control in the Red Hall. "Anyway, you can't stop the Great Abandonment. It's happening. Look up."

Though we were somewhere deep inside the between place, when I tilted back my head, I saw the first moon had already covered most of the sun. Only a narrow crescent remained.

The first eclipse was nearly total.

Darina would rise within minutes.

"But if I'm not supposed to stop the Great Abandonment, what am I supposed to do?" Fear clutched at me.

"What are you willing to do?" asked the first dragon.

"Anything." Hadn't I already declared that, back in the empire?

"Will you let go?"

"Of what?"

"Anything."

The way she said it sent shivers through me, but I looked at the sky again—sunlight was barely squeezing out now—and I nodded. "I've known for almost two decans that I'd have to let go of my human self," I whispered. "'It is sacrifice that enables change.' I accept that. And I'm ready."

"You're still thinking like a human."

"But what else is there? If I become fully dragon, I give up my family and friends. I give up a future with the boy I love. I give up everything I ever wanted, and I do it for them. To save them. To make sure *they* have family and friends and a future."

The first dragon merely tilted her head.

And then I knew.

It wasn't my humanity they needed, but the part that had never been mine to begin with. The chosen part. The dragon part.

"Do you know what that—"

"Yes," she said. "I know what it means."

No more power over noorestones. I could deal with that. I'd lived most of my life not being able to affect noorestones, although the way they burned away my anxiety . . . I would miss that. No, it was the other part that ripped open my soul.

My connection with dragons. With Kelsine and Hush and Lex and all the others I'd met and loved. And—mostly—with LaLa. My sweet dragon flower, who'd saved me over and over again. Who gave me joy and laughter and love.

She was my heart. How could I give up my heart?

"You need to decide," said the first dragon. "The first eclipse is nearly complete."

"What if I say no?" My voice was rough. "What if that's too much?"

"The gods rise either way," said the first dragon. "You can say no, and what's left of the people of the Fallen Isles will drift across the ocean until they die. Or you can say yes, and you'll be given another chance. Not with the Fallen Gods. No. If you live, you'll see them in the sky. But your people will find a new home."

506

"Will she still know me?" The question came out tiny. Pathetic.

"I don't know."

"This is part of my soul," I whispered. "I can't just rip it out. I can't just stop being what I am."

"You were willing to give up your humanity. Is giving up your dragon soul so much worse?"

"*Yes.*" The word was a sob. "I've always loved dragons. I always wanted to *be* a dragon. From the moment I was born, my heart beat for them."

"That doesn't have to change. Look at your friend Ilina."

I grabbed at my chest, choking on my own tears. All I could think about was LaLa, my perfect little dragon. Her shiny gold scales, her sweet eyes, and the way she snuggled on top of my chest at night so that our hearts beat together. She'd saved me today, back on Anahera. Though she'd been in the throes of horror and grief, she'd sensed my danger and risked herself to rescue me. Then she'd guided me to the dragon bones, knowing I'd understand her. And when I couldn't go on, she'd grabbed me by the fingers and dragged me. A tiny gold dragon the size of a ferret, and she'd pulled me the rest of the way.

Our bond was everything to me.

She was everything.

"It wouldn't be a sacrifice if you didn't have to give up something precious."

"I know."

"You've always been willing to give up pieces of yourself for the betterment of others. Your voice, your freedom, your life. But there's one thing you've never compromised on."

Dragons. Fighting to ensure their freedom and safety.

She was right. It was the only sacrifice I could make that would truly matter.

"It's time to decide," she said.

"Can I say good-bye?"

"There's no time."

I wanted to collapse and cry, but she was right. The first moon pinched off the last of the sunlight, and everything went dark.

"It's all right to be sad." The first dragon hugged me. "It makes you human."

My whole body trembled with sorrow and fear and all the uncertain days that loomed ahead of me. "I thought dragons weren't meant to be comforting."

The first dragon scoffed. "Don't be silly. No one tells a dragon how to be."

I wasn't ready, not nearly, but then we were hurled out of the noorestone space, and I was in the dragon sanctuary once again. I stood where I'd been before, my hands pressed to the tower wall, but now every single noorestone was black, burned out, and my body buzzed with energy. Fire.

It was in me now.

But first . . .

The drone of bugs filled the cool air, and dawn seemed to shine from every horizon: from across the sea, from the abandoned city, and from the immense Skyfell Mountains. But above, stars glittered during full day.

And the sun— That was incredible. A halo of fire encircled the black moon, and strands of light arced out into ghostly filaments. I'd never seen anything like it before, this phenomenon of night during the day, and a glow on every horizon. I could have stared up forever, just being amazed, but before I'd had my fill, the island lurched and began to rise.

This was it. The last moments of the Great Abandonment.

I pulled myself away from the ruins and ran for the *Drakontos celestus*, but she was me and I was her, so it took no time at all to find my way between the wings, and then I launched into the sky. My final flight.

A horrible *crack* rent the air, Darina rising, but I kept flying up and away, into the sky, watching for the moment the sun started to reappear.

And then it happened.

A bead of bright white pierced the edge of the eclipse, and sunlight poured back in.

I imagined all the eclipses before this, how triumphant this moment must have been. The return of the sun. The victory of light over dark.

But this was no ordinary eclipse. For a few moments, the moon had taken away the light. But now that the day was back, we'd lost something else.

I looked over my shoulder, toward the place where the Fallen Isles had been just moments before.

Now, there was nothing but empty ocean, dotted with tiny vessels struggling to stay upright as waves rose up, unimpeded by land. No homes. No islands. No gods.

And one more eclipse.

CHAPTER FORTY-TWO

THE SECOND ECLIPSE BEGAN BEFORE THE FIRST WAS even finished.

To everyone else, all the survivors on the ships and rafts and dragons, it must have been a terrifying sight. A moment of victory. The day returning, only for darkness to claim the sky once more.

But when I looked up, I saw two moons crossing the sun, its light like scythes through their darkness. The effect was eerie. Beautiful. Ominous.

Below me, waves crashed into one another, the whole ocean adjusting to the absence of islands. Did Apolla see a difference in the empire? Did the other continents and islands around the world notice?

Just as the first dragon had said, the gods were gone.

They'd held on, waiting until totality was almost over before vanishing. Maybe that was Darina's doing; maybe the goddess of love knew how much I needed those last moments to take in the truth and absorb the magnitude of this sacrifice. I'd think about that later, if there was a later.

First I had to find my dragon.

I had to reach her, hold her, promise that I still loved her more than anything in the world. Before our connection was forever muted, I *needed* her to understand what she meant to me and how my heart would never heal from this.

The moons moved across the sun's face, but there was still time. There *was*. If the gods hadn't left until the instant the sun came back, then I had that long, too.

I touched my heart, pounding in time with the *Drakontos celestus*, and searched the sky for a tiny golden dragon. One among thousands.

When I reached, hundreds of dragons reached back. I could feel them all—*titanuses*, *maiors*, *ignituses*, and *sols*. A thousand smaller species sparked in my mind, their souls open in greeting, and for a moment I was stunned. Shocked. Overwhelmed by the number of dragons all turning their minds toward me.

They soared through the sky, roaring at the darkening sun, skimming through the water where the gods used to be. Others carried people still, circling as though lost without land to navigate by. And more just flew higher and higher, dropping back down when the air became too thin to breathe.

Oh, no.

They were trying to get to the stars. They were trying to get to their gods.

I *ached* for them, and maybe I should have stopped to explain how humans had ruined everything, but I couldn't stop searching. LaLa was out there somewhere, and our time was short.

Through dragons' eyes, I saw ships all across the water, packed tight with people clutching anything stable just to stay upright; the sea shifted madly beneath them, rolling with the loss of the islands. Water roared in grief, just as loud as the dragons.

Then I saw the fleet where I'd left Aaru and the others, sailing east like I'd ordered. Hristo and Ilina were hugging each other, both crying, while Mother and Zara stood at the rail and stared out at all the nothing. Gerel and Chenda struggled to create some kind of order out of the chaos, calling out instructions and working together like they'd been born for this day.

Aaru, too, was busy, tapping with Safa and the other Idrisi girls, but the silence was gone. The gods had taken their gifts up into the sky. Now great waves rolled unimpeded across the ocean, ready to swallow the ships whole.

Light shifted as the moons slipped across the sun; the first was almost gone, just a dark blot on the edge of a yellow crescent. And swiftly, that blot vanished, leaving only the second.

Finally, through the tangle of dragon minds—all their grief and shock and determination—I found LaLa. She

513

and Crystal were nuzzling Kelsine, comforting their friend after all she'd been through, but when LaLa sensed me reaching for her, she didn't hesitate. She shot into the air, flapping as hard as her tiny wings would take her.

I surged toward her, my heart pounding wildly with hope. *I'm coming*, I thought. *I'm coming.*

My wings were huge, and I could fly faster than any other dragon on Noore. Even so, time was short, and no matter how I willed the space between us to fold and bring me to her sooner, the world wouldn't move just because I asked.

Wings straining, lungs heaving, I flew for her, and she flew for me. I could feel her, pushing harder than she ever had in her life, just as determined to reach me in time.

Ocean rolled beneath, and the sky darkened around, but my heart was an arrow pointed straight for LaLa. Even as light squeezed around the second moon—long enough for me to make out ships in the distance—I strained my entire body, human and dragon, to get to her before the eclipse was finished.

Everything went dark.

I flew faster.

Even now, I could feel her pulling closer, her wings beating frantically, her heart racing. We could find each other in the dark, my precious dragon flower and me. We could.

"LaLa!" I called. There was only one last thing that mattered now, and that was holding her.

Light glowed on every horizon, shining off the edges of the angry ocean. Stars gleamed overhead, and the halo of sunlight shone around the moon again, eerie and awe-inspiring.

How long was totality?

How long did we have left?

A tiny cry sounded in the distance: LaLa.

Her voice pierced my heart, and we were close—so close—I could almost feel her in my arms. I could almost hear her throaty purr and smell the smoke on her breath.

I flew, sensing the weight of the moons overhead, and the sunlight beginning to bend around the curve, and this all-horizons dawn starting to shatter. There wasn't enough time. There'd never *been* enough time, but I hadn't listened to the first dragon's warnings.

LaLa called out again, and a small burst of fire shone in the distance.

Moments. There were but moments before the sun returned. I had to do it now—*now*—but I hadn't reached LaLa yet. I hadn't said good-bye.

She screeched again, flapping her wings so hard that her heart felt ready to burst. We were *so* close, and we needed only a moment more. Just a moment.

But it was too late. Sunlight hovered on the other side of the moon.

A gasp.

A promise.

An ending.

515

"LaLa!" I screamed and reached out my hand for her, but this was my choice: the world, or holding her again. I knew, of course, I'd be able to hold her after this, but it would never be the same. Our connection would be severed. And I hadn't said good-bye before—

My eyes ached with tears, and my throat squeezed so tight I could barely breathe. She was only a few seconds away.

We didn't have a few seconds.

"I'm sorry," I whispered, and I shifted course. I dove straight for the sea.

IT WAS DIFFERENT than I thought it'd be.

Even though I plunged into the ocean, pressure building and water boiling around me, a part of me soared up and up—so high that stars shivered back in terror, so huge that galaxies swirled in my wake.

Fire filled up my heart, burning with inferno fury, and for a moment, I thought it wouldn't happen. I *hoped* it wouldn't. I hoped I wasn't too late, and I could go back for LaLa, and—

That was not what I wanted. Not really.

I dove deeper, my dragon soul and me, and broke through the skin of the world, into an ocean of magma that pushed restlessly for release. Nothing drowned me. Nothing crushed me. Nothing burned me. I was the *Drakontos celestus*, the first and the last made one. And where I entered, a fissure opened in the bottom of the ocean and molten rock burst through.

Bright red flared. Seawater bubbled, hardening the rush of lava, but more molten rock pushed through the thin new crust.

And there, in the depths, in the dark, in that space between totality and a golden bead shining out of pure blackness, my dragon soul grew, mixing with the magma as it spread across the seafloor, up ridges, down abysses, and all over the dark and strange world below.

More fissures opened, releasing gas and lava, destruction and creation all in one, until at last the bottom of the sea began to breach the waves above.

Ocean life darted away from the heat, from the lifting, but not everything was fast enough. Shrimps and crabs and strangely luminous fish—and a host of other deep-sea mysteries—rose up into the open air, and steam rushed into the sky.

Small points of land formed under the waves, growing larger as the fire of creation continued below. The tiny islands rose higher, becoming mountain peaks and ridges. Hollows formed, holding water, and long stretches of hills and flatland. Wind swept through the valleys, while waves crashed against anything they could reach, already eroding this new world.

I urged it higher, and then the land caught ships on its craggy, steaming rocks, while exhausted birds found places to rest. Dragons deposited people in the first places they landed, and still the islands grew upward until they merged into one, filled with mountains and canyons and steppes. Water rolled down from the tallest places, forming lakes and rivers and underground aquifers, and although I didn't understand *how*, I knew this water was fresh enough to drink.

Equally mysterious were the plants that sprouted and grew in a matter of moments, and the bugs and lizards and squirrels that darted through a forest. But it happened. Maybe it was Harta's last gift. Regardless, I urged it onward.

This was the shadow soul of the dragon: a new island, a new home, a new chance to do better than everyone who came before us.

Then sunlight broke around the moon, and light poured onto the nascent land.

My dragon soul broke off, but I held on, hoping, wishing—

But I needed to breathe. I needed to go home.

I let go.

SOMEWHERE, ON A brand-new beach, I opened my eyes.

Sand dunes piled up around me.

Sunlight warmed my skin.

Waves crashed across my bare toes.

Palm trees swayed and creaked in the breeze.

And above, the sky yawned blue, wide open and blinding. I squinted and looked away, blinking until the sunspots faded.

Aside from not being able to look at the sun anymore, I felt . . . strangely fine.

For several long minutes, I searched inside myself, feeling around for the dragon soul, or the place where it should be. It *had* been there—I remembered flying and wielding noorestones and feeling what dragons felt—but there wasn't even a phantom ache as evidence of its existence.

I just . . . couldn't feel noorestones humming in the back of my mind, or find the threads that used to connect me to dragons. It was all just gone, as though it had never been there, but it *had*. I *remembered*. But the rest of me had expanded to fill the available space.

Tears slipped down the sides of my face, not because I wanted the loss to hurt more, but because it *should* have. I'd been a dragon—part dragon—and now I was not. Now I was just a girl. Just Mira. Forever.

Pressure stirred on my chest, and suddenly I realized I wasn't alone.

A small, warm body curled against my heart, scales gleaming gold as the sun fell toward the water. She was trembling, so I stretched out my hand and held her in place as I sat up, careful of the sharp scales against my fragile human skin.

LaLa uncurled herself and gazed up at me, her eyes bright and gold and perfect. She gave a small *meep*, and though I couldn't feel her worry as I used to, it was clear in her posture and tone, and the way she tilted her head.

"I wish I'd been faster to get to you," I whispered.

She just looked at me, clicking.

Gently, I stroked down her spine, gazing at this little miracle. She'd found me here. Even without my dragon soul, she'd found me and planted herself on her favorite place to sleep.

It would be different between us—between me and all the dragons—but if LaLa could find me, if she was with me now, then there was hope. Other people, like Ilina and her family, understood dragons just fine. And hadn't that been what I'd done before all of this? Read body language, found ways to train and communicate together? I just had to go back to that. It wouldn't be the same, but I hadn't lost dragons completely.

And it wasn't only me. Everyone's god gifts were gone now. Everyone would need to compensate for the lack of divine abilities if they wanted to survive in this new world.

"We'll be all right," I whispered, and kissed LaLa's nose.

She yawned and jumped to the ground, where she shoved her face into the sand and blew fire. Then she jerked her head back, as though surprised that fiery sand was hot.

It felt strange between us still, like a wall had been erected between my mind and hers. But I'd come to know other people in spite of walls; overcoming this would be no different.

I watched LaLa play for a bit longer, and just as I was

gathering myself to head inland and look for other people, a ship appeared on the horizon.

Hope stirred through me as I found my feet, scooping LaLa out of the sand. As the ship grew closer, LaLa surged into the air with frantic squeaks and chitters, and I lifted my arms in greeting. Gifts or no gifts, I knew who was coming.

The ship was the *Chance Encounter*; I'd know Captain Pentoba's colors anywhere. But even without that, my soul pulled in the direction of the people I loved. I couldn't see them from this distance, but I could feel the way our hearts aligned as my friends spotted me standing here on this beach. Waves drowned out their happy cries, but I could see their excitement in the way they jumped and waved.

As afternoon eased into evening, the ship pulled closer and boats were lowered into the water. LaLa and Crystal were playing in the air between us, blowing fire and clicking at one another like two little gossips, while I let my imagination run wild with our futures.

Ilina and I would open a new sanctuary, both of us getting our greatest wish for a life filled with helping dragons. And the moment a new island rose from the depths, Chenda had probably started considering all the possibilities for a new and fair government—something that would represent and honor all the survivors of the Great Abandonment. Including dragons.

And as for Aaru and me . . .

We had a chance after all. More than a chance.

Shadows fell longer, and bugs buzzed with the third evening today, and finally my friends reached the shallows. I ran out to meet them, splashing water in all directions, and within minutes they surrounded me and we were all hugging one another, laughing and crying. Ilina, Hristo, Chenda, Gerel, Zara, Safa, and Aaru: they were all here.

"Where's Mother?" I asked.

"She thought she should wait on the ship for now," Zara said. "I think she understands that this is our moment."

I hugged my sister again, so wildly happy to see her, and to hear her include herself in our group. She did belong. She'd always belonged.

After we dragged the boats to the beach and everyone finished running around the soft new sand, we sprawled out on the shore and I told my friends about the first dragon, the eclipse, and the sacrifice of my dragon soul.

"Wow." Chenda sat next to Gerel, both of them holding hands. "Are you—"

I nodded quickly, because I wasn't all right yet, but I would be, and for now I didn't want to dampen this glorious feeling of being reunited with my friends—my family. "How did you find me here?"

"Crystal." Ilina stroked her *raptus*, who'd fallen asleep on her knee. "She was looking for LaLa."

A pang of sadness passed through me, but then fingers slipped across the sand and twisted with mine. Aaru. ::**Do you see them?**::

Darkness had fallen, and now stars appeared in the sky. There was Suna, the Judge, and Lesya, the Weaver, and Zabel, the Hero. They all shone brightly in the moonless night, familiar and comforting.

Then I saw the new patterns: a figure that might have been a man hunched over; a woman, heavy with child; two people gazing into each other's eyes. When I looked harder, they were all there, all seven Fallen Gods, reunited with the Upper Gods.

Maybe they were Risen Gods now.

::I see them.::

I turned my head to find Aaru looking at me, warmth in his gaze. ::Earlier, I wanted to ask something.::

"Yes," I whispered.

The hum of quiet conversation silenced, and everyone turned toward us.

"You don't even know what I was going to ask." Aaru sat up.

"It doesn't matter." I took his hand. ::As long as we're together, my answer is yes.::

He smiled and quickly—a little self-consciously—leaned forward to kiss me. It must have been difficult to show affection without the ability to call up silence and feel alone, but we would all need to learn to live our lives under our own powers now. Clearly, he was already practicing.

I kissed him back, there in front of everyone, and only when an immense roar shook the sky did I pull away.

Dark wings blocked out starlight as a great *Drakontos titanus* sailed overhead. She called again, declaring territory, perhaps, and my heart soared as I took LaLa into my arms again, just in case she was afraid of the bigger dragon above.

When the *titanus* was gone, I said, "I've been thinking that since it was my dragon soul that made this island, I should be the one who gets to name it."

"We're not naming the island LaLa," Hristo said.

"Or Mira." Zara smirked. "You've already had enough things named after you."

I laughed and gazed around at everyone: Gerel and Chenda, leaning toward one another; Safa, watching Aaru's hand as he interpreted for her; Hristo, resting his cheek on the top of Ilina's head; and Zara, running her fingers through the soft sand. Here we were. The best friends I'd ever have. The best *sisters* I'd ever have. I loved them all so much my heart ached with it.

"No, neither of those. LaLa and Mira are fantastic names, but they're already taken." I pulled myself up and opened my arms to the starlit beach, the dragon-echoing sky, and this whole world I couldn't wait to explore. "Welcome to Celestus: the Isle of Dragons."

ACKNOWLEDGMENTS

THERE'S ALWAYS SOMETHING A LITTLE INTIMIDATING about writing the acknowledgments pages, especially for the last book in a series. I don't want to overlook anyone's contribution, but I know I will never be able to thank every single person who's made a difference in the life and growth of this trilogy. Still, I will do my best to show as much appreciation and gratitude as possible.

First, my agent, Lauren MacLeod, who was an absolute hero for this book and likes being first. I know I always say what a champion she is, but it's true. Writing books never gets easier (sorry, everyone who was hoping), but having a smart and supportive agent has been an asset—especially with this series.

The HarperCollins side of this book included amazing people like my editors, Maria Barbo and Stephanie Guerdan, who made this book shine like dragon scales; Joel Tippie, who designed these phenomenal covers; and, of course, Katherine Tegen.

As Mira is surrounded by a group of strong and supportive friends, so am I. Some helped with plotting and sensitivity reads, while others provided emotional support and general enthusiasm. No matter what, this book would not be what it is without every one of these people:

Brodi Ashton, Martina Boone, Adrienne Bowling, Erin Bowman, Valerie Cole, Pintip Dunn, Dana Elmendorf, Cynthia Hand, Deborah Hawkins, Stacey Lee, Myra McEntire, Aminah Mae Safi, Alexa Santiago, Francina Simone, Laurel Symonds, Alana Whitman, and Fran Wilde.

The #FantasyOnFriday girl gang, C. J. Redwine, Erin Summerill, Mary Weber, Danielle Paige, Kristen Ciccarelli, Tricia Levenseller, Beth Revis, Amy A. Bartol, Evelyn Skye, Nadine Brandes, and Livia Blackburne.

Special thanks to the entire OQ Support Group, including Tiffie van Bordeveld, Christina Termini, Sarah Kershaw, Christy Hayes, Julie Daly, Bonnie Wagner, Suna Jung, and Nisha Dey. You went above and beyond with your support for this series, including work on promotion, art, and amplification, and I can't say how incredibly grateful I am. Thank you.

Extra thanks to the readers who preordered the book

very early—as soon as it was available!—and requested it from their libraries:

Aldara Thomas, Zahra Linsky, Emma Elizabeth, Kelsey Culver, Laramie Hearn, Christi Viljoen, Emily Peterson, Yulia @bookspired, rachelsfictionncats, Liz and Rachel, Felicia Mathews, Danielle Kent, Lady Julia Hope Hoffmeister, Marie-Kristin Reubert, Adrianne Sautter, Bronwyn Karoline, Meike Linders, Alysha Welliver, Victoria Violette, Ashleigh @ashleighsbookshelf, Katelyn Fowler, Wren Hardwick @FablesAndWren, Melonie Hill, Rachel Booth, Hannah Vermeulen, Lauren James, Sandra Arechaederra, Christy Jane, Tabitha, Lynnae Andersen, Layla Crowie, T. S. Addleston, Maura Trice, Lisa ten Brummelhuis, Breanna Boyer, Aaliyah, Savannah Grace, Soleil Bourdon, Fer Bañuelos, April Schiavoni Kucker, AuntBreESQReads, Vivian Tran, Carrie Frith, Brooke Dimery, Wendy Liu, Nisha Dey, Casey Tomlinson, Christina Loewe, Ruth Meeker, Anna Cole, Leah Lutheran, B. Jones, Cade Roach, Sullivan McPig, Julia Dziennik and Pixi Stix, Ayla den Ouden, Jana at That Artsy Reader Girl, Kim Claesen @Teemuke, Jess C., Shyra Dawson, Angelica Sorrels, Dennise Pendergrass, Vicky Chen, Kimberly Kosydor-Blotevogel, Nicole Charette, Peyton and Abigail Boutwell, Ashley Cotov Ruiz, Roxanne Haney, Andrea Higgins, Michelle Einhorn, Bonnie Lynn Wagner, Shayna Nash, Ashley Nelson, Alana Whitman, Anna T. Davis, Veronica Mitchell, Carina Olsen, Nora Ouahi, Meghan Doberstein, Michelle Worthing, Emily Ruth Morris, Cara

Beining, Mary Hinson, Candy Smith, Shayna Nash, Nicole Curry, Kristen Coffin, and Nori Horvitz.

I can't forget the incredible OwlCrate team, for their continued support of the Fallen Isles trilogy, and my dear friends at One More Page Books in Arlington, VA.

And, as always, I must thank my husband, sister, and mother, and—at last—you: the reader who followed Mira to the end.